PENGUIN ENGLISH LIBRARY

Treasure Island and The Ebb-Tide

Robert Louis Stevenson was born in Edinburgh in 1850. The son of a prosperous civil engineer, he was expected to follow the family profession but was finally allowed to study law at Edinburgh University. Stevenson reacted forcibly against the Presbyterianism of both his city's professional classes and his devout parents, but the influence of Calvinism on his childhood informed the preoccupation with predestination and fascination with evil that are so powerfully explored in much of his fiction. Stevenson suffered from a severe respiratory disease from his twenties onwards, leading him to settle in the gentle climate of Samoa with his American wife, Fanny Osbourne.

Dr Jekyll and Mr Hyde is also published in the Penguin English Library.

Treasure Island
and *The Ebb-Tide*

ROBERT LOUIS STEVENSON

...

PENGUIN ENGLISH
LIBRARY

PENGUIN BOOKS

Published by the Penguin Group
Penguin Books Ltd, 80 Strand, London WC2R ORL, England
Penguin Group (USA) Inc., 375 Hudson Street, New York, New York 10014, USA
Penguin Group (Canada), 90 Eglinton Avenue East, Suite 700, Toronto, Ontario, Canada M4P 2Y3
(a division of Pearson Penguin Canada Inc.)
Penguin Ireland, 25 St Stephen's Green, Dublin 2, Ireland (a division of Penguin Books Ltd)
Penguin Group (Australia), 707 Collins Street, Melbourne, Victoria 3008, Australia
(a division of Pearson Australia Group Pty Ltd)
Penguin Books India Pvt Ltd, 11 Community Centre, Panchsheel Park, New Delhi – 110 017, India
Penguin Group (NZ), 67 Apollo Drive, Rosedale, Auckland 0632, New Zealand
(a division of Pearson New Zealand Ltd)
Penguin Books (South Africa) (Pty) Ltd, Block D, Rosebank Office Park,
181 Jan Smuts Avenue, Parktown North, Gauteng 2193, South Africa

Penguin Books Ltd, Registered Offices: 80 Strand, London WC2R ORL, England

www.penguin.com

Treasure Island first published 1883
Published in Penguin Red Classics 2008
The Ebb-Tide first published 1894
This collection first published in the Penguin English Library 2012

008

Front cover illustration: Coralie Bickford-Smith

Set in 11/13 pt Dante MT Std
Typeset by Jouve (UK), Milton Keynes

Printed and bound in Great Britain by Clays Ltd, Elcograf S.p.A.

ISBN: 978-0-141-19914-6

www.greenpenguin.co.uk

Contents

Contents

Contents

THE EBB-TIDE
by Robert Louis Stevenson and Lloyd Osbourne

PART I
The Trio

PART II
The Quartette

TREASURE ISLAND.

BY

ROBERT LOUIS STEVENSON.

———•••———

CASSELL & COMPANY, LIMITED:

LONDON, PARIS & NEW YORK.

[ALL RIGHTS RESERVED.]

1883.

PART ONE

The Old Buccaneer

Chapter One

The Old Sea Dog at the 'Admiral Benbow'

Squire Trelawney, Dr Livesey, and the rest of these gentlemen having asked me to write down the whole particulars about Treasure Island, from the beginning to the end, keeping nothing back but the bearings of the island, and that only because there is still treasure not yet lifted, I take up my pen in the year of grace 17—, and go back to the time when my father kept the 'Admiral Benbow' inn, and the brown old seaman, with the sabre cut, first took up his lodging under our roof.

I remember him as if it were yesterday, as he came plodding to the inn door, his sea-chest following behind him in a hand-barrow; a tall, strong, heavy, nut-brown man; his tarry pigtail falling over the shoulders of his soiled blue coat; his hands ragged and scarred, with black, broken nails; and the sabre cut across one cheek, a dirty, livid white. I remember him looking round the cove and whistling to himself as he did so, and then breaking out in that old sea-song that he sang so often afterwards: –

'Fifteen men on the dead man's chest –
Yo-ho-ho, and a bottle of rum!'

in the high, old tottering voice that seemed to have been tuned and broken at the capstan bars. Then he rapped on the door with a bit of stick like a handspike that he carried, and when my father appeared, called roughly for a glass of rum. This, when it was brought to him, he drank slowly, like a connoisseur, lingering on the taste, and still looking about him at the cliffs and up at our signboard.

'This is a handy cove,' says he, at length; 'and a pleasant sitty-ated grog-shop. Much company, mate?'

My father told him no, very little company, the more was the pity.

'Well, then,' said he, 'this is the berth for me. Here you, matey,' he cried to the man who trundled the barrow; 'bring up alongside and help up my chest. I'll stay here a bit,' he continued. 'I'm a plain man; rum and bacon and eggs is what I want, and that head up there for to watch ships off. What you mought call me? You mought call me captain. Oh, I see what you're at – there;' and he threw down three or four gold pieces on the threshold. 'You can tell me when I've worked through that,' says he, looking as fierce as a commander.

And, indeed, bad as his clothes were, and coarsely as he spoke, he had none of the appearance of a man who sailed before the mast; but seemed like a mate or skipper, accustomed to be obeyed or to strike. The man who came with the barrow told us the mail had set him down the morning before at the 'Royal George;' that he had inquired what inns there were along the coast, and hearing ours well spoken of, I suppose, and described as lonely, had chosen it from the others for his place of residence. And that was all we could learn of our guest.

He was a very silent man by custom. All day he hung round the cove, or upon the cliffs, with a brass telescope; all evening he sat in a corner of the parlour next the fire, and drank rum and water very strong. Mostly he would not speak when spoken to; only look up sudden and fierce, and blow through his nose like a fog-horn; and we and the people who came about our house soon learned to let him be. Every day, when he came back from his stroll, he would ask if any seafaring men had gone by along the road? At first we thought it was the want of company of his own kind that made him ask this question; but at last we began to see he was desirous to avoid them. When a seaman put up at the 'Admiral Benbow' (as now and then some did, making by the coast road for Bristol), he would look in at him through the curtained door before he entered the parlour; and he was always

4

sure to be as silent as a mouse when any such was present. For me, at least, there was no secret about the matter; for I was, in a way, a sharer in his alarms. He had taken me aside one day, and promised me a silver fourpenny on the first of every month if I would only keep my 'weather-eye open for a seafaring man with one leg,' and let him know the moment he appeared. Often enough, when the first of the month came round, and I applied to him for my wage, he would only blow through his nose at me, and stare me down; but before the week was out he was sure to think better of it, bring me my fourpenny piece, and repeat his orders to look out for 'the seafaring man with one leg.'

How that personage haunted my dreams, I need scarcely tell you. On stormy nights, when the wind shook the four corners of the house, and the surf roared along the cove and up the cliffs, I would see him in a thousand forms, and with a thousand diabolical expressions. Now the leg would be cut off at the knee, now at the hip; now he was a monstrous kind of a creature who had never had but the one leg, and that in the middle of his body. To see him leap and run and pursue me over hedge and ditch was the worst of nightmares. And altogether I paid pretty dear for my monthly fourpenny piece, in the shape of these abominable fancies.

But though I was so terrified by the idea of the seafaring man with one leg, I was far less afraid of the captain himself than anybody else who knew him. There were nights when he took a deal more rum and water than his head would carry; and then he would sometimes sit and sing his wicked, old, wild sea-songs, minding nobody; but sometimes he would call for glasses round, and force all the trembling company to listen to his stories or bear a chorus to his singing. Often I have heard the house shaking with 'Yo-ho-ho, and a bottle of rum;' all the neighbours joining in for dear life, with the fear of death upon them, and each singing louder than the other, to avoid remark. For in these fits he was the most over-riding companion ever known; he would slap his hand on the table for silence all round; he would fly up in a passion of anger at a question, or sometimes because none was put, and so he judged the company was not following his story. Nor would he allow any one to leave the inn till he had drunk himself sleepy and reeled off to bed.

His stories were what frightened people worst of all. Dreadful stories they were; about hanging, and walking the plank, and storms at sea, and the Dry Tortugas, and wild deeds and places on the Spanish Main. By his own account he must have lived his life among some of the wickedest men that God ever allowed upon the sea; and the language in which he told these stories shocked our plain country people almost as much as the crimes that he described. My father was always saying the inn would be ruined, for people would soon cease coming there to be tyrannised over and put down, and sent shivering to their beds; but I really believe his presence did us good. People were frightened at the time, but on looking back they rather liked it; it was a fine excitement in a quiet country life; and there was even a party of the younger men who pretended to admire him, calling him a 'true sea-dog,' and a 'real old salt,' and such like names, and saying there was the sort of man that made England terrible at sea.

In one way, indeed, he bade fair to ruin us; for he kept on staying week after week, and at last month after month, so that all the money had been long exhausted, and still my father never plucked up the heart to insist on having more. If ever he mentioned it, the captain blew through his nose so loudly, that you might say he roared, and stared my poor father out of the room. I have seen him wringing his hands after such a rebuff, and I am sure the annoyance and the terror he lived in must have greatly hastened his early and unhappy death.

All the time he lived with us the captain made no change whatever in his dress but to buy some stockings from a hawker. One of the cocks of his hat having fallen down, he let it hang from that day forth, though it was a great annoyance when it blew.

I remember the appearance of his coat, which he patched himself up-stairs in his room, and which, before the end, was nothing but patches. He never wrote or received a letter, and he never spoke with any but the neighbours, and with these, for the most part, only when drunk on rum. The great sea-chest none of us had ever seen open.

He was only once crossed, and that was towards the end, when my poor father was far gone in a decline that took him off. Dr Livesey came late one afternoon to see the patient, took a bit of dinner from my mother, and went into the parlour to smoke a pipe until his horse should come down from the hamlet, for we had no stabling at the old 'Benbow.' I followed him in, and I remember observing the contrast the neat, bright doctor, with his powder as white as snow, and his bright, black eyes and pleasant manners, made with the coltish country folk, and above all, with that filthy, heavy, bleared scarecrow of a pirate of ours, sitting far gone in rum, with his arms on the table. Suddenly he – the captain, that is – began to pipe up his eternal song: –

> 'Fifteen men on the dead man's chest –
> Yo-ho-ho, and a bottle of rum!
> Drink and the devil had done for the rest –
> Yo-ho-ho, and a bottle of rum!'

At first I had supposed 'the dead man's chest' to be that identical big box of his up-stairs in the front room, and the thought had been mingled in my nightmares with that of the one-legged seafaring man. But by this time we had all long ceased to pay any particular notice to the song; it was new, that night, to nobody but Dr Livesey, and on him I observed it did not produce an agreeable effect, for he looked up for a moment quite angrily before he went on with his talk to old Taylor, the gardener, on a new cure for the rheumatics. In the meantime, the captain gradually brightened up at his own music, and at last flapped his hand upon the table before him in a way we all knew to mean – silence. The voices stopped at once, all but Dr Livesey's; he went on as before, speaking clear and kind, and drawing briskly at his pipe between every word or two. The captain glared at him for a while, flapped his hand again, glared still harder, and at last broke out with a villainous, low oath: 'Silence, there, between decks!'

'Were you addressing me, sir?' says the doctor; and when the ruffian had told him, with another oath, that this was so, 'I have only one thing to say to you, sir,' replies the doctor, 'that if you keep on drinking rum, the world will soon be quit of a very dirty scoundrel!'

The old fellow's fury was awful. He sprang to his feet, drew and opened a sailor's clasp-knife, and, balancing it open on the palm of his hand, threatened to pin the doctor to the wall.

The doctor never so much as moved. He spoke to him, as before, over his shoulder, and in the same tone of voice; rather high, so that all the room might hear, but perfectly calm and steady:–

'If you do not put that knife this instant in your pocket, I promise, upon my honour, you shall hang at the next assizes.'

Then followed a battle of looks between them; but the captain soon knuckled under, put up his weapon, and resumed his seat, grumbling like a beaten dog.

'And now, sir,' continued the doctor, 'since I now know there's such a fellow in my district, you may count I'll have an eye upon you day and night. I'm not a doctor only; I'm a magistrate; and if I catch a breath of complaint against you, if it's only for a piece of incivility like to-night's, I'll take effectual means to have you hunted down and routed out of this. Let that suffice.'

Soon after Dr Livesey's horse came to the door, and he rode away; but the captain held his peace that evening, and for many evenings to come.

Chapter Two

Black Dog Appears and Disappears

It was not very long after this that there occurred the first of the mysterious events that rid us at last of the captain, though not, as you will see, of his affairs. It was a bitter cold winter, with long, hard frosts and heavy gales; and it was plain from the first that my poor father was little likely to see the spring. He sank daily, and my mother and I had all the inn upon our hands; and were kept busy enough, without paying much regard to our unpleasant guest.

It was one January morning, very early – a pinching, frosty morning – the cove all grey with hoar-frost, the ripple lapping softly on the stones, the sun still low and only touching the hill-tops and shining far to seaward. The captain had risen earlier than usual, and set out down the beach, his cutlass swinging under the broad skirts of the old blue coat, his brass telescope under his arm, his hat tilted back upon his head. I remember his breath hanging like smoke in his wake as he strode off, and the last sound I heard of him, as he turned the big rock, was a loud snort of indignation, as though his mind was still running upon Dr Livesey.

Well, mother was up-stairs with father; and I was laying the breakfast-table against the captain's return, when the parlour door opened, and a man stepped in on whom I had never set my eyes before. He was a pale, tallowy creature, wanting two fingers of the left hand; and, though he wore a cutlass, he did not look much like a fighter. I had always my eye open for seafaring men, with one leg or two, and I remember this one puzzled me. He was not sailorly, and yet he had a smack of the sea about him too.

I asked him what was for his service, and he said he would take rum; but as I was going out of the room to fetch it he sat down upon a table, and motioned me to draw near. I paused where I was with my napkin in my hand.

'Come here, sonny,' says he. 'Come nearer here.'

I took a step nearer.

'Is this here table for my mate, Bill?' he asked, with a kind of leer.

I told him I did not know his mate Bill; and this was for a person who stayed in our house, whom we called the captain.

'Well,' said he, 'my mate Bill would be called the captain, as like as not. He has a cut on one cheek, and a mighty pleasant way with him, particularly in drink, has my mate, Bill. We'll put it, for argument like, that your captain has a cut on one cheek – and we'll put it, if you like, that that cheek's the right one. Ah, well! I told you. Now, is my mate Bill in this here house?'

I told him he was out walking.

'Which way, sonny? Which way is he gone?'

And when I had pointed out the rock and told him how the captain was likely to return, and how soon, and answered a few other questions, 'Ah,' said he, 'this'll be as good as drink to my mate Bill.'

The expression of his face as he said these words was not at all pleasant, and I had my own reasons for thinking that the stranger was mistaken, even supposing he meant what he said. But it was no affair of mine, I thought; and, besides, it was difficult to know what to do. The stranger kept hanging about just inside the inn door, peering round the corner like a cat waiting for a mouse. Once I stepped out myself into the road, but he immediately called me back, and, as I did not obey quick enough for his fancy, a most horrible change came over his tallowy face, and he ordered me in, with an oath that made me jump. As soon as I was back again he returned to his former manner, half fawning, half sneering, patted me on the shoulder, told me I was a good boy, and he had taken quite a fancy to me. 'I have a son of my own,' said he, 'as like you as two blocks, and he's all the pride of my 'art. But the great thing for boys is discipline, sonny – discipline. Now, if you had sailed along of Bill, you wouldn't have stood there to be spoke to twice – not you. That was never Bill's way, nor the way of sich as sailed with him. And here, sure enough, is my mate Bill, with a spy-glass under his arm, bless his old 'art, to be sure. You and me'll just go back into the parlour, sonny, and get behind the door, and we'll give Bill a little surprise – bless his 'art, I say again.'

So saying, the stranger backed along with me into the parlour, and put me behind him in the corner, so that we were both hidden by the open door. I was very uneasy and alarmed, as you may fancy, and it rather added to my fears to observe that the stranger was certainly frightened himself. He cleared the hilt of his cutlass and loosened the blade in the sheath; and all the time we were waiting there he kept swallowing as if he felt what we used to call a lump in the throat.

At last in strode the captain, slammed the door behind him, without looking to the right or left, and marched straight across the room to where his breakfast awaited him.

'Bill,' said the stranger, in a voice that I thought he had tried to make bold and big.

The captain spun round on his heel and fronted us; all the brown had gone out of his face, and even his nose was blue; he had the look of a man who sees a ghost, or the evil one, or something worse, if anything can be; and, upon my word, I felt sorry to see him, all in a moment, turn so old and sick.

'Come, Bill, you know me; you know an old shipmate, Bill, surely,' said the stranger.

The captain made a sort of gasp.

'Black Dog!' said he.

'And who else?' returned the other, getting more at his ease. 'Black Dog as ever was, come for to see his old shipmate Billy, at the "Admiral Benbow" inn. Ah, Bill, Bill, we have seen a sight of times, us two, since I lost them two talons,' holding up his mutilated hand.

'Now, look here,' said the captain; 'you've run me down; here I am; well, then, speak up: what is it?'

'That's you, Bill,' returned Black Dog, 'you're in the right of it, Billy. I'll have a glass of rum from this dear child here, as I've took such a liking to; and we'll sit down, if you please, and talk square, like old shipmates.'

When I returned with the rum, they were already seated on either side of the captain's breakfast-table – Black Dog next to the door, and sitting sideways, so as to have one eye on his old ship-mate, and one, as I thought, on his retreat.

He bade me go, and leave the door wide open. 'None of your keyholes for me, sonny,' he said; and I left them together, and retired into the bar.

For a long time, though I certainly did my best to listen, I could hear nothing but a low gabbling; but at last the voices began to grow higher, and I could pick up a word or two, mostly oaths, from the captain.

'No, no, no, no; and an end of it!' he cried once. And again, 'If it comes to swinging, swing all, say I.'

Then all of a sudden there was a tremendous explosion of oaths and other noises – the chair and table went over in a lump, a clash of steel followed, and then a cry of pain, and the next instant I saw Black Dog in full flight, and the captain hotly pursuing, both with drawn cutlasses, and the former streaming blood from the left shoulder. Just at the door, the captain aimed at the fugitive one last tremendous cut, which would certainly have split him to the chine had it not been intercepted by our big signboard of Admiral Benbow. You may see the notch on the lower side of the frame to this day.

That blow was the last of the battle. Once out upon the road, Black Dog, in spite of his wound, showed a wonderful clean pair of heels, and disappeared over the edge of the hill in half a min-ute. The captain, for his part, stood staring at the signboard like a bewildered man. Then he passed his hand over his eyes several times, and at last turned back into the house.

'Jim,' says he, 'rum;' and as he spoke, he reeled a little, and caught himself with one hand against the wall.

'Are you hurt?' cried I.

'Rum,' he repeated. 'I must get away from here. Rum! rum!'

I ran to fetch it; but I was quite unsteadied by all that had fallen out, and I broke one glass and fouled the tap, and while I was still getting in my own way, I heard a loud fall in the parlour, and, running in, beheld the captain lying full length upon the floor. At the same instant my mother, alarmed by the cries and fighting, came running down-stairs to help me. Between us we raised his head. He was breathing very loud and hard; but his eyes were closed, and his face a horrible colour.

'Dear, deary me,' cried my mother, 'what a disgrace upon the house! And your poor father sick!'

In the meantime, we had no idea what to do to help the captain, nor any other thought but that he had got his death-hurt in the scuffle with the stranger. I got the rum, to be sure, and tried to put it down his throat; but his teeth were tightly shut, and his jaws as strong as iron. It was a happy relief for us when the door opened and Doctor Livesey came in, on his visit to my father.

'Oh, doctor,' we cried, 'what shall we do? Where is he wounded?'

'Wounded? A fiddle-stick's end!' said the doctor. 'No more wounded than you or I. The man has had a stroke, as I warned him. Now, Mrs Hawkins, just you run upstairs to your husband, and tell him, if possible, nothing about it. For my part, I must do my best to save this fellow's trebly worthless life; and Jim, you get me a basin.'

When I got back with the basin, the doctor had already ripped up the captain's sleeve, and exposed his great sinewy arm. It was tattooed in several places. 'Here's luck,' 'A fair wind,' and 'Billy Bones his fancy,' were very neatly and clearly executed on the forearm; and up near the shoulder there was a sketch of a gallows and a man hanging from it – done, as I thought, with great spirit.

'Prophetic,' said the doctor, touching this picture with his finger. 'And now, Master Billy Bones, if that be your name, we'll have a look at the colour of your blood. Jim,' he said, 'are you afraid of blood?'

'No, sir,' said I.

'Well, then,' said he, 'you hold the basin;' and with that he took his lancet and opened a vein.

A great deal of blood was taken before the captain opened his eyes and looked mistily about him. First he recognised the doctor with an unmistakable frown; then his glance fell upon me, and he looked relieved. But suddenly his colour changed, and he tried to raise himself, crying: –

'Where's Black Dog?'

'There is no Black Dog here,' said the doctor, 'except what you have on your own back. You have been drinking rum; you have had a stroke, precisely as I told you; and I have just, very much against my own will, dragged you headforemost out of the grave. Now, Mr Bones –'

'That's not my name,' he interrupted.

'Much I care,' returned the doctor. 'It's the name of a buccaneer of my acquaintance; and I call you by it for the sake of shortness, and what I have to say to you is this: one glass of rum won't kill you, but if you take one you'll take another and another, and I stake my wig if you don't break off short, you'll die – do you understand that? – die, and go to your own place, like the man in the Bible. Come, now, make an effort. I'll help you to your bed for once.'

Between us, with much trouble, we managed to hoist him upstairs, and laid him on his bed, where his head fell back on the pillow, as if he were almost fainting.

'Now, mind you,' said the doctor, 'I clear my conscience – the name of rum for you is death.'

besides, I was reassured by the doctor's words, now quoted to me, and rather offended by the offer of a bribe.

'I want none of your money,' said I, 'but what you owe my father. I'll get you one glass, and no more.'

When I brought it to him, he seized it greedily, and drank it out.

'Ay, ay,' said he, 'that's some better, sure enough. And now, matey, did that doctor say how long I was to lie here in this old berth?'

'A week at least,' said I.

'Thunder!' he cried. 'A week! I can't do that; they'd have the black spot on me by then. The lubbers is going about to get the wind of me this blessed moment; lubbers as couldn't keep what they got, and want to nail what is another's. Is that seamanly behaviour, now, I want to know? But I'm a saving soul. I never wasted good money of mine, nor lost it neither; and I'll trick 'em again. I'm not afraid on 'em. I'll shake out another reef, matey, and daddle 'em again.'

As he was thus speaking, he had risen from bed with great difficulty, holding to my shoulder with a grip that almost made me cry out, and moving his legs like so much dead weight. His words, spirited as they were in meaning, contrasted sadly with the weakness of the voice in which they were uttered. He paused when he had got into a sitting position on the edge.

'That doctor's done me,' he murmured. 'My ears is singing. Lay me back.'

Before I could do much to help him he had fallen back again to his former place, where he lay for a while silent.

'Jim,' he said, at length, 'you saw that seafaring man to-day?'

'Black Dog?' I asked.

'Ah! Black Dog,' says he. '*He's* a bad 'un; but there's worse that put him on. Now, if I can't get away nohow, and they tip me the black spot, mind you, it's my old sea-chest they're after; you get on a horse – you can, can't you? Well, then, you get on a horse, and go to – well, yes, I will! – to that eternal Doctor swab, and tell him to pipe all hands – magistrates and sich – and he'll lay 'em aboard at the "Admiral Benbow" – all old Flint's crew, man and boy, all on 'em that's left. I was first mate, I was, old Flint's first mate, and I'm the on'y one as knows the place. He gave it me at Savannah, when he lay a-dying, like as if I was to now, you see. But you won't peach unless they get the black spot on me, or unless you see that Black Dog again, or a seafaring man with one leg, Jim – him above all.'

'But what is the black spot, Captain?' I asked.

'That's a summons, mate. I'll tell you if they get that. But you keep your weather-eye open, Jim, and I'll share with you equals, upon my honour.'

He wandered a little longer, his voice growing weaker; but soon after I had given him his medicine, which he took like a child, with the remark, 'If ever a seaman wanted drugs, it's me,' he fell at last into a heavy, swoon-like sleep, in which I left him. What I should have done had all gone well I do not know. Probably I should have told the whole story to the doctor; for I was in mortal fear lest the captain should repent of his confessions and make an end of me. But as things fell out, my poor father died quite suddenly that evening, which put all other matters on one side. Our natural distress, the visits of the neighbours, the arranging of the funeral, and all the work of the inn to be carried on in the meanwhile, kept me so busy that I had scarcely time to think of the captain, far less to be afraid of him.

He got down-stairs next morning, to be sure, and had his meals as usual, though he ate little, and had more, I am afraid, than his usual supply of rum, for he helped himself out of the bar, scowling and blowing through his nose, and no one dared to cross him. On the night before the funeral he was as drunk as ever; and it was shocking, in that house of mourning, to hear him singing away at his ugly old sea-song; but, weak as he was, we were all in the fear of death for him, and the doctor was suddenly taken up with a case many miles away, and was never near the house after my father's death. I have said the captain was weak; and indeed he seemed rather to grow weaker than regain his strength. He clambered up and down-stairs, and went from the parlour to the bar and back again, and sometimes put his nose out of doors to smell the sea, holding on to the walls as he went for support, and breathing hard and fast like a man on a steep mountain. He never particularly addressed me, and it is my belief he had as good as forgotten his confidences; but his temper was more flighty, and, allowing for his bodily weakness, more violent than ever. He had an alarming way now when he was drunk of drawing his cutlass and laying it bare before him on the table. But, with all that, he minded people less, and seemed shut up in his own thoughts and rather wandering. Once, for instance, to our extreme wonder, he piped up to a different air, a kind of country love-song, that he must have learned in his youth before he had begun to follow the sea.

So things passed until, the day after the funeral, and about three o'clock of a bitter, foggy, frosty afternoon, I was standing at the door for a moment, full of sad thoughts about my father, when I saw some one drawing slowly near along the road. He was plainly blind, for he tapped before him with a stick, and wore a great green shade over his eyes and nose; and he was hunched, as if with age or weakness, and wore a huge old tattered sea-cloak with a hood, that made him appear positively deformed. I never saw in my life a more dreadful looking figure. He stopped a little from the inn, and, raising his voice in an odd sing-song, addressed the air in front of him: –

'Will any kind friend inform a poor blind man, who has lost the precious sight of his eyes in the gracious defence of his native country, England, and God bless King George! – where or in what part of this country he may now be?'

'You are at the "Admiral Benbow," Black Hill Cove, my good man,' said I.

'I hear a voice,' said he – 'a young voice. Will you give me your hand, my kind young friend, and lead me in?'

I held out my hand, and the horrible, soft-spoken, eyeless

creature gripped it in a moment like a vice. I was so much startled that I struggled to withdraw; but the blind man pulled me close up to him with a single action of his arm.

'Now, boy,' he said, 'take me in to the captain.'

'Sir,' said I, 'upon my word I dare not.'

'Oh,' he sneered, 'that's it! Take me in straight, or I'll break your arm.'

And he gave it, as he spoke, a wrench that made me cry out.

'Sir,' said I, 'it is for yourself I mean. The captain is not what he used to be. He sits with a drawn cutlass. Another gentleman –'

'Come, now, march,' interrupted he; and I never heard a voice so cruel, and cold, and ugly as that blind man's. It cowed me more than the pain; and I began to obey him at once, walking straight in at the door and towards the parlour, where our sick old buccaneer was sitting, dazed with rum. The blind man clung close to me, holding me in one iron fist, and leaning almost more of his weight on me than I could carry. 'Lead me straight up to him, and when I'm in view, cry out, "Here's a friend for you, Bill." If you don't, I'll do this;' and with that he gave me a twitch that I thought would have made me faint. Between this and that, I was so utterly terrified of the blind beggar that I forgot my terror of the captain, and as I opened the parlour door, cried out the words he had ordered in a trembling voice.

The poor captain raised his eyes, and at one look the rum went out of him, and left him staring sober. The expression of his face was not so much of terror as of mortal sickness. He made a movement to rise, but I do not believe he had enough force left in his body.

'Now, Bill, sit where you are,' said the beggar. 'If I can't see, I can hear a finger stirring. Business is business. Hold out your left hand. Boy, take his left hand by the wrist, and bring it near to my right.'

We both obeyed him to the letter, and I saw him pass something from the hollow of the hand that held his stick into the palm of the captain's, which closed upon it instantly.

'And now that's done,' said the blind man; and at the words he suddenly left hold of me, and with incredible accuracy and nimbleness, skipped out of the parlour and into the road, where, as I still stood motionless, I could hear his stick go tap-tap-tapping into the distance.

It was some time before either I or the captain seemed to gather our senses; but at length, and about at the same moment, I released his wrist, which I was still holding, and he drew in his hand and looked sharply into the palm.

'Ten o'clock!' he cried. 'Six hours. We'll do them yet;' and he sprang to his feet.

Even as he did so, he reeled, put his hand to his throat, stood swaying for a moment, and then, with a peculiar sound, fell from his whole height face foremost to the floor.

I ran to him at once, calling to my mother. But haste was all in vain. The captain had been struck dead by thundering apoplexy. It is a curious thing to understand, for I had certainly never liked the man, though of late I had begun to pity him, but as soon as I saw that he was dead, I burst into a flood of tears. It was the second death I had known, and the sorrow of the first was still fresh in my heart.

Chapter Four

The Sea-Chest

I lost no time, of course, in telling my mother all that I knew, and perhaps should have told her long before, and we saw ourselves at once in a difficult and dangerous position. Some of the man's money – if he had any – was certainly due to us; but it was not likely that our captain's shipmates, above all the two specimens seen by me, Black Dog and the blind beggar, would be inclined to give up their booty in payment of the dead man's debts. The captain's order to mount at once and ride for Doctor Livesey would have left my mother alone and unprotected, which was not to be thought of. Indeed, it seemed impossible for either of us to remain much longer in the house: the fall of coals in the kitchen grate, the very ticking of the clock, filled us with alarms. The neighbourhood, to our ears, seemed haunted by approaching footsteps; and what between the dead body of the captain on the parlour floor, and the thought of that detestable blind beggar hovering near at hand, and ready to return, there were moments when, as the saying goes, I jumped in my skin for terror. Something must speedily be resolved upon; and it occurred to us at last to go forth together and seek help in the neighbouring hamlet. No sooner said than done. Bare-headed as we were, we ran out at once in the gathering evening and the frosty fog.

The hamlet lay not many hundred yards away though out of view, on the other side of the next cove; and what greatly encouraged me, it was in an opposite direction from that whence the blind man had made his appearance, and whither he had presumably returned. We were not many minutes on the road, though we sometimes stopped to lay hold of each other and hearken.

But there was no unusual sound – nothing but the low wash of the ripple and the croaking of the inmates of the wood.

It was already candle-light when we reached the hamlet, and I shall never forget how much I was cheered to see the yellow shine in doors and windows; but that, as it proved, was the best of the help we were likely to get in that quarter. For – you would have thought men would have been ashamed of themselves – no soul would consent to return with us to the 'Admiral Benbow.' The more we told of our troubles, the more – man, woman, and child – they clung to the shelter of their houses. The name of Captain Flint, though it was strange to me, was well enough known to some there, and carried a great weight of terror. Some of the men who had been to field-work on the far side of the 'Admiral Benbow' remembered, besides, to have seen several strangers on the road, and, taking them to be smugglers, to have bolted away; and one at least had seen a little lugger in what we called Kitt's Hole. For that matter, any one who was a comrade of the captain's was enough to frighten them to death. And the short and the long of the matter was, that while we could get several who were willing enough to ride to Dr Livesey's, which lay in another direction, not one would help us to defend the inn.

They say cowardice is infectious; but then argument is, on the other hand, a great emboldener; and so when each had said his say, my mother made them a speech. She would not, she declared, lose money that belonged to her fatherless boy; 'if none of the rest of you dare,' she said, 'Jim and I dare. Back we will go, the way we came, and small thanks to you big, hulking, chicken-hearted men. We'll have that chest open, if we die for it. And I'll thank you for that bag, Mrs Crossley, to bring back our lawful money in.'

Of course, I said I would go with my mother; and of course they all cried out at our foolhardiness; but even then not a man would go along with us. All they would do was to give me a loaded pistol, lest we were attacked; and to promise to have horses ready saddled, in case we were pursued on our return; while one lad was to ride forward to the doctor's in search of armed assistance.

My heart was beating finely when we two set forth in the cold night upon this dangerous venture. A full moon was beginning to rise and peered redly through the upper edges of the fog, and this increased our haste, for it was plain, before we came forth again, that all would be as bright as day, and our departure exposed to the eyes of any watchers. We slipped along the hedges, noiseless and swift, nor did we see or hear anything to increase our terrors, till, to our relief, the door of the 'Admiral Benbow' had closed behind us.

I slipped the bolt at once, and we stood and panted for a moment in the dark, alone in the house with the dead captain's body. Then my mother got a candle in the bar, and, holding each other's hands, we advanced into the parlour. He lay as we had left him, on his back, with his eyes open, and one arm stretched out.

'Draw down the blind, Jim,' whispered my mother; 'they might come and watch outside. And now,' said she, when I had done so, 'we have to get the key off *that*; and who's to touch it, I should like to know!' and she gave a kind of sob as she said the words.

I went down on my knees at once. On the floor close to his hand there was a little round of paper, blackened on the one side. I could not doubt that this was the *black spot*; and taking it up, I found written on the other side, in a very good, clear hand, this short message: 'You have till ten to-night.'

'He had till ten, mother,' said I; and just as I said it, our old clock began striking. This sudden noise startled us shockingly; but the news was good, for it was only six.

'Now, Jim,' she said, 'that key.'

I felt in his pockets, one after another. A few small coins, a thimble, and some thread and big needles, a piece of pigtail tobacco bitten away at the end, his gully with the crooked handle, a pocket compass, and a tinder-box, were all that they contained, and I began to despair.

'Perhaps it's round his neck,' suggested my mother.

Overcoming a strong repugnance, I tore open his shirt at the neck, and there, sure enough, hanging to a bit of tarry string, which I cut with his own gully, we found the key. At this triumph we were filled with hope, and hurried up-stairs, without delay, to the little room where he had slept so long, and where his box had stood since the day of his arrival.

It was like any other seaman's chest on the outside, the initial 'B.' burned on the top of it with a hot iron, and the corners somewhat smashed and broken as by long, rough usage.

'Give me the key,' said my mother; and though the lock was very stiff, she had turned it and thrown back the lid in a twinkling.

A strong smell of tobacco and tar rose from the interior, but nothing was to be seen on the top except a suit of very good clothes, carefully brushed and folded. They had never been worn, my mother said. Under that, the miscellany began – a quadrant, a tin canikin, several sticks of tobacco, two brace of very handsome pistols, a piece of bar silver, an old Spanish watch and some other trinkets of little value and mostly of foreign make, a pair of compasses mounted with brass, and five or six curious West Indian shells. I have often wondered since why he should have carried about these shells with him in his wandering, guilty, and hunted life.

In the meantime, we had found nothing of any value but the silver and the trinkets, and neither of these were in our way. Underneath there was an old boat-cloak, whitened with sea-salt on many a harbour-bar. My mother pulled it up with impatience, and there lay before us, the last things in the chest, a bundle tied up in oilcloth, and looking like papers, and a canvas bag, that gave forth, at a touch, the jingle of gold.

'I'll show these rogues that I'm an honest woman,' said my mother. 'I'll have my dues, and not a farthing over. Hold Mrs

Crossley's bag.' And she began to count over the amount of the captain's score from the sailor's bag into the one that I was holding.

It was a long, difficult business, for the coins were of all countries and sizes – doubloons, and louis-d'ors, and guineas, and pieces of eight, and I know not what besides, all shaken together at random. The guineas, too, were about the scarcest, and it was with these only that my mother knew how to make her count.

When we were about half way through, I suddenly put my hand upon her arm; for I had heard in the silent, frosty air, a sound that brought my heart into my mouth – the tap-tapping of the blind man's stick upon the frozen road. It drew nearer and nearer, while we sat holding our breath. Then it struck sharp on the inn door, and then we could hear the handle being turned, and the bolt rattling as the wretched being tried to enter; and then there was a long time of silence both within and without. At last the tapping re-commenced, and, to our indescribable joy and gratitude, died slowly away again until it ceased to be heard.

'Mother,' said I, 'take the whole and let's be going;' for I was sure the bolted door must have seemed suspicious, and would bring the whole hornet's nest about our ears; though how thankful I was that I had bolted it, none could tell who had never met that terrible blind man.

But my mother, frightened as she was, would not consent to take a fraction more than was due to her, and was obstinately unwilling to be content with less. It was not yet seven, she said, by a long way; she knew her rights and she would have them; and she was still arguing with me, when a little low whistle sounded a good way off upon the hill. That was enough, and more than enough, for both of us.

'I'll take what I have,' she said, jumping to her feet.

'And I'll take this to square the count,' said I, picking up the oilskin packet.

Next moment we were both groping down-stairs, leaving the

candle by the empty chest; and the next we had opened the door and were in full retreat. We had not started a moment too soon. The fog was rapidly dispersing; already the moon shone quite clear on the high ground on either side; and it was only in the exact bottom of the dell and round the tavern door that a thin veil still hung unbroken to conceal the first steps of our escape. Far less than half-way to the hamlet, very little beyond the bottom of the hill, we must come forth into the moonlight. Nor was this all; for the sound of several footsteps running came already to our ears, and as we looked back in their direction, a light tossing to and fro and still rapidly advancing, showed that one of the newcomers carried a lantern.

'My dear,' said my mother suddenly, 'take the money and run on. I am going to faint.'

This was certainly the end for both of us, I thought. How I cursed the cowardice of the neighbours; how I blamed my poor mother for her honesty and her greed, for her past foolhardiness and present weakness! We were just at the little bridge, by good fortune; and I helped her, tottering as she was, to the edge of the bank, where, sure enough, she gave a sigh and fell on my shoulder. I do not know how I found the strength to do it at all, and I am afraid it was roughly done; but I managed to drag her down the bank and a little way under the arch. Farther I could not move her, for the bridge was too low to let me do more than crawl below it. So there we had to stay – my mother almost entirely exposed, and both of us within earshot of the inn.

Chapter Five

The Last of the Blind Man

My curiosity, in a sense, was stronger than my fear; for I could not remain where I was, but crept back to the bank again, whence, sheltering my head behind a bush of broom, I might command the road before our door. I was scarcely in position ere my enemies began to arrive, seven or eight of them, running hard, their feet beating out of time along the road, and the man with the lantern some paces in front. Three men ran together, hand in hand; and I made out, even through the mist, that the middle man of this trio was the blind beggar. The next moment his voice showed me that I was right.

'Down with the door!' he cried.

'Ay, ay, sir!' answered two or three; and a rush was made upon the 'Admiral Benbow,' the lantern-bearer following; and then I could see them pause, and hear speeches passed in a lower key, as if they were surprised to find the door open. But the pause was brief, for the blind man again issued his commands. His voice sounded louder and higher, as if he were afire with eagerness and rage.

'In, in, in!' he shouted, and cursed them for their delay.

Four or five of them obeyed at once, two remaining on the road with the formidable beggar. There was a pause, then a cry of surprise, and then a voice shouting from the house: –

'Bill's dead.'

But the blind man swore at them again for their delay.

'Search him, some of you shirking lubbers, and the rest of you aloft and get the chest,' he cried.

I could hear their feet rattling up our old stairs, so that the house must have shook with it. Promptly afterwards, fresh sounds of astonishment arose; the window of the captain's room was thrown open with a slam and a jingle of broken glass; and a man leaned out into the moonlight, head and shoulders, and addressed the blind beggar on the road below him.

'Pew,' he cried, 'they've been before us. Some one's turned the chest out alow and aloft.'

'Is it there?' roared Pew.

'The money's there.'

The blind man cursed the money.

'Flint's fist, I mean,' he cried.

'We don't see it here nohow,' returned the man.

'Here, you below there, is it on Bill?' cried the blind man again.

At that, another fellow, probably he who had remained below to search the captain's body, came to the door of the inn. 'Bill's been overhauled a' ready,' said he, 'nothin' left.'

'It's these people of the inn – it's that boy. I wish I had put his eyes out!' cried the blind man, Pew. 'They were here no time ago – they had the door bolted when I tried it. Scatter, lads, and find 'em.'

'Sure enough, they left their glim here,' said the fellow from the window.

'Scatter and find 'em! Rout the house out!' reiterated Pew, striking with his stick upon the road.

Then there followed a great to-do through all our old inn, heavy feet pounding to and fro, furniture thrown over, doors kicked in, until the very rocks re-echoed, and the men came out again, one after another, on the road, and declared that we were nowhere to be found. And just then the same whistle that had alarmed my mother and myself over the dead captain's money was once more clearly audible through the night, but this time twice repeated. I had thought it to be the blind man's trumpet, so to speak, summoning his crew to the assault; but I now found that it was a signal from the hillside towards the hamlet, and, from its effect upon the buccaneers, a signal to warn them of approaching danger.

'There's Dirk again,' said one. 'Twice! We'll have to budge, mates.'

'Budge, you skulk!' cried Pew. 'Dirk was a fool and a coward from the first – you wouldn't mind him. They must be close by; they can't be far; you have your hands on it. Scatter and look for them, dogs! Oh, shiver my soul,' he cried, 'if I had eyes!'

This appeal seemed to produce some effect, for two of the fellows began to look here and there among the lumber, but half-heartedly, I thought, and with half an eye to their own danger all the time, while the rest stood irresolute on the road.

'You have your hands on thousands, you fools, and you hang a leg! You'd be as rich as kings if you could find it, and you know it's here, and you stand there skulking. There wasn't one of you dared face Bill, and I did it – a blind man! And I'm to lose my chance for you! I'm to be a poor, crawling beggar, sponging for rum, when I might be rolling in a coach! If you had the pluck of a weevil in a biscuit you would catch them still.'

'Hang it, Pew, we've got the doubloons!' grumbled one.

'They might have hid the blessed thing,' said another. 'Take the Georges, Pew, and don't stand here squalling.'

Squalling was the word for it, Pew's anger rose so high at these objections; till at last, his passion completely taking the upper hand, he struck at them right and left in his blindness, and his stick sounded heavily on more than one.

These, in their turn, cursed back at the blind miscreant, threatened him in horrid terms, and tried in vain to catch the stick and wrest it from his grasp.

This quarrel was the saving of us, for while it was still raging, another sound came from the top of the hill on the side of the hamlet – the tramp of horses galloping. Almost at the same time a pistol-shot, flash and report, came from the hedge side. And that was plainly the last signal of danger; for the buccaneers turned at once and ran, separating in every direction, one seaward along the cove, one slant across the hill, and so on, so that in half a minute not a sign of them remained but Pew. Him they had deserted, whether in sheer panic or out of revenge for his ill words and blows, I know not; but there he remained behind, tapping up and down the road in a frenzy, and groping and calling for his comrades. Finally he took the wrong turn, and ran a few steps past me, towards the hamlet, crying: –

'Johnny, Black Dog, Dirk,' and other names, 'you won't leave old Pew, mates – not old Pew!'

Just then the noise of horses topped the rise, and four or five riders came in sight in the moonlight, and swept at full gallop down the slope.

At this Pew saw his error, turned with a scream, and ran straight for the ditch, into which he rolled. But he was on his feet again in a second, and made another dash, now utterly bewildered, right under the nearest of the coming horses.

The rider tried to save him, but in vain. Down went Pew with a cry that rang high into the night; and the four hoofs trampled and spurned him and passed by. He fell on his side, then gently collapsed upon his face, and moved no more.

I leaped to my feet and hailed the riders. They were pulling up, at any rate, horrified at the accident; and I soon saw what they were. One, tailing out behind the rest, was a lad that had gone from the hamlet to Dr Livesey's; the rest were revenue officers, whom he had met by the way, and with whom he had had the intelligence to return at once. Some news of the lugger in Kitt's Hole had found its way to Supervisor Dance, and set him forth that night in our direction, and to that circumstance my mother and I owed our preservation from death.

Pew was dead, stone dead. As for my mother, when we had carried her up to the hamlet, a little cold water and salts and that soon brought her back again, and she was none the worse for her terror, though she still continued to deplore the balance of the money. In the meantime the supervisor rode on, as fast as he could, to Kitt's Hole; but his men had to dismount and grope down the dingle, leading, and sometimes supporting, their horses, and in continual fear of ambushes; so it was no great matter for surprise that when they got down to the Hole the lugger was already under way, though still close in. He hailed her. A voice replied, telling him to keep out of the moonlight, or he would get some lead in him, and at the same time a bullet whistled close by his arm. Soon after, the lugger doubled the point and disappeared. Mr Dance stood there, as he said, 'like a fish out of water,' and all he could do was to despatch a man to B— to warn the cutter. 'And that,' said he, 'is just about as good as nothing. They've got off clean, and there's an end. Only,' he added, 'I'm glad I trod on Master Pew's corns;' for by this time he had heard my story.

I went back with him to the 'Admiral Benbow,' and you cannot imagine a house in such a state of smash; the very clock had been thrown down by these fellows in their furious hunt after my mother and myself; and though nothing had actually been taken away except the captain's money-bag and a little silver from the till, I could see at once that we were ruined. Mr Dance could make nothing of the scene.

'They got the money, you say? Well, then, Hawkins, what in fortune were they after? More money, I suppose?'

'No, sir; not money, I think,' replied I. 'In fact, sir, I believe I have the thing in my breast-pocket; and, to tell you the truth, I should like to get it put in safety.'

'To be sure, boy; quite right,' said he. 'I'll take it, if you like.'

'I thought, perhaps, Dr Livesey –' I began.

'Perfectly right,' he interrupted, very cheerily, 'perfectly right – a gentleman and a magistrate. And, now I come to think of it, I might as well ride round there myself and report to him or squire. Master Pew's dead, when all's done; not that I regret it, but he's dead, you see, and people will make it out against an officer of his Majesty's revenue, if make it out they can. Now, I'll tell you, Hawkins: if you like, I'll take you along.'

I thanked him heartily for the offer, and we walked back to the hamlet where the horses were. By the time I had told mother of my purpose they were all in the saddle.

'Dogger,' said Mr Dance, 'you have a good horse; take up this lad behind you.'

As soon as I was mounted, holding on to Dogger's belt, the supervisor gave the word, and the party struck out at a bouncing trot on the road to Dr Livesey's house.

Chapter Six

The Captain's Papers

We rode hard all the way, till we drew up before Dr Livesey's door. The house was all dark to the front.

Mr Dance told me to jump down and knock, and Dogger gave me a stirrup to descend by. The door was opened almost at once by the maid.

'Is Dr Livesey in?' I asked.

No, she said; he had come home in the afternoon, but had gone up to the Hall to dine and pass the evening with the squire.

'So there we go, boys,' said Mr Dance.

This time, as the distance was short, I did not mount, but ran with Dogger's stirrup-leather to the lodge gates, and up the long, leafless, moonlit avenue to where the white line of the Hall buildings looked on either hand on great old gardens. Here Mr Dance dismounted, and, taking me along with him, was admitted at a word into the house.

The servant led us down a matted passage, and showed us at the end into a great library, all lined with bookcases and busts upon the top of them, where the squire and Dr Livesey sat, pipe in hand, on either side of a bright fire.

I had never seen the squire so near at hand. He was a tall man, over six feet high, and broad in proportion, and he had a bluff, rough-and-ready face, all roughened and reddened and lined in his long travels. His eyebrows were very black, and moved readily, and this gave him a look of some temper, not bad, you would say, but quick and high.

'Come in, Mr Dance,' says he, very stately and condescending.

'Good evening, Dance,' says the doctor, with a nod. 'And good evening to you, friend Jim. What good wind brings you here?'

The supervisor stood up straight and stiff, and told his story like a lesson; and you should have seen how the two gentlemen leaned forward and looked at each other, and forgot to smoke in their surprise and interest. When they heard how my mother went back to the inn, Dr Livesey fairly slapped his thigh, and the squire cried 'Bravo!' and broke his long pipe against the grate. Long before it was done, Mr Trelawney (that, you will remember, was the squire's name) had got up from his seat, and was striding about the room, and the doctor, as if to hear the better, had taken off his powdered wig, and sat there, looking very strange indeed with his own close-cropped, black poll.

At last Mr Dance finished the story.

'Mr Dance,' said the squire, 'you are a very noble fellow. And as for riding down that black, atrocious miscreant, I regard it as an act of virtue, sir, like stamping on a cockroach. This lad Hawkins is a trump, I perceive. Hawkins, will you ring that bell? Mr Dance must have some ale.'

'And so, Jim,' said the doctor, 'you have the thing that they were after, have you?'

'Here it is, sir,' said I, and gave him the oilskin packet.

The doctor looked it all over, as if his fingers were itching to open it; but, instead of doing that, he put it quietly in the pocket of his coat.

'Squire,' said he, 'when Dance has had his ale he must, of course, be off on his Majesty's service; but I mean to keep Jim Hawkins here to sleep at my house, and, with your permission, I propose we should have up the cold pie, and let him sup.'

'As you will, Livesey,' said the squire; 'Hawkins has earned better than cold pie.'

So a big pigeon pie was brought in and put on a side-table, and I made a hearty supper, for I was as hungry as a hawk, while Mr Dance was further complimented, and at last dismissed.

'And now, squire,' said the doctor.

'And now, Livesey,' said the squire in the same breath.

'One at a time, one at a time,' laughed Dr Livesey. 'You have heard of this Flint, I suppose?'

'Heard of him!' cried the squire. 'Heard of him, you say! He was the bloodthirstiest buccaneer that sailed, Blackbeard was a child to Flint. The Spaniards were so prodigiously afraid of him, that, I tell you, sir, I was sometimes proud he was an Englishman. I've seen his top-sails with these eyes, off Trinidad, and the cowardly son of a rum-puncheon that I sailed with put back – put back, sir, into Port of Spain.'

'Well, I've heard of him myself, in England,' said the doctor. 'But the point is, had he money?'

'Money!' cried the squire. 'Have you heard the story? What were these villains after but money? What do they care for but money? For what would they risk their rascal carcasses but money?'

'That we shall soon know,' replied the doctor. 'But you are so confoundedly hot-headed and exclamatory that I cannot get a word in. What I want to know is this: Supposing that I have here in my pocket some clue to where Flint buried his treasure, will that treasure amount to much?'

'Amount, sir!' cried the squire. 'It will amount to this: if we have the clue you talk about, I fit out a ship in Bristol dock, and take you and Hawkins here along, and I'll have that treasure if I search a year.'

'Very well,' said the doctor. 'Now, then, if Jim is agreeable, we'll open the packet;' and he laid it before him on the table.

The bundle was sewn together, and the doctor had to get out his instrument-case, and cut the stitches with his medical scissors. It contained two things – a book and a sealed paper.

'First of all we'll try the book,' observed the doctor.

The squire and I were both peering over his shoulder as he opened it, for Dr Livesey had kindly motioned me to come round from the side-table, where I had been eating, to enjoy the sport of the search. On the first page there were only some scraps of writing, such as a man with a pen in his hand might make for idleness or practice. One was the same as the tattoo mark, 'Billy Bones his fancy;' then there was 'Mr W. Bones, mate.' 'No more rum.' 'Off Palm Key he got itt;' and some other snatches, mostly single words and unintelligible. I could not help wondering who it was that had 'got itt,' and what 'itt' was that he got. A knife in his back as like as not.

'Not much instruction there,' said Dr Livesey, as he passed on.

The next ten or twelve pages were filled with a curious series of entries. There was a date at one end of the line and at the other a sum of money, as in common account-books; but instead of explanatory writing, only a varying number of crosses between the two. On the 12th of June, 1745, for instance, a sum of seventy pounds had plainly become due to some one, and there was nothing but six crosses to explain the cause. In a few cases, to be sure, the name of a place would be added, as 'Offe Caraccas;' or a mere entry of latitude and longitude, as '62° 17′ 20″, 19° 2′ 40″.'

The record lasted over nearly twenty years, the amount of the separate entries growing larger as time went on, and at the end a grand total had been made out after five or six wrong additions, and these words appended, 'Bones, his pile.'

'I can't make head or tail of this,' said Dr Livesey.

'The thing is as clear as noonday,' cried the squire. 'This is the black-hearted hound's account-book. These crosses stand for the names of ships or towns that they sank or plundered. The sums are the scoundrel's share, and where he feared an ambiguity, you see he added something clearer. "Offe Caraccas," now; you see, here was some unhappy vessel boarded off that coast. God help the poor souls that manned her – coral long ago.'

'Right!' said the doctor. 'See what it is to be a traveller. Right! And the amounts increase, you see, as he rose in rank.'

There was little else in the volume but a few bearings of places noted in the blank leaves towards the end, and a table for reducing French, English, and Spanish moneys to a common value.

'Thrifty man!' cried the doctor. 'He wasn't the one to be cheated.'

'And now,' said the squire, 'for the other.'

The paper had been sealed in several places with a thimble by way of seal; the very thimble, perhaps, that I had found in the captain's pocket. The doctor opened the seals with great care, and there fell out the map of an island, with latitude and longitude, soundings, names of hills, and bays and inlets, and every particular that would be needed to bring a ship to a safe anchorage upon its shores. It was about nine miles long and five across, shaped, you might say, like a fat dragon standing up, and had two fine land-locked harbours, and a hill in the centre part marked 'The Spy-glass.' There were several additions of a later date; but, above all, three crosses of red ink – two on the north part of the island, one in the south-west, and, beside this last, in the same red ink, and in a small, neat hand, very different from the captain's tottery characters, these words: – 'Bulk of treasure here.'

Over on the back the same hand had written this further information: –

'Tall tree, Spy-glass shoulder, bearing a point to the N. of N. N. E.

'Skeleton Island E. S. E. and by E.

'Ten feet.

'The bar silver is in the north cache; you can find it by the trend of the east hummock, ten fathoms south of the black crag with the face on it.

'The arms are easy found, in the sand hill, N. point of north inlet cape, bearing E. and a quarter N.

'J. F.'

That was all; but brief as it was, and, to me, incomprehensible, it filled the squire and Dr Livesey with delight.

'Livesey,' said the squire, 'you will give up this wretched practice at once. To-morrow I start for Bristol. In three weeks' time – three weeks! – two weeks – ten days – we'll have the best ship, sir, and the choicest crew in England. Hawkins shall come as cabin-boy. You'll make a famous cabin-boy, Hawkins. You, Livesey, are ship's doctor; I am admiral. We'll take Redruth, Joyce, and Hunter. We'll have favourable winds, a quick passage, and not the least difficulty in finding the spot, and money to eat – to roll in – to play duck and drake with ever after.'

'Trelawney,' said the doctor, 'I'll go with you; and I'll go bail for it, so will Jim, and be a credit to the undertaking. There's only one man I'm afraid of.'

'And who's that?' cried the squire. 'Name the dog, sir!'

'You,' replied the doctor; 'for you cannot hold your tongue. We are not the only men who know of this paper. These fellows who attacked the inn to-night – bold, desperate blades, for sure – and the rest who stayed aboard that lugger, and more, I dare say, not far off, are, one and all, through thick and thin, bound that they'll get that money. We must none of us go alone till we get to sea. Jim and I shall stick together in the meanwhile: you'll take Joyce and Hunter when you ride to Bristol, and, from first to last, not one of us must breathe a word of what we've found.'

'Livesey,' returned the squire, 'you are always in the right of it. I'll be as silent as the grave.'

PART TWO

The Sea Cook

Chapter Seven

I Go to Bristol

It was longer than the squire imagined ere we were ready for the sea, and none of our first plans – not even Dr Livesey's, of keeping me beside him – could be carried out as we intended. The doctor had to go to London for a physician to take charge of his practice; the squire was hard at work at Bristol; and I lived on at the Hall under the charge of old Redruth, the gamekeeper, almost a prisoner, but full of sea-dreams and the most charming anticipations of strange islands and adventures. I brooded by the hour together over the map, all the details of which I well remembered. Sitting by the fire in the housekeeper's room, I approached that island in my fancy, from every possible direction; I explored every acre of its surface; I climbed a thousand times to that tall hill they call the Spy-glass, and from the top enjoyed the most wonderful and changing prospects. Sometimes the isle was thick with savages, with whom we fought; sometimes full of dangerous animals that hunted us; but in all my fancies nothing occurred to me so strange and tragic as our actual adventures.

So the weeks passed on, till one fine day there came a letter addressed to Dr Livesey, with this addition, 'To be opened, in the case of his absence, by Tom Redruth, or young Hawkins.' Obeying this order, we found, or rather, I found – for the gamekeeper was a poor hand at reading anything but print – the following important news: –

'Old Anchor Inn, Bristol, March 1, 17–.

'Dear Livesey, – As I do not know whether you are at the Hall or still in London, I send this in double to both places.

43

'The ship is bought and fitted. She lies at anchor, ready for sea. You never imagined a sweeter schooner – a child might sail her – two hundred tons; name, Hispaniola.

'I got her through my old friend, Blandly, who has proved himself throughout the most surprising trump. The admirable fellow literally slaved in my interest, and so, I may say, did every one in Bristol, as soon as they got wind of the port we sailed for – treasure, I mean.'

'Redruth,' said I, interrupting the letter, 'Doctor Livesey will not like that. The squire has been talking, after all.'

'Well, who's a better right?' growled the gamekeeper. 'A pretty rum go if squire ain't to talk for Doctor Livesey, I should think.'

At that I gave up all attempt at commentary, and read straight on: –

'Blandly himself found the Hispaniola, and by the most admirable management got her for the merest trifle. There is a class of men in Bristol monstrously prejudiced against Blandly. They go the length of declaring that this honest creature would do anything for money, that the Hispaniola belonged to him, and that he sold it me absurdly high – the most transparent calumnies. None of them dare, however, to deny the merits of the ship.

'So far there was not a hitch. The workpeople, to be sure – riggers and what not – were most annoyingly slow; but time cured that. It was the crew that troubled me.

'I wished a round score of men – in case of natives, buccaneers, or the odious French – and I had the worry of the deuce itself to find so much as half a dozen, till the most remarkable stroke of fortune brought me the very man that I required.

'I was standing on the dock, when, by the merest accident, I fell in talk with him. I found he was an old sailor, kept a public-house, knew all the seafaring men in Bristol, had lost his health ashore, and wanted a good berth as cook to get to sea again. He had hobbled down there that morning, he said, to get a smell of the salt.

'I was monstrously touched – so would you have been – and, out of pure pity, I engaged him on the spot to be ship's cook. Long John Silver, he is called, and has lost a leg; but that I regarded as a recommendation, since he lost it in his country's service, under the immortal Hawke. He has no pension, Livesey. Imagine the abominable age we live in!

'Well, sir, I thought I had only found a cook, but it was a crew I had discovered. Between Silver and myself we got together in a few days a company of the toughest old salts imaginable – not pretty to look at, but fellows, by their faces, of the most indomitable spirit. I declare we could fight a frigate.

'Long John even got rid of two out of the six or seven I had already engaged. He showed me in a moment that they were just the sort of fresh-water swabs we had to fear in an adventure of importance.

'I am in the most magnificent health and spirits, eating like a bull, sleeping like a tree, yet I shall not enjoy a moment till I hear my old tarpaulins tramping round the capstan. Seaward ho! Hang the treasure! It's the glory of the sea that has turned my head. So now, Livesey, come post; do not lose an hour, if you respect me.

'Let young Hawkins go at once to see his mother, with Redruth for a guard; and then both come full speed to Bristol.

'John Trelawney.

'Postscript. – I did not tell you that Blandly, who, by the way, is to send a consort after us if we don't turn up by the end of August, had found an admirable fellow for sailing-master – a stiff man, which I regret, but, in all other respects, a treasure. Long John Silver unearthed a very competent man for a mate, a man named Arrow. I have a boatswain who pipes, Livesey; so things shall go man-o'-war fashion on board the good ship Hispaniola.

'I forgot to tell you that Silver is a man of substance; I know
of my own knowledge that he has a banker's account, which has
never been overdrawn. He leaves his wife to manage the inn;
and as she is a woman of colour, a pair of old bachelors like you
and I may be excused for guessing that it is the wife, quite as
much as the health, that sends him back to roving.

'J. T.

'P. P. S. – Hawkins may stay one night with his mother.

'J. T.'

You can fancy the excitement into which that letter put me. I was
half beside myself with glee; and if ever I despised a man, it was
old Tom Redruth, who could do nothing but grumble and lam-
ent. Any of the under-gamekeepers would gladly have changed
places with him; but such was not the squire's pleasure, and the
squire's pleasure was like law among them all. Nobody but old
Redruth would have dared so much as even to grumble.

The next morning he and I set out on foot for the 'Admiral Benbow,' and there I found my mother in good health and spirits. The
captain, who had so long been a cause of so much discomfort,
was gone where the wicked cease from troubling. The squire had
had everything repaired, and the public rooms and the sign
repainted, and had added some furniture – above all a beautiful
arm-chair for mother in the bar. He had found her a boy as an
apprentice also, so that she should not want help while I was gone.

It was on seeing that boy that I understood, for the first time,
my situation. I had thought up to that moment of the adventures
before me, not at all of the home that I was leaving; and now, at
sight of this clumsy stranger, who was to stay here in my place
beside my mother, I had my first attack of tears. I am afraid I led
that boy a dog's life; for as he was new to the work, I had a hundred opportunities of setting him right and putting him down,
and I was not slow to profit by them.

The night passed, and the next day, after dinner, Redruth and I were afoot again, and on the road. I said good-bye to mother and the cove where I had lived since I was born, and the dear old 'Admiral Benbow' – since he was repainted, no longer quite so dear. One of my last thoughts was of the captain, who had so often strode along the beach with his cocked hat, his sabre-cut cheek, and his old brass telescope. Next moment we had turned the corner, and my home was out of sight.

The mail picked us up about dusk at the 'Royal George' on the heath. I was wedged in between Redruth and a stout old gentleman, and in spite of the swift motion and the cold night air, I must have dozed a great deal from the very first, and then slept like a log up hill and down dale through stage after stage; for when I was awakened, at last, it was by a punch in the ribs, and I opened my eyes, to find that we were standing still before a large building in a city street, and that the day had already broken a long time.

'Where are we?' I asked.

'Bristol,' said Tom. 'Get down.'

Mr Trelawney had taken up his residence at an inn far down the docks, to superintend the work upon the schooner. Thither we had now to walk, and our way, to my great delight, lay along the quays and beside the great multitude of ships of all sizes and rigs and nations. In one, sailors were singing at their work; in another, there were men aloft, high over my head, hanging to threads that seemed no thicker than a spider's. Though I had lived by the shore all my life, I seemed never to have been near the sea till then. The smell of tar and salt was something new. I saw the most wonderful figureheads, that had all been far over the ocean. I saw, besides, many old sailors, with rings in their ears, and whiskers curled in ringlets, and tarry pigtails, and their swaggering, clumsy sea-walk; and if I had seen as many kings or archbishops I could not have been more delighted.

And I was going to sea myself; to sea in a schooner, with a

piping boatswain, and pig-tailed singing seamen; to sea, bound for an unknown island, and to seek for buried treasures!

While I was still in this delightful dream, we came suddenly in front of a large inn, and met Squire Trelawney, all dressed out like a sea-officer, in stout blue cloth, coming out of the door with a smile on his face, and a capital imitation of a sailor's walk.

'Here you are,' he cried, 'and the doctor came last night from London. Bravo! the ship's company complete!'

'Oh, sir,' cried I, 'when do we sail?'

'Sail!' says he. 'We sail to-morrow!'

Chapter Eight

At the Sign of the 'Spy-glass'

When I had done breakfasting the squire gave me a note addressed to John Silver, at the sign of the 'Spy-glass,' and told me I should easily find the place by following the line of the docks, and keeping a bright look-out for a little tavern with a large brass telescope for sign. I set off, overjoyed at this opportunity to see some more of the ships and seamen, and picked my way among a great crowd of people and carts and bales, for the dock was now at its busiest, until I found the tavern in question.

It was a bright enough little place of entertainment. The sign was newly painted; the windows had neat red curtains; the floor was cleanly sanded. There was a street on each side, and an open door on both, which made the large, low room pretty clear to see in, in spite of clouds of tobacco smoke.

The customers were mostly seafaring men; and they talked so loudly that I hung at the door, almost afraid to enter.

As I was waiting, a man came out of a side room, and, at a glance, I was sure he must be Long John. His left leg was cut off close by the hip, and under the left shoulder he carried a crutch, which he managed with wonderful dexterity, hopping about upon it like a bird. He was very tall and strong, with a face as big as a ham – plain and pale, but intelligent and smiling. Indeed, he seemed in the most cheerful spirits, whistling as he moved about among the tables, with a merry word or a slap on the shoulder for the more favoured of his guests.

Now, to tell you the truth, from the very first mention of Long John in Squire Trelawney's letter, I had taken a fear in my mind that he might prove to be the very one-legged sailor whom I had watched for so long at the old 'Benbow.' But one look at the man before me was enough. I had seen the captain, and Black Dog, and the blind man Pew, and I thought I knew what a buccaneer was like – a very different creature, according to me, from this clean and pleasant-tempered landlord.

I plucked up courage at once, crossed the threshold, and walked right up to the man where he stood, propped on his crutch, talking to a customer.

'Mr Silver, sir?' I asked, holding out the note.

'Yes, my lad,' said he; 'such is my name, to be sure. And who may you be?' And then as he saw the squire's letter, he seemed to me to give something almost like a start.

'Oh!' said he, quite loud, and offering his hand, 'I see. You are our new cabin-boy; pleased I am to see you.'

And he took my hand in his large firm grasp.

Just then one of the customers at the far side rose suddenly and made for the door. It was close by him, and he was out in the street in a moment. But his hurry had attracted my notice, and I recognised him at a glance. It was the tallow-faced man, wanting two fingers, who had come first to the 'Admiral Benbow.'

'Oh,' I cried, 'stop him! it's Black Dog!'

'I don't care two coppers who he is,' cried Silver. 'But he hasn't paid his score. Harry, run and catch him.'

One of the others who was nearest the door leaped up, and started in pursuit.

'If he were Admiral Hawke he shall pay his score,' cried Silver; and then, relinquishing my hand – 'Who did you say he was?' he asked. 'Black what?'

'Dog, sir,' said I. 'Has Mr Trelawney not told you of the buccaneers? He was one of them.'

'So?' cried Silver. 'In my house! Ben, run and help Harry. One of those swabs, was he? Was that you drinking with him, Morgan? Step up here.'

The man whom he called Morgan – an old, grey-haired, mahogany-faced sailor – came forward pretty sheepishly, rolling his quid.

'Now, Morgan,' said Long John, very sternly; 'you never clapped your eyes on that Black – Black Dog before, did you, now?'

'Not I, sir,' said Morgan, with a salute.

'You didn't know his name, did you?'

'No, sir.'

'By the powers, Tom Morgan, it's as good for you!' exclaimed the landlord. 'If you had been mixed up with the like of that, you would never have put another foot in my house, you may lay to that. And what was he saying to you?'

'I don't rightly know, sir,' answered Morgan.

'Do you call that a head on your shoulders, or a blessed dead-eye?' cried Long John. 'Don't rightly know, don't you! Perhaps you don't happen to rightly know who you was speaking to, perhaps? Come, now, what was he jawing – v'yages, cap'ns, ships? Pipe up! What was it?'

'We was a-talkin' of keel-hauling,' answered Morgan.

'Keel-hauling, was you? and a mighty suitable thing, too, and you may lay to that. Get back to your place for a lubber, Tom.'

And then, as Morgan rolled back to his seat, Silver added to me in a confidential whisper, that was very flattering, as I thought: –

'He's quite an honest man, Tom Morgan, on'y stupid. And now,' he ran on again, aloud, 'let's see – Black Dog? No, I don't know the name, not I. Yet I kind of think I've – yes, I've seen the swab. He used to come here with a blind beggar, he used.'

'That he did, you may be sure,' said I. 'I knew that blind man, too. His name was Pew.'

'It was!' cried Silver, now quite excited. 'Pew! That were his name for certain. Ah, he looked a shark, he did! If we run down this Black Dog, now, there'll be news for Cap'n Trelawney! Ben's a good runner; few seamen run better than Ben. He should run him down, hand over hand, by the powers! He talked o' keel-hauling, did he? *I'll* keel-haul him!'

All the time he was jerking out these phrases he was stumping up and down the tavern on his crutch, slapping tables with his hand, and giving such a show of excitement as would have convinced on Old Bailey judge or a Bow Street runner. My suspicions had been thoroughly re-awakened on finding Black Dog at the 'Spy-glass,' and I watched the cook narrowly. But he was too deep, and too ready, and too clever for me, and by the time the two men had come back out of breath, and confessed that they had lost the track in a crowd, and been scolded like thieves, I would have gone bail for the innocence of Long John Silver.

'See here, now, Hawkins,' said he, 'here's a blessed hard thing on a man like me, now, ain't it? There's Cap'n Trelawney – what's he to think? Here I have this confounded son of a Dutchman sitting in my own house, drinking of my own rum! Here you comes and tells me of it plain; and here I let him give us all the slip before my blessed dead-lights! Now, Hawkins, you do me justice with the cap'n. You're a lad, you are, but you're as smart as paint. I see that when you first came in. Now, here it is: What could I do, with this old timber I hobble on? When I was an master mariner I'd have come up alongside of him, hand over hand, and broached him to in a brace of old shakes, I would; but now –'

And then, all of a sudden, he stopped, and his jaw dropped as though he had remembered something.

'The score!' he burst out. 'Three goes o' rum! Why, shiver my timbers, if I hadn't forgotten my score!'

And, falling on a bench, he laughed until the tears ran down his cheeks. I could not help joining; and we laughed together, peal after peal, until the tavern rang again.

'Why, what a precious old sea-calf I am!' he said, at last, wiping his cheeks. 'You and me should get on well, Hawkins, for I'll take my davy I should be rated ship's boy. But, come, now, stand by to go about. This won't do. Dooty is dooty, messmates. I'll put on my old cocked hat, and step along of you to Cap'n Trelawney, and report this here affair. For, mind you, it's serious, young Hawkins; and neither you nor me's come out of it with what I should make so bold as to call credit. Nor you neither, says you;

not smart – none of the pair of us smart. But dash my buttons! that was a good 'un about my score.'

And he began to laugh again, and that so heartily, that though I did not see the joke as he did, I was again obliged to join him in his mirth.

On our little walk along the quays, he made himself the most interesting companion, telling me about the different ships that we passed by, their rig, tonnage, and nationality, explaining the work that was going forward – how one was discharging, another taking in cargo, and a third making ready for sea; and every now and then telling me some little anecdote of ships or seamen, or repeating a nautical phrase till I had learned it perfectly. I began to see that here was one of the best of possible shipmates.

When we got to the inn, the squire and Dr Livesey were seated together, finishing a quart of ale with a toast in it, before they should go aboard the schooner on a visit of inspection.

Long John told the story from first to last, with a great deal of spirit and the most perfect truth. 'That was how it were, now, weren't it, Hawkins?' he would say, now and again, and I could always bear him entirely out.

The two gentlemen regretted that Black Dog had got away; but we all agreed there was nothing to be done, and after he had been complimented, Long John took up his crutch and departed.

'All hands aboard by four this afternoon,' shouted the squire, after him.

'Ay, ay, sir,' cried the cook, in the passage.

'Well, squire,' said Dr Livesey, 'I don't put much faith in your discoveries, as a general thing; but I will say this, John Silver suits me.'

'The man's a perfect trump,' declared the squire.

'And now,' added the doctor, 'Jim may come on board with us, may he not?'

'To be sure he may,' says the squire. 'Take your hat, Hawkins, and we'll see the ship.'

Chapter Nine

Powder and Arms

The *Hispaniola* lay some way out, and we went under the figure-heads and round the sterns of many other ships, and their cables sometimes grated underneath our keel, and sometimes swung above us. At last, however, we got alongside, and were met and saluted as we stepped aboard by the mate, Mr Arrow, a brown old sailor, with earrings in his ears and a squint. He and the squire were very thick and friendly, but I soon observed that things were not the same between Mr Trelawney and the captain.

This last was a sharp-looking man, who seemed angry with everything on board, and was soon to tell us why, for we had hardly got down into the cabin when a sailor followed us.

'Captain Smollett, sir, axing to speak with you,' said he.

'I am always at the captain's orders. Show him in,' said the squire.

The captain, who was close behind his messenger, entered at once, and shut the door behind him.

'Well, Captain Smollett, what have you to say? All well, I hope; all shipshape and seaworthy?'

'Well, sir,' said the captain, 'better speak plain, I believe, even at the risk of offence. I don't like this cruise; I don't like the men; and I don't like my officer. That's short and sweet.'

'Perhaps, sir, you don't like the ship?' inquired the squire, very angry, as I could see.

'I can't speak as to that, sir, not having seen her tried,' said the captain. 'She seems a clever craft; more I can't say.'

'Possibly, sir, you may not like your employer, either?' says the squire.

But here Dr Livesey cut in.

'Stay a bit,' said he, 'stay a bit. No use of such questions as that but to produce ill-feeling. The captain has said too much or he has said too little, and I'm bound to say that I require an explanation of his words. You don't, you say, like this cruise. Now, why?'

'I was engaged, sir, on what we call sealed orders, to sail this ship for that gentleman where he should bid me,' said the captain. 'So far so good. But now I find that every man before the mast knows more than I do. I don't call that fair, now, do you?'

'No,' said Dr Livesey, 'I don't.'

'Next,' said the captain, 'I learn we are going after treasure – hear it from my own hands, mind you. Now, treasure is ticklish work; I don't like treasure voyages on any account; and I don't like them, above all, when they are secret, and when (begging your pardon, Mr Trelawney) the secret has been told to the parrot.'

'Silver's parrot?' asked the squire.

'It's a way of speaking,' said the captain. 'Blabbed, I mean. It's my belief neither of you gentlemen know what you are about; but I'll tell you my way of it – life or death, and a close run.'

'That is all clear, and, I daresay, true enough,' replied Dr Livesey. 'We take the risk; but we are not so ignorant as you believe us. Next, you say you don't like the crew. Are they not good seamen?'

'I don't like them, sir,' returned Captain Smollett. 'And I think I should have had the choosing of my own hands, if you go to that.'

'Perhaps you should,' replied the doctor. 'My friend should, perhaps, have taken you along with him; but the slight, if there be one, was unintentional. And you don't like Mr Arrow?'

'I don't, sir. I believe he's a good seaman; but he's too free with the crew to be a good officer. A mate should keep himself to himself – shouldn't drink with the men before the mast!'

'Do you mean he drinks?' cried the squire.

'No, sir,' replied the captain; 'only that he's too familiar.'

'Well, now, and the short and long of it, captain?' asked the doctor. 'Tell us what you want.'

'Well, gentlemen, are you determined to go on this cruise?'

'Like iron,' answered the squire.

'Very good,' said the captain. 'Then, as you've heard me very patiently, saying things that I could not prove, hear me a few words more. They are putting the powder and the arms in the fore hold. Now, you have a good place under the cabin; why not put them there? – first point. Then you are bringing four of your own people with you, and they tell me some of them are to be berthed forward. Why not give them the berths here beside the cabin? – second point.'

'Any more?' asked Mr Trelawney.

'One more,' said the captain. 'There's been too much blabbing already.'

'Far too much,' agreed the doctor.

'I'll tell you what I've heard myself,' continued Captain Smollett: 'that you have a map of an island; that there's crosses on the map to show where treasure is; and that the island lies –' And then he named the latitude and longitude exactly.

'I never told that,' cried the squire, 'to a soul!'

'The hands know it, sir,' returned the captain.

'Livesey, that must have been you or Hawkins,' cried the squire.

'It doesn't much matter who it was,' replied the doctor. And I could see that neither he nor the captain paid much regard to Mr Trelawney's protestations. Neither did I, to be sure, he was so loose a talker; yet in this case I believe he was really right, and that nobody had told the situation of the island.

'Well, gentlemen,' continued the captain, 'I don't know who has this map; but I make it a point, it shall be kept secret even from me and Mr Arrow. Otherwise I would ask you to let me resign.'

'I see,' said the doctor. 'You wish us to keep this matter dark, and to make a garrison of the stern part of the ship, manned with my friend's own people, and provided with all the arms and powder on board. In other words, you fear a mutiny.'

'Sir,' said Captain Smollett, 'with no intention to take offence, I deny your right to put words into my mouth. No captain, sir, would be justified in going to sea at all if he had ground enough to say that. As for Mr Arrow, I believe him thoroughly honest; some of the men are the same; all may be for what I know. But I am responsible for the ship's safety and the life of every man Jack aboard of her. I see things going, as I think, not quite right. And I ask you to take certain precautions, or let me resign my berth. And that's all.'

'Captain Smollett,' began the doctor, with a smile, 'did ever you hear the fable of the mountain and the mouse? You'll excuse me, I dare say, but you remind me of that fable. When you came in here I'll stake my wig you meant more than this.'

'Doctor,' said the captain, 'you are smart. When I came in here I meant to get discharged. I had no thought that Mr Trelawney would hear a word.'

'No more I would,' cried the squire. 'Had Livesey not been here I should have seen you to the deuce. As it is, I have heard you. I will do as you desire; but I think the worse of you.'

'That's as you please, sir,' said the captain. 'You'll find I do my duty.'

And with that he took his leave.

'Trelawney,' said the doctor, 'contrary to all my notions, I believe you have managed to get two honest men on board with you – that man and John Silver.'

'Silver, if you like,' cried the squire; 'but as for that intolerable humbug, I declare I think his conduct unmanly, unsailorly, and downright un-English.'

'Well,' says the doctor, 'we shall see.'

When we came on deck, the men had begun already to take

out the arms and powder, yo-ho-ing at their work, while the captain and Mr Arrow stood by superintending.

The new arrangement was quite to my liking. The whole schooner had been overhauled; six berths had been made astern, out of what had been the after-part of the main hold; and this set of cabins was only joined to the galley and forecastle by a sparred passage on the port side. It had been originally meant that the captain, Mr Arrow, Hunter, Joyce, the doctor, and the squire, were to occupy these six berths. Now, Redruth and I were to get two of them, and Mr Arrow and the captain were to sleep on deck in the companion, which had been enlarged on each side till you might almost have called it a round-house. Very low it was still, of course; but there was room to swing two hammocks, and even the mate seemed pleased with the arrangement. Even he, perhaps, had been doubtful as to the crew, but that is only guess; for, as you shall hear, we had not long the benefit of his opinion.

We were all hard at work, changing the powder and the berths, when the last man or two, and Long John along with them, came off in a shore-boat.

The cook came up the side like a monkey for cleverness, and, as soon as he saw what was doing, 'So ho, mates!' says he, 'what's this?'

'We're a-changing of the powder, Jack,' answers one.

'Why, by the powers,' cried Long John, 'if we do, we'll miss the morning tide!'

'My orders!' said the captain shortly. 'You may go below, my man. Hands will want supper.'

'Ay, ay, sir,' answered the cook; and, touching his forelock, he disappeared at once in the direction of his galley.

'That's a good man, captain,' said the doctor.

'Very likely, sir,' replied Captain Smollett. 'Easy with that, men – easy,' he ran on, to the fellows who were shifting the powder; and then suddenly observing me examining the swivel we carried amidships, a long brass nine – 'Here, you ship's boy,' he cried, 'out o' that! Off with you to the cook and get some work.'

And then as I was hurrying off I heard him say, quite loudly, to the doctor: –

'I'll have no favourites on my ship.'

I assure you I was quite of the squire's way of thinking, and hated the captain deeply.

Chapter Ten

The Voyage

All that night we were in a great bustle getting things stowed in their place, and boatfuls of the squire's friends, Mr Blandly and the like, coming off to wish him a good voyage and a safe return. We never had a night at the 'Admiral Benbow' when I had half the work; and I was dog-tired when, a little before dawn, the boatswain sounded his pipe, and the crew began to man the capstan-bars. I might have been twice as weary, yet I would not have left the deck; all was so new and interesting to me – the brief commands, the shrill note of the whistle, the men bustling to their places in the glimmer of the ship's lanterns.

'Now, Barbecue, tip us a stave,' cried one voice.

'The old one,' cried another.

'Ay, ay, mates,' said Long John, who was standing by, with his crutch under his arm, and at once broke out in the air and words I knew so well –

'Fifteen men on the dead man's chest' –

And then the whole crew bore chorus: –

'Yo-ho-ho, and a bottle of rum!'

And at the third 'ho!' drove the bars before them with a will.

Even at that exciting moment it carried me back to the old 'Admiral Benbow' in a second; and I seemed to hear the voice of the captain piping in the chorus. But soon the anchor was short up; soon it was hanging dripping at the bows; soon the sails began to draw, and the land and shipping to flit by on either side; and before I could lie down to snatch an hour of slumber the *Hispaniola* had begun her voyage to the Isle of Treasure.

I am not going to relate that voyage in detail. It was fairly prosperous. The ship proved to be a good ship, the crew were capable seamen, and the captain thoroughly understood his business. But before we came the length of Treasure Island, two or three things had happened which require to be known.

Mr Arrow, first of all, turned out even worse than the captain had feared. He had no command among the men, and people did what they pleased with him. But that was by no means the worst of it; for after a day or two at sea he began to appear on deck with hazy eye, red cheeks, stuttering tongue, and other marks of drunkenness. Time after time he was ordered below in disgrace. Sometimes he fell and cut himself; sometimes he lay all day long in his little bunk at one side of the companion; sometimes for a day or two he would be almost sober and attend to his work at least passably.

In the meantime, we could never make out where he got the drink. That was the ship's mystery. Watch him as we pleased, we could do nothing to solve it; and when we asked him to his face, he would only laugh, if he were drunk, and if he were sober, deny solemnly that he ever tasted anything but water.

He was not only useless as an officer, and a bad influence amongst the men, but it was plain that at this rate he must soon kill himself outright; so nobody was much surprised, nor very sorry, when one dark night, with a head sea, he disappeared entirely and was seen no more.

'Overboard!' said the captain. 'Well, gentlemen, that saves the trouble of putting him in irons.'

But there we were, without a mate; and it was necessary, of course, to advance one of the men. The boatswain, Job Anderson, was the likeliest man aboard, and, though he kept his old title, he served in a way as mate. Mr Trelawney had followed the sea, and his knowledge made him very useful, for he often took a watch himself in easy weather. And the coxswain, Israel Hands, was a careful, wily, old, experienced seaman, who could be trusted at a pinch with almost anything.

He was a great confidant of Long John Silver, and so the mention of his name leads me on to speak of our ship's cook, Barbecue, as the men called him.

Aboard ship he carried his crutch by a lanyard round his neck, to have both hands as free as possible. It was something to see him wedge the foot of the crutch against a bulkhead, and, propped against it, yielding to every movement of the ship, get on with his cooking like some one safe ashore. Still more strange was it to see him in the heaviest of weather cross the deck. He had a line or two rigged up to help him across the widest spaces – Long John's earrings, they were called; and he would hand himself from one place to another, now using the crutch, now trailing it alongside by the lanyard, as quickly as another man could walk. Yet some of the men who had sailed with him before expressed their pity to see him so reduced.

'He's no common man, Barbecue,' said the coxswain to me. 'He had good schooling in his young days, and can speak like a book when so minded; and brave – a lion's nothing alongside of Long John! I seen him grapple four, and knock their heads together – him unarmed.'

All the crew respected and even obeyed him. He had a way of talking to each, and doing everybody some particular service. To me he was unweariedly kind; and always glad to see me in the galley, which he kept as clean as a new pin; the dishes hanging up burnished, and his parrot in a cage in one corner.

'Come away, Hawkins,' he would say; 'come and have a yarn with John. Nobody more welcome than yourself, my son. Sit you down and hear the news. Here's Cap'n Flint – I calls my parrot Cap'n Flint, after the famous buccaneer – here's Cap'n Flint predicting success to our v'yage. Wasn't you, cap'n?'

And the parrot would say, with great rapidity, 'Pieces of eight!

pieces of eight! pieces of eight!' till you wondered that it was not out of breath, or till John threw his handkerchief over the cage.

'Now, that bird,' he would say, 'is, may be, two hundred years old, Hawkins – they lives for ever mostly; and if anybody's seen more wickedness, it must be the devil himself. She's sailed with England, the great Cap'n England, the pirate. She's been at Madagascar, and at Malabar, and Surinam, and Providence, and Portobello. She was at the fishing up of the wrecked plate ships. It's there she learned "Pieces of eight," and little wonder; three hundred and fifty thousand of 'em, Hawkins! She was at the boarding of the Viceroy of the Indies out of Goa, she was; and to look at her you would think she was a babby. But you smelt powder – didn't you, cap'n?'

'Stand by to go about,' the parrot would scream.

'Ah, she's a handsome craft, she is,' the cook would say, and give her sugar from his pocket, and then the bird would peck at the bars and swear straight on, passing belief for wickedness. 'There,' John would add, 'you can't touch pitch and not be mucked, lad. Here's this poor old innocent bird o' mine swearing blue fire, and none the wiser, you may lay to that. She would swear the same, in a manner of speaking, before chaplain.' And John would touch his forelock with a solemn way he had, that made me think he was the best of men.

In the meantime, the squire and Captain Smollett were still on pretty distant terms with one another. The squire made no bones about the matter; he despised the captain. The captain, on his part, never spoke but when he was spoken to, and then sharp and short and dry, and not a word wasted. He owned, when driven into a corner, that he seemed to have been wrong about the crew, that some of them were as brisk as he wanted to see, and all had behaved fairly well. As for the ship, he had taken a downright fancy to her. 'She'll lie a point nearer the wind than a man has a right to expect of his own married wife, sir. But,' he would add, 'all I say is we're not home again, and I don't like the cruise.'

The squire, at this, would turn away and march up and down the deck, chin in air.

'A trifle more of that man,' he would say, 'and I shall explode.'

We had some heavy weather, which only proved the qualities of the *Hispaniola*. Every man on board seemed well content, and they must have been hard to please if they had been otherwise; for it is my belief there was never a ship's company so spoiled since Noah put to sea. Double grog was going on the least excuse; there was duff on odd days, as, for instance, if the squire heard it was any man's birthday; and always a barrel of apples standing broached in the waist, for any one to help himself that had a fancy.

'Never knew good come of it yet,' the captain said to Dr Livesey. 'Spoil foc's'le hands, make devils. That's my belief.'

But good did come of the apple barrel, as you shall hear; for if it had not been for that, we should have had no note of warning, and might all have perished by the hand of treachery.

This was how it came about.

We had run up the trades to get the wind of the island we were after – I am not allowed to be more plain – and now we were running down for it with a bright look-out day and night. It was about the last day of our outward voyage, by the largest computation; some time that night, or, at latest, before noon of the morrow, we should sight the Treasure Island. We were heading S. S. W., and had a steady breeze abeam and a quiet sea. The *Hispaniola* rolled steadily, dipping her bowsprit now and then with a whiff of spray. All was drawing alow and aloft; every one was in the bravest spirits, because we were now so near an end of the first part of our adventure.

Now, just after sundown, when all my work was over, and I was on my way to my berth, it occurred to me that I should like an apple. I ran on deck. The watch was all forward looking out for the island. The man at the helm was watching the luff of the sail, and whistling away gently to himself; and that was the only sound excepting the swish of the sea against the bows and around the sides of the ship.

In I got bodily into the apple barrel, and found there was scarce an apple left; but, sitting down there in the dark, what with the sound of the waters and the rocking movement of the ship, I had either fallen asleep, or was on the point of doing so, when a heavy man sat down with rather a clash close by. The barrel shook as he leaned his shoulders against it, and I was just about to jump up when the man began to speak. It was Silver's voice, and, before I had heard a dozen words, I would not have shown myself for all the world, but lay there, trembling and listening, in the extreme of fear and curiosity; for from these dozen words I understood that the lives of all the honest men aboard depended upon me alone.

Chapter Eleven

What I Heard in the Apple Barrel

'No, not I,' said Silver. 'Flint was cap'n; I was quartermaster, along of my timber leg. The same broadside I lost my leg, old Pew lost his dead-lights. It was a master surgeon, him that ampytated me – out of college and all – Latin by the bucket, and what not; but he was hanged like a dog, and sun-dried like the rest, at Corso Castle. That was Roberts' men, that was, and comed of changing names to their ships – *Royal Fortune* and so on. Now, what a ship was christened, so let her stay, I says. So it was with the *Cassandra*, as brought us all safe home from Malabar, after England took the Viceroy of the Indies; so it was with the old *Walrus*, Flint's old ship, as I've seen a-muck with the red blood and fit to sink with gold.'

'Ah!' cried another voice, that of the youngest hand on board, and evidently full of admiration, 'he was the flower of the flock, was Flint!'

'Davis was a man, too, by all accounts,' said Silver. 'I never sailed along of him; first with England, then with Flint, that's my story; and now here on my own account, in a manner of speaking. I laid by nine hundred safe, from England, and two thousand after Flint. That ain't bad for a man before the mast – all safe in bank. 'Tain't earning now, it's saving does it, you may lay to that. Where's all England's men now? I dunno. Where's Flint's? Why, most on 'em aboard here, and glad to get the duff – been begging before that, some on 'em. Old Pew, as had lost his sight, and might have thought shame, spends twelve hundred pound in a year, like a lord in Parliament. Where is he now? Well, he's dead now and under hatches; but for two year before that, shiver my timbers! the man was starving. He begged, and he stole, and he cut throats, and starved at that, by the powers!'

'Well, it ain't much use, after all,' said the young seaman.

''Tain't much use for fools, you may lay to it – that, nor nothing,' cried Silver. 'But now, you look here: you're young, you are, but you're as smart as paint. I see that when I set my eyes on you, and I'll talk to you like a man.'

You may imagine how I felt when I heard this abominable old rogue addressing another in the very same words of flattery as he had used to myself. I think, if I had been able, that I would have killed him through the barrel. Meantime, he ran on, little supposing he was overheard.

'Here it is about gentlemen of fortune. They lives rough, and they risk swinging, but they eat and drink like fighting-cocks, and when a cruise is done, why, it's hundreds of pounds instead of hundreds of farthings in their pockets. Now, the most goes for rum and a good fling, and to sea again in their shirts. But that's not the course I lay. I puts it all away, some here, some there, and none too much anywheres, by reason of suspicion. I'm fifty, mark you; once back from this cruise, I set up gentleman in earnest. Time enough, too, says you. Ah, but I've lived easy in the meantime; never denied myself o'nothing heart desires, and slep' soft and ate dainty all my days, but when at sea. And how did I begin? Before the mast, like you!'

'Well,' said the other, 'but all the other money's gone now, ain't it? You daren't show face in Bristol after this.'

'Why, where might you suppose it was?' asked Silver, derisively.

'At Bristol, in banks and places,' answered his companion.

'It were,' said the cook; 'it were when we weighed anchor. But my old missis has it all by now. And the "Spy-glass" is sold, lease and goodwill and rigging; and the old girl's off to meet me. I would tell you where, for I trust you; but it 'u'd make jealousy among the mates.'

'And can you trust your missis?' asked the other.

'Gentlemen of fortune,' returned the cook, 'usually trusts little among themselves, and right they are, you may lay to it. But I have a way with me, I have. When a mate brings a slip on his cable – one as knows me, I mean – it won't be in the same world with old John. There was some that was feared of Pew, and some that was feared of Flint; but Flint his own self was feared of me. Feared he was, and proud. They was the roughest crew afloat, was Flint's; the devil himself would have been feared to go to sea with them. Well, now, I tell you, I'm not a boasting man, and you seen yourself how easy I keep company; but when I was quartermaster, *lambs* wasn't the word for Flint's old buccaneers. Ah, you may be sure of yourself in old John's ship.'

'Well, I tell you now,' replied the lad, 'I didn't half a quarter like the job till I had this talk with you, John; but there's my hand on it now.'

'And a brave lad you were, and smart, too,' answered Silver, shaking hands so heartily that all the barrel shook, 'and a finer figurehead for a gentleman of fortune I never clapped my eyes on.'

By this time I had begun to understand the meaning of their terms. By a 'gentleman of fortune' they plainly meant neither more nor less than a common pirate, and the little scene that I had overheard was the last act in the corruption of one of the honest hands – perhaps of the last one left aboard. But on this point I was soon to be relieved, for Silver giving a little whistle, a third man strolled up and sat down by the party.

'Dick's square,' said Silver.

'Oh, I know'd Dick was square,' returned the voice of the coxswain, Israel Hands. 'He's no fool, is Dick.' And he turned his quid and spat. 'But, look here,' he went on, 'here's what I want to know, Barbecue: how long are we a-going to stand off and on like a blessed bumboat? I've had a'most enough o' Cap'n Smollett; he's hazed me long enough, by thunder! I want to go into that cabin, I do. I want their pickles and wines, and that.'

'Israel,' said Silver, 'your head ain't much account, nor ever was. But you're able to hear, I reckon; leastways, your ears is big enough. Now, here's what I say: you'll berth forward, and you'll live hard, and you'll speak soft, and you'll keep sober, till I give the word; and you may lay to that, my son.'

'Well, I don't say no, do I?' growled the coxswain. 'What I say is, when? That's what I say.'

'When! by the powers!' cried Silver. 'Well, now, if you want to know, I'll tell you when. The last moment I can manage; and that's when. Here's a first-rate seaman, Cap'n Smollett, sails the blessed ship for us. Here's this squire and doctor with a map and such – I don't know where it is, do I? No more do you, says you. Well, then, I mean this squire and doctor shall find the stuff, and help us to get it aboard, by the powers! Then we'll see. If I was sure of you all, sons of double Dutchmen, I'd have Cap'n Smollett navigate us half-way back again before I struck.'

'Why, we're all seamen aboard here, I should think,' said the lad Dick.

'We're all foc's'le hands, you mean,' snapped Silver. 'We can steer a course, but who's to set one? That's what all you gentlemen split on, first and last. If I had my way, I'd have Cap'n Smollett work us back into the trades at least; then we'd have no blessed miscalculations and a spoonful of water a day. But I know the sort you are. I'll finish with 'em at the island, as soon's the blunt's on board, and a pity it is. But you're never happy till you're drunk. Split my sides, I've a sick heart to sail with the likes of you!'

'Easy all, Long John,' cried Israel. 'Who's a-crossin' of you?'

'Why, how many tall ships, think ye, now, have I seen laid aboard? and how many brisk lads drying in the sun at Execution Dock?' cried Silver, 'and all for this same hurry and hurry and hurry. You hear me? I seen a thing or two at sea, I have. If you would on'y lay your course, and a p'int to windward, you would ride in carriages, you would. But not you! I know you. You'll have your mouthful of rum to-morrow, and go hang.'

'Everybody know'd you was a kind of a chapling, John; but there's others as could hand and steer as well as you,' said Israel.

'They liked a bit o' fun, they did. They wasn't so high and dry, nohow, but took their fling, like jolly companions every one.'

'So?' says Silver. 'Well, and where are they now? Pew was that sort, and he died a beggar-man. Flint was, and he died of rum at Savannah. Ah, they was a sweet crew, they was! on'y, where are they?'

'But,' asked Dick, 'when we do lay 'em athwart, what are we to do with 'em, anyhow?'

'There's the man for me!' cried the cook, admiringly. 'That's what I call business. Well, what would you think? Put 'em ashore like maroons? That would have been England's way. Or cut 'em down like that much pork? That would have been Flint's or Billy Bones's.'

'Billy was the man for that,' said Israel. ' "Dead men don't bite," says he. Well, he's dead now hisself; he knows the long and short on it now; and if ever a rough hand come to port, it was Billy.'

'Right you are,' said Silver, 'rough and ready. But mark you here: I'm an easy man – I'm quite the gentleman, says you; but this time it's serious. Dooty is dooty, mates. I give my vote – death. When I'm in Parlyment, and riding in my coach, I don't want none of these sea-lawyers in the cabin a-coming home, unlooked for, like the devil at prayers. Wait is what I say; but when the time comes, why let her rip!'

'John,' cries the coxswain, 'you're a man!'

'You'll say so, Israel, when you see,' said Silver. 'Only one thing I claim – I claim Trelawney. I'll wring his calf's head off his body with these hands, Dick!' he added, breaking off, 'you just jump up, like a sweet lad, and get me an apple, to wet my pipe like.'

You may fancy the terror I was in! I should have leaped out and run for it, if I had found the strength; but my limbs and heart alike misgave me. I heard Dick begin to rise, and then some one seemingly stopped him, and the voice of Hands exclaimed: –

'Oh, stow that! Don't you get sucking of that bilge, John. Let's have a go of the rum.'

'Dick,' said Silver, 'I trust you. I've a gauge on the keg, mind. There's the key; you fill a pannikin and bring it up.'

Terrified as I was, I could not help thinking to myself that this must have been how Mr Arrow got the strong waters that destroyed him.

Dick was gone but a little while, and during his absence Israel spoke straight on in the cook's ear. It was but a word or two that I could catch, and yet I gathered some important news; for, besides other scraps that tended to the same purpose, this whole clause was audible: 'Not another man of them'll jine.' Hence there were still faithful men on board.

When Dick returned, one after another of the trio took the pannikin and drank – one 'To luck;' another with a 'Here's to old Flint;' and Silver himself saying, in a kind of song, 'Here's to ourselves, and hold your luff, plenty of prizes and plenty of duff.'

Just then a sort of brightness fell upon me in the barrel, and, looking up, I found the moon had risen, and was silvering the mizzen-top and shining white on the luff of the fore-sail; and almost at the same time the voice of the look-out shouted, 'Land ho!'

Chapter Twelve

Council of War

There was a great rush of feet across the deck. I could hear people tumbling up from the cabin and the foc's'le; and, slipping in an instant outside my barrel, I dived behind the fore-sail, made a double towards the stern, and came out upon the open deck in time to join Hunter and Dr Livesey in the rush for the weather bow.

There all hands were already congregated. A belt of fog had lifted almost simultaneously with the appearance of the moon. Away to the south-west of us we saw two low hills, about a couple of miles apart, and rising behind one of them a third and higher hill, whose peak was still buried in the fog. All three seemed sharp and conical in figure.

So much I saw, almost in a dream, for I had not yet recovered from my horrid fear of a minute or two before. And then I heard the voice of Captain Smollett issuing orders. The *Hispaniola* was laid a couple of points nearer the wind, and now sailed a course that would just clear the island on the east.

'And now, men,' said the captain, when all was sheeted home, 'has any one of you ever seen that land ahead?'

'I have, sir,' said Silver. 'I've watered there with a trader I was cook in.'

'The anchorage is on the south, behind an islet, I fancy?' asked the captain.

'Yes, sir; Skeleton Island they calls it. It were a main place for pirates once, and a hand we had on board knowed all their names for it. That hill to the nor'ard they calls the Fore-mast Hill; there are three hills in a row running south'ard – fore, main, and mizzen, sir. But the main – that's the big 'un, with the cloud on it – they usually calls the Spy-glass, by reason of a lookout they kept when they was in the anchorage cleaning; for it's there they cleaned their ships, sir, asking your pardon.'

'I have a chart here,' says Captain Smollett. 'See if that's the place.'

Long John's eyes burned in his head as he took the chart; but, by the fresh look of the paper, I knew he was doomed to disappointment. This was not the map we found in Billy Bones's chest, but an accurate copy, complete in all things – names and heights and soundings – with the single exception of the red crosses and the written notes. Sharp as must have been his annoyance, Silver had the strength of mind to hide it.

'Yes, sir,' said he, 'this is the spot, to be sure; and very prettily drawn out. Who might have done that, I wonder? The pirates were too ignorant, I reckon. Ay, here it is: "Capt. Kidd's Anchorage" – just the name my shipmate called it. There's a strong current runs along the south, and then away nor'ard up the west coast. Right you was, sir,' says he, 'to haul your wind and keep the weather of the island. Leastways, if such was your intention as to enter and careen, and there ain't no better place for that in these waters.'

'Thank you, my man,' says Captain Smollett. 'I'll ask you, later on, to give us a help. You may go.'

I was surprised at the coolness with which John avowed his knowledge of the island; and I own I was half-frightened when I saw him drawing nearer to myself. He did not know, to be sure, that I had overheard his council from the apple barrel, and yet I had, by this time, taken such a horror of his cruelty, duplicity, and power, that I could scarce conceal a shudder when he laid his hand upon my arm.

'Ah,' says he, 'this here is a sweet spot, this island – a sweet spot for a lad to get ashore on. You'll bathe, and you'll climb trees, and you'll hunt goats, you will; and you'll get aloft on them hills like a goat yourself. Why, it makes me young again. I was going to forget my timber leg, I was. It's a pleasant thing to be young, and have ten toes, and you may lay to that. When you want to go a bit of exploring, you just ask old John, and he'll put up a snack for you to take along.'

And clapping me in the friendliest way upon the shoulder, he hobbled off forward, and went below.

Captain Smollett, the squire, and Dr Livesey were talking together on the quarter-deck, and, anxious as I was to tell them my story, I durst not interrupt them openly. While I was still casting about in my thoughts to find some probable excuse, Dr Livesey called me to his side. He had left his pipe below, and being a slave to tobacco, had meant that I should fetch it; but as soon as I was near enough to speak and not to be overheard, I broke out immediately: – 'Doctor, let me speak. Get the captain and squire down to the cabin, and then make some pretence to send for me. I have terrible news.'

The doctor changed countenance a little, but next moment he was master of himself.

'Thank you, Jim,' said he, quite loudly, 'that was all I wanted to know,' as if he had asked me a question.

And with that he turned on his heel and rejoined the other two. They spoke together for a little, and though none of them started, or raised his voice, or so much as whistled, it was plain enough that Dr Livesey had communicated my request; for the next thing that I heard was the captain giving an order to Job Anderson, and all hands were piped on deck.

'My lads,' said Captain Smollett, 'I've a word to say to you. This land that we have sighted is the place we have been sailing for. Mr Trelawney, being a very open-handed gentleman, as we all know, has just asked me a word or two, and as I was able to tell him that every man on board had done his duty, alow and aloft, as I never ask to see it done better, why, he and I and the doctor are going below to the cabin to drink *your* health and luck, and you'll have grog served out for you to drink *our* health and luck. I'll tell you what I think of this: I think it handsome. And if you think as I do, you'll give a good sea cheer for the gentleman that does it.'

The cheer followed – that was a matter of course; but it rang out so full and hearty, that I confess I could hardly believe these same men were plotting for our blood.

'One more cheer for Cap'n Smollett,' cried Long John, when the first had subsided.

And this also was given with a will.

On the top of that the three gentlemen went below, and not long after, word was sent forward that Jim Hawkins was wanted in the cabin.

I found them all three seated round the table, a bottle of Spanish wine and some raisins before them, and the doctor smoking away, with his wig on his lap, and that, I knew, was a sign that he was agitated. The stern window was open, for it was a warm night, and you could see the moon shining behind on the ship's wake.

'Now, Hawkins,' said the squire, 'you have something to say. Speak up.'

I did as I was bid, and as short as I could make it, told the whole details of Silver's conversation. Nobody interrupted me till I was done, nor did any one of the three of them make so much as a movement, but they kept their eyes upon my face from first to last.

'Jim,' said Dr Livesey, 'take a seat.'

And they made me sit down at table beside them, poured me out a glass of wine, filled my hands with raisins, and all three, one after the other, and each with a bow, drank my good health, and their service to me, for my luck and courage.

'Now, captain,' said the squire, 'you were right and I was wrong. I own myself an ass, and I await your orders.'

'No more an ass than I, sir,' returned the captain. 'I never heard of a crew that meant to mutiny but what showed signs before, for any man that had an eye in his head to see the mischief and take steps according. But this crew,' he added, 'beats me.'

'Captain,' said the doctor, 'with your permission, that's Silver. A very remarkable man.'

'He'd look remarkably well from a yard-arm, sir,' returned the captain. 'But this is talk; this don't lead to anything. I see three or four points, and with Mr Trelawney's permission, I'll name them.'

'You, sir, are the captain. It is for you to speak,' says Mr Trelawney, grandly.

'First point,' began Mr Smollett. 'We must go on, because we can't turn back. If I gave the word to go about, they would rise at once. Second point, we have time before us – at least, until this treasure's found. Third point, there are faithful hands. Now, sir, it's got to come to blows sooner or later; and what I propose is, to take time by the forelock, as the saying is, and come to blows some fine day when they least expect it. We can count, I take it, on your own home servants, Mr Trelawney?'

'As upon myself,' declared the squire.

'Three,' reckoned the captain, 'ourselves make seven, counting Hawkins, here. Now, about the honest hands?'

'Most likely Trelawney's own men,' said the doctor; 'those he had picked up for himself, before he lit on Silver.'

'Nay,' replied the squire, 'Hands was one of mine.'

'I did think I could have trusted Hands,' added the captain.

'And to think that they're all Englishmen!' broke out the squire. 'Sir, I could find it in my heart to blow the ship up.'

'Well, gentleman,' said the captain, 'the best that I can say is not much. We must lay to, if you please, and keep a bright look out. It's trying on a man, I know. It would be pleasanter to come to blows. But there's no help for it till we know our men. Lay to, and whistle for a wind, that's my view.'

'Jim here,' said the doctor, 'can help us more than any one. The men are not shy with him, and Jim is a noticing lad.'

'Hawkins, I put prodigious faith in you,' added the squire.

I began to feel pretty desperate at this, for I felt altogether help-less; and yet, by an odd train of circumstances, it was indeed through me that safety came. In the meantime, talk as we pleased, there were only seven out of the twenty-six on whom we knew we could rely; and out of these seven one was a boy, so that the grown men on our side were six to their nineteen.

PART THREE

My Shore Adventure

Chapter Thirteen

How My Shore Adventure Began

The appearance of the island when I came on deck next morning was altogether changed. Although the breeze had now utterly ceased, we had made a great deal of way during the night, and were now lying becalmed about half a mile to the south-east of the low eastern coast. Grey-coloured woods covered a large part of the surface. This even tint was indeed broken up by streaks of yellow sandbreak in the lower lands, and by many tall trees of the pine family, out-topping the others – some singly, some in clumps; but the general colouring was uniform and sad. The hills ran up clear above the vegetation in spires of naked rock. All were strangely shaped, and the Spy-glass, which was by three or four hundred feet the tallest on the island, was likewise the strangest in configuration, running up sheer from almost every side, and then suddenly cut off at the top like a pedestal to put a statue on.

The *Hispaniola* was rolling scuppers under in the ocean swell. The booms were tearing at the blocks, the rudder was banging to and fro, and the whole ship creaking, groaning, and jumping like a manufactory. I had to cling tight to the backstay, and the world turned giddily before my eyes; for though I was a good enough sailor when there was way on, this standing still and being rolled about like a bottle was a thing I never learned to stand without a qualm or so, above all in the morning, on an empty stomach.

Perhaps it was this – perhaps it was the look of the island, with its grey, melancholy woods, and wild stone spires, and the surf that we could both see and hear foaming and thundering on the steep beach – at least, although the sun shone bright and hot, and the shore birds were fishing and crying all around us, and you would have thought any one would have been glad to get to land after being so long at sea, my heart sank, as the saying is, into my boots; and from that first look onward, I hated the very thought of Treasure Island.

We had a dreary morning's work before us, for there was no sign of any wind, and the boats had to be got out and manned, and the ship warped three or four miles round the corner of the island, and up the narrow passage to the haven behind Skeleton Island. I volunteered for one of the boats, where I had, of course, no business. The heat was sweltering, and the men grumbled fiercely over their work. Anderson was in command of my boat, and instead of keeping the crew in order, he grumbled as loud as the worst.

'Well,' he said, with an oath, 'it's not for ever.'

I thought this was a very bad sign; for, up to that day, the men had gone briskly and willingly about their business; but the very sight of the island had relaxed the cords of discipline.

All the way in, Long John stood by the steersman and conned the ship. He knew the passage like the palm of his hand; and though the man in the chains got everywhere more water than was down in the chart, John never hesitated once.

'There's a strong scour with the ebb,' he said, 'and this here passage has been dug out, in a manner of speaking, with a spade.'

We brought up just where the anchor was in the chart, about a third of a mile from each shore, the mainland on one side, and Skeleton Island on the other. The bottom was clean sand. The plunge of our anchor sent up clouds of birds wheeling and crying over the woods; but in less than a minute they were down again, and all was once more silent.

The place was entirely land-locked, buried in woods, the trees coming right down to high-water mark, the shores mostly flat, and the hilltops standing round at a distance in a sort of amphitheatre, one here, one there. Two little rivers, or, rather, two swamps, emptied out into this pond, as you might call it; and the foliage round that part of the shore had a kind of poisonous brightness. From the ship, we could see nothing of the house or stockade, for they were quite buried among trees; and if it had not been for the chart on the companion, we might have been the first that had ever anchored there since the island arose out of the seas.

There was not a breath of air moving, nor a sound but that of the surf booming half a mile away along the beaches and against the rocks outside. A peculiar stagnant smell hung over the anchorage – a smell of sodden leaves and rotting tree trunks. I observed the doctor sniffing and sniffing, like some one tasting a bad egg.

'I don't know about treasure,' he said, 'but I'll stake my wig there's fever here.'

If the conduct of the men had been alarming in the boat, it became truly threatening when they had come aboard. They lay about the deck growling together in talk. The slightest order was received with a black look, and grudgingly and carelessly obeyed. Even the honest hands must have caught the infection, for there was not one man aboard to mend another. Mutiny, it was plain, hung over us like a thunder-cloud.

And it was not only we of the cabin party who perceived the danger. Long John was hard at work going from group to group, spending himself in good advice, and as for example no man could have shown a better. He fairly outstripped himself in will-ingness and civility; he was all smiles to every one. If an order were given, John would be on his crutch in an instant, with the cheeriest 'Ay, ay, sir!' in the world; and when there was nothing else to do, he kept up one song after another, as if to conceal the discontent of the rest.

Of all the gloomy features of that gloomy afternoon, this obvious anxiety on the part of Long John appeared the worst.

We held a council in the cabin.

'Sir,' said the captain, 'if I risk another order, the whole ship 'll come about our ears by the run. You see, sir, here it is. I get a rough answer, do I not? Well, if I speak back, pikes will be going in two shakes; if I don't, Silver will see there's something under that, and the game's up. Now, we've only one man to rely on.'

'And who is that?' asked the squire.

'Silver, sir,' returned the captain; 'he's as anxious as you and I to smother things up. This is a tiff; he'd soon talk 'em out of it if he had the chance, and what I propose to do is to give him the chance. Let's allow the men an afternoon ashore. If they all go, why, we'll fight the ship. If they none of them go, well, then, we hold the cabin, and God defend the right. If some go, you mark my words, sir, Silver 'll bring 'em aboard again as mild as lambs.'

It was so decided; loaded pistols were served out to all the sure men; Hunter, Joyce, and Redruth were taken into our confidence, and received the news with less surprise and a better spirit than we had looked for, and then the captain went on deck and addressed the crew.

'My lads,' said he, 'we've had a hot day, and are all tired and out of sorts. A turn ashore 'll hurt nobody – the boats are still in the water; you can take the gigs, and as many as please may go ashore for the afternoon. I'll fire a gun half an hour before sundown.'

I believe the silly fellows must have thought they would break their shins over treasure as soon as they were landed; for they all came out of their sulks in a moment, and gave a cheer that started the echo in a far-away hill, and sent the birds once more flying and squalling round the anchorage.

The captain was too bright to be in the way. He whipped out of sight in a moment, leaving Silver to arrange the party; and I fancy it was as well he did so. Had he been on deck, he could no longer so much as have pretended not to understand the situation. It was as plain as day. Silver was the captain, and a mighty rebellious crew he had of it. The honest hands – and I was soon to see it proved that there were such on board – must have been very stupid fellows. Or, rather, I suppose the truth was this, that all hands were disaffected by the example of the ringleaders – only some more, some less; and a few, being good fellows in the main, could neither be led nor driven any further. It is one thing to be idle and skulk, and quite another to take a ship and murder a number of innocent men.

At last, however, the party was made up. Six fellows were to stay on board, and the remaining thirteen, including Silver, began to embark.

Then it was that there came into my head the first of the mad notions that contributed so much to save our lives. If six men were left by Silver, it was plain our party could not take and fight the ship; and since only six were left, it was equally plain that the cabin party had no present need of my assistance. It occurred to me at once to go ashore. In a jiffy I had slipped over the side, and curled up in the fore-sheets of the nearest boat, and almost at the same moment she shoved off.

No one took notice of me, only the bow oar saying, 'Is that you, Jim? Keep your head down.' But Silver, from the other boat, looked sharply over and called out to know if that were me; and from that moment I began to regret what I had done.

The crews raced for the beach; but the boat I was in, having some start, and being at once the lighter and the better manned, shot far ahead of her consort, and the bow had struck among the shore-side trees, and I had caught a branch and swung myself out, and plunged into the nearest thicket, while Silver and the rest were still a hundred yards behind.

'Jim, Jim!' I heard him shouting.

But you may suppose I paid no heed; jumping, ducking, and breaking through, I ran straight before my nose, till I could run no longer.

Chapter Fourteen

The First Blow

I was so pleased at having given the slip to Long John, that I began to enjoy myself and look around me with some interest on the strange land that I was in.

I had crossed a marshy tract full of willows, bulrushes, and odd, outlandish, swampy trees; and I had now come out upon the skirts of an open piece of undulating, sandy country, about a mile long, dotted with a few pines, and a great number of contorted trees, not unlike the oak in growth, but pale in the foliage, like willows. On the far side of the open stood one of the hills, with two quaint, craggy peaks, shining vividly in the sun.

I now felt for the first time the joy of exploration. The isle was uninhabited; my shipmates I had left behind, and nothing lived in front of me but dumb brutes and fowls. I turned hither and thither among the trees. Here and there were flowering plants, unknown to me; here and there I saw snakes, and one raised his head from a ledge of rock and hissed at me with a noise not unlike the spinning of a top. Little did I suppose that he was a deadly enemy, and that the noise was the famous rattle.

Then I came to a long thicket of these oak-like trees – live, or evergreen, oaks, I heard afterwards they should be called – which grew low along the sand like brambles, the boughs curiously twisted, the foliage compact, like thatch. The thicket stretched down from the top of one of the sandy knolls, spreading and growing taller as it went, until it reached the margin of the broad, reedy fen, through which the nearest of the little rivers soaked its way into the anchorage. The marsh was steaming in the strong sun, and the outline of the Spy-glass trembled through the haze.

All at once there began to go a sort of bustle among the

bulrushes; a wild duck flew up with a quack, another followed, and soon over the whole surface of the marsh a great cloud of birds hung screaming and circling in the air. I judged at once that some of my shipmates must be drawing near along the borders of the fen. Nor was I deceived; for soon I heard the very distant and low tones of a human voice, which, as I continued to give ear, grew steadily louder and nearer.

This put me in a great fear, and I crawled under cover of the nearest live-oak, and squatted there, hearkening, as silent as a mouse.

Another voice answered; and then the first voice, which I now recognised to be Silver's, once more took up the story, and ran on for a long while in a stream, only now and again interrupted by the other. By the sound they must have been talking earnestly, and almost fiercely; but no distinct word came to my hearing.

At last the speakers seemed to have paused, and perhaps to have sat down; for not only did they cease to draw any nearer, but the birds themselves began to grow more quiet, and to settle again to their places in the swamp.

And now I began to feel that I was neglecting my business; that since I had been so foolhardy as to come ashore with these desperadoes, the least I could do was to overhear them at their councils; and that my plain and obvious duty was to draw as close as I could manage, under the favourable ambush of the crouching trees.

I could tell the direction of the speakers pretty exactly, not only by the sound of their voices, but by the behaviour of the few birds that still hung in alarm above the heads of the intruders.

Crawling on all-fours, I made steadily but slowly towards them; till at last, raising my head to an aperture among the leaves, I could see clear down into a little green dell beside the marsh, and closely set about with trees, where Long John Silver and another of the crew stood face to face in conversation.

The sun beat full upon them. Silver had thrown his hat beside him on the ground, and his great, smooth, blond face, all shining with heat, was lifted to the other man's in a kind of appeal.

'Mate,' he was saying, 'it's because I thinks gold dust of you – gold dust, and you may lay to that! If I hadn't took to you like pitch, do you think I'd have been here a-warning of you? All's up – you can't make nor mend; it's to save your neck that I'm a-speaking, and if one of the wild 'uns knew it, where 'ud I be, Tom – now, tell me, where 'ud I be?'

'Silver,' said the other man – and I observed he was not only red in the face, but spoke as hoarse as a crow, and his voice shook, too, like a taut rope – 'Silver,' says he, 'you're old, and you're honest, or has the name for it; and you've money, too, which lots of poor sailors hasn't; and you're brave, or I'm mistook. And will you tell me you'll let yourself be led away with that kind of a mess of swabs? not you! As sure as God sees me, I'd sooner lose my hand. If I turn agin my dooty –'

And then all of a sudden he was interrupted by a noise. I had found one of the honest hands – well, here, at that same moment, came news of another. Far away out in the marsh there arose, all of a sudden, a sound like the cry of anger, then another on the back of it; and then one horrid, long-drawn scream. The rocks of the Spy-glass re-echoed it a score of times; the whole troop of marsh-birds rose again, darkening heaven, with a simultaneous whirr; and long after that death yell was still ringing in my brain, silence had re-established its empire, and only the rustle of the redescending birds and the boom of the distant surges disturbed the languor of the afternoon.

Tom had leaped at the sound, like a horse at the spur; but Silver had not winked an eye. He stood where he was, resting lightly on his crutch, watching his companion like a snake about to spring.

'John!' said the sailor, stretching out his hand.

'Hands off!' cried Silver, leaping back a yard, as it seemed to me, with the speed and security of a trained gymnast.

'Hands off, if you like, John Silver,' said the other. 'It's a black conscience that can make you feared of me. But, in heaven's name, tell me what was that?'

'That?' returned Silver, smiling away, but warier than ever, his eye a mere pin-point in his big face, but gleaming like a crumb of glass. 'That? Oh, I reckon that'll be Alan.'

And at this poor Tom flashed out like a hero.

'Alan!' he cried. 'Then rest his soul for a true seaman! And as for you, John Silver, long you've been a mate of mine, but you're mate of mine no more. If I die like a dog, I'll die in my dooty. You've killed Alan, have you? Kill me, too, if you can. But I defies you.'

And with that, this brave fellow turned his back directly on the cook, and set off walking for the beach. But he was not destined to go far. With a cry, John seized the branch of a tree, whipped the crutch out of his armpit, and sent that uncouth missile hurtling through the air. It struck poor Tom, point foremost, and with stunning violence, right between the shoulders in the middle of his back. His hands flew up, he gave a sort of gasp, and fell.

Whether he were injured much or little, none could ever tell. Like enough, to judge from the sound, his back was broken on the spot. But he had no time given him to recover. Silver, agile as a monkey, even without leg or crutch, was on the top of him next moment, and had twice buried his knife up to the hilt in that defenceless body. From my place of ambush, I could hear him pant aloud as he struck the blows.

I do not know what it rightly is to faint, but I do know that for the next little while the whole world swam away from before me in a whirling mist; Silver and the birds, and the tall Spy-glass hilltop, going round and round and topsy-turvy before my eyes, and all manner of bells ringing and distant voices shouting in my ear.

When I came again to myself, the monster had pulled himself together, his crutch under his arm, his hat upon his head. Just before him Tom lay motionless upon the sward; but the murderer minded him not a whit, cleansing his blood-stained knife the while upon a wisp of grass. Everything else was unchanged, the sun still shining mercilessly on the steaming marsh and the tall pinnacle of the mountain, and I could scarce persuade myself that murder had been actually done, and a human life cruelly cut short a moment since, before my eyes.

But now John put his hand into his pocket, brought out a whistle, and blew upon it several modulated blasts, that rang far across the heated air. I could not tell, of course, the meaning of the signal; but it instantly awoke my fears. More men would be coming. I might be discovered. They had already slain two of the honest people; after Tom and Alan, might not I come next?

Instantly I began to extricate myself and crawl back again, with what speed and silence I could manage, to the more open portion of the wood. As I did so, I could hear hails coming and going between the old buccaneer and his comrades, and this sound of danger lent me wings. As soon as I was clear of the thicket, I ran as I never ran before, scarce minding the direction of my flight, so long as it led me from the murderers; and as I ran, fear grew and grew upon me, until it turned into a kind of frenzy.

Indeed, could any one be more entirely lost than I? When the gun fired, how should I dare to go down to the boats among those fiends, still smoking from their crime? Would not the first of them who saw me wring my neck like a snipe's? Would not my absence itself be an evidence to them of my alarm, and therefore of my fatal knowledge? It was all over, I thought. Good-bye to the *Hispaniola*; good-bye to the squire, the doctor, and the captain! There was nothing left for me but death by starvation, or death by the hands of the mutineers.

All this while, as I say, I was still running, and, without taking any notice, I had drawn near to the foot of the little hill with the two peaks, and had got into a part of the island where the live-oaks grew more widely apart, and seemed more like forest trees in their bearing and dimensions. Mingled with these were a few scattered pines, some fifty, some nearer seventy, feet high. The air, too, smelt more freshly than down beside the marsh.

And here a fresh alarm brought me to a standstill with a thumping heart.

Chapter Fifteen

The Man of the Island

From the side of the hill, which was here steep and stony, a spout of gravel was dislodged, and fell rattling and bounding through the trees. My eyes turned instinctively in that direction, and I saw a figure leap with great rapidity behind the trunk of a pine. What it was, whether bear or man or monkey, I could in no wise tell. It seemed dark and shaggy; more I knew not. But the terror of this new apparition brought me to a stand.

I was now, it seemed, cut off upon both sides; behind me the murderers, before me this lurking nondescript. And immediately I began to prefer the dangers that I knew to those I knew not. Silver himself appeared less terrible in contrast with this creature of the woods, and I turned on my heel, and, looking sharply behind me over my shoulder, began to retrace my steps in the direction of the boats.

Instantly the figure reappeared, and, making a wide circuit, began to head me off. I was tired, at any rate; but had I been as fresh as when I rose, I could see it was in vain for me to contend in speed with such an adversary. From trunk to trunk the creature flitted like a deer, running manlike on two legs, but unlike any man that I had ever seen, stooping almost double as it ran. Yet a man it was, I could no longer be in doubt about that.

I began to recall what I had heard of cannibals. I was within an ace of calling for help. But the mere fact that he was a man, however wild, had somewhat reassured me, and my fear of Silver began to revive in proportion. I stood still, therefore, and cast about for some method of escape; and as I was so thinking, the recollection of my pistol flashed into my mind. As soon as I remembered I was not defenceless, courage glowed again in my heart; and I set my face resolutely for this man of the island, and walked briskly towards him.

He was concealed, by this time, behind another tree trunk; but he must have been watching me closely, for as soon as I began to move in his direction he reappeared and took a step to meet me. Then he hesitated, drew back, came forward again, and at last, to my wonder and confusion, threw himself on his knees and held out his clasped hands in supplication.

At that I once more stopped.

'Who are you?' I asked.

'Ben Gunn,' he answered, and his voice sounded hoarse and awkward, like a rusty lock. 'I'm poor Ben Gunn, I am; and I haven't spoke with a Christian these three years.'

I could now see that he was a white man like myself, and that his features were even pleasing. His skin, wherever it was exposed, was burnt by the sun; even his lips were black, and his fair eyes looked quite startling in so dark a face. Of all the beggar-men that I had seen or fancied, he was the chief for raggedness. He was clothed with tatters of old ship's canvas and old sea cloth; and this extraordinary patchwork was all held together by a system of the most various and incongruous fastenings, brass buttons, bits of stick, and loops of tarry gaskin. About his waist he wore an old brass-buckled leather belt, which was the one thing solid in his whole accoutrement.

'Three years!' I cried. 'Were you shipwrecked?'

'Nay, mate,' said he – 'marooned.'

I had heard the word, and I knew it stood for a horrible kind of punishment common enough among the buccaneers, in which the offender is put ashore with a little powder and shot, and left behind on some desolate and distant island.

'Marooned three years agone,' he continued, 'and lived on goats since then, and berries, and oysters. Wherever a man is, says I, a man can do for himself. But, mate, my heart is sore for

Christian diet. You mightn't happen to have a piece of cheese about you, now? No? Well, many's the long night I've dreamed of cheese – toasted, mostly – and woke up again, and here I were.'

'If ever I can get aboard again,' said I, 'you shall have cheese by the stone.'

All this time he had been feeling the stuff of my jacket, smoothing my hands, looking at my boots, and generally, in the intervals of his speech, showing a childish pleasure in the presence of a fellow-creature. But at my last words he perked up into a kind of startled slyness.

'If ever you can get aboard again, says you?' he repeated. 'Why, now, who's to hinder you?'

'Not you, I know,' was my reply.

'And right you was,' he cried. 'Now you – what do you call yourself, mate?'

'Jim,' I told him.

'Jim, Jim,' says he, quite pleased apparently. 'Well, now, Jim, I've lived that rough as you'd be ashamed to hear of. Now, for instance, you wouldn't think I had had a pious mother – to look at me?' he asked.

'Why, no, not in particular,' I answered.

'Ah, well,' said he, 'but I had – remarkable pious. And I was a civil, pious boy, and could rattle off my catechism that fast, as you couldn't tell one word from another. And here's what it come to, Jim, and it begun with chuck-farthen on the blessed grave-stones! That's what it begun with, but it went further'n that; and so my mother told me, and predicked the whole, she did, the pious woman! But it were Providence that put me here. I've thought it all out in this here lonely island, and I'm back on piety. You don't catch me tasting rum so much; but just a thimbleful for luck, of course, the first chance I have. I'm bound I'll be good, and I see the way to. And, Jim' – looking all round him, and lowering his voice to a whisper – 'I'm rich.'

I now felt sure that the poor fellow had gone crazy in his solitude, and I suppose I must have shown the feeling in my face; for he repeated the statement hotly: –

'Rich! rich! I says. And I'll tell you what: I'll make a man of you, Jim. Ah, Jim, you'll bless your stars, you will, you was the first that found me!'

And at this there came suddenly a lowering shadow over his face, and he tightened his grasp upon my hand, and raised a forefinger threateningly before my eyes.

'Now, Jim, you tell me true: that ain't Flint's ship?' he asked.

At this I had a happy inspiration. I began to believe that I had found an ally, and I answered him at once.

'It's not Flint's ship, and Flint is dead; but I'll tell you true, as you ask me – there are some of Flint's hands aboard; worse luck for the rest of us.'

'Not a man – with one – leg?' he gasped.

'Silver?' I asked.

'Ah, Silver!' says he; 'that were his name.'

'He's the cook; and the ringleader, too.'

He was still holding me by the wrist, and at that he gave it quite a wring.

'If you was sent by Long John,' he said, 'I'm as good as pork, and I know it. But where was you, do you suppose?'

I had made my mind up in a moment, and by way of answer told him the whole story of our voyage, and the predicament in which we found ourselves. He heard me with the keenest interest, and when I had done he patted me on the head.

'You're a good lad, Jim,' he said; 'and you're all in a clove hitch, ain't you? Well, you just put your trust in Ben Gunn – Ben Gunn's the man to do it. Would you think it likely, now, that your squire would prove a liberal-minded one in case of help – him being in a clove hitch, as you remark?'

I told him the squire was the most liberal of men.

'Ay, but you see,' returned Ben Gunn, 'I didn't mean giving me a gate to keep, and a shuit of livery clothes, and such; that's not my mark, Jim. What I mean is, would he be likely to come down to the toon of, say one thousand pounds out of money that's as good as a man's own already?'

'I am sure he would,' said I. 'As it was, all hands were to share.'

'*And* a passage home?' he added, with a look of great shrewdness.

'Why,' I cried, 'the squire's a gentleman. And besides, if we got rid of the others, we should want you to help work the vessel home.'

'Ah,' said he, 'so you would.' And he seemed very much relieved.

'Now, I'll tell you what,' he went on. 'So much I'll tell you, and no more. I were in Flint's ship when he buried the treasure; he and six along – six strong seamen. They was ashore nigh on a week, and us standing off and on in the old *Walrus*. One fine day up went the signal, and here come Flint by himself in a little boat, and his head done up in a blue scarf. The sun was getting up, and mortal white he looked about the cutwater. But, there he was, you mind, and the six all dead – dead and buried. How he done it, not a man aboard us could make out. It was battle, murder, and sudden death, leastways – him against six. Billy Bones was the mate; Long John, he was quartermaster; and they asked him where the treasure was. "Ah," says he, "you can go ashore, if you like, and stay," he says; 'but as for the ship, she'll beat up for more, by thunder!' That's what he said.

'Well, I was in another ship three years back, and we sighted this island. "Boys," said I, "here's Flint's treasure; let's land and find it." The cap'n was displeased at that; but my messmates were all of a mind, and landed. Twelve days they looked for it, and every day they had the worse word for me, until one fine morning all hands went aboard. "As for you, Benjamin Gunn," says they, "here's a musket," they says, "and a spade, and pickaxe. You can stay here, and find Flint's money for yourself," they says.

'Well, Jim, three years have I been here, and not a bite of

Christian diet from that day to this. But now, you look here; look at me. Do I look like a man before the mast? No, says you. Nor I weren't, neither, I says.'

And with that he winked and pinched me hard.

'Just you mention them words to your squire, Jim' – he went on: 'Nor he weren't, neither – that's the words. Three years he were the man of this island, light and dark, fair and rain; and sometimes he would, maybe, think upon a prayer (says you), and sometimes he would, maybe, think of his old mother, so be as she's alive (you'll say); but the most part of Gunn's time (this is what you'll say) – the most part of his time was took up with another matter. And then you'll give him a nip, like I do.'

And he pinched me again in the most confidential manner.

'Then,' he continued – 'then you'll up, and you'll say this: – Gunn is a good man (you'll say), and he puts a precious sight more confidence – a precious sight, mind that – in a gen'leman born than in these gen'lemen of fortune, having been one hisself.'

'Well,' I said, 'I don't understand one word that you've been saying. But that's neither here nor there; for how am I to get on board?'

'Ah,' said he, 'that's the hitch, for sure. Well, there's my boat, that I made with my two hands. I keep her under the white rock. If the worst come to the worst, we might try that after dark. Hi!' he broke out, 'what's that?'

For just then, although the sun had still an hour or two to run, all the echoes of the island awoke and bellowed to the thunder of a cannon.

'They have begun to fight!' I cried. 'Follow me.'

And I began to run towards the anchorage, my terrors all forgotten; while, close at my side, the marooned man in his goatskins trotted easily and lightly.

'Left, left,' says he; 'keep to your left hand, mate Jim! Under the trees with you! Theer's where I killed my first goat. They don't come down here now; they're all mast-headed on them mountings

for the fear of Benjamin Gunn. Ah! and there's the cetemery' –
cemetery, he must have meant. 'You see the mounds? I come here
and prayed, nows and thens, when I thought maybe a Sunday
would be about doo. It weren't quite a chapel, but it seemed more
solemn like; and then, says you, Ben Gunn was short-handed – no
chapling, nor so much as a Bible and a flag, you says.'

So he kept talking as I ran, neither expecting nor receiving any
answer.

The cannon-shot was followed, after a considerable interval,
by a volley of small arms.

Another pause, and then, not a quarter of a mile in front of
me, I beheld the Union Jack flutter in the air above a wood.

PART FOUR

The Stockade

PART FOUR

The Stockade

Chapter Sixteen

Narrative Continued by the Doctor:
How the Ship Was Abandoned

It was about half-past one – three bells in the sea phrase – that the two boats went ashore from the *Hispaniola*. The captain, the squire, and I were talking matters over in the cabin. Had there been a breath of wind, we should have fallen on the six mutineers who were left aboard with us, slipped our cable, and away to sea. But the wind was wanting; and, to complete our helplessness, down came Hunter with the news that Jim Hawkins had slipped into a boat and was gone ashore with the rest.

It never occurred to us to doubt Jim Hawkins; but we were alarmed for his safety. With the men in the temper they were in, it seemed an even chance if we should see the lad again. We ran on deck. The pitch was bubbling in the seams; the nasty stench of the place turned me sick; if ever a man smelt fever and dysentery, it was in that abominable anchorage. The six scoundrels were sitting grumbling under a sail in the forecastle; ashore we could see the gigs made fast, and a man sitting in each, hard by where the river runs in. One of them was whistling 'Lillibullero.'

Waiting was a strain; and it was decided that Hunter and I should go ashore with the jolly-boat, in quest of information.

The gigs had leaned to their right; but Hunter and I pulled straight in, in the direction of the stockade upon the chart. The two who were left guarding their boats seemed in a bustle at our appearance; 'Lillibullero' stopped off, and I could see the pair discussing what they ought to do. Had they gone and told Silver, all might have turned out differently; but they had their orders, I suppose, and decided to sit quietly where they were and hark back again to 'Lillibullero.'

There was a slight bend in the coast, and I steered so as to put it between us; even before we landed we had thus lost sight of the gigs. I jumped out and came as near running as I durst, with a big silk handkerchief under my hat for coolness' sake, and a brace of pistols ready primed for safety.

I had not gone a hundred yards when I reached the stockade.

This was how it was: a spring of clear water rose almost at the top of a knoll. Well, on the knoll, and enclosing the spring, they had clapped a stout log-house, fit to hold two score of people on a pinch, and loopholed for musketry on every side. All round this they had cleared a wide space, and then the thing was completed by a paling six feet high, without door or opening, too strong to pull down without time and labour, and too open to shelter the besiegers. The people in the log-house had them in every way; they stood quiet in shelter and shot the others like partridges. All they wanted was a good watch and food; for, short of a complete surprise, they might have held the place against a regiment.

What particularly took my fancy was the spring. For, though we had a good enough place of it in the cabin of the *Hispaniola*, with plenty of arms and ammunition, and things to eat, and excellent wines, there had been one thing overlooked – we had no water. I was thinking this over, when there came ringing over the island the cry of a man at the point of death. I was not new to violent death – I have served his Royal Highness the Duke of Cumberland, and got a wound myself at Fontenoy – but I know my pulse went dot and carry one. 'Jim Hawkins is gone,' was my first thought.

It is something to have been an old soldier, but more still to have been a doctor. There is no time to dilly-dally in our work. And so now I made up my mind instantly, and with no time lost returned to the shore, and jumped on board the jolly-boat.

By good fortune Hunter pulled a good oar. We made the water fly; and the boat was soon alongside, and I aboard the schooner.

I found them all shaken, as was natural. The squire was sitting down, as white as a sheet, thinking of the harm he had led us to, the good soul! and one of the six forecastle hands was little better.

'There's a man,' says Captain Smollett, nodding towards him, 'new to this work. He came nigh-hand fainting, doctor, when he heard the cry. Another touch of the rudder and that man would join us.'

I told my plan to the captain, and between us we settled on the details of its accomplishment.

We put old Redruth in the gallery between the cabin and the forecastle, with three or four loaded muskets and a mattress for protection. Hunter brought the boat round under the stern-port, and Joyce and I set to work loading her with powder-tins, muskets, bags of biscuits, kegs of pork, a cask of cognac, and my invaluable medicine-chest.

In the meantime, the squire and the captain stayed on deck, and the latter hailed the coxswain, who was the principal man aboard.

'Mr Hands,' he said, 'here are two of us with a brace of pistols each. If any one of you six makes a signal of any description, that man's dead.'

They were a good deal taken aback; and, after a little consultation, one and all tumbled down the fore companion, thinking, no doubt, to take us on the rear. But when they saw Redruth waiting for them in the sparred gallery, they went about ship at once, and a head popped out again on deck.

'Down, dog!' cries the captain.

And the head popped back again; and we heard no more, for the time, of these six very faint-hearted seamen.

By this time, tumbling things in as they came, we had the jolly-boat loaded as much as we dared. Joyce and I got out through the stern-port, and we made for shore again, as fast as oars could take us.

This second trip fairly aroused the watchers along shore. 'Lilli-bullero' was dropped again; and just before we lost sight of them behind the little point, one of them whipped ashore and disappeared. I had half a mind to change my plan and destroy their boats, but I feared that Silver and the others might be close at hand, and all might very well be lost by trying for too much.

We had soon touched land in the same place as before, and set to provision the block house. All three made the first journey, heavily laden, and tossed our stores over the palisade. Then, leaving Joyce to guard them – one man, to be sure, but with half a dozen muskets – Hunter and I returned to the jolly-boat, and loaded ourselves once more. So we proceeded without pausing to take breath, till the whole cargo was bestowed, when the two servants took up their position in the block house, and I, with all my power, sculled back to the *Hispaniola*.

That we should have risked a second boat-load seems more daring than it really was. They had the advantage of numbers, of course, but we had the advantage of arms. Not one of the men ashore had a musket, and before they could get within range for pistol shooting, we flattered ourselves we should be able to give a good account of a half-dozen at least.

The squire was waiting for me at the stern window, all his faintness gone from him. He caught the painter and made it fast, and we fell to loading the boat for our very lives. Pork, powder, and biscuit was the cargo, with only a musket and a cutlass apiece for the squire and me and Redruth and the captain. The rest of the arms and powder we dropped overboard in two fathoms and a half of water, so that we could see the bright steel shining far below us in the sun, on the clean, sandy bottom.

By this time the tide was beginning to ebb, and the ship was swinging round to her anchor. Voices were heard faintly halloaing in the direction of the two gigs; and though this reassured us for Joyce and Hunter, who were well to the eastward, it warned our party to be off.

Redruth retreated from his place in the gallery, and dropped into the boat, which we then brought round to the ship's counter, to be handier for Captain Smollett.

'Now, men,' said he, 'do you hear me?'

There was no answer from the forecastle.

'It's to you, Abraham Gray – it's to you I am speaking.'

Still no reply.

'Gray,' resumed Mr Smollett, a little louder, 'I am leaving this ship, and I order you to follow your captain. I know you are a good man at bottom, and I daresay not one of the lot of you's as bad as he makes out. I have my watch here in my hand; I give you thirty seconds to join me in.'

There was a pause.

'Come, my fine fellow,' continued the captain, 'don't hang so long in stays. I'm risking my life, and the lives of these good gentlemen, every second.'

There was a sudden scuffle, a sound of blows, and out burst Abraham Gray with a knife-cut on the side of the cheek, and came running to the captain, like a dog to the whistle.

'I'm with you, sir,' said he.

And the next moment he and the captain had dropped aboard of us, and we had shoved off and given way.

We were clear out of the ship; but not yet ashore in our stockade.

Chapter Seventeen

Narrative Continued by the Doctor:
The Jolly-boat's Last Trip

This fifth trip was quite different from any of the others. In the first place, the little gallipot of a boat that we were in was gravely overloaded. Five grown men, and three of them – Trelawney, Redruth, and the captain – over six feet high, was already more than she was meant to carry. Add to that the powder, pork, and bread-bags. The gunwale was lipping astern. Several times we shipped a little water, and my breeches and the tails of my coat were all soaking wet before we had gone a hundred yards.

The captain made us trim the boat, and we got her to lie a little more evenly. All the same, we were afraid to breathe.

In the second place, the ebb was now making – a strong rippling current running westward through the basin, and then south'ard and seaward down the straits by which we had entered in the morning. Even the ripples were a danger to our overloaded craft; but the worst of it was that we were swept out of our true course, and away from our proper landing-place behind the point. If we let the current have its way we should come ashore beside the gigs, where the pirates might appear at any moment.

'I cannot keep her head for the stockade, sir,' said I to the captain. I was steering, while he and Redruth, two fresh men, were at the oars. 'The tide keeps washing her down. Could you pull a little stronger?'

'Not without swamping the boat,' said he. 'You must bear up, sir, if you please – bear up until you see you're gaining.'

I tried, and found by experiment that the tide kept sweeping us westward until I had laid her head due east, or just about right angles to the way we ought to go.

'We'll never get ashore at this rate,' said I.

'If it's the only course that we can lie, sir, we must even lie it,' returned the captain. 'We must keep up-stream. You see, sir,' he went on, 'if once we dropped to leeward of the landing-place, it's hard to say where we should get ashore, besides the chance of being boarded by the gigs; whereas, the way we go the current must slacken, and then we can dodge back along the shore.'

'The current's less a'ready, sir,' said the man Gray, who was sitting in the fore-sheets; 'you can ease her off a bit.'

'Thank you, my man,' said I, quite as if nothing had happened; for we had all quietly made up our minds to treat him like one of ourselves.

Suddenly the captain spoke up again, and I thought his voice was a little changed.

'The gun!' said he.

'I have thought of that,' said I, for I made sure he was thinking of a bombardment of the fort. 'They could never get the gun ashore, and if they did, they could never haul it through the woods.'

'Look astern, doctor,' replied the captain.

We had entirely forgotten the long nine; and there, to our horror, were the five rogues busy about her, getting off her jacket, as they called the stout tarpaulin cover under which she sailed. Not only that, but it flashed into my mind at the same moment that the round-shot and the powder for the gun had been left behind, and a stroke with an axe would put it all into the possession of the evil ones aboard.

'Israel was Flint's gunner,' said Gray, hoarsely.

At any risk, we put the boat's head direct for the landing-place. By this time we had got so far out of the run of the current that we kept steerage way even at our necessarily gentle rate of rowing, and I could keep her steady for the goal. But the worst of it was, that with the course I now held, we turned our broadside instead of our stern to the *Hispaniola*, and offered a target like a barn door.

I could hear, as well as see, that brandy-faced rascal, Israel Hands, plumping down a round-shot on the deck.

'Who's the best shot?' asked the captain.

'Mr Trelawney, out and away,' said I.

'Mr Trelawney, will you please pick me off one of these men, sir? Hands, if possible,' said the captain.

Trelawney was as cool as steel. He looked to the priming of his gun.

'Now,' cried the captain, 'easy with that gun, sir, or you'll swamp the boat. All hands stand by to trim her when he aims.'

The squire raised his gun, the rowing ceased, and we leaned over to the other side to keep the balance, and all was so nicely contrived that we did not ship a drop.

They had the gun, by this time, slewed round upon the swivel, and Hands, who was at the muzzle with the rammer, was, in consequence, the most exposed. However, we had no luck; for just as Trelawney fired, down he stooped, the ball whistled over him, and it was one of the other four who fell.

The cry he gave was echoed, not only by his companions on board, but by a great number of voices from the shore, and looking in that direction I saw the other pirates trooping out from among the trees and tumbling into their places in the boats.

'Here come the gigs, sir,' said I.

'Give way then,' cried the captain. 'We mustn't mind if we swamp her now. If we can't get ashore, all's up.'

'Only one of the gigs is being manned, sir,' I added, 'the crew of the other most likely going round by shore to cut us off.'

'They'll have a hot run, sir,' returned the captain. 'Jack ashore, you know. It's not them I mind; it's the round-shot. Carpet bowls! My lady's maid couldn't miss. Tell us, squire, when you see the match, and we'll hold water.'

In the meanwhile we had been making headway at a good pace for a boat so overloaded, and we had shipped but little water in the process. We were now close in; thirty or forty strokes and we should beach her; for the ebb had already disclosed a narrow belt of sand below the clustering trees. The gig was no longer to be feared; the little point had already concealed it from our eyes. The ebb-tide, which had so cruelly delayed us, was now making reparation, and delaying our assailants. The one source of danger was the gun.

'If I durst,' said the captain, 'I'd stop and pick off another man.'

But it was plain that they meant nothing should delay their shot. They had never so much as looked at their fallen comrade, though he was not dead, and I could see him trying to crawl away.

'Ready!' cried the squire.

'Hold!' cried the captain, quick as an echo.

And he and Redruth backed with a great heave that sent her stern bodily under water. The report fell in at the same instant of time. This was the first that Jim heard, the sound of the squire's shot not having reached him. Where the ball passed, not one of us precisely knew; but I fancy it must have been over our heads, and that the wind of it may have contributed to our disaster.

At any rate, the boat sank by the stern, quite gently, in three feet of water, leaving the captain and myself, facing each other, on our feet. The other three took complete headers, and came up again, drenched and bubbling.

So far there was no great harm. No lives were lost, and we could wade ashore in safety. But there were all our stores at the bottom, and, to make things worse, only two guns out of five remained in a state for service. Mine I had snatched from my knees and held over my head, by a sort of instinct. As for the captain, he had carried his over his shoulder by a bandoleer, and, like a wise man, lock uppermost. The other three had gone down with the boat.

To add to our concern, we heard voices already drawing near us in the woods along shore; and we had not only the danger of being cut off from the stockade in our half-crippled state, but the fear before us whether, if Hunter and Joyce were attacked by half a dozen, they would have the sense and conduct to stand firm. Hunter was steady, that we knew; Joyce was a doubtful case – a pleasant, polite man for a valet, and to brush one's clothes, but not entirely fitted for a man of war.

With all this in our minds, we waded ashore as fast as we could, leaving behind us the poor jolly-boat, and a good half of all our powder and provisions.

Chapter Eighteen

Narrative Continued by the Doctor:
End of the First Day's Fighting

We made our best speed across the strip of wood that now divided us from the stockade; and at every step we took the voices of the buccaneers rang nearer. Soon we could hear their footfalls as they ran, and the cracking of the branches as they breasted across a bit of thicket.

I began to see we should have a brush for it in earnest, and looked to my priming.

'Captain,' said I, 'Trelawney is the dead shot. Give him your gun; his own is useless.'

They exchanged guns, and Trelawney, silent and cool as he had been since the beginning of the bustle, hung a moment on his heel to see that all was fit for service. At the same time, observing Gray to be unarmed, I handed him my cutlass. It did all our hearts good to see him spit in his hand, knit his brows, and make the blade sing through the air. It was plain from every line of his body that our new hand was worth his salt.

Forty paces farther we came to the edge of the wood and saw the stockade in front of us. We struck the enclosure about the middle of the south side, and, almost at the same time, seven mutineers – Job Anderson, the boatswain, at their head – appeared in full cry at the south-western corner.

They paused, as if taken aback; and before they recovered, not only the squire and I, but Hunter and Joyce from the block house, had time to fire. The four shots came in rather a scattering volley; but they did the business: one of the enemy actually fell, and the rest, without hesitation, turned and plunged into the trees.

After reloading, we walked down the outside of the palisade to see to the fallen enemy. He was stone dead – shot through the heart.

We began to rejoice over our good success, when just at that moment a pistol cracked in the bush, a ball whistled close past my ear, and poor Tom Redruth stumbled and fell his length on the ground. Both the squire and I returned the shot; but as we had nothing to aim at, it is probable we only wasted powder. Then we reloaded, and turned our attention to poor Tom.

The captain and Gray were already examining him; and I saw with half an eye that all was over.

I believe the readiness of our return volley had scattered the mutineers once more, for we were suffered without further molestation to get the poor old gamekeeper hoisted over the stockade, and carried, groaning and bleeding, into the log-house.

Poor old fellow, he had not uttered one word of surprise, complaint, fear, or even acquiescence, from the very beginning of our troubles till now, when we had laid him down in the log-house to die. He had lain like a Trojan behind his mattress in the gallery; he had followed every order silently, doggedly, and well; he was the oldest of our party by a score of years; and now, sullen, old, serviceable servant, it was he that was to die.

The squire dropped down beside him on his knees and kissed his hand, crying like a child.

'Be I going, doctor?' he asked.

'Tom, my man,' said I, 'you're going home.'

'I wish I had had a lick at them with the gun first,' he replied.

'Tom,' said the squire, 'say you forgive me, won't you?'

'Would that be respectful like, from me to you, squire?' was the answer. 'Howsoever, so be it, amen!'

After a little while of silence, he said he thought somebody might read a prayer. 'It's the custom, sir,' he added, apologetically. And not long after, without another word, he passed away.

In the meantime the captain, whom I had observed to be wonderfully swollen about the chest and pockets, had turned out a great many various stores – the British colours, a Bible, a coil of stoutish rope, pen, ink, the log-book, and pounds of tobacco. He had found a longish fir-tree lying felled and trimmed in the enclosure, and, with the help of Hunter, he had set it up at the corner of the log-house where the trunks crossed and made an angle. Then, climbing on the roof, he had with his own hand bent and run up the colours.

This seemed mightily to relieve him. He re-entered the log-house, and set about counting up the stores, as if nothing else existed. But he had an eye on Tom's passage for all that; and as soon as all was over, came forward with another flag, and reverently spread it on the body.

'Don't you take on, sir,' he said, shaking the squire's hand. 'All's well with him; no fear for a hand that's been shot down in his duty to captain and owner. It mayn't be good divinity, but it's a fact.'

Then he pulled me aside.

'Dr Livesey,' he said, 'in how many weeks do you and squire expect the consort?'

I told him it was a question, not of weeks, but of months; that if we were not back by the end of August, Blandly was to send to find us; but neither sooner nor later. 'You can calculate for yourself,' I said.

'Why, yes,' returned the captain, scratching his head, 'and making a large allowance, sir, for all the gifts of Providence, I should say we were pretty close hauled.'

'How do you mean?' I asked.

'It's a pity, sir, we lost that second load. That's what I mean,' replied the captain. 'As for powder and shot, we'll do. But the rations are short, very short – so short, Doctor Livesey, that we're, perhaps, as well without that extra mouth.'

And he pointed to the dead body under the flag.

Just then, with a roar and a whistle, a round-shot passed high above the roof of the log-house and plumped far beyond us in the wood.

'Oho!' said the captain. 'Blaze away! You've little enough powder already, my lads.'

At the second trial, the aim was better, and the ball descended inside the stockade, scattering a cloud of sand, but doing no further damage.

'Captain,' said the squire, 'the house is quite invisible from the ship. It must be the flag they are aiming at. Would it not be wiser to take it in?'

'Strike my colours!' cried the captain. 'No, sir, not I;' and, as soon as he had said the words, I think we all agreed with him. For it was not only a piece of stout, seamanly, good feeling; it was good policy besides, and showed our enemies that we despised their cannonade.

All through the evening they kept thundering away. Ball after ball flew over or fell short, or kicked up the sand in the enclosure; but they had to fire so high that the shot fell dead and buried itself in the soft sand. We had no ricochet to fear; and though one popped in through the roof of the log-house and out again through the floor, we soon got used to that sort of horse-play, and minded it no more than cricket.

'There is one thing good about all this,' observed the captain: 'the wood in front of us is likely clear. The ebb has made a good while; our stores should be uncovered. Volunteers to go and bring in pork.'

Gray and Hunter were the first to come forward. Well armed, they stole out of the stockade; but it proved a useless mission. The mutineers were bolder than we fancied, or they put more trust in Israel's gunnery. For four or five of them were busy carrying off our stores, and wading out with them to one of the gigs that lay close by, pulling an oar or so to hold her steady against the current. Silver was in the stern-sheets in command; and every man of them was now provided with a musket from some secret magazine of their own.

The captain sat down to his log, and here is the beginning of the entry: –

'Alexander Smollett, master; David Livesey, ship's doctor; Abraham Gray, carpenter's mate; John Trelawney, owner; John Hunter and Richard Joyce, owner's servants, landsmen – being all that is left faithful of the ship's company – with stores for ten days at short rations, came ashore this day, and flew British colours on the log-house in Treasure Island. Thomas Redruth, owner's servant, landsman, shot by the mutineers; James Hawkins, cabin-boy –'

And at the same time I was wondering over poor Jim Hawkins's fate.

A hail on the land side.

'Somebody hailing us,' said Hunter, who was on guard.

'Doctor! squire! captain! Hullo, Hunter, is that you?' came the cries.

And I ran to the door in time to see Jim Hawkins, safe and sound, come climbing over the stockade.

Chapter Nineteen

Narrative Resumed by Jim Hawkins: The Garrison in the Stockade

As soon as Ben Gunn saw the colours he came to a halt, stopped me by the arm, and sat down.

'Now,' said he, 'there's your friends, sure enough.'

'Far more likely it's the mutineers,' I answered.

'That!' he cried. 'Why, in a place like this, where nobody puts in but gen'lemen of fortune, Silver would fly the Jolly Roger, you don't make no doubt of that. No; that's your friends. There's been blows, too, and I reckon your friends has had the best of it; and here they are ashore in the old stockade, as was made years and years ago by Flint. Ah, he was the man to have a headpiece, was Flint! Barring rum, his match were never seen. He were afraid of none, not he; on'y Silver – Silver was that genteel.'

'Well,' said I, 'that may be so, and so be it; all the more reason that I should hurry on and join my friends.'

'Nay, mate,' returned Ben, 'not you. You're a good boy, or I'm mistook; but you're on'y a boy, all told. Now, Ben Gunn is fly. Rum wouldn't bring me there, where you're going – not rum wouldn't, till I see your born gen'leman, and gets it on his word of honour. And you won't forget my words: "A precious sight (that's what you'll say), a precious sight more confidence" – and then nips him.'

And he pinched me the third time with the same air of cleverness.

'And when Ben Gunn is wanted, you know where to find him, Jim. Just wheer you found him to-day. And him that comes is to have a white thing in his hand: and he's to come alone. Oh! and you'll say this: "Ben Gunn," says you, "has reasons of his own."'

'Well,' said I, 'I believe I understand. You have something to propose, and you wish to see the squire or the doctor; and you're to be found where I found you. Is that all?'

'And when? says you,' he added. 'Why, from about noon observation to about six bells.'

'Good,' said I, 'and now may I go?'

'You won't forget?' he inquired, anxiously. 'Precious sight, and reasons of his own, says you. Reasons of his own; that's the mainstay; as between man and man. Well, then' – still holding me – 'I reckon you can go, Jim. And, Jim, if you was to see Silver, you wouldn't go for to sell Ben Gunn? wild horses wouldn't draw it from you? No, says you. And if them pirates camp ashore, Jim, what would you say but there'd be widders in the morning?'

Here he was interrupted by a loud report, and a cannon ball came tearing through the trees and pitched in the sand, not a hundred yards from where we two were talking. The next moment each of us had taken to his heels in a different direction.

For a good hour to come frequent reports shook the island, and balls kept crashing through the woods. I moved from hiding-place to hiding-place, always pursued, or so it seemed to me, by these terrifying missiles. But towards the end of the bombardment, though still I durst not venture in the direction of the stockade, where the balls fell oftenest, I had begun, in a manner, to pluck up my heart again; and after a long detour to the east, crept down among the shore-side trees.

The sun had just set, the sea breeze was rustling and tumbling in the woods, and ruffling the grey surface of the anchorage; the tide, too, was far out, and great tracts of sand lay uncovered; the air, after the heat of the day, chilled me through my jacket.

The *Hispaniola* still lay where she had anchored; but, sure enough, there was the Jolly Roger – the black flag of piracy – flying from her peak. Even as I looked, there came another red flash and another report, that sent the echoes clattering, and one more round shot whistled through the air. It was the last of the cannonade.

I lay for some time, watching the bustle which succeeded the attack. Men were demolishing something with axes on the beach near the stockade; the poor jolly-boat, I afterwards discovered. Away, near the mouth of the river, a great fire was glowing among the trees, and between that point and the ship one of the gigs kept coming and going, the men, whom I had seen so gloomy, shouting at the oars like children. But there was a sound in their voices which suggested rum.

At length I thought I might return towards the stockade. I was pretty far down on the low, sandy spit that encloses the anchorage to the east, and is joined at half-water to Skeleton Island; and now, as I rose to my feet, I saw some distance further down the spit, and rising from among low bushes, an isolated rock, pretty high, and peculiarly white in colour. It occurred to me that this might be the white rock of which Ben Gunn had spoken, and that some day or other a boat might be wanted, and I should know where to look for one.

Then I skirted among the woods until I had regained the rear, or shoreward side, of the stockade, and was soon warmly welcomed by the faithful party.

I had soon told my story, and began to look about me. The log-house was made of unsquared trunks of pine – roof, walls, and floor. The latter stood in several places as much as a foot or a foot and a half above the surface of the sand. There was a porch at the door, and under this porch the little spring welled up into an artificial basin of a rather odd kind – no other than a great ship's kettle of iron, with the bottom knocked out, and sunk 'to her bearings,' as the captain said, among the sand.

Little had been left beside the framework of the house; but in one corner there was a stone slab laid down by way of hearth, and an old rusty iron basket to contain the fire.

The slopes of the knoll and all the inside of the stockade had been cleared of timber to build the house, and we could see by the stumps what a fine and lofty grove had been destroyed. Most of the soil had been washed away or buried in drift after the removal of the trees; only where the streamlet ran down from the kettle a thick bed of moss and some ferns and little creeping bushes were still green among the sand. Very close around the stockade – too close for defence, they said – the wood still flourished high and dense, all of fir on the land side, but towards the sea with a large admixture of live-oaks.

The cold evening breeze, of which I have spoken, whistled through every chink of the rude building, and sprinkled the floor with a continual rain of fine sand. There was sand in our eyes, sand in our teeth, sand in our suppers, sand dancing in the spring at the bottom of the kettle, for all the world like porridge beginning to boil. Our chimney was a square hole in the roof; it was but a little part of the smoke that found its way out, and the rest eddied about the house, and kept us coughing and piping the eye.

Add to this that Gray, the new man, had his face tied up in a bandage for a cut he had got in breaking away from the mutineers; and that poor old Tom Redruth, still unburied, lay along the wall, stiff and stark, under the Union Jack.

If we had been allowed to sit idle, we should all have fallen in the blues, but Captain Smollett was never the man for that. All hands were called up before him, and he divided us into watches. The doctor, and Gray, and I, for one; the squire, Hunter, and Joyce, upon the other. Tired though we all were, two were sent our for firewood; two more were set to dig a grave for Redruth; the doctor was named cook; I was put sentry at the door; and the captain himself went from one to another, keeping up our spirits and lending a hand wherever it was wanted.

From time to time the doctor came to the door for a little air and to rest his eyes, which were almost smoked out of his head; and whenever he did so, he had a word for me.

'That man Smollett,' he said once, 'is a better man than I am. And when I say that it means a deal, Jim.'

Another time he came and was silent for a while. Then he put his head on one side, and looked at me.

'Is this Ben Gunn a man?' he asked.

'I do not know, sir,' said I. 'I am not very sure whether he's sane.'

'If there's any doubt about the matter, he is,' returned the doctor. 'A man who has been three years biting his nails on a desert island, Jim, can't expect to appear as sane as you or me. It doesn't lie in human nature. Was it cheese you said he had a fancy for?'

'Yes, sir, cheese,' I answered.

'Well, Jim,' says he, 'just see the good that comes of being dainty in your food. You've seen my snuff-box, haven't you? And you never saw me take snuff; the reason being that in my snuff-box I carry a piece of Parmesan cheese – a cheese made in Italy, very nutritious. Well, that's for Ben Gunn!'

Before supper was eaten we buried old Tom in the sand, and stood round him for a while bare-headed in the breeze. A good deal of firewood had been got in, but not enough for the captain's fancy; and he shook his head over it, and told us we 'must get back to this to-morrow rather livelier.' Then, when we had eaten our pork, and each had a good stiff glass of brandy grog, the three chiefs got together in a corner to discuss our prospects.

It appears they were at their wit's end what to do, the stores being so low that we must have been starved into surrender long before help came. But our best hope, it was decided, was to kill off the buccaneers until they either hauled down their flag or ran away with the *Hispaniola*. From nineteen they were already reduced to fifteen, two others were wounded, and one, at least – the man shot beside the gun – severely wounded, if he were not dead. Every time we had a crack at them, we were to take it, saving our own lives, with the extremest care. And, besides that, we had two able allies – rum and the climate.

As for the first, though we were about half a mile away, we could hear them roaring and singing late into the night; and as for the second, the doctor staked his wig that, camped where they were in the marsh, and unprovided with remedies, the half of them would be on their backs before a week.

'So,' he added, 'if we are not all shot down first, they'll be glad to be packing in the schooner. It's always a ship, and they can get to buccaneering again, I suppose.'

'First ship that ever I lost,' said Captain Smollett.

I was dead tired, as you may fancy; and when I got to sleep, which was not till after a great deal of tossing, I slept like a log of wood.

The rest had long been up, and had already breakfasted and increased the pile of firewood by about half as much again, when I was wakened by a bustle and the sound of voices.

'Flag of truce!' I heard some one say; and then, immediately after, with a cry of surprise, 'Silver himself!'

And, at that, up I jumped, and, rubbing my eyes, ran to a loop-hole in the wall.

Chapter Twenty

Silver's Embassy

Sure enough, there were two men just outside the stockade, one of them waving a white cloth; the other, no less a person than Silver himself, standing placidly by.

It was still quite early, and the coldest morning that I think I ever was abroad in; a chill that pierced into the marrow. The sky was bright and cloudless overhead, and the tops of the trees shone rosily in the sun. But where Silver stood with his lieutenant all was still in shadow, and they waded knee deep in a low, white vapour that had crawled during the night out of the morass. The chill and the vapour taken together told a poor tale of the island. It was plainly a damp, feverish, unhealthy spot.

'Keep indoors, men,' said the captain. 'Ten to one this is a trick.'

Then he hailed the buccaneer.

'Who goes? Stand, or we fire.'

'Flag of truce,' cried Silver.

The captain was in the porch, keeping himself carefully out of the way of a treacherous shot should any be intended. He turned and spoke to us: –

'Doctor's watch on the look out. Dr Livesey, take the north side, if you please; Jim, the east; Gray, west. The watch below, all hands to load muskets. Lively, men, and careful.'

And then he turned again to the mutineers.

'And what do you want with your flag of truce?' he cried.

This time it was the other man who replied.

'Cap'n Silver, sir, to come on board and make terms,' he shouted.

'Cap'n Silver! Don't know him. Who's he?' cried the captain. And we could hear him adding to himself: 'Cap'n, is it? My heart, and here's promotion!'

Long John answered for himself.

'Me, sir. These poor lads have chosen me cap'n, after your desertion, sir' – laying a particular emphasis upon the word 'desertion.' 'We're willing to submit, if we can come to terms, and no bones about it. All I ask is your word, Cap'n Smollett, to let me safe and sound out of this here stockade, and one minute to get out o' shot before a gun is fired.'

'My man,' said Captain Smollett, 'I have not the slightest desire to talk to you. If you wish to talk to me, you can come, that's all. If there's any treachery, it'll be on your side, and the Lord help you.'

'That's enough, cap'n,' shouted Long John, cheerily. 'A word from you's enough. I know a gentleman, and you may lay to that.'

We could see the man who carried the flag of truce attempting to hold Silver back. Nor was that wonderful, seeing how cavalier had been the captain's answer. But Silver laughed at him aloud, and slapped him on the back, as if the idea of alarm had been absurd. Then he advanced to the stockade, threw over his crutch, got a leg up, and with great vigour and skill succeeded in surmounting the fence and dropping safely to the other side.

I will confess that I was far too much taken up with what was going on to be of the slightest use as sentry; indeed, I had already deserted my eastern loophole, and crept up behind the captain, who had now seated himself on the threshold, with his elbows on his knees, his head in his hands, and his eyes fixed on the water, as it bubbled out of the old iron kettle in the sand. He was whistling to himself, 'Come, Lasses and Lads.'

Silver had terrible hard work getting up the knoll. What with the steepness of the incline, the thick tree stumps, and the soft sand, he and his crutch were as helpless as a ship in stays. But he stuck to it like a man in silence, and at last arrived before the captain, whom he saluted in the handsomest style. He was tricked out in his best; an immense blue coat, thick with brass buttons, hung as low as to his knees, and a fine laced hat was set on the back of his head.

'Here you are, my man,' said the captain, raising his head. 'You had better sit down.'

'You ain't a-going to let me inside, cap'n?' complained Long John. 'It's a main cold morning, to be sure, sir, to sit outside upon the sand.'

'Why, Silver,' said the captain, 'if you had pleased to be an honest man, you might have been sitting in your galley. It's your own doing. You're either my ship's cook – and then you were treated handsome – or Cap'n Silver, a common mutineer and pirate, and then you can go hang!'

'Well, well, cap'n,' returned the sea cook, sitting down as he was bidden on the sand, 'you'll have to give me a hand up again, that's all. A sweet pretty place you have of it here. Ah, there's Jim! The top of the morning to you, Jim. Doctor, here's my service. Why, there you all are together like a happy family, in a manner of speaking.'

'If you have anything to say, my man, better say it,' said the captain.

'Right you were, Cap'n Smollett,' replied Silver. 'Dooty is dooty, to be sure. Well, now, you look here, that was a good lay of yours last night. I don't deny it was a good lay. Some of you pretty handy with a hand-spike-end. And I'll not deny neither but what some of my people was shook – maybe all was shook; maybe I was shook myself; maybe that's why I'm here for terms. But you mark me, cap'n, it won't do twice, by thunder! We'll have to do sentry-go, and ease off a point or so on the rum. Maybe you think we were all a sheet in the wind's eye. But I'll tell you I was sober; I was on'y dog tired; and if I'd awoke a second sooner I'd 'a' caught you at the act, I would. He wasn't dead when I got round to him, not he.'

'Well?' says Captain Smollett, as cool as can be.

All that Silver said was a riddle to him, but you would never have guessed it from his tone. As for me, I began to have an inkling. Ben Gunn's last words came back to my mind. I began to suppose that he had paid the buccaneers a visit while they all lay drunk together round their fire, and I reckoned up with glee that we had only fourteen enemies to deal with.

'Well, here it is,' said Silver. 'We want that treasure, and we'll have it – that's our point! You would just as soon save your lives, I reckon; and that's yours. You have a chart, haven't you?'

'That's as may be,' replied the captain.

'Oh, well, you have, I know that,' returned Long John. 'You needn't be so husky with a man; there ain't a particle of service in that, and you may lay to it. What I mean is, we want your chart. Now, I never meant you no harm, myself.'

'That won't do with me, my man,' interrupted the captain. 'We know exactly what you meant to do, and we don't care; for now, you see, you can't do it.'

And the captain looked at him calmly, and proceeded to fill a pipe.

'If Abe Gray –' Silver broke out.

'Avast there! cried Mr Smollett. 'Gray told me nothing, and I asked him nothing; and what's more, I would see you and him and this whole island blown clean out of the water into blazes first. So there's my mind for you, my man, on that.'

This little whiff of temper seemed to cool Silver down. He had been growing nettled before, but now he pulled himself together.

'Like enough,' said he. 'I would set no limits to what gentlemen might consider shipshape, or might not, as the case were. And, seein' as how you are about to take a pipe, cap'n, I'll make so free as do likewise.'

And he filled a pipe and lighted it; and the two men sat silently smoking for quite a while, now looking each other in the face, now stopping their tobacco, now leaning forward to spit. It was as good as the play to see them.

'Now,' resumed Silver, 'here it is. You give us the chart to get the treasure by, and drop shooting poor seamen, and stoving of their heads in while asleep. You do that, and we'll offer you a choice.

Either you come aboard along of us, once the treasure shipped, and then I'll give you my affy-davy, upon my word of honour, to clap you somewhere safe ashore. Or, if that ain't to your fancy, some of my hands being rough, and having old scores, on account of hazing, then you can stay here, you can. We'll divide stores with you, man for man; and I'll give my affy-davy, as before, to speak the first ship I sight, and send 'em here to pick you up. Now you'll own that's talking. Handsomer you couldn't look to get, not you. And I hope' – raising his voice – 'that all hands in this here block house will overhaul my words, for what is spoke to one is spoke to all.'

Captain Smollett rose from his seat, and knocked out the ashes of his pipe in the palm of his left hand.

'Is that all?' he asked.

'Every last word, by thunder!' answered John. 'Refuse that, and you've seen the last of me but musket-balls.'

'Very good,' said the captain. 'Now you'll hear me. If you'll come up one by one, unarmed, I'll engage to clap you all in irons, and take you home to a fair trial in England. If you won't, my name is Alexander Smollett, I've flown my sovereign's colours, and I'll see you all to Davy Jones. You can't find the treasure. You can't sail the ship – there's not a man among you fit to sail the ship. You can't fight us – Gray, there, got away from five of you. Your ship's in irons, Master Silver; you're on a lee shore, and so you'll find. I stand here and tell you so; and they're the last good words you'll get from me; for, in the name of heaven, I'll put a bullet in your back when next I meet you. Tramp, my lad. Bundle out of this, please, hand over hand, and double quick.'

Silver's face was a picture; his eyes started in his head with wrath. He shook the fire out of his pipe.

'Give me a hand up!' he cried.

'Not I,' returned the captain.

'Who'll give me a hand up?' he roared.

Not a man among us moved. Growling the foulest imprecations, he crawled along the sand till he got hold of the porch and could hoist himself again upon his crutch. Then he spat into the spring.

'There!' he cried, 'that's what I think of ye. Before an hour's out, I'll stove in your old block house like a rum puncheon. Laugh, by thunder, laugh! Before an hour's out, ye'll laugh upon the other side. Them that die'll be the lucky ones.'

And with a dreadful oath he stumbled off, ploughed down the sand, was helped across the stockade, after four or five failures, by the man with the flag of truce, and disappeared in an instant afterwards among the trees.

Chapter Twenty-One

The Attack

As soon as Silver disappeared, the captain, who had been closely watching him, turned towards the interior of the house, and found not a man of us at his post but Gray. It was the first time we had ever seen him angry.

'Quarters!' he roared. And then, as we all slunk back to our places, 'Gray,' he said, 'I'll put your name in the log; you've stood by your duty like a seaman. Mr Trelawney, I'm surprised at you, sir. Doctor, I thought you had worn the king's coat! If that was how you served at Fontenoy, sir, you'd have been better in your berth.'

The doctor's watch were all back at their loopholes, the rest were busy loading the spare muskets, and every one with a red face, you may be certain, and a flea in his ear, as the saying is.

The captain looked on for a while in silence. Then he spoke.

'My lads,' said he, 'I've given Silver a broadside. I pitched it in red-hot on purpose; and before the hour's out, as he said, we shall be boarded. We're outnumbered, I needn't tell you that, but we fight in shelter; and, a minute ago, I should have said we fought with discipline. I've no manner of doubt that we can drub them, if you choose.'

Then he went the rounds, and saw, as he said, that all was clear.

On the two short sides of the house, east and west, there were only two loopholes; on the south side where the porch was, two again; and on the north side, five. There was a round score of muskets for the seven of us; the firewood had been built into four piles – tables, you might say – one about the middle of each side, and on each of these tables some ammunition and four loaded muskets were laid ready to the hand of the defenders. In the middle, the cutlasses lay ranged.

'Toss out the fire,' said the captain; 'the chill is past, and we musn't have smoke in our eyes.'

The iron fire basket was carried bodily out by Mr Trelawney, and the embers smothered among sand.

'Hawkins hasn't had his breakfast. Hawkins, help yourself, and back to your post to eat it,' continued Captain Smollett. 'Lively, now, my lad; you'll want it before you've done. Hunter, serve out a round of brandy to all hands.'

And while this was going on, the captain completed, in his own mind, the plan of the defence.

'Doctor, you will take the door,' he resumed. 'See, and don't expose yourself; keep within, and fire through the porch. Hunter, take the east side, there. Joyce, you stand by the west, my man. Mr Trelawney, you are the best shot – you and Gray will take this long north side, with the five loopholes; it's there the danger is. If they can get up to it, and fire in upon us through our own ports, things would begin to look dirty. Hawkins, neither you nor I are much account at the shooting; we'll stand by to load and bear a hand.'

As the captain had said, the chill was past. As soon as the sun had climbed above our girdle of trees, it fell with all its force upon the clearing, and drank up the vapours at a draught. Soon the sand was baking, and the resin melting in the logs of the block house. Jackets and coats were flung aside; shirts thrown open at the neck, and rolled up to the shoulders; and we stood there, each at his post, in a fever of heat and anxiety.

An hour passed away.

'Hang them!' said the captain. 'This is as dull as the doldrums. Gray, whistle for a wind.'

And just at that moment came the first news of the attack.

'If you please, sir,' said Joyce, 'if I see any one am I to fire?'

'I told you so!' cried the captain.

'Thank you, sir,' returned Joyce, with the same quiet civility.

Nothing followed for a time; but the remark had set us all on the alert, straining ears and eyes – the musketeers with their pieces balanced in their hands, the captain out in the middle of the block house, with his mouth very tight and a frown on his face.

So some seconds passed, till suddenly Joyce whipped up his musket and fired. The report had scarcely died away ere it was repeated and repeated from without in a scattering volley, shot behind shot, like a string of geese, from every side of the enclosure. Several bullets struck the log-house, but not one entered; and, as the smoke cleared away and vanished, the stockade and the woods around it looked as quiet and empty as before. Not a bough waved, not the gleam of a musket-barrel betrayed the presence of our foes.

'Did you hit your man?' asked the captain.

'No, sir,' replied Joyce. 'I believe not, sir.'

'Next best thing to tell the truth,' muttered Captain Smollett. 'Load his gun, Hawkins. How many should you say there were on your side, doctor?'

'I know precisely,' said Dr Livesey. 'Three shots were fired on this side. I saw the three flashes – two close together – one farther to the west.'

'Three!' repeated the captain. 'And how many on yours, Mr Trelawney?'

But this was not so easily answered. There had come many from the north – seven, by the squire's computation; eight or nine, according to Gray. From the east and west only a single shot had been fired. It was plain, therefore, that the attack would be developed from the north, and that on the other three sides we were only to be annoyed by a show of hostilities. But Captain Smollett made no change in his arrangements. If the mutineers succeeded in crossing the stockade, he argued, they would take possession of any unprotected loophole, and shoot us down like rats in our own stronghold.

Nor had we much time left to us for thought. Suddenly, with a loud huzza, a little cloud of pirates leaped from the woods on the north side, and ran straight on the stockade. At the same moment, the fire was once more opened from the woods, and a rifle ball sang through the doorway, and knocked the doctor's musket into bits.

The boarders swarmed over the fence like monkeys. Squire and Gray fired again and yet again; three men fell, one forwards into the enclosure, two back on the outside. But of these, one was evidently more frightened than hurt, for he was on his feet again in a crack, and instantly disappeared among the trees.

Two had bit the dust, one had fled, four had made good their footing inside our defences; while from the shelter of the woods seven or eight men, each evidently supplied with several muskets, kept up a hot though useless fire on the log-house.

The four who had boarded made straight before them for the building, shouting as they ran, and the men among the trees shouted back to encourage them. Several shots were fired; but, such was the hurry of the marksmen, not one appears to have taken effect. In a moment, the four pirates had swarmed up the mound and were upon us.

The head of Job Anderson, the boatswain, appeared at the middle loophole.

'At 'em, all hands – all hands!' he roared, in a voice of thunder.

At the same moment, another pirate grasped Hunter's musket by the muzzle, wrenched it from his hands, plucked it through the loophole, and, with one stunning blow, laid the poor fellow senseless on the floor. Meanwhile a third, running unharmed all round the house, appeared suddenly in the doorway, and fell with his cutlass on the doctor.

Our position was utterly reversed. A moment since we were firing, under cover, at an exposed enemy; now it was we who lay uncovered, and could not return a blow.

The log-house was full of smoke, to which we owed our comparative safety. Cries and confusion, the flashes and reports of pistol shots, and one loud groan, rang in my ears.

'Out, lads, out, and fight 'em in the open! Cutlasses!' cried the captain.

I snatched a cutlass from the pile, and some one, at the same time snatching another, gave me a cut across the knuckles which I hardly felt. I dashed out of the door into the clear sunlight. Some one was close behind, I knew not whom. Right in front, the doctor was pursuing his assailant down the hill, and, just as my eyes fell upon him, beat down his guard, and sent him sprawling on his back, with a great slash across the face.

'Round the house, lads! round the house!' cried the captain; and even in the hurly-burly I perceived a change in his voice.

Mechanically, I obeyed, turned eastwards, and with my cutlass raised, ran round the corner of the house. Next moment I was face to face with Anderson. He roared aloud, and his hanger went up above his head, flashing in the sunlight. I had not time to be afraid, but, as the blow still hung impending, leaped in a trice upon one side, and missing my foot in the soft sand, rolled headlong down the slope.

When I had first sallied from the door, the other mutineers had been already swarming up the palisade to make an end of us. One man, in a red night-cap, with his cutlass in his mouth, had even got upon the top and thrown a leg across. Well, so short had been the interval, that when I found my feet again all was in the same posture, the fellow with the red night-cap still half way over, another still just showing his head above the top of the stockade. And yet, in this breath of time, the fight was over, and the victory was ours.

Gray, following close behind me, had cut down the big boatswain ere he had time to recover from his last blow. Another had been shot at a loophole in the very act of firing into the house, and now lay in agony, the pistol still smoking in his hand. A third, as I had seen, the doctor had disposed of at a blow. Of the four who had scaled the palisade, one only remained unaccounted for, and he, having left his cutlass on the field, was now clambering out again with the fear of death upon him.

'Fire – fire from the house!' cried the doctor. 'And you, lads, back into cover.'

But his words were unheeded, no shot was fired, and the last boarder made good his escape, and disappeared with the rest into the wood. In three seconds nothing remained of the attacking party but the five who had fallen, four on the inside, and one on the outside, of the palisade.

The doctor and Gray and I ran full speed for shelter. The survivors would soon be back where they had left their muskets, and at any moment the fire might recommence.

The house was by this time somewhat cleared of smoke, and we saw at a glance the price we had paid for victory. Hunter lay beside his loophole, stunned; Joyce by his, shot through the head, never to move again; while right in the centre, the squire was supporting the captain, one as pale as the other.

'The captain's wounded,' said Mr Trelawney.

'Have they run?' asked Mr Smollett.

'All that could, you may be bound,' returned the doctor; 'but there's five of them will never run again.'

'Five!' cried the captain. 'Come, that's better. Five against three leaves us four to nine. That's better odds than we had at starting. We were seven to nineteen then, or thought we were, and that's as bad to bear.'*

* The mutineers were soon only eight in number, for the man shot by Mr Trelawney on board the schooner died that same evening of his wound. But this was, of course, not known till after by the faithful party.

PART FIVE

My Sea Adventure

Chapter Twenty-Two

How My Sea Adventure Began

There was no return of the mutineers – not so much as another shot out of the woods. They had 'got their rations for that day' as the captain put it, and we had the place to ourselves and a quiet time to overhaul the wounded and get dinner. Squire and I cooked outside in spite of the danger, and even outside we could hardly tell what we were at, for horror of the loud groans that reached us from the doctor's patients.

Out of the eight men who had fallen in the action, only three still breathed – that one of the pirates who had been shot at the loophole, Hunter, and Captain Smollett; and of these the first two were as good as dead; the mutineer, indeed, died under the doctor's knife, and Hunter, do what we could, never recovered consciousness in this world. He lingered all day, breathing loudly like the old buccaneer at home in his apoplectic fit; but the bones of his chest had been crushed by the blow and his skull fractured in falling, and some time in the following night, without sign or sound, he went to his Maker.

As for the captain, his wounds were grievous indeed, but not dangerous. No organ was fatally injured. Anderson's ball – for it was Job that shot him first – had broken his shoulder-blade and touched the lung, not badly; the second had only torn and displaced some muscles in the calf. He was sure to recover, the doctor said, but, in the meantime and for weeks to come, he must not walk nor move his arm, nor so much as speak when he could help it.

My own accidental cut across the knuckles was a flea-bite. Doctor Livesey patched it up with plaster, and pulled my ears for me into the bargain.

After dinner the squire and the doctor sat by the captain's side a while in consultation; and when they had talked to their hearts' content, it being then a little past noon, the doctor took up his hat and pistols, girt on a cutlass, put the chart in his pocket, and with a musket over his shoulder, crossed the palisade on the north side, and set off briskly through the trees.

Gray and I were sitting together at the far end of the block house, to be out of earshot of our officers consulting; and Gray took his pipe out of his mouth and fairly forgot to put it back again, so thunder-struck he was at this occurrence.

'Why, in the name of Davy Jones,' said he, 'is Dr Livesey mad?'

'Why, no,' says I. 'He's about the last of this crew for that, I take it.'

'Well, shipmate,' said Gray, 'mad he may not be; but if *he's* not, you mark my words, *I* am.'

'I take it,' replied I, 'the doctor has his idea; and if I am right, he's going now to see Ben Gunn.'

I was right, as appeared later; but, in the meantime, the house being stifling hot, and the little patch of sand inside the palisade ablaze with midday sun, I began to get another thought into my head, which was not by any means so right. What I began to do was to envy the doctor, walking in the cool shadow of the woods, with the birds about him, and the pleasant smell of the pines, while I sat grilling, with my clothes stuck to the hot resin, and so much blood about me, and so many poor dead bodies lying all around, that I took a disgust of the place that was almost as strong as fear.

All the time I was washing out the block house, and then washing up the things from dinner, this disgust and envy kept growing stronger and stronger, till at last, being near a bread-bag, and no one then observing me, I took the first step towards my escapade, and filled both pockets of my coat with biscuit.

I was a fool, if you like, and certainly I was going to do a foolish, over-bold act; but I was determined to do it with all the precautions in my power. These biscuits, should anything befall me, would keep me, at least, from starving till far on in the next day.

The next thing I laid hold of was a brace of pistols, and as I already had a powder-horn and bullets, I felt myself well supplied with arms.

As for the scheme I had in my head, it was not a bad one in itself. I was to go down the sandy spit that divides the anchorage on the east from the open sea, find the white rock I had observed last evening, and ascertain whether it was there or not that Ben Gunn had hidden his boat; a thing quite worth doing, as I still believe. But as I was certain I should not be allowed to leave the enclosure, my only plan was to take French leave, and slip out when nobody was watching; and that was so bad a way of doing it as made the thing itself wrong. But I was only a boy, and I had made my mind up.

Well, as things at last fell out, I found an admirable opportunity. The squire and Gray were busy helping the captain with his bandages; the coast was clear; I made a bolt for it over the stockade and into the thickest of the trees, and before my absence was observed I was out of cry of my companions.

This was my second folly, far worse than the first, as I left but two sound men to guard the house; but like the first, it was a help towards saving all of us.

I took my way straight for the east coast of the island, for I was determined to go down the sea side of the spit to avoid all chance of observation from the anchorage. It was already late in the afternoon, although still warm and sunny. As I continued to thread the tall woods I could hear from far before me not only the continuous thunder of the surf, but a certain tossing of foliage and grinding of boughs which showed me the sea breeze had set in higher than usual. Soon cool draughts of air began to reach me; and a few steps farther I came forth into the open borders of the grove, and saw the sea lying blue and sunny to the horizon, and the surf tumbling and tossing its foam along the beach.

I have never seen the sea quiet round Treasure Island. The sun might blaze overhead, the air be without a breath, the surface smooth and blue, but still these great rollers would be running along all the external coast, thundering and thundering by day and night; and I scarce believe there is one spot in the island where a man would be out of earshot of their noise.

I walked along beside the surf with great enjoyment, till thinking I was now got far enough to the south, I took the cover of some thick bushes, and crept warily up to the ridge of the spit.

Behind me was the sea, in front the anchorage. The sea breeze, as though it had the sooner blown itself out by its unusual violence, was already at an end; it had been succeeded by light, variable airs from the south and south-east, carrying great banks of fog; and the anchorage, under lee of Skeleton Island, lay still and leaden as when first we entered it. The *Hispaniola*, in that unbroken mirror, was exactly portrayed from the truck to the water-line, the Jolly Roger hanging from her peak.

Alongside lay one of the gigs, Silver in the stern-sheets – him I could always recognise – while a couple of men were leaning over the stern bulwarks, one of them with a red cap – the very rogue that I had seen some hours before stride-legs upon the palisade. Apparently they were talking and laughing, though at that distance – upwards of a mile – I could, of course, hear no word of what was said. All at once, there began the most horrid, unearthly screaming, which at first startled me badly, though I had soon remembered the voice of Captain Flint, and even thought I could make out the bird by her bright plumage as she sat perched upon her master's wrist.

Soon after the jolly-boat shoved off and pulled for shore, and the man with the red cap and his comrade went below by the cabin companion.

Just about the same time the sun had gone down behind the Spy-glass, and as the fog was collecting rapidly, it began to grow dark in earnest. I saw I must lose no time if I were to find the boat that evening.

The white rock, visible enough above the brush, was still some eighth of a mile further down the spit, and it took me a goodish while to get up with it, crawling, often on all-fours, among the scrub. Night had almost come when I laid my hand on its rough sides. Right below it there was an exceedingly small hollow of green turf, hidden by banks and a thick underwood about knee-deep, that grew there very plentifully; and in the centre of the dell, sure enough, a little tent of goat-skins, like what the gipsies carry about with them in England.

I dropped into the hollow, lifted the side of the tent, and there was Ben Gunn's boat – home-made if ever anything was home-made: a rude, lop-sided framework of tough wood, and stretched upon that a covering of goat-skin, with the hair inside. The thing was extremely small, even for me, and I can hardly imagine that it could have floated with a full-sized man. There was one thwart set as low as possible, a kind of stretcher in the bows, and a double paddle for propulsion.

I had not then seen a coracle, such as the ancient Britons made, but I have seen one since, and I can give you no fairer idea of Ben Gunn's boat than by saying it was like the first and the worst coracle ever made by man. But the great advantage of the coracle it certainly possessed, for it was exceedingly light and portable.

Well, now that I had found the boat, you would have thought I had had enough of truantry for once; but, in the meantime, I had taken another notion, and become so obstinately fond of it, that I would have carried it out, I believe, in the teeth of Captain Smollett himself. This was to slip out under cover of the night, cut the *Hispaniola* adrift, and let her go ashore where she fancied. I had quite made up my mind that the mutineers, after their repulse of the morning, had nothing nearer their hearts than to up anchor and away to sea; this, I thought, it would be a fine thing to prevent, and now that I had seen how they left their watchmen unprovided with a boat, I thought it might be done with little risk.

Down I sat to wait for darkness, and made a hearty meal of biscuit. It was a night out of ten thousand for my purpose. The fog had now buried all heaven. As the last rays of daylight dwindled and disappeared, absolute blackness settled down on Treasure Island. And when, at last, I shouldered the coracle, and groped my way stumblingly out of the hollow where I had supped, there were but two points visible on the whole anchorage.

One was the great fire on shore, by which the defeated pirates lay carousing in the swamp. The other, a mere blur of light upon the darkness, indicated the position of the anchored ship. She had swung round to the ebb – her bow was now towards me – the only lights on board were in the cabin; and what I saw was merely a reflection on the fog of the strong rays that flowed from the stern window.

The ebb had already run some time, and I had to wade through a long belt of swampy sand, where I sank several times above the ankle, before I came to the edge of the retreating water, and wading a little way in, with some strength and dexterity, set my coracle, keel downwards, on the surface.

Chapter Twenty-Three

The Ebb-tide Runs

The coracle – as I had ample reason to know before I was done with her – was a very safe boat for a person of my height and weight, both buoyant and clever in a seaway; but she was the most cross-grained lop-sided craft to manage. Do as you pleased, she always made more leeway than anything else, and turning round and round was the manœuvre she was best at. Even Ben Gunn himself has admitted that she was 'queer to handle till you knew her way.'

Certainly I did not know her way. She turned in every direction but the one I was bound to go; the most part of the time we were broadside on, and I am very sure I never should have made the ship at all but for the tide. By good fortune, paddle as I pleased, the tide was still sweeping me down; and there lay the *Hispaniola* right in the fair way, hardly to be missed.

First she loomed before me like a blot of something yet blacker than darkness, then her spars and hull began to take shape, and the next moment, as it seemed (for, the further I went, the brisker grew the current of the ebb), I was alongside of her hawser, and had laid hold.

The hawser was as taut as a bowstring, and the current so strong she pulled upon her anchor. All round the hull, in the blackness, the rippling current bubbled and chattered like a little mountain stream. One cut with my sea-gully, and the *Hispaniola* would go humming down the tide.

So far so good; but it next occurred to my recollection that a taut hawser, suddenly cut, is a thing as dangerous as a kicking horse. Ten to one, if I were so foolhardy as to cut the *Hispaniola* from her anchor, I and the coracle would be knocked clean out of the water.

This brought me to a full stop, and if fortune had not again particularly favoured me, I should have had to abandon my design. But the light airs which had begun blowing from the south-east and south had hauled round after nightfall into the south-west. Just while I was meditating, a puff came, caught the *Hispaniola*, and forced her up into the current; and to my great joy, I felt the hawser slacken in my grasp, and the hand by which I held it dip for a second under water.

With that I made my mind up, took out my gully, opened it with my teeth, and cut one strand after another, till the vessel swung only by two. Then I lay quiet, waiting to sever these last when the strain should be once more lightened by a breath of wind.

All this time I had heard the sound of loud voices from the cabin; but, to say truth, my mind had been so entirely taken up with other thoughts that I had scarcely given ear. Now, however, when I had nothing else to do, I began to pay more heed.

One I recognised for the coxswain's, Israel Hands, that had been Flint's gunner in former days. The other was, of course, my friend of the red night-cap. Both men were plainly the worse of drink, and they were still drinking; for, even while I was listening, one of them, with a drunken cry, opened the stern window and threw out something, which I divined to be an empty bottle. But they were not only tipsy; it was plain that they were furiously angry. Oaths flew like hailstones, and every now and then there came forth such an explosion as I thought was sure to end in blows. But each time the quarrel passed off, and the voices grumbled lower for a while, until the next crisis came, and, in its turn, passed away without result.

On shore, I could see the glow of the great camp fire burning warmly through the shore-side trees. Some one was singing, a dull, old, droning sailor's song, with a droop and a quaver at the end of every verse, and seemingly no end to it at all but the patience of the singer. I had heard it on the voyage more than once, and remembered these words: –

> 'But one man of her crew alive,
> What put to sea with seventy-five.'

And I thought it was a ditty rather too dolefully appropriate for a company that had met such cruel losses in the morning. But, indeed, from what I saw, all these buccaneers were as callous as the sea they sailed on.

At last the breeze came; the schooner sidled and drew nearer in the dark; I felt the hawser slacken once more, and with a good, tough effort, cut the last fibres through.

The breeze had but little action on the coracle, and I was almost instantly swept against the bows of the *Hispaniola*. At the same time the schooner began to turn upon her heel, spinning slowly, end for end, across the current.

I wrought like a fiend, for I expected every moment to be swamped; and since I found I could not push the coracle directly off, I now shoved straight astern. At length I was clear of my dangerous neighbour; and just as I gave the last impulsion, my hands came across a light cord that was trailing overboard across the stern bulwarks. Instantly I grasped it.

Why I should have done so I can hardly say. It was at first mere instinct; but once I had it in my hands and found it fast, curiosity began to get the upper hand, and I determined I should have one look through the cabin window.

I pulled in hand over hand on the cord, and, when I judged myself near enough, rose at infinite risk to about half my height, and thus commanded the roof and a slice of the interior of the cabin.

By this time the schooner and her little consort were gliding pretty swiftly through the water; indeed, we had already fetched up level with the camp fire. The ship was talking, as sailors say, loudly, treading the innumerable ripples with an incessant weltering splash; and until I got my eye above the window-sill I could not comprehend why the watchmen had taken no alarm. One glance, however, was sufficient; and it was only one glance that I durst take from that unsteady skiff. It showed me Hands and his companion locked together in deadly wrestle, each with a hand upon the other's throat.

I dropped upon the thwart again, none too soon, for I was near overboard. I could see nothing for the moment, but these two furious, encrimsoned faces, swaying together under the smoky lamp; and I shut my eyes to let them grow once more familiar with the darkness.

The endless ballad had come to an end at last, and the whole diminished company about the camp fire had broken into the chorus I had heard so often: –

> 'Fifteen men on the dead man's chest –
> Yo-ho-ho, and a bottle of rum!
> Drink and the devil had done for the rest –
> Yo-ho-ho, and a bottle of rum!'

I was just thinking how busy drink and the devil were at that very moment in the cabin of the *Hispaniola*, when I was surprised by a sudden lurch of the coracle. At the same moment she yawed sharply and seemed to change her course. The speed in the meantime had strangely increased.

I opened my eyes at once. All round me were little ripples, combing over with a sharp, bristling sound and slightly phosphorescent. The *Hispaniola* herself, a few yards in whose wake I was still being whirled along, seemed to stagger in her course, and I saw her spars toss a little against the blackness of the night; nay, as I looked longer, I made sure she also was wheeling to the southward.

I glanced over my shoulder, and my heart jumped against my ribs. There, right behind me, was the glow of the camp fire. The current had turned at right angles, sweeping round along with it the tall schooner and the little dancing coracle; ever quickening, ever bubbling higher, ever muttering louder, it went spinning through the narrows for the open sea.

Suddenly the schooner in front of me gave a violent yaw, turning, perhaps, through twenty degrees; and almost at the same moment one shout followed another from on board; I could hear feet pounding on the companion ladder; and I knew that the two drunkards had at last been interrupted in their quarrel and awakened to a sense of their disaster.

I lay down flat in the bottom of that wretched skiff, and devoutly recommended my spirit to its Maker. At the end of the straits, I made sure we must fall into some bar of raging breakers, where all my troubles would be ended speedily; and though I could, perhaps, bear to die, I could not bear to look upon my fate as it approached.

So I must have lain for hours, continually beaten to and fro upon the billows, now and again wetted with flying sprays, and never ceasing to expect death at the next plunge. Gradually weariness grew upon me; a numbness, an occasional stupor, fell upon my mind even in the midst of my terrors; until sleep at last supervened, and in my sea-tossed coracle I lay and dreamed of home and the old 'Admiral Benbow.'

Chapter Twenty-Four

The Cruise of the Coracle

It was broad day when I awoke, and found myself tossing at the south-west end of Treasure Island. The sun was up, but was still hid from me behind the great bulk of the Spy-glass, which on this side descended almost to the sea in formidable cliffs.

Haulbowline Head and Mizzen-mast Hill were at my elbow; the hill bare and dark, the head bound with cliffs forty or fifty feet high, and fringed with great masses of fallen rock. I was scarce a quarter of a mile to seaward, and it was my first thought to paddle in and land.

That notion was soon given over. Among the fallen rocks the breakers spouted and bellowed; loud reverberations, heavy sprays flying and falling, succeeded one another from second to second; and I saw myself, if I ventured nearer, dashed to death upon the rough shore, or spending my strength in vain to scale the beetling crags.

Nor was that all; for crawling together on flat tables of rock, or letting themselves drop into the sea with loud reports, I beheld huge slimy monsters – soft snails, as it were, of incredible bigness – two or three score of them together, making the rocks to echo with their barkings.

I have understood since that they were sea lions, and entirely harmless. But the look of them, added to the difficulty of the shore and the high running of the surf, was more than enough to disgust me of that landing place. I felt willing rather to starve at sea than to confront such perils.

In the meantime I had a better chance, as I supposed, before me. North of Haulbowline Head, the land runs in a long way, leaving, at low tide, a long stretch of yellow sand. To the north of that, again, there comes another cape – Cape of the Woods, as it was marked upon the chart – buried in tall green pines, which descended to the margin of the sea.

I remembered what Silver had said about the current that sets northward along the whole west coast of Treasure Island; and seeing from my position that I was already under its influence, I preferred to leave Haulbowline Head behind me, and reserve my strength for an attempt to land upon the kindlier-looking Cape of the Woods.

There was a great, smooth swell upon the sea. The wind blowing steady and gentle from the south, there was no contrariety between that and the current, and the billows rose and fell unbroken.

Had it been otherwise, I must long ago have perished; but as it was, it is surprising how easily and securely my little and light boat could ride. Often, as I still lay at the bottom, and kept no more than an eye above the gunwale, I would see a big blue summit heaving close above me; yet the coracle would but bounce a little, dance as if on springs, and subside on the other side into the trough as lightly as a bird.

I began after a little to grow very bold, and sat up to try my skill at paddling. But even a small change in the disposition of the weight will produce violent changes in the behaviour of a coracle. And I had hardly moved before the boat, giving up at once her gentle dancing movement, ran straight down a slope of water so steep that it made me giddy, and struck her nose, with a spout of spray, deep into the side of the next wave.

I was drenched and terrified, and fell instantly back into my old position, whereupon the coracle seemed to find her head again, and led me as softly as before among the billows. It was plain she was not to be interfered with, and at that rate, since I could in no way influence her course, what hope had I left of reaching land?

I began to be horribly frightened, but I kept my head, for all that. First, moving with all care, I gradually baled out the coracle with my sea-cap; then getting my eye once more above the gun-wale, I set myself to study how it was she managed to slip so quietly through the rollers.

I found each wave, instead of the big, smooth glossy mountain it looks from shore, or from a vessel's deck, was for all the world like any range of hills on the dry land, full of peaks and smooth places and valleys. The coracle, left to herself, turning from side to side, threaded, so to speak, her way through these lower parts, and avoided the steep slopes and higher, toppling summits of the wave.

'Well, now,' thought I to myself, 'it is plain I must lie where I am, and not disturb the balance; but it is plain, also, that I can put the paddle over the side, and from time to time, in smooth places, give her a shove or two towards land.' No sooner thought upon than done. There I lay on my elbows, in the most trying attitude, and every now and again gave a weak stroke or two to turn her head to shore.

It was very tiring, and slow work, yet I did visibly gain ground; and, as we drew near the Cape of the Woods, though I saw I must infallibly miss that point, I had still made some hundred yards of easting. I was, indeed, close in. I could see the cool, green tree-tops swaying together in the breeze, and I felt sure I should make the next promontory without fail.

It was high time, for I now began to be tortured with thirst. The glow of the sun from above, its thousand-fold reflection from the waves, the sea-water that fell and dried upon me, caking my very lips with salt, combined to make my throat burn and my brain ache. The sight of the trees so near at hand had almost made me sick with longing; but the current had soon carried me past the point; and, as the next reach of sea opened out, I beheld a sight that changed the nature of my thoughts.

Right in front of me, not half a mile away, I beheld the *Hispaniola* under sail. I made sure, of course, that I should be taken; but I was so distressed for want of water, that I scarce knew whether to be glad or sorry at the thought; and, long before I had come to a conclusion, surprise had taken entire possession of my mind, and I could do nothing but stare and wonder.

The *Hispaniola* was under her main-sail and two jibs, and the beautiful white canvas shone in the sun like snow or silver. When I first sighted her, all her sails were drawing; she was laying a course about north-west; and I presumed the men on board were going round the island on their way back to the anchorage. Presently she began to fetch more and more to the westward, so that I thought they had sighted me and were going about in chase. At last, however, she fell right into the wind's eye, was taken dead aback, and stood there a while helpless, with her sails shivering.

'Clumsy fellows,' said I; 'they must still be drunk as owls.' And I thought how Captain Smollett would have set them skipping.

Meanwhile, the schooner gradually fell off, and filled again upon another tack, sailed swiftly for a minute or so, and brought up once more dead in the wind's eye. Again and again was this repeated. To and fro, up and down, north, south, east, and west, the *Hispaniola* sailed by swoops and dashes, and at each repetition ended as she had begun, with idly flapping canvas. It became plain to me that nobody was steering. And, if so, where were the men? Either they were dead drunk, or had deserted her, I thought, and perhaps if I could get on board, I might return the vessel to her captain.

The current was bearing coracle and schooner southward at an equal rate. As for the latter's sailing, it was so wild and intermittent, and she hung each time so long in irons, that she certainly gained nothing, if she did not even lose. If only I dared to sit up and paddle, I made sure that I could overhaul her. The scheme had an air of adventure that inspired me, and the thought of the water-breaker beside the fore companion doubled my growing courage.

Up I got, was welcomed almost instantly by another cloud of spray, but this time stuck to my purpose; and set myself, with all my strength and caution, to paddle after the unsteered *Hispaniola*. Once I shipped a sea so heavy that I had to stop and bail, with my heart fluttering like a bird; but gradually I got into the way of the thing, and guided my coracle among the waves, with only now and then a blow upon her bows and a dash of foam in my face.

I was now gaining rapidly on the schooner; I could see the brass glisten on the tiller as it banged about; and still no soul appeared upon her decks. I could not choose but suppose she was deserted. If not, the men were lying drunk below, where I might batten them down, perhaps, and do what I chose with the ship.

For some time she had been doing the worst thing possible for me – standing still. She headed nearly due south, yawing, of course, all the time. Each time she fell off her sails partly filled, and these brought her, in a moment, right to the wind again. I have said this was the worst thing possible for me; for helpless as she looked in this situation, with the canvas cracking like cannon, and the blocks trundling and banging on the deck, she still continues to run away from me, not only with the speed of the current, but by the whole amount of her leeway, which was naturally great.

But now, at last, I had my chance. The breeze fell, for some seconds, very low, and the current gradually turning her, the *Hispaniola* revolved slowly round her centre, and at last presented me her stern, with the cabin window still gaping open, and the lamp over the table still burning on into the day. The main-sail hung drooped like a banner. She was stock-still, but for the current.

For the last little while I had even lost; but now, redoubling my efforts, I began once more to overhaul the chase.

I was not a hundred yards from her when the wind came again in a clap; she filled on the port tack, and was off again, stooping and skimming like a swallow.

My first impulse was one of despair, but my second was towards joy. Round she came, till she was broadside on to me – round still

till she had covered a half, and then two-thirds, and then three-quarters of the distance that separated us. I could see the waves boiling white under her forefoot. Immensely tall she looked to me from my low station in the coracle.

And then, of a sudden, I began to comprehend. I had scarce time to think – scarce time to act and save myself. I was on the summit of one swell when the schooner came stooping over the next. The bowsprit was over my head. I sprang to my feet, and leaped, stamping the coracle under water. With one hand I caught the jib-boom, while my foot was lodged between the stay and the brace; and as I still clung there panting, a dull blow told me that the schooner had charged down upon and struck the coracle, and that I was left without retreat on the *Hispaniola*.

Chapter Twenty-Five

I Strike the Jolly Roger

I had scarce gained a position on the bowsprit, when the flying jib flapped and filled upon the other tack, with a report like a gun. The schooner trembled to her keel under the reverse; but next moment, the other sails still drawing, the jib flapped back again, and hung idle.

This had nearly tossed me off into the sea; and now I lost no time, crawled back along the bowsprit, and tumbled head foremost on the deck.

I was on the lee side of the forecastle, and the mainsail, which was still drawing, concealed from me a certain portion of the after-deck. Not a soul was to be seen. The planks, which had not been swabbed since the mutiny, bore the print of many feet; and an empty bottle, broken by the neck, tumbled to and fro like a live thing in the scuppers.

Suddenly the *Hispaniola* came right into the wind. The jibs behind me cracked aloud; the rudder slammed to; the whole ship gave a sickening heave and shudder, and at the same moment the main-boom swung inboard, the sheet groaning in the blocks, and showed me the lee after-deck.

There were the two watchmen, sure enough: red-cap on his back, as stiff as a handspike, with his arms stretched out like those of a crucifix, and his teeth showing through his open lips; Israel Hands propped against the bulwarks, his chin on his chest, his hands lying open before him on the deck, his face as white, under its tan, as a tallow candle.

For a while the ship kept bucking and sidling like a vicious horse, the sails filling, now on one tack, now on another, and the boom swinging to and fro till the mast groaned aloud under the strain. Now and again, too, there would come a cloud of light sprays over the bulwark, and a heavy blow of the ship's bows against the swell: so much heavier weather was made of it by this great rigged ship than by my home-made, lop-sided coracle, now gone to the bottom of the sea.

At every jump of the schooner, red cap slipped to and fro; but – what was ghastly to behold – neither his attitude nor his fixed teeth-disclosing grin was anyway disturbed by this rough usage. At every jump, too, Hands appeared still more to sink into himself and settle down upon the deck, his feet sliding ever the farther out, and the whole body canting towards the stern, so that his face became, little by little, hid from me; and at last I could see nothing beyond his ear and the frayed ringlet of one whisker.

At the same time, I observed, around both of them, splashes of dark blood upon the planks, and began to feel sure that they had killed each other in their drunken wrath.

While I was thus looking and wondering, in a calm moment, when the ship was still, Israel Hands turned partly round, and, with a low moan, writhed himself back to the position in which I had seen him first. The moan, which told of pain and deadly weakness, and the way in which his jaw hung open, went right to my heart. But when I remembered the talk I had overheard from the apple barrel, all pity left me.

I walked aft until I reached the main-mast.

'Come aboard, Mr Hands,' I said, ironically.

He rolled his eyes round heavily; but he was too far gone to express surprise. All he could do was to utter one word, 'Brandy.'

It occurred to me there was no time to lose; and, dodging the boom as it once more lurched across the deck, I slipped aft, and down the companion stairs into the cabin.

It was such a scene of confusion as you can hardly fancy. All the lockfast places had been broken open in quest of the chart. The floor was thick with mud, where ruffians had sat down to drink or consult after wading in the marshes round their camp. The bulk-heads, all painted in clear white, and beaded round with gilt, bore a pattern of dirty hands. Dozens of empty bottles clinked together in corners to the rolling of the ship. One of the doctor's medical books lay open on the table, half of the leaves gutted out, I suppose, for pipelights. In the midst of all this the lamp still cast a smoky glow, obscure and brown as umber.

I went into the cellar; all the barrels were gone, and of the bottles a most surprising number had been drunk out and thrown away. Certainly, since the mutiny began, not a man of them could ever have been sober.

Foraging about, I found a bottle with some brandy left, for Hands; and for myself I routed out some biscuit, some pickled fruits, a great bunch of raisins, and a piece of cheese. With these I came on deck, put down my own stock behind the rudder head, and well out of the coxswain's reach, went forward to the water-breaker, and had a good, deep drink of water, and then, and not till then, gave Hands the brandy.

He must have drunk a gill before he took the bottle from his mouth.

'Aye,' said he, 'by thunder, but I wanted some o' that!'

I had sat down already in my own corner and begun to eat.

'Much hurt?' I asked him.

He grunted, or, rather, I might say, he barked.

'If that doctor was aboard,' he said, 'I'd be right enough in a couple of turns; but I don't have no manner of luck, you see, and that's what's the matter with me. As for that swab, he's good and dead, he is,' he added, indicating the man with the red cap. 'He warn't no seaman, anyhow. And where mought you have come from?'

'Well,' said I, 'I've come aboard to take possession of this ship, Mr Hands; and you'll please regard me as your captain until further notice.'

He looked at me sourly enough, but said nothing. Some of the colour had come back into his cheeks, though he still looked very sick, and still continued to slip out and settle down as the ship banged about.

'By-the-by,' I continued, 'I can't have these colours, Mr Hands; and, by your leave, I'll strike 'em. Better none than these.'

And, again dodging the boom, I ran to the colour lines, handed down their cursed black flag, and chucked it overboard.

'God save the king!' said I, waving my cap; 'and there's an end to Captain Silver!'

He watched me keenly and slyly, his chin all the while on his breast.

'I reckon,' he said at last – 'I reckon, Cap'n Hawkins, you'll kind of want to get ashore, now. S'pose we talks.'

'Why, yes,' says I, 'with all my heart, Mr Hands. Say on.' And I went back to my meal with a good appetite.

'This man,' he began, nodding feebly at the corpse – 'O'Brien were his name – a rank Irelander – this man and me got the canvas on her, meaning for to sail her back. Well, *he's* dead now, he is – as dead as bilge; and who's to sail this ship, I don't see. Without I gives you a hint, you ain't that man, as far's I can tell. Now, look here, you gives me food and drink, and a old scarf or ankecher to tie my wound up, you do; and I'll tell you how to sail her; and that's about square all round, I take it.'

'I'll tell you one thing,' says I: 'I'm not going back to Captain Kidd's anchorage. I mean to get into North Inlet, and beach her quietly there.'

'To be sure you did,' he cried. 'Why, I ain't sich an infernal lubber, after all. I can see, can't I? I've tried my fling, I have, and I've lost, and it's you has the wind of me. North Inlet? Why, I haven't no ch'ice, not I! I'd help you sail her up to Execution Dock, by thunder! so I would.'

Well, as it seemed to me, there was some sense in this. We struck our bargain on the spot. In three minutes I had the *Hispaniola* sailing easily before the wind along the coast of Treasure

Island, with good hopes of turning the northern point ere noon, and beating down again as far as North Inlet before high water, when we might beach her safely, and wait till the subsiding tide permitted us to land.

Then I lashed the tiller and went below to my own chest, where I got a soft silk handkerchief of my mother's. With this, and with my aid, Hands bound up the great bleeding stab he had received in the thigh, and after he had eaten a little and had a swallow or two more of the brandy, he began to pick up visibly, sat straighter up, spoke louder and clearer, and looked in every way another man.

The breeze served us admirably. We skimmed before it like a bird, the coast of the island flashing by, and the view changing every minute. Soon we were past the high lands and bowling beside low, sandy country, sparsely dotted with dwarf pines, and soon we were beyond that again, and had turned the corner of the rocky hill that ends the island on the north.

I was greatly elated with my new command, and pleased with the bright, sunshiny weather and these different prospects of the coast. I had now plenty of water and good things to eat, and my conscience, which had smitten me hard for my desertion, was quieted by the great conquest I had made. I should, I think, have had nothing left me to desire but for the eyes of the coxswain as they followed me derisively about the deck, and the odd smile that appeared continually on his face. It was a smile that had in it something both of pain and weakness – a haggard, old man's smile; but there was, besides that, a grain of derision, a shadow of treachery in his expression as he craftily watched, and watched, and watched me at my work.

Chapter Twenty-Six

Israel Hands

The wind, serving us to a desire, now hauled into the west. We could run so much the easier from the north-east corner of the island to the mouth of the North Inlet. Only, as we had no power to anchor, and dared not beach her till the tide had flowed a good deal farther, time hung on our hands. The coxswain told me how to lay the ship to; after a good many trials I succeeded, and we both sat in silence, over another meal.

'Cap'n,' said he, at length, with that same uncomfortable smile, 'here's my old shipmate, O'Brien; s' pose you was to heave him overboard. I ain't particular as a rule, and I don't take no blame for settling his hash; but I don't reckon him ornamental, now, do you?'

'I'm not strong enough, and I don't like the job; and there he lies, for me,' said I.

'This here's an unlucky ship – this *Hispaniola*, Jim,' he went on, blinking. 'There's a power of men been killed in this *Hispaniola* – a sight o' poor seamen dead and gone since you and me took ship to Bristol. I never seen sich dirty luck, not I. There was this here O'Brien, now – he's dead, ain't he? Well, now, I'm no scholar, and you're a lad as can read and figure; and, to put it straight, do you take it as a dead man is dead for good, or do he come alive again?'

'You can kill the body, Mr Hands, but not the spirit; you must know that already,' I replied. 'O'Brien there is in another world, and maybe watching us.'

'Ah!' says he. 'Well, that's unfort'nate – appears as if killing parties was a waste of time. Howsomever, sperrits don't reckon for much, by what I've seen. I'll chance it with the sperrits, Jim. And now, you've spoke up free, and I'll take it kind if you'd step down into that there cabin and get me a – well, a – shiver my timbers! I can't hit the name on 't; well, you get me a bottle of wine, Jim – this here brandy's too strong for my head.'

Now, the coxswain's hesitation seemed to be unnatural; and as for the notion of his preferring wine to brandy, I entirely disbelieved it. The whole story was a pretext. He wanted me to leave the deck – so much was plain; but with what purpose I could in no way imagine. His eyes never met mine; they kept wandering to and fro, up and down, now with a look to the sky, now with a flitting glance upon the dead O'Brien. All the time he kept smiling, and putting his tongue out in the most guilty, embarrassed manner, so that a child could have told that he was bent on some deception. I was prompt with my answer, however, for I saw where my advantage lay; and that with a fellow so densely stupid I could easily conceal my suspicions to the end.

'Some wine?' I said. 'Far better. Will you have white or red?'

'Well, I reckon it's about the blessed same to me, shipmate,' he replied; 'so it's strong, and plenty of it, what's the odds?'

'All right,' I answered. 'I'll bring you port, Mr Hands. But I'll have to dig for it.'

With that I scuttled down the companion with all the noise I could, slipped off my shoes, ran quietly along the sparred gallery, mounted the forecastle ladder, and popped my head out of the fore companion. I knew he would not expect to see me there; yet I took every precaution possible; and certainly the worst of my suspicions proved too true.

He had risen from his position to his hands and knees; and, though his leg obviously hurt him pretty sharply when he moved – for I could hear him stifle a groan – yet it was at a good, rattling rate that he trailed himself across the deck. In half a minute he had reached the port scuppers, and picked, out of a coil of rope, a long knife, or rather a short dirk, discoloured to the hilt with blood. He looked upon it for a moment, thrusting forth his under jaw, tried the point upon his hand, and then, hastily concealing it in the bosom of his jacket, trundled back again into his old place against the bulwark.

This was all that I required to know. Israel could move about; he was now armed; and if he had been at so much trouble to get rid of me, it was plain that I was meant to be the victim. What he would do afterwards – whether he would try to crawl right across the island from North Inlet to the camp among the swamps, or whether he would fire Long Tom, trusting that his own comrades might come first to help him, was, of course, more than I could say.

Yet I felt sure that I could trust him in one point, since in that our interests jumped together, and that was in the disposition of the schooner. We both desired to have her stranded safe enough, in a sheltered place, and so that, when the time came, she could be got off again with as little labour and danger as might be; and until that was done I considered that my life would certainly be spared.

While I was thus turning the business over in my mind, I had not been idle with my body. I had stolen back to the cabin, slipped once more into my shoes, and laid my hand at random on a bottle of wine, and now, with this for an excuse, I made my reappearance on the deck.

Hands lay as I had left him, all fallen together in a bundle, and with his eyelids lowered, as though he were too weak to bear the light. He looked up, however, at my coming, knocked the neck off the bottle, like a man who had done the same thing often, and took a good swig, with his favourite toast of 'Here's luck!' Then he lay quiet for a little, and then, pulling out a stick of tobacco, begged me to cut him a quid.

'Cut me a junk o' that,' says he, 'for I haven't no knife, and hardly strength enough, so be as I had. Ah, Jim, Jim, I reckon I've missed stays! Cut me a quid, as'll likely be the last, lad; for I'm for my long home, and no mistake.'

'Well,' said I, 'I'll cut you some tobacco; but if I was you and thought myself so badly, I would go to my prayers, like a Christian man.'

'Why?' said he. 'Now, you tell me why.'

'Why?' I cried. 'You were asking me just now about the dead. You've broken your trust; you've lived in sin and lies and blood; there's a man you killed lying at your feet this moment; and you ask me why! For God's mercy, Mr Hands, that's why.'

I spoke with a little heat, thinking of the bloody dirk he had hidden in his pocket, and designed, in his ill thoughts, to end me with. He, for his part, took a great draught of the wine, and spoke with the most unusual solemnity.

'For thirty years,' he said, 'I've sailed the seas, and seen good and bad, better and worse, fair weather and foul, provisions running out, knives going, and what not. Well, now I tell you, I never seen good come o' goodness yet. Him as strikes first is my fancy; dead men don't bite; them's my views – amen, so be it. And now, you look here,' he added, suddenly changing his tone, 'we've had about enough of this foolery. The tide's made good enough by now. You just take my orders, Cap'n Hawkins, and we'll sail slap in and be done with it.'

All told, we had scarce two miles to run; but the navigation was delicate, the entrance to this northern anchorage was not only narrow and shoal, but lay east and west, so that the schooner must be nicely handled to be got in. I think I was a good, prompt subaltern, and I am very sure that Hands was an excellent pilot; for we went about and about, and dodged in, shaving the banks, with a certainty and a neatness that were a pleasure to behold.

Scarcely had we passed the heads before the land closed around us. The shores of North Inlet were as thickly wooded as those of the southern anchorage; but the space was longer and narrower, and more like, what in truth it was, the estuary of a river. Right before us, at the southern end, we saw the wreck of a ship in the last stages of dilapidation. It had been a great vessel of three masts, but had lain so long exposed to the injuries of the weather, that it was hung about with great webs of dripping seaweed, and on the deck of it shore bushes had taken root, and now flourished thick with flowers. It was a sad sight, but it showed us that the anchorage was calm.

'Now,' said Hands, 'look there; there's a pet bit for to beach a ship in. Fine flat sand, never a catspaw, trees all around of it, and flowers a-blowing like a garding on that old ship.'

'And once beached,' I inquired, 'how shall we get her off again?'

'Why, so,' he replied: 'you take a line ashore there on the other side at low water: take a turn about one o' them big pines; bring it back, take a turn round the capstan, and lie-to for the tide. Come high water, all hands take a pull upon the line, and off she comes as sweet as natur'. And now, boy, you stand by. We're near the bit now, and she's too much way on her. Starboard a little – so – steady – starboard – larboard a little – steady – steady!'

So he issued his commands, which I breathlessly obeyed; till, all of a sudden, he cried, 'Now, my hearty, luff!' And I put the helm hard up, and the *Hispaniola* swung round rapidly, and ran stem on for the low wooded shore.

The excitement of these last manœuvres had somewhat inter-fered with the watch I had kept hitherto, sharply enough, upon the coxswain. Even then I was still so much interested, waiting for the ship to touch, that I had quite forgot the peril that hung over my head, and stood craning over the starboard bulwarks and watching the ripples spreading wide before the bows. I might have fallen without a struggle for my life, had not a sudden dis-quietude seized upon me, and made me turn my head. Perhaps I had heard a creak, or seen his shadow moving with the tail of my eye; perhaps it was an instinct like a cat's; but, sure enough, when I looked round, there was Hands, already half-way towards me, with the dirk in his right hand.

We must both have cried out aloud when our eyes met; but while mine was the shrill cry of terror, his was a roar of fury like a charging bull's. At the same instant he threw himself forward, and I leaped sideways towards the bows. As I did so, I let go of the tiller, which sprang sharp to leeward; and I think this saved my life, for it struck Hands across the chest, and stopped him, for the moment, dead.

Before he could recover, I was safe out of the corner where he had me trapped, with all the deck to dodge about. Just forward of the main-mast I stopped, drew a pistol from my pocket, took a cool aim, though he had already turned and was once more coming directly after me, and drew the trigger. The hammer fell, but there followed neither flash nor sound; the priming was useless with sea water. I cursed myself for my neglect. Why had not I, long before, reprimed and reloaded my only weapons? Then I should not have been as now, a mere fleeing sheep before this butcher.

Wounded as he was, it was wonderful how fast he could move, his grizzled hair tumbling over his face, and his face itself as red as a red ensign with his haste and fury. I had no time to try my other pistol, nor, indeed, much inclination, for I was sure it would be useless. One thing I saw plainly: I must not simply retreat before him, or he would speedily hold me boxed into the bows, as a moment since he had so nearly boxed me in the stern. Once so caught, and nine or ten inches of the blood-stained dirk would be my last experience on this side of eternity. I placed my palms against the main-mast, which was of a goodish bigness, and waited, every nerve upon the stretch.

Seeing that I meant to dodge, he also paused; and a moment or two passed in feints on his part, and corresponding movements upon mine. It was such a game as I had often played at home about the rocks of Black Hill Cove; but never before, you may be sure, with such a wildly beating heart as now. Still, as I say, it was a boy's game, and I thought I could hold my own at it, against an elderly seaman with a wounded thigh. Indeed, my courage had begun to rise so high, that I allowed myself a few darting thoughts on what would be the end of the affair; and while I saw certainly that I could spin it out for long, I saw no hope of any ultimate escape.

Well, while things stood thus, suddenly the *Hispaniola* struck, staggered, ground for an instant in the sand, and then, swift as a blow, canted over to the port side, till the deck stood at an angle of forty-five degrees, and about a puncheon of water splashed into the scupper holes, and lay, in a pool, between the deck and bulwark.

We were both of us capsized in a second, and both of us rolled, almost together, into the scuppers; the dead red-cap, with his arms still spread out, tumbling stiffly after us. So near were we, indeed, that my head came against the coxswain's foot with a crack that made my teeth rattle. Blow and all, I was the first afoot again; for Hands had got involved with the dead body. The sudden canting of the ship had made the deck no place for running on; I had to find some new way of escape, and that upon the instant, for my foe was almost touching me. Quick as thought, I sprang into the mizzen shrouds, rattled up hand over hand, and did not draw a breath till I was seated on the cross-trees.

I had been saved by being prompt; the dirk had struck not half a foot below me, as I pursued my upward flight; and there stood Israel Hands with his mouth open and his face upturned to mine, a perfect statue of surprise and disappointment.

Now that I had a moment to myself, I lost no time in changing the priming of my pistol, and then, having one ready for service, and to make assurance doubly sure, I proceeded to draw the load of the other, and recharge it afresh from the beginning.

My new employment struck Hands all of a heap; he began to see the dice going against him; and after an obvious hesitation, he also hauled himself heavily into the shrouds, and, with the dirk in his teeth, began slowly and painfully to mount. It cost him no end of time and groans to haul his wounded leg behind him; and I had quietly finished my arrangements before he was much more than a third of the way up. Then, with a pistol in either hand, I addressed him.

'One more step, Mr Hands,' said I, 'and I'll blow your brains out! Dead men don't bite, you know,' I added, with a chuckle.

He stopped instantly. I could see by the working of his face that he was trying to think, and the process was so slow and laborious that, in my new-found security, I laughed aloud. At last, with a swallow or two, he spoke, his face still wearing the same expression of extreme perplexity. In order to speak he had to take the dagger from his mouth, but, in all else, he remained unmoved.

'Jim,' says he, 'I reckon we're fouled, you and me, and we'll have to sign articles. I'd have had you but for that there lurch: but I don't have no luck, not I; and I reckon I'll have to strike, which comes hard, you see, for a master mariner to a ship's younker like you, Jim.'

I was drinking in his words and smiling away, as conceited as a cock upon a wall, when, all in a breath, back went his right hand over his shoulder. Something sang like an arrow through the air; I felt a blow and then a sharp pang, and there I was pinned by the shoulder to the mast. In the horrid pain and surprise of the moment – I scarce can say it was by my own volition, and I am sure it was without a conscious aim – both my pistols went off, and both escaped out of my hands. They did not fall alone; with a choked cry, the coxswain loosed his grasp upon the shrouds, and plunged head first into the water.

Chapter Twenty-Seven

'Pieces of Eight'

Owing to the cant of the vessel, the masts hung far out over the water, and from my perch on the cross-trees I had nothing below me but the surface of the bay. Hands, who was not so far up, was, in consequence, nearer to the ship, and fell between me and the bulwarks. He rose once to the surface in a lather of foam and blood, and then sank again for good. As the water settled, I could see him lying huddled together on the clean, bright sand in the shadow of the vessel's sides. A fish or two whipped past his body. Sometimes, by the quivering of the water, he appeared to move a little, as if he were trying to rise. But he was dead enough, for all that, being both shot and drowned, and was food for fish in the very place where he had designed my slaughter.

I was no sooner certain of this than I began to feel sick, faint, and terrified. The hot blood was running over my back and chest. The dirk, where it had pinned my shoulder to the mast, seemed to burn like a hot iron; yet it was not so much these real sufferings that distressed me, for these, it seemed to me, I could bear without a murmur; it was the horror I had upon my mind of falling from the cross-trees into that still green water beside the body of the coxswain.

I clung with both hands till my nails ached, and I shut my eyes as if to cover up the peril. Gradually my mind came back again, my pulses quieted down to a more natural time, and I was once more in possession of myself.

It was my first thought to pluck forth the dirk; but either it stuck too hard or my nerve failed me; and I desisted with a violent shudder. Oddly enough, that very shudder did the business. The knife, in fact, had come the nearest in the world to missing me altogether;

it held me by a mere pinch of skin, and this the shudder tore away. The blood ran down the faster, to be sure; but I was my own master again, and only tacked to the mast by my coat and shirt.

These last I broke through with a sudden jerk, and then regained the deck by the starboard shrouds. For nothing in the world would I have again ventured, shaken as I was, upon the overhanging port shrouds, from which Israel had so lately fallen.

I went below, and did what I could for my wound; it pained me a good deal, and still bled freely; but it was neither deep nor dangerous, nor did it greatly gall me when I used my arm. Then I looked around me, and as the ship was now, in a sense, my own, I began to think of clearing it from its last passenger – the dead man, O'Brien.

He had pitched, as I have said, against the bulwarks, where he lay like some horrible, ungainly sort of puppet; life-size, indeed, but how different from life's colour or life's comeliness! In that position, I could easily have my way with him; and as the habit of tragical adventures had worn off almost all my terror for the dead, I took him by the waist as if he had been a sack of bran, and, with one good heave, tumbled him overboard. He went in with a sounding plunge; the red cap came off, and remained floating on the surface; and as soon as the splash subsided, I could see him and Israel lying side by side, both wavering with the tremulous movement of the water. O'Brien, though still quite a young man, was very bald. There he lay, with that bald head across the knees of the man who had killed him, and the quick fishes steering to and fro over both.

I was now alone upon the ship; the tide had just turned. The sun was within so few degrees of setting that already the shadow of the pines upon the western shore began to reach right across the anchorage, and fall in patterns on the deck. The evening breeze had sprung up, and though it was well warded off by the hill with the two peaks upon the east, the cordage had begun to sing a little softly to itself and the idle sails to rattle to and fro.

I began to see a danger to the ship. The jibs I speedily doused and brought tumbling to the deck; but the main-sail was a harder matter. Of course, when the schooner canted over, the boom had swung out-board, and the cap of it and a foot or two of sail hung even under water. I thought this made it still more dangerous; yet the strain was so heavy that I half feared to meddle. At last, I got my knife and cut the halyards. The peak dropped instantly, a great belly of loose canvas floated broad upon the water; and since, pull as I liked, I could not budge the downhall, that was the extent of what I could accomplish. For the rest, the *Hispaniola* must trust to luck, like myself.

By this time the whole anchorage had fallen into shadow – the last rays, I remember, falling through a glade of the wood, and shining bright as jewels, on the flowery mantle of the wreck. It began to be chill; the tide was rapidly fleeting seaward, the schooner settling more and more on her beam-ends.

I scrambled forward and looked over. It seemed shallow enough, and holding the cut hawser in both hands for a last security, I let myself drop softly overboard. The water scarcely reached my waist; the sand was firm and covered with ripple marks, and I waded ashore in great spirits, leaving the *Hispaniola* on her side, with her mainsail trailing wide upon the surface of the bay. About the same time the sun went fairly down, and the breeze whistled low in the dusk among the tossing pines.

At least, and at last, I was off the sea, nor had I returned thence empty handed. There lay the schooner, clear at last from buccaneers and ready for our own men to board and get to sea again. I had nothing nearer my fancy than to get home to the stockade and boast of my achievements. Possibly I might be blamed a bit for my truantry, but the recapture of the *Hispaniola* was a clenching answer, and I hoped that even Captain Smollett would confess I had not lost my time.

So thinking, and in famous spirits, I began to set my face homeward for the block house and my companions. I remembered that the most easterly of the rivers which drain into Captain Kidd's anchorage ran from the two-peaked hill upon my left; and I bent my course in that direction that I might pass the stream while it was small. The wood was pretty open, and keeping along the lower spurs, I had soon turned the corner of that hill, and not long after waded to the mid-calf across the water-course.

This brought me near to where I had encountered Ben Gunn, the maroon; and I walked more circumspectly, keeping an eye on every side. The dusk had come nigh hand completely, and, as I opened out the cleft between the two peaks, I became aware of a wavering glow against the sky, where, as I judged, the man of the island was cooking his supper before a roaring fire. And yet I wondered, in my heart, that he should show himself so careless. For if I could see this radiance, might it not reach the eyes of Silver himself where he camped upon the shore among the marshes?

Gradually the night fell blacker; it was all I could do to guide myself even roughly towards my destination; the double hill behind me and the Spy-glass on my right hand loomed faint and fainter; the stars were few and pale; and in the low ground where I wandered I kept tripping among bushes and rolling into sandy pits.

Suddenly a kind of brightness fell about me. I looked up; a pale glimmer of moonbeams had alighted on the summit of the Spy-glass, and soon after I saw something broad and silvery moving low down behind the trees, and knew the moon had risen.

With this to help me, I passed rapidly over what remained to me of my journey; and, sometimes walking, sometimes running, impatiently drew near to the stockade. Yet, as I began to thread the grove that lies before it, I was not so thoughtless but that I slacked my pace and went a trifle warily. It would have been a poor end of my adventures to get shot down by my own party in mistake.

The moon was climbing higher and higher; its light began to fall here and there in masses through the more open districts of the wood; and right in front of me a glow of a different colour appeared among the trees. It was red and hot, and now and again it was a little darkened – as it were the embers of a bonfire smouldering.

For the life of me, I could not think what it might be.

At last I came right down upon the borders of the clearing. The western end was already steeped in moonshine; the rest, and the block house itself, still lay in a black shadow, chequered with long, silvery streaks of light. On the other side of the house an immense fire had burned itself into clear embers and shed a steady, red reverberation, contrasted strongly with the mellow paleness of the moon. There was not a soul stirring, nor a sound beside the noises of the breeze.

I stopped, with much wonder in my heart, and perhaps a little terror also. It had not been our way to build great fires; we were, indeed, by the captain's orders, somewhat niggardly of firewood; and I began to fear that something had gone wrong while I was absent.

I stole round by the eastern end, keeping close in shadow, and at a convenient place, where the darkness was thickest, crossed the palisade.

To make assurance surer, I got upon my hands and knees, and crawled, without a sound, towards the corner of the house. As I drew nearer, my heart was suddenly and greatly lightened. It is not a pleasant noise in itself, and I have often complained of it at other times; but just then it was like music to hear my friends snoring together so loud and peaceful in their sleep. The sea cry of the watch, that beautiful 'All's well,' never fell more reassuringly on my ear.

In the meantime, there was no doubt of one thing; they kept an infamous bad watch. If it had been Silver and his lads that were now creeping in on them, not a soul would have seen daybreak. That was what it was, thought I, to have the captain wounded; and again I blamed myself sharply for leaving them in that danger with so few to mount guard.

By this time I had got to the door and stood up. All was dark within, so that I could distinguish nothing by the eye. As for sounds, there was the steady drone of the snorers, and a small occasional noise, a flickering or pecking that I could in no way account for.

With my arms before me I walked steadily in. I should lie down in my own place (I thought, with a silent chuckle) and enjoy their faces when they found me in the morning.

My foot struck something yielding – it was a sleeper's leg; and he turned and groaned, but without awakening.

And then, all of a sudden, a shrill voice broke forth out of the darkness:

'Pieces of eight! pieces of eight! pieces of eight! pieces of eight! pieces of eight!' and so forth, without pause or change, like the clacking of a tiny mill.

Silver's green parrot, Captain Flint! It was she whom I had heard pecking at a piece of bark; it was she, keeping better watch than any human being, who thus announced my arrival with her wearisome refrain.

I had no time left me to recover. At the sharp, clipping tone of the parrot, the sleepers awoke and sprang up; and with a mighty oath, the voice of Silver cried: –

'Who goes?'

I turned to run, struck violently against one person, recoiled, and ran full into the arms of a second, who, for his part, closed upon and held me tight.

'Bring a torch, Dick,' said Silver, when my capture was thus assured.

And one of the men left the log-house, and presently returned with a lighted brand.

PART SIX

Captain Silver

Chapter Twenty-Eight

In the Enemy's Camp

The red glare of the torch, lighting up the interior of the block house, showed me the worst of my apprehensions realised. The pirates were in possession of the house and stores: there was the cask of cognac, there were the pork and bread, as before; and, what ten-fold increased my horror, not a sign of any prisoner. I could only judge that all had perished, and my heart smote me sorely that I had not been there to perish with them.

There were six of the buccaneers, all told; not another man was left alive. Five of them were on their feet, flushed and swollen, suddenly called out of the first sleep of drunkenness. The sixth had only risen upon his elbow; he was deadly pale, and the blood-stained bandage round his head told that he had recently been wounded, and still more recently dressed. I remembered the man who had been shot and had run back among the woods in the great attack, and doubted not that this was he.

The parrot sat, preening her plumage, on Long John's shoulder. He himself, I thought, looked somewhat paler and more stern than I was used to. He still wore the fine broadcloth suit in which he had fulfilled his mission, but it was bitterly the worse for wear, daubed with clay and torn with the sharp briers of the wood.

'So,' said he, 'here's Jim Hawkins, shiver my timbers! dropped in, like, eh? Well, come, I take that friendly.'

And thereupon he sat down across the brandy cask, and began to fill a pipe.

'Give me a loan of the link, Dick,' said he; and then, when he had a good light, 'That'll do, lad,' he added; 'stick the glim in the wood heap; and you, gentlemen, bring yourselves to! – you

175

needn't stand up for Mr Hawkins; *he'll* excuse you, you may lay to that. And so, Jim' – stopping the tobacco – 'here you were, and quite a pleasant surprise for poor old John. I see you were smart when first I set my eyes on you; but this here gets away from me clean, it do.'

To all this, as may be well supposed, I made no answer. They had set me with my back against the wall; and I stood there, looking Silver in the face, pluckily enough, I hope, to all outward appearance, but with black despair in my heart.

Silver took a whiff or two of his pipe with great composure, and then ran on again.

'Now, you see, Jim, so be as you *are* here,' says he, 'I'll give you a piece of my mind. I've always liked you, I have, for a lad of spirit, and the picter of my own self when I was young and handsome. I always wanted you to jine and take your share, and die a gentleman, and now, my cock, you've got to. Cap'n Smollett's a fine seaman, as I'll own up to any day, but stiff on discipline. "Dooty is dooty," says he, and right he is. Just you keep clear of the cap'n. The doctor himself is gone dead against you – "ungrateful scamp" was what he said; and the short and the long of the whole story is about here: you can't go back to your own lot, for they won't have you; and, without you start a third ship's company all by yourself, which might be lonely, you'll have to jine with Cap'n Silver.'

So far so good. My friends, then, were still alive, and though I partly believed the truth of Silver's statement, that the cabin party were incensed at me for my desertion, I was more relieved than distressed by what I heard.

'I don't say nothing as to your being in our hands,' continued Silver, 'though there you are, and you may lay to it. I'm all for argyment; I never seen good come out o' threatening. If you like the service, well, you'll jine; and if you don't, Jim, why, you're free to answer no – free and welcome, shipmate; and if fairer can be said by mortal seaman, shiver my sides!'

'Am I to answer then?' I asked, with a very tremulous voice. Through all this sneering talk, I was made to feel the threat of death that overhung me, and my cheeks burned and my heart beat painfully in my breast.

'Lad,' said Silver, 'no one's a-pressing of you. Take your bearings. None of us won't hurry you, mate; time goes so pleasant in your company, you see.'

'Well,' says I, growing a bit bolder, 'if I'm to choose, I declare I have a right to know what's what, and why you're here, and where my friends are.'

'Wot's wot?' repeated one of the buccaneers, in a deep growl. 'Ah, he'd be a lucky one as knowed that!'

'You'll, perhaps, batten down your hatches till you're spoke to, my friend,' cried Silver truculently to this speaker. And then, in his first gracious tones, he replied to me: 'Yesterday morning, Mr Hawkins,' said he, 'in the dog-watch, down came Dr Livesey with a flag of truce. Says he, "Cap'n Silver, you're sold out. Ship's gone." Well, maybe we'd been taking a glass, and a song to help it round. I won't say no. Leastways, none of us had looked out. We looked out, and by thunder! the old ship was gone. I never seen a pack o' fools look fishier; and you may lay to that, if I tells you that looked the fishiest. "Well," says the doctor, "let's bargain." We bargained, him and I, and here we are: stores, brandy, block house, the firewood you was thoughtful enough to cut, and, in a manner of speaking, the whole blessed boat, from crosstrees to keelson. As for them, they've tramped; I don't know where's they are.'

He drew again quietly at his pipe.

'And lest you should take it into that head of yours,' he went on, 'that you was included in the treaty, here's the last word that was said: "How many are you," says I, "to leave?" "Four," says he – "four, and one of us wounded. As for that boy, I don't know where he is, confound him," says he, "nor I don't much care. We're about sick of him." These was his words.'

'Is that all?' I asked.

'Well, it's all that you're to hear, my son,' returned Silver.

'And now I am to choose?'

'And now you are to choose, and you may lay to that,' said Silver.

'Well,' said I, 'I am not such a fool but I know pretty well what I have to look for. Let the worst come to the worst, it's little I care. I've seen too many die since I fell in with you. But there's a thing or two I have to tell you,' I said, and by this time I was quite excited; 'and the first is this: here you are, in a bad way: ship lost, treasure lost, men lost; your whole business gone to wreck; and if you want to know who did it – it was I! I was in the apple barrel the night we sighted land, and I heard you, John, and you, Dick Johnson, and Hands, who is now at the bottom of the sea, and told every word you said before the hour was out. And as for the schooner, it was I who cut her cable, and it was I that killed the men you had aboard of her, and it was I who brought her where you'll never see her more, not one of you. The laugh's on my side; I've had the top of this business from the first; I no more fear you than I fear a fly. Kill me, if you please, or spare me. But one thing I'll say, and no more; if you spare me, bygones are bygones, and when you fellows are in court for piracy, I'll save you all I can. It is for you to choose. Kill another and do yourselves no good, or spare me and keep a witness to save you from the gallows.'

I stopped, for, I tell you, I was out of breath, and, to my wonder, not a man of them moved, but all sat staring at me like as many sheep. And while they were still staring, I broke out again: –

'And now, Mr Silver,' I said, 'I believe you're the best man here, and if things go to the worst, I'll take it kind of you to let the doctor know the way I took it.'

'I'll bear it in mind,' said Silver, with an accent so curious that I could not, for the life of me, decide whether he were laughing at my request, or had been favourably affected by my courage.

'I'll put one to that,' cried the old mahogany-faced seaman – Morgan by name – whom I had seen in Long John's public-house upon the quays of Bristol. 'It was him that knowed Black Dog.'

'Well, and see here,' added the sea-cook. 'I'll put another again to that, by thunder! for it was this same boy that faked the chart from Billy Bones. First and last, we've split upon Jim Hawkins!'

'Then here goes!' said Morgan, with an oath.

And he sprang up, drawing his knife as if he had been twenty.

'Avast, there!' cried Silver. 'Who are you, Tom Morgan? Maybe you thought you was cap'n here, perhaps. By the powers, but I'll teach you better! Cross me, and you'll go where many a good man's gone before you, first and last, these thirty year back – some to the yard-arm, shiver my timbers! and some by the board, and all to feed the fishes. There's never a man looked me between the eyes and seen a good day a'terwards, Tom Morgan, you may lay to that.'

Morgan paused; but a hoarse murmur rose from the others.

'Tom's right,' said one.

'I stood hazing long enough from one,' added another. 'I'll be hanged if I'll be hazed by you, John Silver.'

'Did any of you gentlemen want to have it out with *me?*' roared Silver, bending far forward from his position on the keg, with his pipe still glowing in his right hand. 'Put a name on what you're at; you ain't dumb, I reckon. Him that wants shall get it. Have I lived this many years, and a son of a rum puncheon cock his hat athwart my hawse at the latter end of it? You know the way; you're all gentlemen o' fortune, by your account. Well, I'm ready. Take a cutlass, him that dares, and I'll see the colour of his inside, crutch and all, before that pipe's empty.'

Not a man stirred; not a man answered.

'That's your sort, is it?' he added, returning his pipe to his mouth. 'Well, you're a gay lot to look at, anyway. Not much worth to fight, you ain't. P'r'aps you can understand King George's

English. I'm cap'n here by 'lection. I'm cap'n here because I'm the best man by a long sea-mile. You won't fight, as gentleman o' fortune should; then, by thunder, you'll obey, and you may lay to it! I like that boy, now; I never seen a better boy than that. He's more a man than any pair of rats of you in this here house, and what I say is this: let me see him that'll lay a hand on him – that's what I say, and you may lay to it.'

There was a long pause after this. I stood straight up against the wall, my heart still going like a sledgehammer, but with a ray of hope now shining in my bosom. Silver leant back against the wall, his arms crossed, his pipe in the corner of his mouth, as calm as though he had been in church; yet his eye kept wandering furtively, and he kept the tail of it on his unruly followers. They, on their part, drew gradually together towards the far end of the block house, and the low hiss of their whispering sounded in my ear continuously, like a stream. One after another, they would look up, and the red light of the torch would fall for a second on their nervous faces; but it was not towards me, it was towards Silver that they turned their eyes.

'You seem to have a lot to say,' remarked Silver, spitting far into the air. 'Pipe up and let me hear it, or lay to.'

'Ax your pardon, sir,' returned one of the men, 'you're pretty free with some of the rules; maybe you'll kindly keep an eye upon the rest. This crew's dissatisfied; this crew don't vally bullying a marlinspike; this crew has its rights like other crews, I'll make so free as that; and by your own rules, I take it we can talk together. I ax your pardon, sir, acknowledging you for to be capting at this present; but I claim my right, and steps outside for a council.'

And with an elaborate sea-salute, this fellow, a long, ill-looking, yellow-eyed man of five and thirty, stepped coolly towards the door and disappeared out of the house. One after another, the rest followed his example; each making a salute as he passed; each adding some apology. 'According to rules,' said one. 'Fo'c's'le council,' said Morgan. And so with one remark or another, all marched out, and left Silver and me alone with the torch.

The sea-cook instantly removed his pipe.

'Now, look you here, Jim Hawkins,' he said, in a steady whisper, that was no more than audible, 'you're within half a plank of death, and, what's a long sight worse, of torture. They're going to throw me off. But, you mark, I stand by you through thick and thin. I didn't mean to; no, not till you spoke up. I was about desperate to lose that much blunt, and be hanged into the bargain. But I see you was the right sort. I says to myself: You stand by Hawkins, John, and Hawkins 'll stand by you. You're his last card, and, by the living thunder, John, he's yours! Back to back, says I. You save your witness, and he'll save your neck!'

I began dimly to understand.

'You mean all's lost?' I asked.

'Ay, by gum, I do!' he answered. 'Ship gone, neck gone – that's the size of it. Once I looked into that bay, Jim Hawkins, and seen no schooner – well, I'm tough, but I gave out. As for that lot and their council, mark me, they're outright fools and cowards. I'll save your life – if so be as I can – from them. But, see here, Jim – tit for tat – you save Long John from swinging.'

I was bewildered; it seemed a thing so hopeless he was asking – he, the old buccaneer, the ringleader throughout.

'What I can do, that I'll do,' I said.

'It's a bargain!' cried Long John. 'You speak up plucky, and, by thunder! I've a chance.'

He hobbled to the torch, where it stood propped among the firewood, and took a fresh light to his pipe.

'Understand me, Jim,' he said, returning. 'I've a head on my shoulders, I have. I'm on squire's side now. I know you've got that ship safe somewheres. How you done it, I don't know, but safe it is. I guess Hands and O'Brien turned soft. I never much believed in neither of *them*. Now you mark me. I ask no questions, nor I won't let others. I know when a game's up, I do; and I know a lad that's staunch. Ah, you that's young – you and me might have done a power of good together!'

He drew some cognac from the cask into a tin canikin.

'Will you taste, messmate?' he asked; and when I had refused: 'Well, I'll take a drain myself, Jim,' said he. 'I need a caulker, for there's trouble on hand. And, talking o' trouble, why did that doctor give me the chart, Jim?'

My face expressed a wonder so unaffected that he saw the needlessness of further questions.

'Ah, well, he did, though,' said he. 'And there's something under that, no doubt – something, surely, under that, Jim – bad or good.'

And he took another swallow of the brandy, shaking his great fair head like a man who looks forward to the worst.

Chapter Twenty-Nine

The Black Spot Again

The council of the buccaneers had lasted some time, when one of them re-entered the house, and with a repetition of the same salute, which had in my eyes an ironical air, begged for a moment's loan of the torch. Silver briefly agreed; and this emissary retired again, leaving us together in the dark.

'There's a breeze coming, Jim,' said Silver, who had, by this time, adopted quite a friendly and familiar tone.

I turned to the loophole nearest me and looked out. The embers of the great fire had so far burned themselves out, and now glowed so low and duskily, that I understood why these conspirators desired a torch. About half way down the slope to the stockade, they were collected in a group; one held the light; another was on his knees in their midst, and I saw the blade of an open knife shine in his hand with varying colours, in the moon and torchlight. The rest were all somewhat stooping, as though watching the manoeuvres of this last. I could just make out that he had a book as well as a knife in his hand; and was still wondering how anything so incongruous had come in their possession, when the kneeling figure rose once more to his feet, and the whole party began to move together towards the house.

'Here they come,' said I; and I returned to my former position, for it seemed beneath my dignity that they should find me watching them.

'Well, let 'em come, lad – let 'em come,' said Silver, cheerily. 'I've still a shot in my locker.'

The door opened, and the five men, standing huddled together just inside, pushed one of their number forward. In any other circumstances it would have been comical to see his slow advance, hesitating as he set down each foot, but holding his closed right hand in front of him.

'Step up, lad,' cried Silver. 'I won't eat you. Hand it over, lubber. I know the rules, I do; I won't hurt a depytation.'

Thus encouraged, the buccaneer stepped forth more briskly, and having passed something to Silver, from hand to hand, slipped yet more smartly back again to his companions.

The sea-cook looked at what had been given him.

'The black spot! I thought so,' he observed. 'Where might you have got the paper? Why, hillo! look here, now: this ain't lucky! You've gone and cut this out of a Bible. What fool's cut a Bible?'

'Ah, there!' said Morgan – 'there! Wot did I say? No good'll come o' that, I said.'

'Well, you've about fixed it now, among you,' continued Silver. 'You'll all swing now, I reckon. What soft-headed lubber had a Bible?'

'It was Dick,' said one.

'Dick, was it? Then Dick can get to prayers,' said Silver. 'He's seen his slice of luck, has Dick, and you may lay to that.'

But here the long man with the yellow eyes struck in.

'Belay that talk, John Silver,' he said. 'This crew has tipped you the black spot in full council, as in dooty bound; just you turn it over, as in dooty bound, and see what's wrote there. Then you can talk.'

'Thanky, George,' replied the sea-cook. 'You always was brisk for business, and has the rules by heart, George, as I'm pleased to see. Well, what is it, anyway? Ah! 'Deposed' – that's it, is it? Very pretty wrote, to be sure; like print, I swear. Your hand o' write George? Why, you was gettin' quite a leadin' man in this here crew. You'll be cap'n next, I shouldn't wonder. Just oblige me with that torch again, will you? this pipe don't draw.'

'Come, now,' said George, 'you don't fool this crew no more. You're a funny man, by your account; but you're over now, and you'll maybe step down off that barrel, and help vote.'

'I thought you said you knowed the rules,' returned Silver, contemptuously. 'Leastways, if you don't, I do; and I wait here – and I'm still your cap'n, mind – till you outs with your grievances, and I reply, in the meantime, your black spot ain't worth a biscuit. After that, we'll see.'

'Oh,' replied George, 'you don't be under no kind of apprehension; *we're* all square, we are. First, you've made a hash of this cruise – you'll be a bold man to say no to that. Second, you let the enemy out o' this here trap for nothing. Why did they want out? I dunno; but it's pretty plain they wanted it. Third, you wouldn't let us go at them upon the march. Oh, we see through you, John Silver; you want to play booty, that's what's wrong with you. And then, fourth, there's this here boy.'

'Is that all?' asked Silver, quietly.

'Enough, too,' retorted George. 'We'll all swing and sun-dry for your bungling.'

'Well, now, look here, I'll answer these four p'ints; one after another I'll answer 'em. I made a hash o' this cruise, did I? Well, now, you all know what I wanted; and you all know, if that had been done, that we'd 'a' been aboard the *Hispaniola* this night as ever was, every man of us alive, and fit, and full of good plum-duff, and the treasure in the hold of her, by thunder! Well, who crossed me? Who forced my hand, as was the lawful cap'n? Who tipped me the black spot the day we landed, and began this dance? Ah, it's a fine dance – I'm with you there – and looks mighty like a hornpipe in a rope's end at Execution Dock by London town, it does. But who done it? Why, it was Anderson, and Hands, and you, George Merry! And you're the last above board of that same meddling crew; and you have the Davy Jones's insolence to up and stand for cap'n over me – you, that sank the lot of us! By the powers! but this tops the stiffest yarn to nothing.'

Silver paused, and I could see by the faces of George and his late comrades that these words had not been said in vain.

'That's for number one,' cried the accused, wiping the sweat from his brow, for he had been talking with a vehemence that shook the house. 'Why, I give you my word, I'm sick to speak to you. You've neither sense nor memory, and I leave it to fancy where your mothers was that let you come to sea. Sea! Gentlemen o' fortune! I reckon tailors is your trade.'

'Go on, John,' said Morgan. 'Speak up to the others.'

'Ah, the others!' returned John. 'They're a nice lot, ain't they? You say this cruise is bungled. Ah! by gum, if you could understand how bad it's bungled, you would see! We're that near the gibbet that my neck's stiff with thinking on it. You've seen 'em, maybe, hanged in chains, birds about 'em, seamen p'inting 'em out as they go down with the tide. "Who's that?" says one. "That! Why, that's John Silver. I knowed him well," says another. And you can hear the chains a-jangle as you go about and reach for the other buoy. Now, that's about where we are, every mother's son of us, thanks to him, and Hands, and Anderson, and other ruination fools of you. And if you want to know about number four, and that boy, why, shiver my timbers! isn't he a hostage? Are we a-going to waste a hostage? No, not us; he might be our last chance, and I shouldn't wonder. Kill that boy? not me, mates! And number three? Ah, well, there's a deal to say to number three. Maybe you don't count it nothing to have a real college doctor come to see you every day – you, John, with your head broke – or you, George Merry, that had the ague shakes upon you not six hours agone, and has your eyes the colour of lemon peel to this same moment on the clock? And may be, perhaps, you didn't know there was a consort coming, either? But there is; and not so long till then; and we'll see who'll be glad to have a hostage when it comes to that. And as for number two, and why I made a bargain – well, you came crawling on your knees to me to make it – on your knees you came, you was that downhearted – and you'd have starved, too, if I hadn't – but that's a trifle! you look there – that's why!'

And he cast down upon the floor a paper that I instantly

recognised – none other than the chart on yellow paper, with the three red crosses, that I had found in the oilcloth at the bottom of the captain's chest. Why the doctor had given it to him was more than I could fancy.

But if it were inexplicable to me, the appearance of the chart was incredible to the surviving mutineers. They leaped upon it like cats upon a mouse. It went from hand to hand, one tearing it from another; and by the oaths and the cries and the childish laughter with which they accompanied their examination, you would have thought, not only they were fingering the very gold, but were at sea with it, besides, in safety.

'Yes,' said one, 'that's Flint, sure enough. J. F., and a score below, with a clove hitch to it; so he done ever.'

'Mighty pretty,' said George. 'But how are we to get away with it, and us no ship?'

Silver suddenly sprang up, and supporting himself with a hand against the wall: 'Now I give you warning, George,' he cried. 'One more word of your sauce, and I'll call you down and fight you. How? Why, how do I know? You had ought to tell me that – you and the rest, that lost me my schooner, with your interference, burn you! But not you, you can't; you hain't got the invention of a cockroach. But civil you can speak, and shall, George Merry, you may lay to that.'

'That's fair enow,' said the old man Morgan.

'Fair! I reckon so,' said the sea-cook. 'You lost the ship; I found the treasure. Who's the better man at that? And now I resign, by thunder! Elect whom you please to be your cap'n now; I'm done with it.'

'Silver!' they cried. 'Barbecue for ever! Barbecue for cap'n!'

'So that's the toon, is it?' cried the cook. 'George, I reckon you'll have to wait another turn, friend; and lucky for you as I'm not a revengeful man. But that was never my way. And now, ship-mates, this black spot? 'Tain't much good now, is it? Dick's crossed his luck and spoiled his Bible, and that's about all.'

'It'll do to kiss the book on still, won't it?' growled Dick, who was evidently uneasy at the curse he had brought upon himself.

'A Bible with a bit cut out!' returned Silver, derisively. 'Not it. It don't bind no more'n a ballad-book.'

'Don't it, though?' cried Dick, with a sort of joy. 'Well, I reckon that's worth having, too.'

'Here, Jim – here's a cur'osity for you,' said Silver; and he tossed me the paper.

It was a round, about the size of a crown piece. One side was blank, for it had been the last leaf; the other contained a verse or two of Revelation – these words among the rest, which struck sharply home upon my mind: 'Without are dogs and murderers.' The printed side had been blackened with wood ash, which already began to come off and soil my fingers; on the blank side had been written with the same material the one word 'Depposed.' I have that curiosity beside me at this moment; but not a trace of writing now remains beyond a single scratch, such as a man might make with his thumb-nail.

That was the end of the night's business. Soon after, with a drink all round, we lay down to sleep, and the outside of Silver's vengeance was to put George Merry up for sentinel, and threaten him with death if he should prove unfaithful.

It was long ere I could close an eye, and Heaven knows I had matter enough for thought in the man whom I had slain that afternoon, in my own most perilous position, and, above all, in the remarkable game that I saw Silver now engaged upon – keeping the mutineers together with one hand, and grasping, with the other, after every means, possible and impossible, to make his peace and save his miserable life. He himself slept peacefully, and snored aloud; yet my heart was sore for him, wicked as he was, to think on the dark perils that environed, and the shameful gibbet that awaited him.

Chapter Thirty

On Parole

I was wakened – indeed, we were all wakened, for I could see even the sentinel shake himself together from where he had fallen against the door-post – by a clear, hearty voice hailing us from the margin of the wood: –

'Block house, ahoy!' it cried. 'Here's the doctor.'

And the doctor it was. Although I was glad to hear the sound, yet my gladness was not without admixture. I remembered with confusion my insubordinate and stealthy conduct; and when I saw where it had brought me – among what companions and surrounded by what dangers – I felt ashamed to look him in the face.

He must have risen in the dark, for the day had hardly come; and when I ran to a loophole and looked out, I saw him standing, like Silver once before, up to the mid-leg in creeping vapour.

'You, doctor! Top o' the morning to you, sir!' cried Silver, broad awake and beaming with good nature in a moment. 'Bright and early, to be sure; and it's the early bird, as the saying goes, that gets the rations. George, shake up your timbers, son, and help Dr Livesey over the ship's side. All a-doin' well, your patients was – all well and merry.'

So he pattered on, standing on the hill-top, with his crutch under his elbow, and one hand upon the side of the log-house – quite the old John in voice, manner, and expression.

'We've quite a surprise for you, too, sir,' he continued. 'We've a little stranger here – he! he! A noo boarder and lodger, sir, and looking fit and taut as a fiddle; slep' like a supercargo, he did, right alongside of John – stern to stem we was, all night.'

Dr Livesey was by this time across the stockade and pretty near the cook; and I could hear the alteration in his voice as he said: –

'Not Jim?'

'The very same Jim as ever was,' says Silver.

The doctor stopped outright, although he did not speak, and it was some seconds before he seemed able to move on.

'Well, well,' he said, at last, 'duty first and pleasure afterwards, as you might have said yourself, Silver. Let us overhaul these patients of yours.'

A moment afterwards he had entered the block house, and, with one grim nod to me, proceeded with his work among the sick. He seemed under no apprehension, though he must have known that his life, among these treacherous demons, depended on a hair; and he rattled on to his patients as if he were paying an ordinary professional visit in a quiet English family. His manner, I suppose, reacted on the men; for they behaved to him as if nothing had occurred – as if he were still ship's doctor, and they still faithful hands before the mast.

'You're doing well, my friend,' he said to the fellow with the bandaged head, 'and if ever any person had a close shave, it was you; your head must be as hard as iron. Well, George, how goes it? You're a pretty colour, certainly; why, your liver, man, is upside down. Did you take that medicine? Did he take that medicine, men?'

'Ay, ay, sir, he took it, sure enough,' returned Morgan.

'Because, you see, since I am mutineers' doctor, or prison doctor, as I prefer to call it,' says Doctor Livesey, in his pleasantest way, 'I make it a point of honour not to lose a man for King George (God bless him!) and the gallows.'

The rogues looked at each other, but swallowed the home-thrust in silence.

'Dick don't feel well, sir,' said one.

'Don't he?' replied the doctor. 'Well, step up here, Dick, and let me see your tongue. No, I should be surprised if he did! the man's tongue is fit to frighten the French. Another fever.'

'Ah, there,' said Morgan, 'that comed of sp'iling Bibles.'

'That comed – as you call it – of being arrant asses,' retorted the doctor, 'and not having sense enough to know honest air from poison, and the dry land from a vile, pestiferous slough. I think it most probable – though, of course, it's only an opinion – that you'll all have the deuce to pay before you get that malaria out of your systems. Camp in a bog, would you? Silver, I'm surprised at you. You're less of a fool than many, take you all round; but you don't appear to me to have the rudiments of a notion of the rules of health.

'Well,' he added, after he had dosed them round, and they had taken his prescriptions, with really laughable humility, more like charity school-children than blood-guilty mutineers and pirates – 'well, that's done for to-day. And now I should wish to have a talk with that boy, please.'

And he nodded his head in my direction carelessly.

George Merry was at the door, spitting and spluttering over some bad-tasted medicine; but at the first word of the doctor's proposal he swung round with a deep flush, and cried 'No!' and swore.

Silver struck the barrel with his open hand.

'Si-lence!' he roared, and looked about him positively like a lion. 'Doctor,' he went on, in his usual tones, 'I was a-thinking of that, knowing as how you had a fancy for the boy. We're all humbly grateful for your kindness, and, as you see, puts faith in you, and takes the drugs down like that much grog. And I take it I've found a way as 'll suit all. Hawkins, will you give me your word of honour as a young gentleman – for a young gentleman you are, although poor born – your word of honour not to slip your cable?'

I readily gave the pledge required.

'Then, doctor,' said Silver, 'you just step outside o' that stockade, and once you're there, I'll bring the boy down on the inside, and I reckon you can yarn through the spars. Good day to you, sir, and all our dooties to the squire and Cap'n Smollett.'

The explosion of disapproval, which nothing but Silver's black looks had restrained, broke out immediately the doctor had left the house. Silver was roundly accused of playing double – of trying to make a separate peace for himself – of sacrificing the interests of his accomplices and victims; and, in one word, of the identical, exact thing that he was doing. It seemed to me so obvious, in this case, that I could not imagine how he was to turn their anger. But he was twice the man the rest were; and his last night's victory had given him a huge preponderance on their minds. He called them all the fools and dolts you can imagine, said it was necessary I should talk to the doctor, fluttered the chart in their faces, asked them if they could afford to break the treaty the very day they were bound a-treasure-hunting.

'No, by thunder!' he cried, 'it's us must break the treaty when the time comes; and till then I'll gammon that doctor, if I have to ile his boots with brandy.'

And then he bade them get the fire lit, and stalked out upon his crutch, with his hand on my shoulder, leaving them in a disarray, and silenced by his volubility rather than convinced.

'Slow, lad, slow,' he said. 'They might round upon us in a twinkle of an eye, if we was seen to hurry.'

Very deliberately, then, did we advance across the sand to where the doctor awaited us on the other side of the stockade, and as soon as we were within easy speaking distance, Silver stopped.

'You'll make a note of this here also, doctor,' says he, 'and the boy'll tell you how I saved his life, and were deposed for it, too, and you may lay to that. Doctor, when a man's steering as near the wind as me – playing chuck-farthing with the last breath in his body, like – you wouldn't think it too much, mayhap, to give him one good word? You'll please bear in mind it's not my life only now – it's that boy's into the bargain; and you'll speak me fair, doctor, and give me a bit o' hope to go on, for the sake of mercy.'

Silver was a changed man, once he was out there and had his back to his friends and the block house; his cheeks seemed to have fallen in, his voice trembled; never was a soul more dead in earnest.

'Why, John, you're not afraid?' asked Doctor Livesey.

'Doctor, I'm no coward; no, not I – not *so* much!' and he snapped his fingers. 'If I was I wouldn't say it. But I'll own up fairly, I've the shakes upon me for the gallows. You're a good man and a true; I never seen a better man! And you'll not forget what I done good, not any more than you'll forget the bad, I know. And I step aside – see here – and leave you and Jim alone. And you'll put that down for me, too, for it's a long stretch, is that!'

So saying, he stepped back a little way, till he was out of ear-shot, and there sat down upon a tree-stump and began to whistle; spinning round now and again upon his seat so as to command a sight, sometimes of me and the doctor, and sometimes of his unruly ruffians as they went to and fro in the sand, between the fire – which they were busy rekindling – and the house, from which they brought forth pork and bread to make the breakfast.

'So, Jim,' said the doctor, sadly, 'here you are. As you have brewed, so shall you drink, my boy. Heaven knows, I cannot find it in my heart to blame you; but this much I will say, be it kind or unkind: when Captain Smollett was well, you dared not have gone off; and when he was ill, and couldn't help it, by George, it was down-right cowardly!'

I will own that I here began to weep. 'Doctor,' I said, 'you might spare me. I have blamed myself enough; my life's forfeit anyway, and I should have been dead by now, if Silver hadn't stood for me; and doctor, believe this, I can die – and I daresay I deserve it – but what I fear is torture. If they come to torture me –'

'Jim,' the doctor interrupted, and his voice was quite changed, 'Jim I can't have this. Whip over, and we'll run for it.'

'Doctor,' said I, 'I passed my word.'

'I know, I know,' he cried. 'We can't help that, Jim, now. I'll take it on my shoulders, holus bolus, blame and shame, my boy;

but stay here, I cannot let you. Jump! One jump, and you're out, and we'll run for it like antelopes.'

'No,' I replied, 'you know right well you wouldn't do the thing yourself; neither you, nor squire, nor captain; and no more will I. Silver trusted me; I passed my word, and back I go. But, doctor, you did not let me finish. If they come to torture me, I might let slip a word of where the ship is; for I got the ship, part by luck and part by risking, and she lies in North Inlet, on the southern beach, and just below high water. At half tide she must be high and dry.'

'The ship!' exclaimed the doctor.

Rapidly I described to him my adventures, and he heard me out in silence.

'There is a kind of fate in this,' he observed, when I had done. 'Every step, it's you that saves our lives; and do you suppose by any chance that we are going to let you lose yours? That would be a poor return, my boy. You found out the plot; you found Ben Gunn – the best deed that ever you did, or will do, though you live to ninety. Oh, by Jupiter, and talking of Ben Gunn! why, this is the mischief in person. Silver,' he cried, 'Silver! – I'll give you a piece of advice,' he continued, as the cook drew near again; 'don't you be in any great hurry after that treasure.'

'Why, sir, I do my possible, which that ain't,' said Silver. 'I can only, asking your pardon, save my life and the boy's by seeking for that treasure; and you may lay to that.'

'Well, Silver,' replied the doctor, 'if that is so, I'll go one step further: look out for squalls when you find it.'

'Sir,' said Silver, 'as between man and man, that's too much and too little. What you're after, why you left the block house, why you given me that there chart, I don't know, now, do I? and yet I done your bidding with my eyes shut and never a word of hope! But no, this here's too much. If you won't tell me what you mean plain out, just say so, and I'll leave the helm.'

'No,' said the doctor, musingly, 'I've no right to say more; it's not my secret, you see, Silver, or, I give you my word, I'd tell it you. But I'll go as far with you as I dare go, and a step beyond; for I'll have my wig sorted by the captain or I'm mistaken! And, first, I'll give you a bit of hope: Silver, if we both get alive out of this wolf-trap, I'll do my best to save you, short of perjury.'

Silver's face was radiant. 'You couldn't say more, I'm sure, sir, not if you was my mother,' he cried.

'Well, that's my first concession,' added the doctor. 'My second is a piece of advice: Keep the boy close beside you, and when you need help, halloo. I'm off to seek it for you, and that itself will show you if I speak at random. Good-bye, Jim.'

And Dr Livesey shook hands with me through the stockade, nodded to Silver, and set off at a brisk pace into the wood.

Chapter Thirty-One

The Treasure Hunt – Flint's Pointer

'Jim,' said Silver, when we were alone, 'if I saved your life, you saved mine; and I'll not forget it. I seen the doctor waving you to run for it – with the tail of my eye, I did; and I seen you say no, as plain as hearing. Jim, that's one to you. This is the first glint of hope I had since the attack failed, and I owe it you. And now, Jim, we're to go in for this here treasure-hunting, with sealed orders, too, and I don't like it; and you and me must stick close, back to back like, and we'll save our necks in spite o' fate and fortune.'

Just then a man hailed us from the fire that breakfast was ready, and we were soon seated here and there about the sand over biscuit and fried junk. They had lit a fire fit to roast an ox; and it was now grown so hot that they could only approach it from the windward, and even there not without precaution. In the same wasteful spirit, they had cooked, I suppose, three times more than we could eat; and one of them, with an empty laugh, threw what was left into the fire, which blazed and roared again over this unusual fuel. I never in my life saw men so careless of the morrow; hand to mouth is the only word that can describe their way of doing; and what with wasted food and sleeping sentries, though they were bold enough for a brush and be done with it, I could see their entire unfitness for anything like a prolonged campaign.

Even Silver, eating away, with Captain Flint upon his shoulder, had not a word of blame for their recklessness. And this the more surprised me, for I thought he had never shown himself so cunning as he did then.

'Ay, mates,' said he, 'it's lucky you have Barbecue to think for you with this here head. I got what I wanted, I did. Sure enough, they have the ship. Where they have it, I don't know yet; but once we hit the treasure, we'll have to jump about and find out. And then, mates, us that has the boats, I reckon, has the upper hand.'

Thus he kept running on, with his mouth full of the hot bacon: thus he restored their hope and confidence, and, I more than suspect, repaired his own at the same time.

'As for hostage,' he continued, 'that's his last talk, I guess, with them he loves so dear. I've got my piece o' news, and thanky to him for that; but it's over and done. I'll take him in a line when we go treasure-hunting, for we'll keep him like so much gold, in case of accidents, you mark, and in the meantime. Once we got the ship and treasure both, and off to sea like jolly companions, why, then, we'll talk Mr Hawkins over, we will, and we'll give him his share, to be sure, for all his kindness.'

It was no wonder the men were in a good humour now. For my part, I was horribly cast down. Should the scheme he had now sketched prove feasible, Silver, already doubly a traitor, would not hesitate to adopt it. He had still a foot in either camp, and there was no doubt he would prefer wealth and freedom with the pirates to a bare escape from hanging, which was the best he had to hope on our side.

Nay, and even if things so fell out that he was forced to keep his faith with Dr Livesey, even then what danger lay before us! What a moment that would be when the suspicions of his followers turned to certainty, and he and I should have to fight for dear life – he, a cripple, and I, a boy – against five strong and active seamen!

Add to this double apprehension, the mystery that still hung over the behaviour of my friends; their unexplained desertion of the stockade; their inexplicable cession of the chart; or, harder still to understand, the doctor's last warning to Silver, 'Look out for squalls when you find it;' and you will readily believe how little taste I found in my breakfast, and with how uneasy a heart I set forth behind my captors on the quest for treasure.

We made a curious figure, had any one been there to see us; all in soiled sailor clothes, and all but me armed to the teeth. Silver had two guns slung about him – one before and one behind – besides the great cutlass at his waist, and a pistol in each pocket of his square-tailed coat. To complete his strange appearance, Captain Flint sat perched upon his shoulder and gabbling odds and ends of purposeless sea-talk. I had a line about my waist, and followed obediently after the sea-cook, who held the loose end of the rope, now in his free hand, now between his powerful teeth. For all the world, I was led like a dancing bear.

The other men were variously burthened; some carrying picks and shovels – for that had been the very first necessary they brought ashore from the *Hispaniola* – others laden with pork, bread, and brandy for the mid-day meal. All the stores, I observed, came from our stock; and I could see the truth of Silver's words the night before. Had he not struck a bargain with the doctor, he and his mutineers, deserted by the ship, must have been driven to subsist on clear water and the proceeds of their hunting. Water would have been little to their taste; a sailor is not usually a good shot; and, besides all that, when they were so short of eatables, it was not likely they would be very flush of powder.

Well, thus equipped, we all set out – even the fellow with the broken head, who should certainly have kept in shadow – and straggled, one after another, to the beach, where the two gigs awaited us. Even these bore trace of the drunken folly of the pirates, one in a broken thwart, and both in their muddy and unbailed condition. Both were to be carried along with us, for the sake of safety; and so, with our numbers divided between them, we set forth upon the bosom of the anchorage.

As we pulled over, there was some discussion on the chart. The red cross was, of course, far too large to be a guide; and the terms of the note on the back, as you will hear, admitted of some ambiguity. They ran, the reader may remember, thus: –

'Tall tree, Spy-glass shoulder, bearing a point to the N. of N. N. E.

'Skeleton Island E. S. E. and by E.

'Ten feet.'

A tall tree was thus the principal mark. Now, right before us, the anchorage was bounded by a plateau from two to three hundred feet high, adjoining on the north the sloping southern shoulder of the Spy-glass, and rising again towards the south into the rough, cliffy eminence called the Mizzen-mast Hill. The top of the plateau was dotted thickly with pine trees of varying height. Every here and there, one of a different species rose forty or fifty feet clear above its neighbours, and which of these was the particular 'tall tree' of Captain Flint could only be decided on the spot, and by the readings of the compass.

Yet, although that was the case, every man on board the boats had picked a favourite of his own ere we were half way over, Long John alone shrugging his shoulders and bidding them wait till they were there.

We pulled easily, by Silver's directions, not to weary the hands prematurely; and, after quite a long passage, landed at the mouth of the second river – that which runs down a woody cleft of the Spy-glass. Thence, bending to our left, we began to ascend the slope towards the plateau.

At the first outset, heavy, miry ground and a matted, marish vegetation, greatly delayed our progress; but by little and little the hill began to steepen and become stony under foot, and the wood to change its character and to grow in a more open order. It was, indeed, a most pleasant portion of the island that we were now approaching. A heavy-scented broom and many flowering shrubs had almost taken the place of grass. Thickets of green nutmeg trees were dotted here and there with the red columns and the broad shadow of the pines; and the first mingled their spice with the aroma of the others. The air, besides, was fresh and stirring, and this, under the sheer sunbeams, was a wonderful refreshment to our senses.

The party spread itself abroad, in a fan shape, shouting and leaping to and fro. About the centre, and a good way behind the rest, Silver and I followed – I tethered by my rope, he ploughing, with deep pants, among the sliding gravel. From time to time, indeed, I had to lend him a hand, or he must have missed his footing and fallen backward down the hill.

We had thus proceeded for about half a mile, and were approaching the brow of the plateau, when the man upon the farthest left began to cry aloud, as if in terror. Shout after shout came from him, and the others began to run in his direction.

'He can't 'a' found the treasure,' said old Morgan, hurrying past us from the right, 'for that's clean a-top.'

Indeed, as we found when we also reached the spot, it was something very different. At the foot of a pretty big pine, and involved in a green creeper, which had even partly lifted some of the smaller bones, a human skeleton lay, with a few shreds of clothing, on the ground. I believe a chill struck for a moment to every heart.

'He was a seaman,' said George Merry, who, bolder than the rest, had gone up close, and was examining the rags of clothing. 'Leastways, this is good sea-cloth.'

'Ay, ay,' said Silver, 'like enough; you wouldn't look to find a bishop here, I reckon. But what sort of a way is that for bones to lie? 'Tain't in natur'.'

Indeed, on a second glance, it seemed impossible to fancy that the body was in a natural position. But for some disarray (the work, perhaps, of the birds that had fed upon him, or of the slow-growing creeper that had gradually enveloped his remains) the man lay perfectly straight – his feet pointing in one direction, his hands, raised above his head like a diver's, pointing directly in the opposite.

'I've taken a notion into my old numskull,' observed Silver. 'Here's the compass; there's the tip-top p'int o' Skeleton Island, stickin' out like a tooth. Just take a bearing, will you, along the line of them bones.'

It was done. The body pointed straight in the direction of the island, and the compass read duly E. S. E. and by E.

'I thought so,' cried the cook; 'this here is a p'inter. Right up there is our line for the Pole Star and the jolly dollars. But, by thunder! if it don't make me cold inside to think of Flint. This is one of *his* jokes, and no mistake. Him and these six was alone here; he killed 'em, every man; and this one he hauled here and laid down by compass, shiver my timbers! They're long bones, and the hair's been yellow. Ay, that would be Allardyce. You mind Allardyce, Tom Morgan?'

'Ay, ay,' returned Morgan, 'I mind him; he owed me money, he did, and took my knife ashore with him.'

'Speaking of knives,' said another, 'why don't we find his'n lying round? Flint warn't the man to pick a seaman's pocket; and the birds, I guess, would leave it be.'

'By the powers, and that's true!' cried Silver.

'There ain't a thing left here,' said Merry, still feeling round among the bones, 'not a copper doit nor a baccy box. It don't look nat'ral to me.'

'No, by gum, it don't,' agreed Silver; 'not nat'ral, nor not nice, says you. Great guns! messmates, but if Flint was living, this would be a hot spot for you and me. Six they were, and six are we; and bones is what they are now.'

'I saw him dead with these here dead-lights,' said Morgan. 'Billy took me in. There he laid, with penny-pieces on his eyes.'

'Dead – ay, sure enough he's dead and gone below,' said the fellow with the bandage; 'but if ever sperrit walked, it would be Flint's. Dear heart, but he died bad, did Flint!'

'Ay, that he did,' observed another; 'now he raged, and now he hollered for the rum, and now he sang. "Fifteen Men" were his only song, mates; and I tell you true, I never rightly liked to hear it since. It was main hot, and the windy was open, and I hear that old song comin' out as clear as clear – and the death-haul on the man already.'

'Come, come,' said Silver, 'stow this talk. He's dead, and he don't walk, that I know; leastways, he won't walk by day, and you may lay to that. Care killed a cat. Fetch ahead for the doubloons.'

We started, certainly; but in spite of the hot sun and the staring daylight, the pirates no longer ran separate and shouting through the wood, but kept side by side and spoke with bated breath. The terror of the dead buccaneer had fallen on their spirits.

Chapter Thirty-Two

The Treasure Hunt – The Voice among the Trees

Partly from the damping influence of this alarm, partly to rest Silver and the sick folk, the whole party sat down as soon as they had gained the brow of the ascent.

The plateau being somewhat tilted towards the west, this spot on which we had paused commanded a wide prospect on either hand. Before us, over the tree-tops, we beheld the Cape of the Woods fringed with surf; behind, we not only looked down upon the anchorage and Skeleton Island, but saw – clear across the spit and the eastern lowlands – a great field of open sea upon the east. Sheer above us rose the Spy-glass, here dotted with single pines, there black with precipices. There was no sound but that of the distant breakers, mounting from all round, and the chirp of countless insects in the brush. Not a man, not a sail upon the sea; the very largeness of the view increased the sense of solitude.

Silver, as he sat, took certain bearings with his compass.

'There are three "tall trees,"' said he, 'about in the right line from Skeleton Island. "Spy-glass Shoulder," I take it, means that lower p'int there. It's child's play to find the stuff now. I've half a mind to dine first.'

'I don't feel sharp,' growled Morgan. 'Thinkin' o' Flint – I think it were – as done me.'

'Ah, well, my son, you praise your stars he's dead,' said Silver.

'He were an ugly devil,' cried a third pirate, with a shudder; 'that blue in the face, too!'

'That was how the rum took him,' added Merry. 'Blue! well, I reckon he was blue. That's a true word.'

Ever since they had found the skeleton and got upon this train of thought, they had spoken lower and lower, and they had almost

203

got to whispering by now, so that the sound of their talk hardly interrupted the silence of the wood. All of a sudden, out of the middle of the trees in front of us, a thin, high, trembling voice struck up the well-known air and words: –

'Fifteen men on the dead man's chest –
Yo-ho-ho, and a bottle of rum!'

I never have seen men more dreadfully affected than the pirates. The colour went from their six faces like enchantment; some leaped to their feet, some clawed hold of others; Morgan grovelled on the ground.

'It's Flint, by – !' cried Merry.

The song had stopped as suddenly as it began – broken off, you would have said, in the middle of a note, as though some one had laid his hand upon the singer's mouth. Coming so far through the clear, sunny atmosphere among the green tree-tops, I thought it had sounded airily and sweetly; and the effect on my companions was the stranger.

'Come,' said Silver, struggling with his ashen lips to get the word out, 'this won't do. Stand by to go about. This is a rum start, and I can't name the voice: but it's some one skylarking – some one that's flesh and blood, and you may lay to that.'

His courage had come back as he spoke, and some of the colour to his face along with it. Already the others had begun to lend an ear to this encouragement, and were coming a little to themselves, when the same voice broke out again – not this time singing, but in a faint distant hail, that echoed yet fainter among the clefts of the Spy-glass.

'Darby M'Graw,' it wailed – for that is the word that best describes the sound – 'Darby M'Graw! Darby M'Graw!' again and again and again; and then rising a little higher, and with an oath that I leave out, 'Fetch aft the rum, Darby!'

The buccaneers remained rooted to the ground, their eyes

starting from their heads. Long after the voice had died away they still stared in silence, dreadfully, before them.

'That fixes it!' gasped one. 'Let's go!'

'They was his last words,' moaned Morgan, 'his last words above board.'

Dick had his Bible out, and was praying volubly. He had been well brought up, had Dick, before he came to sea and fell among bad companions.

Still, Silver was unconquered. I could hear his teeth rattle in his head; but he had not yet surrendered.

'Nobody in this here island ever heard of Darby,' he muttered; 'not one but us that's here.' And then, making a great effort, 'Shipmates,' he cried, 'I'm here to get that stuff, and I'll not be beat by man nor devil. I never was feared of Flint in his life, and, by the powers, I'll face him dead. There's seven hundred thousand pound not a quarter of a mile from here. When did ever a gentleman o' fortune show his stern to that much dollars, for a boosy old seaman with a blue mug – and him dead, too?'

But there was no sign of re-awakening courage in his followers; rather, indeed, of growing terror at the irreverence of his words.

'Belay there, John!' said Merry. 'Don't you cross a sperrit.'

And the rest were all too terrified to reply. They would have run away severally had they dared; but fear kept them together, and kept them close by John, as if his daring helped them. He, on his part, had pretty well fought his weakness down.

'Sperrit? Well, maybe,' he said. 'But there's one thing not clear to me. There was an echo. Now, no man ever seen a sperrit with a shadow; well, then, what's he doing with an echo to him, I should like to know? That ain't in natur', surely?'

This argument seemed weak enough to me. But you can never tell what will affect the superstitious, and, to my wonder, George Merry was greatly relieved.

'Well, that's so,' he said. 'You've a head upon your shoulders, John, and no mistake. 'Bout ship, mates! This here crew is on a wrong tack, I do believe. And come to think on it, it was like Flint's voice, I grant you, but not just so clear-away like it, after all. It was liker somebody else's voice now – it was liker –'

'By the powers, Ben Gunn!' roared Silver.

'Ay, and so it were,' cried Morgan, springing on his knees. 'Ben Gunn it were!'

'It don't make much odds, do it, now?' asked Dick. 'Ben Gunn's not here in the body, any more'n Flint.'

But the older hands greeted this remark with scorn.

'Why, nobody minds Ben Gunn,' cried Merry; 'dead or alive, nobody minds him.'

It was extraordinary how their spirits had returned, and how the natural colour had revived in their faces. Soon they were chatting together, with intervals of listening; and not long after, hearing no further sound, they shouldered the tools and set forth again, Merry walking first with Silver's compass to keep them on the right line with Skeleton Island. He had said the truth: dead or alive, nobody minded Ben Gunn.

Dick alone still held his Bible, and looked around him as he went, with fearful glances; but he found no sympathy, and Silver even joked him on his precautions.

'I told you,' said he – 'I told you, you had sp'iled your Bible. If it ain't no good to swear by, what do you suppose a sperrit would give for it? Not that!' and he snapped his big fingers, halting a moment on his crutch.

But Dick was not to be comforted; indeed, it was soon plain to me that the lad was falling sick; hastened by heat, exhaustion, and the shock of his alarm, the fever, predicted by Doctor Livesey, was evidently growing swiftly higher.

It was fine open walking here, upon the summit; our way lay a little down-hill, for, as I have said, the plateau tilted towards the west. The pines, great and small, grew wide apart; and even between the clumps of nutmeg and azalea, wide open spaces baked in the hot sunshine. Striking, as we did, pretty near north-west across the island, we drew, on the one hand, ever nearer under the shoulders of the Spy-glass, and on the other, looked ever wider over that western bay where I had once tossed and trembled in the coracle.

The first of the tall trees was reached, and by the bearing, proved the wrong one. So with the second. The third rose nearly two hundred feet into the air above a clump of underwood; a giant of a vegetable, with a red column as big as a cottage, and a wide shadow around in which a company could have manœuvred. It was conspicuous far to sea both on the east and west, and might have been entered as a sailing mark upon the chart.

But it was not its size that now impressed my companions; it was the knowledge that seven hundred thousand pounds in gold lay somewhere buried below its spreading shadow. The thought of the money, as they drew nearer, swallowed up their previous terrors. Their eyes burned in their heads; their feet grew speedier and lighter; their whole soul was bound up in that fortune, that whole lifetime of extravagance and pleasure, that lay waiting there for each of them.

Silver hobbled, grunting, on his crutch; his nostrils stood out and quivered; he cursed like a madman when the flies settled on his hot and shiny countenance; he plucked furiously at the line that held me to him, and, from time to time, turned his eyes upon me with a deadly look. Certainly he took no pains to hide his thoughts; and certainly I read them like print. In the immediate nearness of the gold, all else had been forgotten; his promise and the doctor's warning were both things of the past; and I could not doubt that he hoped to seize upon the treasure, find and board the *Hispaniola* under cover of night, cut every honest throat about that island, and sail away as he had at first intended, laden with crimes and riches.

Shaken as I was with these alarms, it was hard for me to keep up with the rapid pace of the treasure-hunters. Now and again I stumbled; and it was then that Silver plucked so roughly at the rope and launched at me his murderous glances. Dick, who had dropped behind us, and now brought up the rear, was babbling to himself both prayers and curses, as his fever kept rising. This also added to my wretchedness, and, to crown all, I was haunted by the thought of the tragedy that had once been acted on that plateau, when that ungodly buccaneer with the blue face – he who died at Savannah, singing and shouting for drink – had there, with his own hand, cut down his six accomplices. This grove, that was now so peaceful, must then have rung with cries, I thought; and even with the thought I could believe I heard it ringing still.

We were now at the margin of the thicket.

'Huzza, mates, all together!' shouted Merry; and the foremost broke into a run.

And suddenly, not ten yards further, we beheld them stop. A low cry arose. Silver doubled his pace, digging away with the foot of his crutch like one possessed; and next moment he and I had come also to a dead halt.

Before us was a great excavation, not very recent, for the sides had fallen in and grass had sprouted on the bottom. In this were the shaft of a pick broken in two and the boards of several packing-cases strewn around. On one of these boards I saw, branded with a hot iron, the name *Walrus* – the name of Flint's ship.

All was clear to probation. The *cache* had been found and rifled: the seven hundred thousand pounds were gone!

Chapter Thirty-Three

The Fall of a Chieftain

There never was such an overturn in this world. Each of these six men was as though he had been struck. But with Silver the blow passed almost instantly. Every thought of his soul had been set full-stretch, like a racer, on that money; well, he was brought up in a single second, dead; and he kept his head, found his temper, and changed his plan before the others had had time to realise the disappointment.

'Jim,' he whispered, 'take that, and stand by for trouble.'

And he passed me a double-barrelled pistol.

At the same time he began quietly moving northward, and in a few steps had put the hollow between us two and the other five. Then he looked at me and nodded, as much as to say, 'Here is a narrow corner,' as, indeed, I thought it was. His looks were now quite friendly; and I was so revolted at these constant changes, that I could not forbear whispering, 'So you've changed sides again.'

There was no time left for him to answer in. The buccaneers, with oaths and cries, began to leap, one after another, into the pit, and to dig with their fingers, throwing the boards aside as they did so. Morgan found a piece of gold. He held it up with a perfect spout of oaths. It was a two-guinea piece, and it went from hand to hand among them for a quarter of a minute.

'Two guineas!' roared Merry, shaking it at Silver. 'That's your seven hundred thousand pounds, is it? You're the man for bargains, ain't you? You're him that never bungled nothing, you wooden-headed lubber!'

'Dig away, boys,' said Silver, with the coolest insolence; 'you'll find some pig-nuts and I shouldn't wonder.'

'Pig-nuts!' repeated Merry, in a scream. 'Mates, do you hear that? I tell you, now, that man there knew it all along. Look in the face of him, and you'll see it wrote there.'

'Ah, Merry,' remarked Silver, 'standing for cap'n again? You're a pushing lad, to be sure.'

But this time every one was entirely in Merry's favour. They began to scramble out of the excavation, darting furious glances behind them. One thing I observed, which looked well for us: they all got out upon the opposite side from Silver.

Well, there we stood, two on one side, five on the other, the pit between us, and nobody screwed up high enough to offer the first blow. Silver never moved; he watched them, very upright on his crutch, and looked as cool as ever I saw him. He was brave, and no mistake.

At last, Merry seemed to think a speech might help matters.

'Mates,' says he, 'there's two of them alone there; one's the old cripple that brought us all here and blundered us down to this; the other's that cub that I mean to have the heart of. Now, mates –'

He was raising his arm and his voice, and plainly meant to lead a charge. But just then – crack! crack! crack! – three musket-shots flashed out of the thicket. Merry tumbled head foremost into the excavation; the man with the bandage spun round like a teeto-tum, and fell all his length upon his side, where he lay dead, but still twitching; and the other three turned and ran for it with all their might.

Before you could wink, Long John had fired two barrels of a pistol into the struggling Merry; and as the man rolled up his eyes at him in the last agony, 'George,' said he, 'I reckon I settled you.'

At the same moment the doctor, Gray, and Ben Gunn joined us, with smoking muskets, from among the nutmeg trees.

'Forward!' cried the doctor. 'Double quick, my lads. We must head 'em off the boats.'

And we set off at a great pace, sometimes plunging through the bushes to the chest.

I tell you, but Silver was anxious to keep up with us. The work that man went through, leaping on his crutch till the muscles of his chest were fit to burst, was work no sound man ever equalled; and so thinks the doctor. As it was, he was already thirty yards behind us, and on the verge of strangling, when we reached the brow of the slope.

'Doctor,' he hailed, 'see there! no hurry!'

Sure enough there was no hurry. In a more open part of the plateau, we could see the three survivors still running in the same direction as they had started, right for Mizzen-mast Hill. We were already between them and the boats; and so we four sat down to breathe, while Long John, mopping his face, came slowly up with us.

'Thank ye kindly, doctor,' says he. 'You came in in about the nick, I guess, for me and Hawkins. And so it's you, Ben Gunn!' he added. 'Well, you're a nice one to be sure.'

'I'm Ben Gunn, I am,' replied the maroon, wriggling like an eel in his embarrassment. 'And,' he added, after a long pause, 'how do, Mr Silver? Pretty well, I thank ye, says you.'

'Ben, Ben,' murmured Silver, 'to think as you've done me!'

The doctor sent back Gray for one of the pickaxes, deserted, in their flight, by the mutineers; and then as we proceeded leisurely down hill to where the boats were lying, related, in a few words, what had taken place. It was a story that profoundly interested Silver; and Ben Gunn, the half-idiot maroon, was the hero from beginning to end.

Ben, in his long, lonely wanderings about the island, had found the skeleton – it was he that had rifled it; he had found the treasure; he had dug it up (it was the haft of his pickaxe that lay broken in the excavation); he had carried it on his back, in many weary journeys, from the foot of the tall pine to a cave he had on the two-pointed hill at the north-east angle of the island, and there it had lain stored in safety since two months before the arrival of the *Hispaniola*.

When the doctor had wormed this secret from him, on the

afternoon of the attack, and when, next morning, he saw the anchorage deserted, he had gone to Silver, given him the chart, which was now useless – given him the stores, for Ben Gunn's cave was well supplied with goats' meat salted by himself – given anything and everything to get a chance of moving in safety from the stockade to the two-pointed hill, there to be clear of malaria and keep a guard upon the money.

'As for you, Jim,' he said, 'it went against my heart, but I did what I thought best for those who had stood by their duty; and if you were not one of these, whose fault was it?'

That morning, finding that I was to be involved in the horrid disappointment he had prepared for the mutineers, he had run all the way to the cave, and, leaving the squire to guard the captain, had taken Gray and the maroon, and started, making the diagonal across the island, to be at hand beside the pine. Soon, however, he saw that our party had the start of him; and Ben Gunn, being fleet of foot, had been despatched in front to do his best alone. Then it had occurred to him to work upon the superstitions of his former shipmates; and he was so far successful that Gray and the doctor had come up and were already ambushed before the arrival of the treasure-hunters.

'Ah,' said Silver, 'it were fortunate for me that I had Hawkins here. You would have let old John be cut to bits, and never given it a thought, doctor.'

'Not a thought,' replied Doctor Livesey, cheerily.

And by this time we had reached the gigs. The doctor, with a pickaxe, demolished one of them, and then we all got aboard the other, and set out to go round by sea for North Inlet.

This was a run of eight or nine miles. Silver, though he was almost killed already with fatigue, was set to an oar, like the rest of us, and we were soon skimming swiftly over a smooth sea. Soon we passed out of the straits and doubled the south-east corner of the island, round which, four days ago, we had towed the *Hispaniola*.

As we passed the two-pointed hill, we could see the black mouth of Ben Gunn's cave, and a figure standing by it, leaning on a musket. It was the squire; and we waved a handkerchief and gave him three cheers, in which the voice of Silver joined as heartily as any.

Three miles farther, just inside the mouth of North Inlet, what should we meet but the *Hispaniola*, cruising by herself? The last flood had lifted her; and had there been much wind, or a strong tide current, as in the southern anchorage, we should never have found her more, or found her stranded beyond help. As it was, there was little amiss, beyond the wreck of the mainsail. Another anchor was got ready, and dropped in a fathom and a half of water. We all pulled round again to Rum Cove, the nearest point for Ben Gunn's treasure-house; and then Gray, single-handed, returned with the gig to the *Hispaniola*, where he was to pass the night on guard.

A gentle slope ran up from the beach to the entrance of the cave. At the top, the squire met us. To me he was cordial and kind, saying nothing of my escapade, either in the way of blame or praise. At Silver's polite salute he somewhat flushed.

'John Silver,' he said, 'you're a prodigious villain and impostor – a monstrous impostor, sir. I am told I am not to prosecute you. Well, then, I will not. But the dead men, sir, hang about your neck like millstones.'

'Thank you kindly, sir,' replied Long John, again saluting.

'I dare you to thank me!' cried the squire. 'It is a gross dereliction of my duty. Stand back.'

And thereupon we all entered the cave. It was a large, airy place, with a little spring and a pool of clear water, overhung with ferns. The floor was sand. Before a big fire lay Captain Smollett; and in a far corner, only duskily flickered over by the blaze, I beheld great heaps of coin and quadrilaterals built of bars of gold. That was Flint's treasure that we had come so far to seek, and that had cost already the lives of seventeen men from the *Hispaniola*. How many it had cost in the amassing, what blood and sorrow, what good ships scuttled on the deep, what brave men walking the plank blindfold, what shot of cannon, what shame and lies and cruelty, perhaps no man alive could tell. Yet there were still three upon that island – Silver, and old Morgan, and Ben Gunn – who had each taken his share in these crimes, as each had hoped in vain to share in the reward.

'Come in, Jim,' said the captain. 'You're a good boy in your line, Jim; but I don't think you and me'll go to sea again. You're too much of the born favourite for me. Is that you, John Silver? What brings you here, man?'

'Come back to my dooty, sir,' returned Silver.

'Ah!' said the captain; and that was all he said.

What a supper I had of it that night, with all my friends around me; and what a meal it was, with Ben Gunn's salted goat, and some delicacies and a bottle of old wine from the *Hispaniola*. Never, I am sure, were people gayer or happier. And there was Silver, sitting back almost out of the firelight, but eating heartily, prompt to spring forward when anything was wanted, even joining quietly in our laughter – the same bland, polite, obsequious seaman of the voyage out.

Chapter Thirty-Four

And Last

The next morning we fell early to work, for the transportation of this great mass of gold near a mile by land to the beach, and thence three miles by boat to the *Hispaniola*, was a considerable task for so small a number of workmen. The three fellows still abroad upon the island did not greatly trouble us; a single sentry on the shoulder of the hill was sufficient to insure us against any sudden onslaught, and we thought, besides, they had had more than enough of fighting.

Therefore the work was pushed on briskly. Gray and Ben Gunn came and went with the boat, while the rest, during their absences, piled treasure on the beach. Two of the bars, slung in a rope's-end, made a good load for a grown man – one that he was glad to walk slowly with. For my part, as I was not much use at carrying, I was kept busy all day in the cave, packing the minted money into bread-bags.

It was a strange collection, like Billy Bones's hoard for the diversity of coinage, but so much larger and so much more varied that I think I never had more pleasure than in sorting them. English, French, Spanish, Portuguese, Georges, and Louises, doubloons and double guineas and moidores and sequins, the pictures of all the kings of Europe for the last hundred years, strange Oriental pieces stamped with what looked like wisps of string or bits of spider's web, round pieces and square pieces, and pieces bored through the middle, as if to wear them round your neck – nearly every variety of money in the world must, I think, have found a place in that collection; and for number, I am sure they were like autumn leaves, so that my back ached with stooping and my fingers with sorting them out.

Day after day this work went on; by every evening a fortune had been stowed aboard, but there was another fortune waiting for the morrow; and all this time we heard nothing of the three surviving mutineers.

At last – I think it was on the third night – the doctor and I were strolling on the shoulder of the hill where it overlooks the low-lands of the isle, when, from out the thick darkness below, the wind brought us a noise between shrieking and singing. It was only a snatch that reached our ears, followed by the former silence.

'Heaven forgive them,' said the doctor, "tis the mutineers!'

'All drunk, sir,' struck in the voice of Silver from behind us.

Silver, I should say, was allowed his entire liberty, and, in spite of daily rebuffs, seemed to regard himself once more as quite a privileged and friendly dependent. Indeed, it was remarkable how well he bore these slights, and with what unwearying politeness he kept on trying to ingratiate himself with all. Yet, I think, none treated him better than a dog; unless it was Ben Gunn, who was still terribly afraid of his old quarter-master, or myself, who had really something to thank him for; although for that matter, I suppose, I had reason to think even worse of him than any-body else, for I had seen him meditating a fresh treachery upon the plateau. Accordingly, it was pretty gruffly that the doctor answered him.

'Drunk or raving,' said he.

'Right you were, sir,' replied Silver; 'and precious little odds which, to you and me.'

'I suppose you would hardly ask me to call you a humane man,' returned the doctor, with a sneer, 'and so my feelings may surprise you, Master Silver. But if I were sure they were raving – as I am morally certain one, at least, of them is down with fever – I should leave this camp, and, at whatever risk to my own carcass, take them the assistance of my skill.'

'Ask your pardon, sir, you would be very wrong,' quoth Silver. 'You would lose your precious life, and you may lay to that. I'm on your side now, hand and glove; and I shouldn't wish for to see the party weakened, let alone yourself, seeing as I know what I owes you. But these men down there, they couldn't keep their word – no, not supposing they wished to; and what's more, they couldn't believe as you could.'

'No,' said the doctor. 'You're the man to keep your word, we know that.'

Well, that was about the last news we had of the three pirates. Only once we heard a gunshot a great way off, and supposed them to be hunting. A council was held, and it was decided that we must desert them on the island – to the huge glee, I must say, of Ben Gunn, and with the strong approval of Gray. We left a good stock of powder and shot, the bulk of the salt goat, a few medicines, and some other necessaries, tools, clothing, a spare sail, a fathom or two of rope, and, by the particular desire of the doctor, a handsome present of tobacco.

That was about our last doing on the island. Before that, we had got the treasure stowed, and had shipped enough water and the remainder of the goat meat, in case of any distress; and at last, one fine morning, we weighed anchor, which was about all that we could manage, and stood out of North Inlet, the same colours flying that the captain had flown and fought under at the palisade.

The three fellows must have been watching us closer than we thought for, as we soon had proved. For, coming through the narrows, we had to lie very near the southern point, and there we saw all three of them kneeling together on a spit of sand, with their arms raised in supplication. It went to all our hearts, I think, to leave them in that wretched state; but we could not risk another mutiny; and to take them home for the gibbet would have been a cruel sort of kindness. The doctor hailed them and told them of the stores we had left, and where they were to find them. But they continued to call us by name, and appeal to us, for God's sake, to be merciful, and not leave them to die in such a place.

At last, seeing the ship still bore on her course, and was now swiftly drawing out of earshot, one of them – I know not which it was – leapt to his feet with a hoarse cry, whipped his musket to his shoulder, and sent a shot whistling over Silver's head and through the mainsail.

After that, we kept under cover of the bulwarks, and when next I looked out they had disappeared from the spit, and the spit itself had almost melted out of sight in the growing distance. That was, at least, the end of that; and before noon, to my inexpressible joy, the highest rock of Treasure Island had sunk into the blue round of sea.

We were so short of men, that every one on board had to bear a hand – only the captain lying on a mattress in the stern and giving his orders; for, though greatly recovered he was still in want of quiet. We laid her head for the nearest port in Spanish America, for we could not risk the voyage home without fresh hands; and as it was, what with baffling winds and a couple of fresh gales, we were all worn out before we reached it.

It was just at sundown when we cast anchor in a most beautiful land-locked gulf, and were immediately surrounded by shore boats full of negroes, and Mexican Indians, and half-bloods, selling fruits and vegetables, and offering to dive for bits of money. The sight of so many good-humoured faces (especially the blacks), the taste of the tropical fruits, and above all, the lights that began to shine in the town, made a most charming contrast to our dark and bloody sojourn on the island; and the doctor and the squire, taking me along with them, went ashore to pass the early part of the night. Here they met the captain of an English man-of-war, fell in talk with him, went on board his ship, and, in short, had so agreeable a time, that day was breaking when we came alongside the *Hispaniola*.

Ben Gunn was on deck alone, and, as soon as we came on board, he began, with wonderful contortions, to make us a confession. Silver was gone. The maroon had connived at his escape in a shore boat some hours ago, and he now assured us he had only done so to preserve our lives, which would certainly have been forfeit if 'that man with the one leg had stayed aboard.' But this was not all. The sea-cook had not gone empty-handed. He had cut through a bulkhead unobserved, and had removed one of the sacks of coin, worth, perhaps, three or four hundred guineas, to help him on his further wanderings.

I think we were all pleased to be so cheaply quit of him.

Well, to make a long story short, we got a few hands on board, made a good cruise home, and the *Hispaniola* reached Bristol just as Mr Blandly was beginning to think of fitting out her consort. Five men only of those who had sailed returned with her. 'Drink and the devil had done for the rest,' with a vengeance; although, to be sure, we were not quite in so bad a case as that other ship they sang about:

> 'With one man of her crew alive,
> What put to sea with seventy-five.'

All of us had an ample share of the treasure, and used it wisely or foolishly, according to our natures. Captain Smollett is now retired from the sea. Gray not only saved his money, but, being suddenly smit with the desire to rise, also studied his profession; and he is now mate and part owner of a fine full-rigged ship; married besides, and the father of a family. As for Ben Gunn, he got a thousand pounds, which he spent or lost in three weeks, or, to be more exact, in nineteen days, for he was back begging on the twentieth. Then he was given a lodge to keep, exactly as he had feared upon the island; and he still lives, a great favourite, though something of a butt, with the country boys, and a notable singer in church on Sundays and saints' days.

Of Silver we have heard no more. That formidable seafaring man with one leg has at last gone clean out of my life; but I daresay he met his old negress, and perhaps still lives in comfort with her and Captain Flint. It is to be hoped so, I suppose, for his chances of comfort in another world are very small.

The bar silver and the arms still lie, for all that I know, where Flint buried them; and certainly they shall lie there for me. Oxen and wain-ropes would not bring me back again to that accursed island; and the worst dreams that ever I have are when I hear the surf booming about its coasts, or start upright in bed, with the sharp voice of Captain Flint still ringing in my ears: 'Pieces of eight! pieces of eight!'

The Ebb-Tide

A Trio and Quartette

BY

ROBERT LOUIS STEVENSON AND LLOYD OSBOURNE

'There is a tide in the affairs of men'

PART ONE
The Trio

Chapter One

Night on the Beach

Throughout the island world of the Pacific, scattered men of many European races and from almost every grade of society carry activity and disseminate disease. Some prosper, some vegetate. Some have mounted the steps of thrones and owned islands and navies. Others again must marry for a livelihood; a strapping, merry, chocolate-coloured dame supports them in sheer idleness; and, dressed like natives, but still retaining some foreign element of gait or attitude, still perhaps with some relic (such as a single eye-glass) of the officer and gentleman, they sprawl in palm-leaf verandahs and entertain an island audience with memoirs of the music-hall. And there are still others, less pliable, less capable, less fortunate, perhaps less base, who continue, even in these isles of plenty, to lack bread.

At the far end of the town of Papeete, three such men were seated on the beach under a *purao*-tree.

It was late. Long ago the band had broken up and marched musically home, a motley troop of men and women, merchant clerks and navy officers, dancing in its wake, arms about waist and crowned with garlands. Long ago darkness and silence had gone from house to house about the tiny pagan city. Only the street lamps shone on, making a glow-worm halo in the umbrageous alleys or drawing a tremulous image on the waters of the port. A sound of snoring ran among the piles of lumber by the Government pier. It was wafted ashore from the graceful clipper-bottomed schooners, where they lay moored close in like dinghies, and their crews were stretched upon the deck under the open sky or huddled in a rude tent amidst the disorder of merchandise.

But the men under the *purao* had no thought of sleep. The

same temperature in England would have passed without remark in summer; but it was bitter cold for the South Seas. Inanimate nature knew it, and the bottle of cocoanut oil stood frozen in every bird-cage house about the island; and the men knew it, and shivered. They wore flimsy cotton clothes, the same they had sweated in by day and run the gauntlet of the tropic showers; and to complete their evil case, they had no breakfast to mention, less dinner, and no supper at all.

In the telling South Sea phrase, these three men were *on the beach*. Common calamity had brought them acquainted, as the three most miserable English-speaking creatures in Tahiti; and beyond their misery, they knew next to nothing of each other, not even their true names. For each had made a long apprentice-ship in going downward; and each, at some stage of the descent, had been shamed into the adoption of an *alias*. And yet not one of them had figured in a court of justice; two were men of kindly virtues; and one, as he sat and shivered under the *purao*, had a tattered Virgil in his pocket.

Certainly, if money could have been raised upon the book, Robert Herrick would long ago have sacrificed that last posses-sion; but the demand for literature, which is so marked a feature in some parts of the South Seas, extends not so far as the dead tongues; and the Virgil, which he could not exchange against a meal, had often consoled him in his hunger. He would study it, as he lay with tightened belt on the floor of the old calaboose, seek-ing favourite passages and finding new ones only less beautiful because they lacked the consecration of remembrance. Or he would pause on random country walks; sit on the path side, gaz-ing over the sea on the mountains of Eimeo; and dip into the *Aeneid*, seeking *sortes*. And if the oracle (as is the way of oracles) replied with no very certain nor encouraging voice, visions of England at least would throng upon the exile's memory: the busy schoolroom, the green playing-fields, holidays at home, and the perennial roar of London, and the fireside, and the white head of his father. For it is the destiny of those grave, restrained and classic writers, with whom we make enforced and often painful acquaintanceship at school, to pass into the blood and become native in the memory; so that a phrase of Virgil speaks not so much of Mantua or Augustus, but of English places and the student's own irrevocable youth.

Robert Herrick was the son of an intelligent, active, and ambitious man, small partner in a considerable London house. Hopes were conceived of the boy; he was sent to a good school, gained there an Oxford scholarship, and proceeded in course to the Western University. With all his talent and taste (and he had much of both) Robert was deficient in consistency and intellectual manhood, wandered in bypaths of study, worked at music or at metaphysics when he should have been at Greek, and took at last a paltry degree. Almost at the same time, the London house was disastrously wound up; Mr Herrick must begin the world again as a clerk in a strange office, and Robert relinquish his ambitions and accept with gratitude a career that he detested and despised. He had no head for figures, no interest in affairs, detested the constraint of hours, and despised the aims and the success of merchants. To grow rich was none of his ambitions; rather to do well. A worse or a more bold young man would have refused the destiny; perhaps tried his future with his pen; perhaps enlisted. Robert, more prudent, possibly more timid, consented to embrace that way of life in which he could most readily assist his family. But he did so with a mind divided; fled the neighbourhood of former comrades; and chose, out of several positions placed at his disposal, a clerkship in New York.

His career thenceforth was one of unbroken shame. He did not drink, he was exactly honest, he was never rude to his employers, yet was everywhere discharged. Bringing no interest to his duties, he brought no attention; his day was a tissue of things neglected and things done amiss; and from place to place and from town to town, he carried the character of one thoroughly incompetent. No man can bear the word applied to him without some flush of colour, as indeed there is none other that so emphatically slams in a man's face the door of self-respect. And to Herrick, who was conscious of talents and acquirements, who looked down upon those humble duties in which he was found wanting, the pain was the more exquisite. Early in his fall, he had ceased to be able to make remittances; shortly after, having nothing but failure to communicate, he ceased writing home; and about a year before this tale begins, turned suddenly upon the streets of San Francisco by a vulgar and infuriated German Jew, he had broken the last bonds of self-respect, and upon a sudden impulse, changed his name and invested his last dollar in a passage on the mail brigantine, the *City of Papeete*. With what expectation he had trimmed his flight for the South Seas, Herrick perhaps scarcely knew. Doubtless there were fortunes to be made in pearl and copra; doubtless others not more gifted than himself had climbed in the island world to be queen's consorts and king's ministers. But if Herrick had gone there with any manful purpose, he would have kept his father's name: the *alias* betrayed his moral bankruptcy; he had struck his flag; he entertained no hope to reinstate himself or help his straitened family; and he came to the islands (where he knew the climate to be soft, bread cheap, and manners easy) a skulker from life's battle and his own immediate duty. Failure, he had said, was his portion; let it be a pleasant failure.

It is fortunately not enough to say 'I will be base.' Herrick continued in the islands his career of failure; but in the new scene and under the new name, he suffered no less sharply than before. A place was got, it was lost in the old style; from the long-suffering of the keepers of restaurants he fell to more open charity upon the wayside; as time went on, good-nature became weary, and after a repulse or two, Herrick became shy. There were women enough who would have supported a far worse and a far uglier man; Herrick never met or never knew them: or if he did both, some manlier feeling would revolt, and he preferred starvation. Drenched with rains, broiling by day, shivering by night, a disused and ruinous prison for a bedroom, his diet begged or pilfered out of rubbish heaps, his associates two creatures equally outcast with himself, he had drained for months the cup of penitence. He had known what it was to be resigned, what it was to break forth in a childish fury of rebellion against fate, and what it was to sink into the coma of despair. The time had changed him. He told himself no longer tales of an easy and perhaps agreeable declension; he read his nature otherwise; he had proved himself incapable of rising, and he now learned by experience that he could not stoop to fall. Something that was scarcely pride or strength, that was perhaps only refinement, withheld him from capitulation; but he looked on upon his own misfortune with a growing rage, and sometimes wondered at his patience.

It was now the fourth month completed, and still there was no change or sign of change. The moon, racing through a world of flying clouds of every size and shape and density, some black as inkstains, some delicate as lawn, threw the marvel of her Southern brightness over the same lovely and detested scene: the island mountains crowned with the perennial island cloud, the embowered city studded with rare lamps, the masts in the harbour, the smooth mirror of the lagoon, and the mole of the barrier reef on which the breakers whitened. The moon shone too, with bull's-eye sweeps, on his companions; on the stalwart frame of the American who called himself Brown, and was known to be a master-mariner in some disgrace; and on the dwarfish person, the pale eyes and toothless smile of a vulgar and bad-hearted cockney clerk. Here was society for Robert Herrick! The Yankee skipper was a man at least: he had sterling qualities of tenderness and resolution; he was one whose hand you could take without a blush. But there was no redeeming grace about the other, who called himself sometimes Hay and sometimes Tomkins, and laughed at the discrepancy; who had been employed in every store in Papeete, for the creature was able in his way; who had been discharged from each in turn, for he was wholly vile; who had alienated all his old employers so that they passed him in the street as if he were a dog, and all his old comrades so that they shunned him as they would a creditor.

Not long before, a ship from Peru had brought an influenza, and it now raged in the island, and particularly in Papeete. From all round the *purao* arose and fell a dismal sound of men coughing, and strangling as they coughed. The sick natives, with the islander's impatience of a touch of fever, had crawled from their houses to be cool, and squatting on the shore or on the beached canoes, painfully expected the new day. Even as the crowing of cocks goes about the country in the night from farm to farm, accesses of coughing arose, and spread, and died in the distance, and sprang up again. Each miserable shiverer caught the suggestion from his neighbour, was torn for some minutes by that cruel ecstasy, and left spent and without voice or courage when it passed. If a man had pity to spend, Papeete beach, in that cold night and in that infected season, was a place to spend it on. And of all the sufferers, perhaps the least deserving, but surely the most pitiable, was the London clerk. He was used to another life, to houses, beds, nursing, and the dainties of the sick-room; he lay here now, in the cold open, exposed to the gusting of the wind, and with an empty belly. He was besides infirm; the disease shook him to the vitals; and his companions watched his endurance with surprise. A profound commiseration filled them, and contended with and conquered their abhorrence. The disgust attendant on so ugly a sickness magnified this dislike; at the same time, and with more than compensating strength, shame for a sentiment so inhuman bound them the more straitly to his service; and even the evil they knew of him swelled their solicitude, for the thought of death is always the least supportable when it draws near to the merely sensual and selfish. Sometimes they held him up; sometimes, with mistaken helpfulness, they beat him between the shoulders; and when the poor wretch lay back ghastly and spent after a paroxysm of coughing, they would sometimes peer into his face, doubtfully exploring it for any mark of life. There is no one but has some virtue: that of the clerk was courage; and he would make haste to reassure them in a pleasantry not always decent.

'I'm all right, pals,' he gasped once: 'this is the thing to strengthen the muscles of the larynx.'

'Well, you take the cake!' cried the captain.

'O, I'm good plucked enough,' pursued the sufferer with a broken utterance. 'But it do seem bloomin' hard to me, that I should be the only party down with this form of vice, and the only one to do the funny business. I think one of you other parties might wake up. Tell a fellow something.'

'The trouble is we've nothing to tell, my son,' returned the captain.

'I'll tell you, if you like, what I was thinking,' said Herrick.

'Tell us anything,' said the clerk, 'I only want to be reminded that I ain't dead.'

Herrick took up his parable, lying on his face and speaking slowly and scarce above his breath, not like a man who has anything to say, but like one talking against time.

'Well, I was thinking this,' he began: 'I was thinking I lay on Papeete beach one night – all moon and squalls and fellows coughing – and I was cold and hungry, and down in the mouth, and was about ninety years of age, and had spent two hundred and twenty of them on Papeete beach. And I was thinking I wished I had a ring to rub, or had a fairy godmother, or could raise Beelzebub. And I was trying to remember how you did it. I knew you made a ring of skulls, for I had seen that in the *Freischütz*: and that you took off your coat and turned up your sleeves, for I had seen Formes do that when he was playing Kaspar, and you could see (by the way he went about it) it was a business he had studied; and that you ought to have something to kick up a smoke and a bad smell, I daresay a cigar might do, and that you ought to say the Lord's Prayer backwards. Well, I wondered if I could do that; it seemed rather a feat, you see. And then I wondered if I would say it forward, and I thought I did. Well, no sooner had I got to *world without end*, than I saw a man in a *pariu*, and with a mat under his arm, come along the beach from the town. He was rather a hard-favoured old party, and he limped and crippled, and all the time he kept coughing. At first I didn't cotton to his looks, I thought, and then I got sorry for the old soul because he coughed so hard. I remembered that we had some of that cough mixture the American consul gave the captain for Hay. It never did Hay a ha'porth of service, but I thought it might do the old gentleman's business for him, and stood up. *"Yorana!"* says I. *"Yorana!"* says he. "Look here," I said, "I've got some first-rate stuff in a bottle; it'll fix your cough, savvy? *Harry my** and I'll measure you a tablespoonful in the palm of my hand, for all our plate is at the bankers." So I thought the old party came up, and the nearer he came, the less I took to him. But I had passed my word, you see.'

'Wot is this bloomin' drivel?' interrupted the clerk. 'It's like the rot there is in tracts.'

'It's a story; I used to tell them to the kids at home,' said Herrick. 'If it bores you, I'll drop it.'

'O, cut along!' returned the sick man, irritably, 'It's better than nothing.'

'Well,' continued Herrick, 'I had no sooner given him the cough mixture than he seemed to straighten up and change, and I saw he wasn't a Tahitian after all, but some kind of Arab, and had a long beard on his chin. "One good turn deserves another," says he. "I am a magician out of the *Arabian Nights*, and this mat that I have under my arm is the original carpet of Mohammed Ben Somebody-or-other. Say the word, and you can have a cruise

---

* Come here.

upon the carpet." "You don't mean to say this is the Travelling Carpet?" I cried. "You bet I do," said he. "You've been to America since last I read the *Arabian Nights*," said I, a little suspicious. "I should think so," said he. "Been everywhere. A man with a carpet like this isn't going to moulder in a semi-detached villa." Well, that struck me as reasonable. "All right," I said; "and do you mean to tell me I can get on that carpet and go straight to London, England?" I said, "London, England," captain, because he seemed to have been so long in your part of the world. "In the crack of a whip," said he. I figured up the time. What is the difference between Papeete and London, captain?'

'Taking Greenwich and Point Venus, nine hours, odd minutes and seconds,' replied the mariner.

'Well, that's about what I made it,' resumed Herrick, 'about nine hours. Calling this three in the morning, I made out I would drop into London about noon; and the idea tickled me immensely. "There's only one bother," I said, "I haven't a copper cent. It would be a pity to go to London and not buy the morning *Standard*." "O!" said he, "you don't realize the conveniences of this carpet. You see this pocket? you've only got to stick your hand in, and you pull it out filled with sovereigns." '

'Double-eagles, wasn't it?' inquired the captain.

'That was what it was!' cried Herrick. 'I thought they seemed unusually big, and I remember now I had to go to the money-changers at Charing Cross and get English silver.'

'O, you went there?' said the clerk. 'Wot did you do? Bet you had a B.-and-S.!'

'Well, you see, it was just as the old boy said – like the cut of a whip,' said Herrick. 'The one minute I was here on the beach at three in the morning, the next I was in front of the Golden Cross at midday. At first I was dazzled, and covered my eyes, and there didn't seem the smallest change; the roar of the Strand and the roar of the reef were like the same: hark to it now, and you can hear the cabs and buses rolling and the streets resound! And then at last I could look about, and there was the old place, and no mistake! With the statues in the square, and St Martin's-in-the-Fields, and the bobbies, and the sparrows, and the hacks; and I can't tell you what I felt like. I felt like crying, I believe, or dancing, or jumping clean over the Nelson Column. I was like a fellow caught up out of Hell and flung down into the dandiest part of Heaven. Then I spotted for a hansom with a spanking horse. "A shilling for yourself, if you're there in twenty minutes!" said I to the jarvey. He went a good pace, though of course it was a trifle to the carpet; and in nineteen minutes and a half I was at the door.'

'What door?' asked the captain.

'Oh, a house I know of,' returned Herrick.

'Bet it was a public-house!' cried the clerk, – only these were not his words. 'And w'y didn't you take the carpet there instead of trundling in a growler?'

'I didn't want to startle a quiet street,' said the narrator. 'Bad form. And besides, it was a hansom.'

'Well, and what did you do next?' inquired the captain.

'Oh, I went in,' said Herrick.

'The old folks?' asked the captain.

'That's about it,' said the other, chewing a grass.

'Well, I think you are about the poorest 'and at a yarn!' cried the clerk. 'Crikey, it's like *Ministering Children*! I can tell you there would be more beer and skittles about my little jaunt. I would go and have a B.-and-S. for luck. Then I would get a big ulster with astracan fur, and take my cane and do the la-de-da down Piccadilly. Then I would go to a slap-up restaurant, and have green peas, and a bottle of fizz, and a chump chop – Oh! and I forgot, I'd 'ave some devilled whitebait first – and green gooseberry tart, and 'ot coffee, and some of that form of vice in big bottles with a seal – Benedictine – that's the bloomin' nyme! Then I'd drop into a theatre, and pal on with some chappies, and do the dancing rooms and bars, and that, and wouldn't go 'ome till morning, till daylight doth appear. And the next day I'd have watercresses, 'am, muffin, and fresh butter; wouldn't I just, O my!'

The clerk was interrupted by a fresh attack of coughing.

'Well, now, I'll tell you what I would do,' said the captain: 'I would have none of your fancy rigs with the man driving from the mizzen cross-trees, but a plain fore-and-aft hack cab of the highest registered tonnage. First of all, I would bring up at the market and get a turkey and a sucking-pig. Then I'd go to a wine-merchant's and get a dozen of champagne, and a dozen of some sweet wine, rich and sticky and strong, something in the port or madeira line, the best in the store. Then I'd bear up for a toy-store, and lay out twenty dollars in assorted toys for the piccaninies; and then to a confectioner's and take in cakes and pies and fancy bread, and that stuff with the plums in it; and then to a news-agency and buy all the papers, all the picture ones for the kids, and all the story papers for the old girl about the Earl discovering himself to Anna-Mariar and the escape of the Lady Maude from the private madhouse; and then I'd tell the fellow to drive home.'

'There ought to be some syrup for the kids,' suggested Herrick; 'they like syrup.'

'Yes, syrup for the kids, red syrup at that!' said the captain. 'And those things they pull at, and go pop, and have measly poetry inside. And then I tell you we'd have a thanksgiving-day and Christmas-tree combined. Great Scott, but I would like to see the kids! I guess they would light right out of the house, when they saw daddy driving up. My little Adar – '

The captain stopped sharply.

'Well, keep it up!' said the clerk.

'The damned thing is, I don't know if they ain't starving!' cried the captain.

'They can't be worse off than we are, and that's one comfort,' returned the clerk. 'I defy the devil to make me worse off.'

It seemed as if the devil heard him. The light of the moon had been some time cut off and they had talked in darkness. Now there was heard a roar, which drew impetuously nearer; the face of the lagoon was seen to whiten; and before they had staggered to their feet, a squall burst in rain upon the outcasts. The rage and volume of that avalanche one must have lived in the tropics to conceive; a man panted in its assault, as he might pant under a shower-bath; and the world seemed whelmed in night and water.

They fled, groping for their usual shelter – it might be almost called their home – in the old calaboose; came drenched into its empty chambers; and lay down, three sops of humanity on the cold coral floors, and presently, when the squall was overpast, the others could hear in the darkness the chattering of the clerk's teeth.

'I say, you fellows,' he wailed, 'for God's sake, lie up and try to warm me. I'm blymed if I don't think I'll die else!'

So the three crept together into one wet mass, and lay until day came, shivering and dozing off, and continually re-awakened to wretchedness by the coughing of the clerk.

Chapter Two

Morning on the Beach – The Three Letters

The clouds were all fled, the beauty of the tropic day was spread upon Papeete; and the wall of breaking seas upon the reef, and the palms upon the islet, already trembled in the heat. A French man-of-war was going out, homeward bound; she lay in the middle distance of the port, an ant-heap for activity. In the night a schooner had come in, and now lay far out, hard by the passage; and the yellow flag, the emblem of pestilence, flew on her. From up the coast, a long procession of canoes headed round the point and towards the market, bright as a scarf with the many-coloured clothing of the natives and the piles of fruit. But not even the beauty and the welcome warmth of the morning, not even these naval movements, so interesting to sailors and to idlers, could engage the attention of the outcasts. They were still cold at heart, their mouths sour from the want of sleep, their steps rambling from the lack of food; and they strung like lame geese along the beach in a disheartened silence. It was towards the town they moved; towards the town whence smoke arose, where happier folk were breakfasting; and as they went, their hungry eyes were upon all sides, but they were only scouting for a meal.

A small and dingy schooner lay snug against the quay, with which it was connected by a plank. On the forward deck, under a spot of awning, five Kanakas who made up the crew, were squatted round a basin of fried feis,* and drinking coffee from tin mugs.

'Eight bells: knock off for breakfast!' cried the captain with a miserable heartiness. 'Never tried this craft before; positively my first appearance; guess I'll draw a bumper house.'

---

* *Fei* is the hill banana.

237

He came close up to where the plank rested on the grassy quay; turned his back upon the schooner, and began to whistle that lively air, 'The Irish Washerwoman.' It caught the ears of the Kanaka seamen like a preconcerted signal; with one accord they looked up from their meal and crowded to the ship's side, fei in hand and munching as they looked. Even as a poor brown Pyrenean bear dances in the streets of English towns under his master's baton; even so, but with how much more of spirit and precision, the captain footed it in time to his own whistling, and his long morning shadow capered beyond him on the grass. The Kanakas smiled on the performance; Herrick looked on heavy-eyed, hunger for the moment conquering all sense of shame; and a little farther off, but still hard by, the clerk was torn by the seven devils of the influenza.

The captain stopped suddenly, appeared to perceive his audience for the first time, and represented the part of a man surprised in his private hour of pleasure.

'Hello!' said he.

The Kanakas clapped hands and called upon him to go on.

'No, *sir*!' said the captain. 'No eat, no dance. Savvy?'

'Poor old man!' returned one of the crew. 'Him no eat?'

'Lord, no!' said the captain. 'Like-um too much eat. No got.'

'All right. Me got,' said the sailor; 'you tome here. Plenty tof-fee, plenty fei. Nutha man him tome too.'

'I guess we'll drop right in,' observed the captain; and he and his companions hastened up the plank. They were welcomed on board with the shaking of hands; place was made for them about the basin; a sticky demijohn of molasses was added to the feast in honour of company, and an accordion brought from the fore-castle and significantly laid by the performer's side.

'*Ariana*,'* said he lightly, touching the instrument as he spoke; and he fell to on a long savoury fei, made an end of it, raised his

---

* By-and-bye.

mug of coffee, and nodded across at the spokesman of the crew. 'Here's your health, old man; you're a credit to the South Pacific,' said he.

With the unsightly greed of hounds they glutted themselves with the hot food and coffee; and even the clerk revived and the colour deepened in his eyes. The kettle was drained, the basin cleaned; their entertainers, who had waited on their wants throughout with the pleased hospitality of Polynesians, made haste to bring forward a dessert of island tobacco and rolls of pandanus leaf to serve as paper; and presently all sat about the dishes puffing like Indian Sachems.

'When a man 'as breakfast every day, he don't know what it is,' observed the clerk.

'The next point is dinner,' said Herrick; and then with a passionate utterance: 'I wish to God I was a Kanaka!'

'There's one thing sure,' said the captain. 'I'm about desperate, I'd rather hang than rot here much longer.' And with the word he took the accordion and struck up 'Home, sweet home.'

'O, drop that!' cried Herrick, 'I can't stand that.'

'No more can I,' said the captain. 'I've got to play something though: got to pay the shot, my son.' And he struck up 'John Brown's Body' in a fine sweet baritone: 'Dandy Jim of Carolina', came next; 'Rorin the Bold', 'Swing low, Sweet Chariot', and 'The Beautiful Land' followed. The captain was paying his shot with usury, as he had done many a time before; many a meal had he bought with the same currency from the melodious-minded natives, always, as now, to their delight.

He was in the middle of 'Fifteen Dollars in the Inside Pocket', singing with dogged energy, for the task went sore against the grain, when a sensation was suddenly to be observed among the crew.

'*Tapena Tom harry my*,'* said the spokesman, pointing.

---

* 'Captain Tom is coming.'

And the three beachcombers, following his indication, saw the figure of a man in pyjama trousers and a white jumper approaching briskly from the town.

'That's Tapena Tom, is it?' said the captain, pausing in his music. 'I don't seem to place the brute.'

'We'd better cut,' said the clerk. "E's no good.'

'Well,' said the musician deliberately, 'one can't most generally always tell. I'll try it on, I guess. Music has charms to soothe the savage Tapena, boys. We might strike it rich; it might amount to iced punch in the cabin.'

'Hiced punch? O my!' said the clerk. 'Give him something 'ot, captain. "Way down the Swannee River"; try that.'

'No, *sir*! Looks Scotch,' said the captain; and he struck, for his life, into 'Auld Lang Syne'.

Captain Tom continued to approach with the same business-like alacrity; no change was to be perceived in his bearded face as he came swinging up the plank: he did not even turn his eyes on the performer.

> 'We twa hae paidled in the burn
> Frae morning tide till dine,'

went the song.

Captain Tom had a parcel under his arm, which he laid on the house roof, and then turning suddenly to the strangers: 'Here, you!' he bellowed, 'be off out of that!'

The clerk and Herrick stood not on the order of their going, but fled incontinently by the plank. The performer, on the other hand, flung down the instrument and rose to his full height slowly.

'What's that you say?' he said. 'I've half a mind to give you a lesson in civility.'

'You set up any more of your gab to me,' returned the Scotchman, 'and I'll show ye the wrong side of a jyle. I've heard tell of the three of ye. Ye're not long for here, I can tell ye that. The Government has their eyes upon ye. They make short work of damned beachcombers, I'll say that for the French.'

'You wait till I catch you off your ship!' cried the captain: and then, turning to the crew, 'Good-bye, you fellows!' he said. 'You're gentlemen, anyway! The worst nigger among you would look better upon a quarter-deck than that filthy Scotchman.'

Captain Tom scorned to reply; he watched with a hard smile the departure of his guests; and as soon as the last foot was off the plank, turned to the hands to work cargo.

The beachcombers beat their inglorious retreat along the shore; Herrick first, his face dark with blood, his knees trembling under him with the hysteria of rage. Presently, under the same *purao* where they had shivered the night before, he cast himself down, and groaned aloud, and ground his face into the sand.

'Don't speak to me, don't speak to me. I can't stand it,' broke from him.

The other two stood over him perplexed.

'Wot can't he stand now?' said the clerk. "Asn't he 'ad a meal? *I'm* lickin' my lips.'

Herrick reared up his wild eyes and burning face. 'I can't beg!' he screamed, and again threw himself prone.

'This thing's got to come to an end,' said the captain with an intake of the breath.

'Looks like signs of an end, don't it?' sneered the clerk.

'He's not so far from it, and don't you deceive yourself,' replied the captain. 'Well,' he added in a livelier voice, 'you fellows hang on here, and I'll go and interview my representative.'

Whereupon he turned on his heel, and set off at a swinging sailor's walk towards Papeete.

It was some half-hour later when he returned. The clerk was dozing with his back against the tree: Herrick still lay where he had flung himself; nothing showed whether he slept or waked.

'See, boys!' cried the captain, with that artificial heartiness of his which was at times so painful, 'here's a new idea.' And he produced note-paper, stamped envelopes, and pencils, three of each. 'We can all write home by the mail brigantine; the consul says I can come over to his place and ink up the addresses.'

'Well, that's a start, too,' said the clerk. 'I never thought of that.'

'It was that yarning last night about going home that put me up to it,' said the captain.

'Well, 'and over,' said the clerk. 'I'll 'ave a shy,' and he retired a little distance to the shade of a canoe.

The others remained under the *purao*. Now they would write a word or two, now scribble it out; now they would sit biting at the pencil end and staring seaward; now their eyes would rest on the clerk, where he sat propped on the canoe, leering and coughing, his pencil racing glibly on the paper.

'I can't do it,' said Herrick suddenly. 'I haven't got the heart.'

'See here,' said the captain, speaking with unwonted gravity; 'it may be hard to write, and to write lies at that; and God knows it is; but it's the square thing. It don't cost anything to say you're well and happy, and sorry you can't make a remittance this mail; and if you don't, I'll tell you what I think it is – I think it's about the high-water mark of being a brute beast.'

'It's easy to talk,' said Herrick. 'You don't seem to have written much yourself, I notice.'

'What do you bring in me for?' broke from the captain. His voice was indeed scarce raised above a whisper, but emotion clanged in it. 'What do you know about me? If you had commanded the finest barque that ever sailed from Portland; if you had been drunk in your berth when she struck the breakers in Fourteen Island Group, and hadn't had the wit to stay there and drown, but came on deck, and given drunken orders, and lost six lives – I could understand your talking then! There,' he said more quietly, 'that's my yarn, and now you know it. It's a pretty one for the father of a family. Five men and a woman murdered. Yes,

there was a woman on board, and hadn't no business to be either.
Guess, I sent her to Hell, if there is such a place. I never dared go
home again; and the wife and the little ones went to England to
her father's place. I don't know what's come to them,' he added,
with a bitter shrug.

'Thank you, captain,' said Herrick. 'I never liked you better.'

They shook hands, short and hard, with eyes averted, tenderness swelling in their bosoms.

'Now, boys! to work again at lying!' said the captain.

'I'll give my father up,' returned Herrick with a writhen smile.
'I'll try my sweetheart instead for a change of evils.'

And here is what he wrote: –

'Emma, I have scratched out the beginning to my father, for
I think I can write more easily to you. This is my last farewell to
all, the last you will ever hear or see of an unworthy friend and
son. I have failed in life; I am quite broken down and disgraced.
I pass under a false name; you will have to tell my father that
with all your kindness. It is my own fault. I know, had I chosen,
that I might have done well; and yet I swear to you I tried to
choose. I could not bear that you should think I did not try. For
I loved you all; you must never doubt me in that, you least of all.
I have always unceasingly loved, but what was my love worth?
and what was I worth? I had not the manhood of a common
clerk, I could not work to earn you; I have lost you now, and for
your sake I could be glad of it. When you first came to my
father's house – do you remember those days? – I want you to,
you saw the best of me then, all that was good in me. Do you
remember the day I took your hand and would not let it go –
and the day on Battersea Bridge, when we were looking at a
barge, and I began to tell you one of my silly stories, and broke
off to say I loved you? That was the beginning, and now here is
the end. When you have read this letter, you will go round and
kiss them all good-bye, my father and mother, and the children,

one by one, and poor uncle; and tell them all to forget me, and forget me yourself. Turn the key in the door; let no thought of me return; be done with the poor ghost that pretended he was a man and stole your love. Scorn of myself grinds in me as I write. I should tell you I am well and happy, and want for nothing. I do not exactly make money, or I should send a remittance; but I am well cared for, have friends, live in a beautiful place and climate, such as we have dreamed of together, and no pity need be wasted on me. In such places, you understand, it is easy to live, and live well, but often hard to make sixpence in money. Explain this to my father, he will understand. I have no more to say; only linger, going out, like an unwilling guest. God in heaven bless you. Think of me at the last, here, on a bright beach, the sky and sea immoderately blue, and the great breakers roaring outside on a barrier reef, where a little isle sits green with palms. I am well and strong. It is a more pleasant way to die than if you were crowding about me on a sick-bed. And yet I am dying. This is my last kiss. Forgive, forget the unworthy.'

So far he had written, his paper was all filled, when there returned a memory of evenings at the piano, and that song, the masterpiece of love, in which so many have found the expression of their dearest thoughts. '*Einst, O wunder!*' he added. More was not required; he knew that in his love's heart the context would spring up, escorted with fair images and harmony; of how all through life her name should tremble in his ears, her name be everywhere repeated in the sounds of nature; and when death came, and he lay dissolved, her memory lingered and thrilled among his elements.

> 'Once, O wonder! once from the ashes of my heart
> Arose a blossom –'

Herrick and the captain finished their letters about the same time; each was breathing deep, and their eyes met and were averted as they closed the envelopes.

'Sorry I write so big,' said the captain gruffly. 'Came all of a rush, when it did come.'

'Same here,' said Herrick. 'I could have done with a ream when I got started; but it's long enough for all the good I had to say.'

They were still at the addresses when the clerk strolled up, smirking and twirling his envelope, like a man well pleased. He looked over Herrick's shoulder.

'Hullo,' he said, 'you ain't writing 'ome.'

'I am, though,' said Herrick; 'she lives with my father. Oh, I see what you mean,' he added. 'My real name is Herrick. No more Hay,' – they had both used the same *alias* – 'no more Hay than yours, I daresay.'

'Clean bowled in the middle stump!' laughed the clerk. 'My name's 'Uish if you want to know. Everybody has a false nyme in the Pacific. Lay you five to three the captain 'as.'

'So I have too,' replied the captain; 'and I've never told my own since the day I tore the title-page out of my Bowditch and flung the damned thing into the sea. But I'll tell it to you, boys. John Davis is my name. I'm Davis of the *Sea Ranger*.'

'Dooce you are!' said Huish. 'And what was she? a pirate or a slyver?'

'She was the fastest barque out of Portland, Maine,' replied the captain; 'and for the way I lost her, I might as well have bored a hole in her side with an auger.'

'Oh, you lost her, did you?' said the clerk. ''Ope she was insured?'

No answer being returned to this sally, Huish, still brimming over with vanity and conversation, struck into another subject.

'I've a good mind to read you my letter,' said he. 'I've a good fist with a pen when I choose, and this is a prime lark. She was a barmaid I ran across in Northampton; she was a spanking fine piece, no end of style; and we cottoned at first sight like parties in the play. I suppose I spent the chynge of a fiver on that girl. Well, I 'appened to remember her nyme, so I wrote to her, and told her 'ow I had got rich, and married a queen in the Hislands, and lived in a blooming palace. Such a sight of crammers! I must read you one bit about my opening the nigger parliament in a cocked 'at. It's really prime.'

The captain jumped to his feet. 'That's what you did with the paper that I went and begged for you?' he roared.

It was perhaps lucky for Huish – it was surely in the end unfortunate for all – that he was seized just then by one of his prostrating accesses of cough; his comrades would have else deserted him, so bitter was their resentment. When the fit had passed, the clerk reached out his hand, picked up the letter, which had fallen to the earth, and tore it into fragments, stamp and all.

'Does that satisfy you?' he asked sullenly.

'We'll say no more about it,' replied Davis.

Chapter Three

The Old Calaboose – Destiny at the Door

The old calaboose, in which the waifs had so long harboured, is a low, rectangular enclosure of building at the corner of a shady western avenue and a little townward of the British consulate. Within was a grassy court, littered with wreckage and the traces of vagrant occupation. Six or seven cells opened from the court: the doors, that had once been locked on mutinous whalermen, rotting before them in the grass. No mark remained of their old destination, except the rusty bars upon the windows.

The floor of one of the cells had been a little cleared; a bucket (the last remaining piece of furniture of the three caitiffs) stood full of water by the door, a half cocoanut-shell beside it for a drinking-cup; and on some ragged ends of mat Huish sprawled asleep, his mouth open, his face deathly. The glow of the tropic afternoon, the green of sunbright foliage, stared into that shady place through door and window; and Herrick, pacing to and fro on the coral floor, sometimes paused and laved his face and neck with tepid water from the bucket. His long arrears of suffering, the night's vigil, the insults of the morning, and the harrowing business of the letter, had strung him to that point when pain is almost pleasure, time shrinks to a mere point, and death and life appear indifferent. To and fro he paced like a caged brute; his mind whirling through the universe of thought and memory; his eyes, as he went, skimming the legends on the wall. The crumbling whitewash was all full of them: Tahitian names, and French, and English, and rude sketches of ships under sail and men at fisticuffs.

It came to him of a sudden that he too must leave upon these walls the memorial of his passage. He paused before a clean

247

space, took the pencil out, and pondered. Vanity, so hard to dislodge, awoke in him. We call it vanity at least; perhaps unjustly. Rather it was the bare sense of his existence prompted him; the sense of his life, the one thing wonderful, to which he scarce clung with a finger. From his jarred nerves, there came a strong sentiment of coming change; whether good or ill he could not say: change, he knew no more – change, with inscrutable veiled face, approaching noiseless. With the feeling, came the vision of a concert room, the rich hues of instruments, the silent audience, and the loud voice of the symphony. 'Destiny knocking at the door,' he thought; drew a stave on the plaster, and wrote in the famous phrase from the Fifth Symphony. 'So,' thought he, 'they will know that I loved music and had classical tastes. They? He, I suppose: the unknown, kindred spirit that shall come some day and read my *memor querela*. Ha, he shall have Latin too!' And he added: *terque quaterque beati Queis ante ora patrum.*

He turned again to his uneasy pacing, but now with an irrational and supporting sense of duty done. He had dug his grave that morning; now he had carved his epitaph; the folds of the toga were composed, why should he delay the insignificant trifle that remained to do? He paused and looked long in the face of the sleeping Huish, drinking disenchantment and distaste of life. He nauseated himself with that vile countenance. Could the thing continue? What bound him now? Had he no rights? – only the obligation to go on, without discharge or furlough, bearing the unbearable? *Ich trage unerträgliches*, the quotation rose in his mind; he repeated the whole piece, one of the most perfect of the most perfect of poets; and a phrase struck him like a blow: *Du, stolzes Herz, du hast es ja gewollt.* Where was the pride of his heart? And he raged against himself, as a man bites on a sore tooth, in a heady sensuality of scorn. 'I have no pride, I have no heart, no manhood,' he thought, 'or why should I prolong a life more shameful than the gallows? Or why should I have fallen to it? No pride, no capacity, no force. Not even a bandit! and to be starving here with worse than banditti – with this trivial hell-hound!' His rage against his comrade rose and flooded him, and he shook a trembling fist at the sleeper.

A swift step was audible. The captain appeared upon the threshold of the cell, panting and flushed, and with a foolish face of happiness. In his arms he carried a loaf of bread and bottles of beer; the pockets of his coat were bulging with cigars. He rolled his treasures on the floor, grasped Herrick by both hands, and crowed with laughter.

'Broach the beer!' he shouted. 'Broach the beer, and glory hallelujah!'

'Beer?' repeated Huish, struggling to his feet.

'Beer it is!' cried Davis. 'Beer and plenty of it. Any number of persons can use it (like Lyon's tooth-tablet) with perfect propriety and neatness. Who's to officiate?'

'Leave me alone for that,' said the clerk. He knocked the necks off with a lump of coral, and each drank in succession from the shell.

'Have a weed,' said Davis. 'It's all in the bill.'

'What is up?' asked Herrick.

The captain fell suddenly grave. 'I'm coming to that,' said he. 'I want to speak with Herrick here. You, Hay – or Huish, or whatever your name is – you take a weed and the other bottle, and go and see how the wind is down by the *purao*. I'll call you when you're wanted!'

'Hey? Secrets? That ain't the ticket,' said Huish.

'Look here, my son,' said the captain, 'this is business, and don't you make any mistake about it. If you're going to make trouble, you can have it your own way and stop right here. Only get the thing right: if Herrick and I go, we take the beer. Savvy?'

'Oh, I don't want to shove my oar in,' returned Huish. 'I'll cut right enough. Give me the swipes. You can jaw till you're blue in the face for what I care. I don't think it's the friendly touch: that's all.' And he shambled grumbling out of the cell into the staring sun.

The captain watched him clear of the courtyard; then turned to Herrick.

'What is it?' asked Herrick thickly.

'I'll tell you,' said Davis. 'I want to consult you. It's a chance we've got. What's that?' he cried, pointing to the music on the wall.

'What?' said the other. 'Oh, that! It's music; it's a phrase of Beethoven's I was writing up. It means Destiny knocking at the door.'

'Does it?' said the captain, rather low; and he went near and studied the inscription; 'and this French?' he asked, pointing to the Latin.

'O, it just means I should have been luckier if I had died at home,' returned Herrick impatiently. 'What is this business?'

'Destiny knocking at the door,' repeated the captain; and then, looking over his shoulder, 'Well, Mr Herrick, that's about what it comes to,' he added.

'What do you mean? Explain yourself,' said Herrick.

But the captain was again staring at the music. 'About how long ago since you wrote up this truck?' he asked.

'What does it matter?' exclaimed Herrick. 'I daresay half-an-hour.'

'My God, it's strange!' cried Davis. 'There's some men would call that accidental: not me. That – 'and he drew his thick finger under the music – 'that's what I call Providence.'

'You said we had a chance,' said Herrick.

'Yes, *sir*!' said the captain, wheeling suddenly face to face with his companion. 'I did so. If you're the man I take you for, we have a chance.'

'I don't know what you take me for,' was the reply. 'You can scarce take me too low.'

'Shake hands, Mr Herrick,' said the captain. 'I know you. You're a gentleman and a man of spirit. I didn't want to speak before that bummer there; you'll see why. But to you I'll rip it right out. I got a ship.'

'A ship?' cried Herrick. 'What ship?'

'That schooner we saw this morning off the passage.'

'The schooner with the hospital flag?'

'That's the hooker,' said Davis. 'She's the *Farallone*, hundred and sixty tons register, out of 'Frisco for Sydney, in California champagne. Captain, mate, and one hand all died of the smallpox, same as they had round in the Paumotus, I guess. Captain and mate were the only white men; all the hands Kanakas; seems a queer kind of outfit from a Christian port. Three of them left and a cook; didn't know where they were; I can't think where they were either, if you come to that; Wiseman must have been on the booze, I guess, to sail the course he did. However, there *he* was, dead; and here are the Kanakas as good as lost. They bummed around at sea like the babes in the wood; and tumbled end-on upon Tahiti. The consul here took charge. He offered the berth to Williams; Williams had never had the small-pox and backed down. That was when I came in for the letter-paper; I thought there was something up when the consul asked me to look in again; but I never let on to you fellows, so 's you'd not be disappointed. Consul tried M'Neil; scared of small-pox. He tried Capirati, that Corsican, and Leblue, or whatever his name is, wouldn't lay a hand on it; all too fond of their sweet lives. Last of all, when there wasn't nobody else left to offer it to, he offers it to me. "Brown, will you ship captain and take her to Sydney?" says he. "Let me choose my own mate and another white hand," says I, "for I don't hold with this Kanaka crew racket; give us all two months' advance to get our clothes and instruments out of pawn, and I'll take stock tonight, fill up stores, and get to sea tomorrow before dark!" That's what I said. "That's good enough," says the consul, "and you can count yourself damned lucky, Brown," says he. And he said it pretty meaningful-appearing, too. However, that's all one now. I'll ship Huish before the mast – of course I'll let him berth aft – and I'll ship you mate at seventy-five dollars and two months' advance.'

'Me mate? Why, I'm a landsman!' cried Herrick.

'Guess you've got to learn,' said the captain. 'You don't fancy I'm going to skip and leave you rotting on the beach perhaps? I'm not that sort, old man. And you're handy anyway; I've been ship-mates with worse.'

'God knows I can't refuse,' said Herrick. 'God knows I thank you from my heart.'

'That's all right,' said the captain. 'But it ain't all.' He turned aside to light a cigar.

'What else is there?' asked the other, with a pang of undefinable alarm.

'I'm coming to that,' said Davis, and then paused a little. 'See here,' he began, holding out his cigar between his finger and thumb, 'suppose you figure up what this'll amount to. You don't catch on? Well, we get two months' advance; we can't get away from Papeete – our creditors wouldn't let us go – for less; it'll take us along about two months to get to Sydney; and when we get there, I just want to put it to you squarely: What the better are we?'

'We're off the beach at least,' said Herrick.

'I guess there's a beach at Sydney,' returned the captain; 'and I'll tell you one thing, Mr Herrick – I don't mean to try. No, *sir*! Sydney will never see me.'

'Speak out plain,' said Herrick.

'Plain Dutch,' replied the captain. 'I'm going to own that schooner. It's nothing new; it's done every year in the Pacific. Stephens stole a schooner the other day, didn't he? Hayes and Pease stole vessels all the time. And it's the making of the crowd of us. See here – you think of that cargo. Champagne! why, it's like as if it was put up on purpose. In Peru we'll sell that liquor off at the pier-head, and the schooner after it, if we can find a fool to buy her; and then light out for the mines. If you'll back me up, I stake my life I carry it through.'

'Captain,' said Herrick, with a quailing voice, 'don't do it!'

'I'm desperate,' returned Davis. 'I've got a chance; I may never get another. Herrick, say the word; back me up; I think we've starved together long enough for that.'

'I can't do it. I'm sorry. I can't do it. I've not fallen as low as that,' said Herrick, deadly pale.

'What did you say this morning?' said Davis. 'That you couldn't beg? It's the one thing or the other, my son.'

'Ah, but this is the jail!' cried Herrick. 'Don't tempt me. It's the jail.'

'Did you hear what the skipper said on board that schooner?' pursued the captain. 'Well, I tell you he talked straight. The French have let us alone for a long time; it can't last longer; they've got their eye on us; and as sure as you live, in three weeks you'll be in jail whatever you do. I read it in the consul's face.'

'You forget, captain,' said the young man. 'There is another way. I can die; and to say truth, I think I should have died three years ago.'

The captain folded his arms and looked the other in the face. 'Yes,' said he, 'yes, you can cut your throat; that's a frozen fact; much good may it do you! And where do I come in?'

The light of a strange excitement came in Herrick's face. 'Both of us,' said he, 'both of us together. It's not possible you can enjoy this business. Come,' and he reached out a timid hand, 'a few strokes in the lagoon – and rest!'

'I tell you, Herrick, I'm 'most tempted to answer you the way the man does in the Bible, and say, *"Get thee behind me, Satan!"*' said the captain. 'What! you think I would go drown myself, and I got children starving? Enjoy it? No, by God, I do not enjoy it! but it's the row I've got to hoe, and I'll hoe it till I drop right here. I have three of them, you see, two boys and the one girl, Adar. The trouble is that you are not a parent yourself. I tell you, Herrick, I love you,' the man broke out; 'I didn't take to you at first, you were so anglified and tony, but I love you now; it's a man that loves you stands here and wrestles with you. I can't go to sea with

253

the bummer alone; it's not possible. Go drown yourself, and there goes my last chance – the last chance of a poor miserable beast, earning a crust to feed his family. I can't do nothing but sail ships, and I've no papers. And here I get a chance, and you go back on me! Ah, you've no family, and that's where the trouble is!'

'I have indeed,' said Herrick.

'Yes, I know,' said the captain, 'you think so. But no man's got a family till he's got children. It's only the kids count. There's something about the little shavers . . . I can't talk of them. And if you thought a cent about this father that I hear you talk of, or that sweetheart you were writing to this morning, you would feel like me. You would say, What matter laws, and God, and that? My folks are hard up, I belong to them, I'll get them bread, or, by God! I'll get them wealth, if I have to burn down London for it. That's what you would say. And I'll tell you more: your heart is saying so this living minute. I can see it in your face. You're thinking, Here's poor friendship for the man I've starved along of, and as for the girl that I set up to be in love with, here's a mighty limp kind of a love that won't carry me as far as 'most any man would go for a demijohn of whisky. There's not much *ro*mance to that love, anyway; it's not the kind they carry on about in song-books. But what's the good of my carrying on talking, when it's all in your inside as plain as print? I put the question to you once for all. Are you going to desert me in my hour of need? – you know if I've deserted you – or will you give me your hand, and try a fresh deal, and go home (as like as not) a millionaire? Say no, and God pity me! Say yes, and I'll make the little ones pray for you every night on their bended knees. "God bless Mr Herrick!" that's what they'll say, one after the other, the old girl sitting there holding stakes at the foot of the bed, and the damned little innocents . . .' he broke off. 'I don't often rip out about the kids,' he said; 'but when I do, there's something fetches loose.'

'Captain,' said Herrick faintly, 'is there nothing else?'

'I'll prophesy if you like,' said the captain with renewed vigour.

'Refuse this, because you think yourself too honest, and before a month's out you'll be jailed for a sneak-thief. I give you the word fair. I can see it, Herrick, if you can't; you're breaking down. Don't think, if you refuse this chance, that you'll go on doing the evangelical; you're about through with your stock; and before you know where you are, you'll be right out on the other side. No, it's either this for you; or else it's [New] Caledonia. I bet you never were there, and saw those white, shaved men, in their dust clothes and straw hats, prowling around in gangs in the lamplight at Noumea, they look like wolves, and they look like preachers, and they look like the sick; Huish is a daisy to the best of them. Well, there's your company. They're waiting for you, Herrick, and you got to go; and that's a prophecy.'

And as the man stood and shook through his great stature, he seemed indeed like one in whom the spirit of divination worked and might utter oracles. Herrick looked at him, and looked away; it seemed not decent to spy upon such agitation; and the young man's courage sank.

'You talk of going home,' he objected. 'We could never do that.'

'*We* could,' said the other. 'Captain Brown couldn't, nor Mr Hay, that shipped mate with him couldn't. But what's that to do with Captain Davis or Mr Herrick, you galoot?'

'But Hayes had these wild islands where he used to call,' came the next fainter objection.

'We have the wild islands of Peru,' retorted Davis. 'They were wild enough for Stephens, no longer agone than just last year. I guess they'll be wild enough for us.'

'And the crew?'

'All Kanakas. Come, I see you're right, old man. I see you'll stand by.' And the captain once more offered his hand.

'Have it your own way then,' said Herrick. 'I'll do it: a strange thing for my father's son. But I'll do it. I'll stand by you, man, for good or evil.'

'God bless you!' cried the captain, and stood silent. 'Herrick,' he added with a smile, 'I believe I'd have died in my tracks, if you'd said, No!'

And Herrick, looking at the man, half believed so also.

'And now we'll go break it to the bummer,' said Davis.

'I wonder how he'll take it,' said Herrick.

'Him? Jump at it!' was the reply.

Chapter Four

The Yellow Flag

The schooner *Farallone* lay well out in the jaws of the pass, where the terrified pilot had made haste to bring her to her moorings and escape. Seen from the beach through the thin line of shipping, two objects stood conspicuous to seaward: the little isle, on the one hand, with its palms and the guns and batteries raised forty years before in defence of Queen Pomare's capital; the outcast *Farallone*, upon the other, banished to the threshold of the port, rolling there to her scuppers, and flaunting the plague-flag as she rolled. A few sea-birds screamed and cried about the ship; and within easy range, a man-of-war guard-boat hung off and on and glittered with the weapons of marines. The exuberant daylight and the blinding heaven of the tropics picked out and framed the pictures.

A neat boat, manned by natives in uniform, and steered by the doctor of the port, put from shore towards three of the afternoon, and pulled smartly for the schooner. The foresheets were heaped with sacks of flour, onions, and potatoes, perched among which was Huish dressed as a foremast hand; a heap of chests and cases impeded the action of the oarsmen; and in the stern, by the left hand of the doctor, sat Herrick, dressed in a fresh rig of slops, his brown beard trimmed to a point, a pile of paper novels on his lap, and nursing the while between his feet a chronometer, for which they had exchanged that of the *Farallone*, long since run down and the rate lost.

They passed the guard-boat, exchanging hails with the boatswain's mate in charge, and drew near at last to the forbidden ship. Not a cat stirred, there was no speech of man; and the sea being exceeding high outside, and the reef close to where the schooner lay, the clamour of the surf hung round her like the sound of battle.

'*Ohé la goëlette!*' sang out the doctor, with his best voice.

Instantly, from the house where they had been stowing away stores, first Davis, and then the ragamuffin, swarthy crew made their appearance.

'Hullo, Hay, that you?' said the captain, leaning on the rail. 'Tell the old man to lay her alongside, as if she was eggs. There's a hell of a run of sea here, and his boat's brittle.'

The movement of the schooner was at that time more than usually violent. Now she heaved her side as high as a deep-sea steamer's, and showed the flashing of her copper; now she swung swiftly toward the boat until her scuppers gurgled.

'I hope you have sea-legs,' observed the doctor. 'You will require them.'

Indeed, to board the *Farallone*, in that exposed position where she lay, was an affair of some dexterity. The less precious goods were hoisted roughly in; the chronometer, after repeated failures, was passed gently and successfully from hand to hand; and there remained only the more difficult business of embarking Huish. Even that piece of dead weight (shipped A. B. at eighteen dollars, and described by the captain to the consul as an invaluable man) was at last hauled on board without mishap; and the doctor, with civil salutations, took his leave.

The three co-adventurers looked at each other, and Davis heaved a breath of relief.

'Now let's get this chronometer fixed,' said he, and led the way into the house. It was a fairly spacious place; two state-rooms and a good-sized pantry opened from the main cabin; the bulk-heads were painted white, the floor laid with waxcloth. No litter, no sign of life remained; for the effects of the dead men had been disinfected and conveyed on shore. Only on the table, in a saucer, some sulphur burned, and the fumes set them coughing as they entered. The captain peered into the starboard stateroom, where the bed-clothes still lay tumbled in the bunk, the blanket flung back as they had flung it back from the disfigured corpse before its burial.

'Now, I told these niggers to tumble that truck overboard,' grumbled Davis. 'Guess they were afraid to lay hands on it. Well, they've hosed the place out; that's as much as can be expected, I suppose. Huish, lay on to these blankets.'

'See you blooming well far enough first,' said Huish, drawing back.

'What's that?' snapped the captain. 'I'll tell you, my young friend, I think you make a mistake. I'm captain here.'

'Fat lot I care,' returned the clerk.

'That so?' said Davis. 'Then you'll berth forward with the niggers! Walk right out of this cabin.'

'Oh, I dessay!' said Huish. 'See any green in my eye? A lark's a lark.'

'Well, now, I'll explain this business, and you'll see (once for all) just precisely how much lark there is to it,' said Davis. 'I'm captain, and I'm going to be it. One thing of three. First, you take my orders here as cabin steward, in which case you mess with us. Or second, you refuse, and I pack you forward – and you get as quick as the word's said. Or, third and last, I'll signal that man-of-war and send you ashore under arrest for mutiny.'

'And, of course, I wouldn't blow the gaff? O no!' replied the jeering Huish.

'And who's to believe you, my son?' inquired the captain. 'No, *sir*! There ain't no lark about my captainizing. Enough said. Up with these blankets.'

Huish was no fool, he knew when he was beaten; and he was no coward either, for he stepped to the bunk, took the infected bed-clothes fairly in his arms, and carried them out of the house without a check or tremor.

'I was waiting for the chance,' said Davis to Herrick. 'I needn't do the same with you, because you understand it for yourself.'

'Are you going to berth here?' asked Herrick, following the captain into the stateroom, where he began to adjust the chronometer in its place at the bed-head.

'Not much!' replied he. 'I guess I'll berth on deck. I don't know as I'm afraid, but I've no immediate use for confluent smallpox.'

'I don't know that I'm afraid either,' said Herrick. 'But the thought of these two men sticks in my throat; that captain and mate dying here, one opposite to the other. It's grim. I wonder what they said last?'

'Wiseman and Wishart?' said the captain. 'Probably mighty small potatoes. That's a thing a fellow figures out for himself one way, and the real business goes quite another. Perhaps Wiseman said, "Here, old man, fetch up the gin, I'm feeling powerful rocky." And perhaps Wishart said, "Oh, hell!"'

'Well, that's grim enough,' said Herrick.

'And so it is,' said Davis. 'There; there's that chronometer fixed. And now it's about time to up anchor and clear out.'

He lit a cigar and stepped on deck.

'Here, you! What's *your* name?' he cried to one of the hands, a lean-flanked, clean-built fellow from some far western island, and of a darkness almost approaching to the African.

'Sally Day,' replied the man.

'Devil it is,' said the captain. 'Didn't know we had ladies on board. Well, Sally, oblige me by hauling down that rag there. I'll do the same for you another time.' He watched the yellow bunting as it was eased past the cross-trees and handed down on deck. 'You'll float no more on this ship,' he observed. 'Muster the people aft, Mr Hay,' he added, speaking unnecessarily loud, 'I've a word to say to them.'

It was with a singular sensation that Herrick prepared for the first time to address a crew. He thanked his stars indeed, that they were natives. But even natives, he reflected, might be critics too quick for such a novice as himself; they might perceive some lapse from that precise and cut-and-dry English which prevails on board a ship; it was even possible they understood no other; and he racked his brain, and overhauled his reminiscences of sea romance for some appropriate words.

'Here, men! tumble aft!' he said. 'Lively now! all hands aft!'

They crowded in the alleyway like sheep.

'Here they are, sir,' said Herrick.

For some time the captain continued to face the stern; then turned with ferocious suddenness on the crew, and seemed to enjoy their shrinking.

'Now,' he said, twisting his cigar in his mouth and toying with the spokes of the wheel, 'I'm Captain Brown. I command this ship. This is Mr Hay, first officer. The other white man is cabin steward, but he'll stand watch and do his trick. My orders shall be obeyed smartly. You savvy, "*smartly*"? There shall be no growling about the kaikai, which will be above allowance. You'll put a handle to the mate's name, and tack on "sir" to every order I give you. If you're smart and quick, I'll make this ship comfortable for all hands.' He took the cigar out of his mouth. 'If you're not,' he added, in a roaring voice, 'I'll make it a floating hell. Now, Mr Hay, we'll pick watches, if you please.'

'All right,' said Herrick.

'You will please use "sir" when you address me, Mr Hay,' said the captain. 'I'll take the lady. Step to starboard, Sally.' And then he whispered in Herrick's ear: 'take the old man.'

'I'll take you, there,' said Herrick.

'What's your name?' said the captain. 'What's that you say? Oh, that's not English; I'll have none of your highway gibberish on my ship. We'll call you old Uncle Ned, because you've got no wool on the top of your head, just the place where the wool ought to grow. Step to port, Uncle. Don't you hear Mr Hay has picked you? Then I'll take the white man. White Man, step to starboard. Now which of you two is the cook? You? Then Mr Hay takes your friend in the blue dungaree. Step to port, Dungaree. There, we know who we all are: Dungaree, Uncle Ned, Sally Day,

White Man, and Cook. All F. F. V.'s I guess. And now, Mr Hay, we'll up anchor, if you please.'

'For heaven's sake, tell me some of the words,' whispered Herrick.

An hour later, the *Farallone* was under all plain sail, the rudder hard a-port, and the cheerfully-clanking windlass had brought the anchor home.

'All clear, sir,' cried Herrick from the bow.

The captain met her with the wheel, as she bounded like a stag from her repose, trembling and bending to the puffs. The guard-boat gave a parting hail, the wake whitened and ran out; the *Farallone* was under weigh.

Her berth had been close to the pass. Even as she forged ahead Davis slewed her for the channel between the pier ends of the reef, the breakers sounding and whitening to either hand. Straight through the narrow band of blue, she shot to seaward: and the captain's heart exulted as he felt her tremble underfoot, and (looking back over the taffrail) beheld the roofs of Papeete changing position on the shore and the island mountains rearing higher in the wake.

But they were not yet done with the shore and the horror of the yellow flag. About midway of the pass, there was a cry and a scurry, a man was seen to leap upon the rail, and, throwing his arms over his head, to stoop and plunge into the sea.

'Steady as she goes,' the captain cried, relinquishing the wheel to Huish.

The next moment he was forward in the midst of the Kanakas, belaying-pin in hand.

'Anybody else for shore?' he cried, and the savage trumpeting of his voice, no less than the ready weapon in his hand, struck fear in all. Stupidly they stared after their escaped companion, whose black head was visible upon the water, steering for the land. And the schooner meanwhile slipt like a racer through the pass, and met the long sea of the open ocean with a souse of spray.

'Fool that I was, not to have a pistol ready!' exclaimed Davies. 'Well, we go to sea short-handed, we can't help that. You have a lame watch of it, Mr Hay.'

'I don't see how we are to get along,' said Herrick.

'Got to,' said the captain. 'No more Tahiti for me.'

Both turned instinctively and looked astern. The fair island was unfolding mountain-top on mountain-top; Eimeo, on the port board, lifted her splintered pinnacles; and still the schooner raced to the open sea.

'Think!' cried the captain with a gesture, 'yesterday morning I danced for my breakfast like a poodle dog.'

Chapter Five

The Cargo of Champagne

The ship's head was laid to clear Eimeo to the north, and the captain sat down in the cabin, with a chart, a ruler, and an epitome.

'East a half no'the,' said he, raising his face from his labours. 'Mr Hay, you'll have to watch your dead reckoning; I want every yard she makes on every hair's-breadth of a course. I'm going to knock a hole right straight through the Paumotus, and that's always a near touch. Now, if this South East Trade ever blew out of the S. E., which it don't, we might hope to lie within half a point of our course. Say we lie within a point of it. That'll just about weather Fakarava. Yes, sir, that's what we've got to do, if we tack for it. Brings us through this slush of little islands in the cleanest place: see?' And he showed where his ruler intersected the wide-lying labyrinth of the Dangerous Archipelago. 'I wish it was night, and I could put her about right now; we're losing time and easting. Well, we'll do our best. And if we don't fetch Peru, we'll bring up to Ecuador. All one, I guess. Depreciated dollars down, and no questions asked. A remarkable fine institootion, the South American don.'

Tahiti was already some way astern, the Diadem rising from among broken mountains – Eimeo was already close aboard, and stood black and strange against the golden splendour of the west – when the captain took his departure from the two islands, and the patent log was set.

Some twenty minutes later, Sally Day, who was continually leaving the wheel to peer in at the cabin clock, announced in a shrill cry 'Fo' bell,' and the cook was to be seen carrying the soup into the cabin.

'I guess I'll sit down and have a pick with you,' said Davis to

Herrick. 'By the time I've done, it'll be dark, and we'll clap the hooker on the wind for South America.'

In the cabin at one corner of the table, immediately below the lamp, and on the lee side of a bottle of champagne, sat Huish.

'What's this? Where did that come from?' asked the captain.

'It's fizz, and it came from the after-'old, if you want to know,' said Huish, and drained his mug.

'This'll never do,' exclaimed Davis, the merchant seaman's horror of breaking into cargo showing incongruously forth on board that stolen ship. 'There was never any good came of games like that.'

'You byby!' said Huish. 'A fellow would think (to 'ear him) we were on the square! And look 'ere, you've put this job up 'ansomely for me, 'aven't you? I'm to go on deck and steer while you two sit and guzzle, and I'm to go by a nickname, and got to call you "sir" and "mister". Well, you look here, my bloke: I'll have fizz *ad lib.*, or it won't wash. I tell you that. And you know mighty well, you ain't got any man-of-war to signal now.'

Davis was staggered. 'I'd give fifty dollars this had never happened,' he said weakly.

'Well, it *as* 'appened, you see,' returned Huish. 'Try some; it's devilish good.'

The Rubicon was crossed without another struggle. The captain filled a mug and drank.

'I wish it was beer,' he said with a sigh. 'But there's no denying it's the genuine stuff and cheap at the money. Now, Huish, you clear out and take your wheel.'

The little wretch had gained a point, and he was gay. 'Ay, ay, sir,' said he, and left the others to their meal.

'Pea soup!' exclaimed the captain. 'Blamed if I thought I should taste pea soup again!'

Herrick sat inert and silent. It was impossible after these months of hopeless want to smell the rough, high-spiced sea victuals without lust, and his mouth watered with desire of the champagne. It was no less impossible to have assisted at the scene between Huish and the captain, and not to perceive, with sudden bluntness, the gulf where he had fallen. He was a thief among thieves. He said it to himself. He could not touch the soup. If he had moved at all, it must have been to leave the table, throw himself overboard, and drown – an honest man.

'Here,' said the captain, 'you look sick, old man; have a drop of this.'

The champagne creamed and bubbled in the mug; its bright colour, its lively effervescence, seized his eye. 'It is too late to hesitate,' he thought; his hand took the mug instinctively; he drank, with unquenchable pleasure and desire of more; drained the vessel dry, and set it down with sparkling eyes.

'There is something in life after all!' he cried. 'I had forgot what it was like. Yes, even this is worth while. Wine, food, dry clothes – why, they're worth dying, worth hanging for! Captain, tell me one thing: why aren't all the poor folk foot-pads?'

'Give it up,' said the captain.

'They must be damned good,' cried Herrick. 'There's something here beyond me. Think of that calaboose! Suppose we were sent suddenly back.' He shuddered as stung by a convulsion, and buried his face in his clutching hands.

'Here, what's wrong with you?' cried the captain. There was no reply; only Herrick's shoulders heaved, so that the table was shaken. 'Take some more of this. Here, drink this. I order you to. Don't start crying when you're out of the wood.'

'I'm not crying,' said Herrick, raising his face and showing his dry eyes. 'It's worse than crying. It's the horror of that grave that we've escaped from.'

'Come now, you tackle your soup; that'll fix you,' said Davis kindly. 'I told you you were all broken up. You couldn't have stood out another week.'

'That's the dreadful part of it!' cried Herrick. 'Another week and I'd have murdered some one for a dollar! God! and I know that? And I'm still living? It's some beastly dream.'

'Quietly, quietly! Quietly does it, my son. Take your pea soup. Food, that's what you want,' said Davis.

The soup strengthened and quieted Herrick's nerves; another glass of wine, and a piece of pickled pork and fried banana completed what the soup began; and he was able once more to look the captain in the face.

'I didn't know I was so much run down,' he said.

'Well,' said Davis, 'you were as steady as a rock all day: now you've had a little lunch, you'll be as steady as a rock again.'

'Yes,' was the reply, 'I'm steady enough now, but I'm a queer kind of a first officer.'

'Shucks!' cried the captain. 'You've only got to mind the ship's course, and keep your slate to half a point. A babby could do that, let alone a college graduate like you. There ain't nothing *to* sailoring, when you come to look it in the face. And now we'll go and put her about. Bring the slate; we'll have to start our dead reckoning right away.'

The distance run since the departure was read off the log by the binnacle light and entered on the slate.

'Ready about,' said the captain. 'Give me the wheel, White Man, and you stand by the mainsheet. Boom tackle, Mr Hay, please, and then you can jump forward and attend head sails.'

'Ay, ay, sir,' responded Herrick.

'All clear forward?' asked Davis.

'All clear, sir.'

'Hard a-lee!' cried the captain. 'Haul in your slack as she comes,' he called to Huish. 'Haul in your slack, put your back into it; keep your feet out of the coils.' A sudden blow sent Huish flat along the deck, and the captain was in his place. 'Pick yourself up and keep the wheel hard over!' he roared. 'You wooden fool, you wanted to get killed, I guess. Draw the jib,' he cried a moment later; and then to Huish, 'Give me the wheel again, and see if you can coil that sheet.'

But Huish stood and looked at Davis with an evil countenance. 'Do you know you struck me?' said he.

'Do you know I saved your life?' returned the other, not deigning to look at him, his eyes travelling instead between the compass and the sails. 'Where would you have been, if that boom had swung out and you bundled in the slack? No, *sir*, we'll have no more of you at the mainsheet. Seaport towns are full of mainsheet-men; they hop upon one leg, my son, what's left of them, and the rest are dead. (Set your boom tackle, Mr Hay.) Struck you, did I? Lucky for you I did.'

'Well,' said Huish slowly, 'I dessay there may be somethink in that. 'Ope there is.' He turned his back elaborately on the captain, and entered the house, where the speedy explosion of a champagne cork showed he was attending to his comfort.

Herrick came aft to the captain. 'How is she doing now?' he asked.

'East and by no'the a half no'the,' said Davis. 'It's about as good as I expected.'

'What'll the hands think of it?' said Herrick.

'Oh, they don't think. They ain't paid to,' says the captain.

'There was something wrong, was there not? between you and –' Herrick paused.

'That's a nasty little beast, that's a biter,' replied the captain, shaking his head. 'But so long as you and me hang in, it don't matter.'

Herrick lay down in the weather alleyway; the night was cloudless, the movement of the ship cradled him, he was oppressed besides by the first generous meal after so long a time of famine; and he was recalled from deep sleep by the voice of Davis singing out: 'Eight bells!'

He rose stupidly and staggered aft, where the captain gave him the wheel.

'By the wind,' said the captain. 'It comes a little puffy; when you get a heavy puff, steal all you can to windward, but keep her a good full.'

He stepped towards the house, paused and hailed the forecastle.

'Got such a thing as a concertina forward?' said he. 'Bully for you, Uncle Ned. Fetch it aft, will you?'

The schooner steered very easy; and Herrick, watching the moon-whitened sails, was overpowered by drowsiness. A sharp report from the cabin startled him; a third bottle had been opened; and Herrick remembered the *Sea Ranger* and Fourteen Island Group. Presently the notes of the accordion sounded, and then the captain's voice:

'O honey, with our pockets full of money,
We will trip, trip, trip, we will trip it on the quay,
And I will dance with Kate, and Tom will dance with Sall,
When we're all back from South Amerikee.'

So it went to its quaint air; and the watch below lingered and listened by the forward door, and Uncle Ned was to be seen in the moonlight nodding time; and Herrick smiled at the wheel, his anxieties a while forgotten. Song followed song; another cork exploded; there were voices raised, as though the pair in the cabin were in disagreement; and presently it seemed the breach was healed; for it was now the voice of Huish that struck up, to the captain's accompaniment –

'Up in a balloon, boys,
Up in a balloon,
All among the little stars
And round about the moon.'

A wave of nausea overcame Herrick at the wheel. He wondered why the air, the words (which were yet written with a certain knack), and the voice and accent of the singer, should all jar his spirit like a file on a man's teeth. He sickened at the thought of his two comrades drinking away their reason upon stolen wine, quarrelling and hiccupping and waking up, while the doors of a prison yawned for them in the near future. 'Shall I have sold my honour for nothing?' he thought; and a heat of rage and resolution glowed in his bosom – rage against his comrades – resolution to carry through this business if it might be carried; pluck profit out of shame, since the shame at least was now inevitable; and come home, home from South America – how did the song go? – 'with his pockets full of money'.

> 'O honey, with our pockets full of money,
> We will trip, trip, trip, we will trip it on the quay:'

so the words ran in his head; and the honey took on visible form, the quay rose before him and he knew it for the lamplit Embankment, and he saw the lights of Battersea bridge bestride the sullen river. All through the remainder of his trick, he stood entranced, reviewing the past. He had been always true to his love, but not always sedulous to recall her. In the growing calamity of his life, she had swum more distant, like the moon in mist. The letter of farewell, the dishonourable hope that had surprised and corrupted him in his distress, the changed scene, the sea, the night and the music – all stirred him to the roots of manhood. 'I *will* win her,' he thought, and ground his teeth. 'Fair or foul, what matters if I win her?'

'Fo' bell, matey. I think um fo' bell' – he was suddenly recalled by these words in the voice of Uncle Ned.

'Look in at the clock, Uncle,' said he. He would not look himself, from horror of the tipplers.

'Him past, matey,' repeated the Hawaiian.

'So much the better for you, Uncle,' he replied; and he gave up the wheel, repeating the directions as he had received them.

He took two steps forward and remembered his dead reckoning. 'How has she been heading?' he thought; and he flushed from head to foot. He had not observed or had forgotten; here was the old incompetence; the slate must be filled up by guess. 'Never again!' he vowed to himself in silent fury, 'never again. It shall be no fault of mine if this miscarry.' And for the remainder of his watch, he stood close by Uncle Ned, and read the face of the compass as perhaps he had never read a letter from his sweetheart.

All the time, and spurring him to the more attention, song, loud talk, fleering laughter and the occasional popping of a cork, reached his ears from the interior of the house; and when the port watch was relieved at midnight, Huish and the captain appeared upon the quarter-deck with flushed faces and uneven steps, the former laden with bottles, the latter with two tin mugs. Herrick silently passed them by. They hailed him in thick voices, he made no answer, they cursed him for a churl, he paid no heed although his belly quivered with disgust and rage. He closed-to the door of the house behind him, and cast himself on a locker in the cabin – not to sleep he thought – rather to think and to despair. Yet he had scarce turned twice on his uneasy bed, before a drunken voice hailed him in the ear, and he must go on deck again to stand the morning watch.

The first evening set the model for those that were to follow. Two cases of champagne scarce lasted the four-and-twenty hours, and almost the whole was drunk by Huish and the captain. Huish seemed to thrive on the excess; he was never sober, yet never wholly tipsy; the food and the sea air had soon healed him of his disease, and he began to lay on flesh. But with Davis things went worse. In the drooping, unbuttoned figure that sprawled all day upon the lockers, tippling and reading novels; in the fool who made of the evening watch a public carouse on the quarter-deck, it would have been hard to recognize the vigorous seaman of Papeete roads. He kept himself reasonably well in hand till he had taken the sun and yawned and blotted through his calculations; but from the moment he rolled up the chart, his hours were passed in slavish self-indulgence or in hoggish slumber. Every other branch of his duty was neglected, except maintaining a stern discipline about the dinner-table. Again and again Herrick would hear the cook called aft, and see him running with fresh tins, or carrying away again a meal that had been totally condemned. And the more the captain became sunk in drunkenness, the more delicate his palate showed itself. Once, in the forenoon, he had a bo'sun's chair rigged over the rail, stripped to his trousers, and went overboard with a pot of paint. 'I don't like the way this schooner's painted,' said he, 'and I taken a down upon her name.' But he tired of it in half an hour, and the schooner went on her way with an incongruous patch of colour on the stern, and the word *Farallone* part obliterated and part looking through. He refused to stand either the middle or the morning watch. It was fine-weather sailing, he said; and asked, with a laugh, 'Who ever heard of the old man standing watch himself?' To the dead reckoning which Herrick still tried to keep, he would pay not the least attention nor afford the least assistance.

'What do we want of dead reckoning?' he asked. 'We get the sun all right, don't we?'

'We mayn't get it always though,' objected Herrick. 'And you told me yourself you weren't sure of the chronometer.'

'Oh, there ain't no flies in the chronometer!' cried Davis.

'Oblige me so far, captain,' said Herrick stiffly. 'I am anxious to keep this reckoning, which is a part of my duty; I do not know what to allow for current, nor how to allow for it. I am too inexperienced; and I beg of you to help me.'

'Never discourage zealous officer,' said the captain, unrolling the chart again, for Herrick had taken him over his day's work and while he was still partly sober. 'Here it is: look for yourself; anything from west to west no' the-west, and anyways from 5 to

25 miles. That's what the A'm'ralty chart says; I guess you don't expect to get on ahead of your own Britishers?'

'I am trying to do my duty, Captain Brown,' said Herrick, with a dark flush, 'and I have the honour to inform you that I don't enjoy being trifled with.'

'What in thunder do you want?' roared Davis. 'Go and look at the blamed wake. If you're trying to do your duty, why don't you go and do it? I guess it's no business of mine to go and stick my head over the ship's rump? I guess it's yours. And I'll tell you what it is, my fine fellow, I'll trouble you not to come the dude over me. You're insolent, that's what's wrong with you. Don't you crowd me, Mr Herrick, Esquire.'

Herrick tore up his papers, threw them on the floor, and left the cabin.

'He's turned a bloomin' swot, ain't he?' sneered Huish.

'He thinks himself too good for his company, that's what ails Herrick, Esquire,' raged the captain. 'He thinks I don't understand when he comes the heavy swell. Won't sit down with us, won't he? won't say a civil word? I'll serve the son of a gun as he deserves. By God, Huish, I'll show him whether he's too good for John Davis!'

'Easy with the names, cap',' said Huish, who was always the more sober. 'Easy over the stones, my boy!'

'All right, I will. You're a good sort, Huish. I didn't take to you at first, but I guess you're right enough. Let's open another bottle,' said the captain; and that day, perhaps because he was excited by the quarrel, he drank more recklessly, and by four o'clock was stretched insensible upon the locker.

Herrick and Huish supped alone, one after the other, opposite his flushed and snorting body. And if the sight killed Herrick's hunger, the isolation weighed so heavily on the clerk's spirit, that he was scarce risen from table ere he was currying favour with his former comrade.

Herrick was at the wheel when he approached, and Huish leaned confidentially across the binnacle.

'I say, old chappie,' he said, 'you and me don't seem to be such pals somehow.'

Herrick gave her a spoke or two in silence; his eye, as it skirted from the needle to the luff of the foresail, passed the man by without speculation. But Huish was really dull, a thing he could support with difficulty, having no resources of his own. The idea of a private talk with Herrick, at this stage of their relations, held out particular inducements to a person of his character. Drink besides, as it renders some men hypersensitive, made Huish callous. And it would almost have required a blow to make him quit his purpose.

'Pretty business, ain't it?' he continued; 'Dyvis on the lush? Must say I thought you gave it 'im A1 today. He didn't like it a bit; took on hawful after you were gone. – "'Ere," says I, "'old on, easy on the lush," I says. "'Errick was right, and you know it. Give 'im a chanst," I says. – "'Uish," sezee, "don't you gimme no more of your jaw, or I'll knock your bloomin' eyes out." Well, wot can I do, 'Errick? But I tell you, I don't 'arf like it. It looks to me like the *Sea Rynger* over again.'

Still Herrick was silent.

'Do you 'ear me speak?' asked Huish sharply. 'You're pleasant, ain't you?'

'Stand away from that binnacle,' said Herrick.

The clerk looked at him, long and straight and black; his figure seemed to writhe like that of a snake about to strike; then he turned on his heel, went back to the cabin and opened a bottle of champagne. When eight bells were cried, he slept on the floor beside the captain on the locker; and of the whole starboard watch, only Sally Day appeared upon the summons. The mate proposed to stand the watch with him, and let Uncle Ned lie down; it would make twelve hours on deck, and probably sixteen, but in this fair-weather sailing, he might safely sleep between his tricks of wheel, leaving orders to be called on any sign of squalls. So far he could trust the men, between whom and himself a close relation had sprung up. With Uncle Ned he held long nocturnal conversations, and the old man told him his simple and hard story of exile, suffering, and injustice among cruel whites. The cook, when he found Herrick messed alone, produced for him unexpected and sometimes unpalatable dainties, of which he forced himself to eat. And one day, when he was forward, he was surprised to feel a caressing hand run down his shoulder, and to hear the voice of Sally Day crooning in his ear: 'You gootch man!' He turned, and, choking down a sob, shook hands with the negrito. They were kindly, cheery, childish souls. Upon the Sunday each brought forth his separate Bible – for they were all men of alien speech even to each other, and Sally Day communicated with his mates in English only, each read or made believe to read his chapter, Uncle Ned with spectacles on his nose; and they would all join together in the singing of missionary hymns. It was thus a cutting reproof to compare the islanders and the whites aboard the *Farallone*. Shame ran in Herrick's blood to remember what employment he was on, and to see these poor souls – and even Sally Day, the child of cannibals, in all likelihood a cannibal himself – so faithful to what they knew of good. The fact that he was held in grateful favour by these innocents served like blinders to his conscience, and there were times when he was inclined, with Sally Day, to call himself a good man. But the height of his favour was only now to appear. With one voice, the crew protested; ere Herrick knew what they were doing, the cook was aroused and came a willing volunteer; all hands clustered about their mate with expostulations and caresses; and he was bidden to lie down and take his customary rest without alarm.

'He tell you tlue,' said Uncle Ned. 'You sleep. Evely man hea he do all light. Evely man he like you too much.'

Herrick struggled, and gave way; choked upon some trivial

words of gratitude; and walked to the side of the house, against which he leaned, struggling with emotion.

Uncle Ned presently followed him and begged him to lie down.

'It's no use, Uncle Ned,' he replied. 'I couldn't sleep. I'm knocked over with all your goodness.'

'Ah, no call me Uncle Ned no mo'!' cried the old man. 'No my name! My name Taveeta, all-e-same Taveeta King of Islael. Wat for he call that Hawaii? I think no savvy nothing – all-e-same Wise-a-mana.'

It was the first time the name of the late captain had been mentioned, and Herrick grasped the occasion. The reader shall be spared Uncle Ned's unwieldy dialect, and learn in less embarrassing English, the sum of what he now communicated. The ship had scarce cleared the Golden Gates before the captain and mate had entered on a career of drunkenness, which was scarcely interrupted by their malady and only closed by death. For days and weeks they had encountered neither land nor ship; and seeing themselves lost on the huge deep with their insane conductors, the natives had drunk deep of terror.

At length they made a low island, and went in; and Wiseman and Wishart landed in the boat.

There was a great village, a very fine village, and plenty Kanakas in that place; but all mighty serious; and from every here and there in the back parts of the settlement, Taveeta heard the sounds of island lamentation. 'I no savvy *talk* that island,' said he. 'I savvy hear um *cly*. I think, Hum! too many people die here!' But upon Wiseman and Wishart the significance of that barbaric keening was lost. Full of bread and drink, they rollicked along unconcerned, embraced the girls who had scarce energy to repel them, took up and joined (with drunken voices) in the death wail, and at last (on what they took to be an invitation) entered under the roof of a house in which was a considerable concourse of people sitting silent. They stooped below the eaves, flushed and laughing; within a minute they came forth again with changed faces and silent tongues; and as the press severed to make way for them, Taveeta was able to perceive, in the deep shadow of the house, the sick man raising from his mat a head already defeatured by disease. The two tragic triflers fled without hesitation for their boat, screaming on Taveeta to make haste; they came aboard with all speed of oars, raised anchor and crowded sail upon the ship with blows and curses, and were at sea again – and again drunk – before sunset. A week after, and the last of the two had been committed to the deep. Herrick asked Taveeta where that island was, and he replied that, by what he gathered of folks' talk as they went up together from the beach, he supposed it must be one of the Paumotus. This was in itself probable enough, for the Dangerous Archipelago had been swept that year from east to west by devastating smallpox; but Herrick thought it a strange course to lie from Sydney. Then he remembered the drink.

'Were they not surprised when they made the island?' he asked.

'Wise-a-mana he say "dam! what this?"' was the reply.

'O, that's it then,' said Herrick. 'I don't believe they knew where they were.'

'I think so too,' said Uncle Ned. 'I think no savvy. This one mo' betta,' he added, pointing to the house where the drunken captain slumbered: 'Take-a-sun all-e-time.'

The implied last touch completed Herrick's picture of the life and death of his two predecessors; of their prolonged, sordid, sodden sensuality as they sailed, they knew not whither, on their last cruise. He held but a twinkling and unsure belief in any future state; the thought of one of punishment he derided; yet for him (as for all) there dwelt a horror about the end of the brutish man. Sickness fell upon him at the image thus called up; and when he compared it with the scene in which himself was acting, and considered the doom that seemed to brood upon the schooner, a horror that was almost superstitious fell upon him. And yet the strange thing was, he did not falter. He who had proved his incapacity in so many fields, being now falsely placed amid duties which he did not understand, without help, and it might be said without countenance, had hitherto surpassed expectation; and even the shameful misconduct and shocking disclosures of that night seemed but to nerve and strengthen him. He had sold his honour; he vowed it should not be in vain; 'it shall be no fault of mine if this miscarry,' he repeated. And in his heart he wondered at himself. Living rage no doubt supported him; no doubt also, the sense of the last cast, of the ships burned, of all doors closed but one, which is so strong a tonic to the merely weak, and so deadly a depressent to the merely cowardly.

For some time the voyage went otherwise well. They weathered Fakarava with one board; and the wind holding well to the southward and blowing fresh, they passed between Raraka and Katiu, and ran some days north-east by east-half-east under the lee of Takume and Honden, neither of which they made. In about 14° South and between 134° and 135° West, it fell a dead calm with rather a heavy sea. The captain refused to take in sail, the helm was lashed, no watch was set, and the *Farallone* rolled and banged for three days, according to observation, in almost the same place. The fourth morning, a little before day, a breeze sprang up and rapidly freshened. The captain had drunk hard the night before; he was far from sober when he was roused; and when he came on deck for the first time at half-past eight, it was plain he had already drunk deep again at breakfast. Herrick avoided his eye; and resigned the deck with indignation to a man more than half-seas over.

By the loud commands of the captain and the singing out of fellows at the ropes, he could judge from the house that sail was being crowded on the ship; relinquished his half-eaten breakfast; and came on deck again, to find the main and the jib topsails set, and both watches and the cook turned out to hand the staysail. The *Farallone* lay already far over; the sky was obscured with misty scud; and from the windward an ominous squall came flying up, broadening and blackening as it rose.

Fear thrilled in Herrick's vitals. He saw death hard by; and if not death, sure ruin. For if the *Farallone* lived through the coming squall, she must surely be dismasted. With that their enterprise was at an end, and they themselves bound prisoners to the very evidence of their crime. The greatness of the peril and his own alarm sufficed to silence him. Pride, wrath, and shame raged without issue in his mind; and he shut his teeth and folded his arms close.

The captain sat in the boat to windward, bellowing orders and insults, his eyes glazed, his face deeply congested; a bottle set between his knees, a glass in his hand half empty. His back was to the squall, and he was at first intent upon the setting of the sail. When that was done, and the great trapezium of canvas had begun to draw and to trail the lee-rail of the *Farallone* level with the foam, he laughed out an empty laugh, drained his glass, sprawled back among the lumber in the boat, and fetched out a crumpled novel.

Herrick watched him, and his indignation glowed red-hot. He glanced to windward where the squall already whitened the near sea and heralded its coming with a singular and dismal sound. He glanced at the steersman, and saw him clinging to the spokes with a face of a sickly blue. He saw the crew were running to their stations without orders. And it seemed as if something broke in his brain; and the passion of anger, so long restrained, so long eaten in secret, burst suddenly loose and shook him like a sail. He stepped across to the captain and smote his hand heavily on the drunkard's shoulder.

'You brute,' he said, in a voice that tottered, 'look behind you!'

'Wha's that?' cried Davis, bounding in the boat and upsetting the champagne.

'You lost the *Sea Ranger* because you were a drunken sot,' said Herrick. 'Now you're going to lose the *Farallone*. You're going to drown here the same way as you drowned others, and be damned. And your daughter shall walk the streets, and your sons be thieves like their father.'

For the moment, the words struck the captain white and foolish. 'My God!' he cried, looking at Herrick as upon a ghost; 'my God, Herrick!'

'Look behind you, then!' reiterated the assailant.

The wretched man, already partly sobered, did as he was told, and in the same breath of time leaped to his feet. 'Down staysail!' he trumpeted. The hands were thrilling for the order, and the great sail came with a run, and fell half overboard among the racing foam. 'Jib topsail-halyards! Let the stays'l be,' he said again.

But before it was well uttered, the squall shouted aloud and fell, in a solid mass of wind and rain commingled, on the *Farallone*; and she stooped under the blow, and lay like a thing dead. From the mind of Herrick reason fled; he clung in the weather rigging, exulting; he was done with life, and he gloried in the release; he gloried in the wild noises of the wind and the choking onslaught of the rain; he gloried to die so, and now, amid this coil of the elements. And meanwhile, in the waist up to his knees in water – so low the schooner lay – the captain was hacking at the foresheet with a pocket-knife. It was a question of seconds, for the *Farallone* drank deep of the encroaching seas. But the hand of the captain had the advance; the foresail boom tore apart the last strands of the sheet and crashed to leeward; the *Farallone* leaped up into the wind and righted; and the peak and throat halyards, which had long been let go, began to run at the same instant.

For some ten minutes more she careered under the impulse of the squall; but the captain was now master of himself and of his ship, and all danger at an end. And then, sudden as a trick-change upon the stage, the squall blew by, the wind dropped into light airs, the sun beamed forth again upon the tattered schooner; and the captain, having secured the fore-sail boom and set a couple of hands to the pump, walked aft, sober, a little pale, and with the sodden end of a cigar still stuck between his teeth even as the squall had found it. Herrick followed him; he could scarce recall the violence of his late emotions, but he felt there was a scene to go through, and he was anxious and even eager to go through with it.

The captain, turning at the house end, met him face to face, and averted his eyes. 'We've lost the two tops'ls and the stays'l,' he gabbled. 'Good business, we didn't lose any sticks. I guess you think we're all the better without the kites.'

'That's not what I'm thinking,' said Herrick, in a voice strangely quiet, that yet echoed confusion in the captain's mind.

'I know that,' he cried, holding up his hand. 'I know what you're thinking. No use to say it now. I'm sober.'

'I have to say it, though,' returned Herrick.

'Hold on, Herrick; you've said enough,' said Davis. 'You've said what I would take from no man breathing but yourself; only I know it's true.'

'I have to tell you, Captain Brown,' pursued Herrick, 'that I resign my position as mate. You can put me in irons or shoot me, as you please; I will make no resistance, only, I decline in any way to help or to obey you; and I suggest you should put Mr Huish in my place. He will make a worthy first officer to your captain, sir.' He smiled, bowed, and turned to walk forward.

'Where are you going, Herrick?' cried the captain, detaining him by the shoulder.

'To berth forward with the men, sir,' replied Herrick, with the same hateful smile. 'I've been long enough aft here with you – gentlemen.'

'You're wrong there,' said Davis. 'Don't you be too quick with me; there ain't nothing wrong but the drink – it's the old story, man! Let me get sober once, and then you'll see,' he pleaded.

'Excuse me, I desire to see no more of you,' said Herrick.

The captain groaned aloud. 'You know what you said about my children?' he broke out.

'By rote. In case you wish me to say it you again?' asked Herrick.

'Don't!' cried the captain, clapping his hands to his ears. 'Don't make me kill a man I care for! Herrick, if you see me put a glass to my lips again till we're ashore, I give you leave to put a bullet through me; I beg you to it! You're the only man aboard whose carcase is worth losing; do you think I don't know that? do you think I ever went back on you? I always knew you were in the right of it – drunk or sober, I knew that. What do you want? – an oath? Man, you're clever enough to see that this is sure-enough earnest.'

'Do you mean there shall be no more drinking?' asked Herrick, 'neither by you nor Huish? that you won't go on stealing my profits and drinking my champagne that I gave my honour for? and that you'll attend to your duties, and stand watch and watch, and bear your proper share of the ship's work, instead of leaving it all on the shoulders of a landsman, and making yourself the butt and scoff of native seamen? Is that what you mean? If it is, be so good as say it categorically.'

'You put these things in a way hard for a gentleman to swallow,' said the captain. 'You wouldn't have me say I was ashamed of myself? Trust me this once; I'll do the square thing, and there's my hand on it.'

'Well, I'll try it once,' said Herrick. 'Fail me again . . .'

'No more now!' interrupted Davis. 'No more, old man! Enough said. You've a riling tongue when your back's up, Herrick. Just be glad we're friends again, the same as what I am; and go tender on the raws; I'll see as you don't repent it. We've been mighty near death this day – don't say whose fault it was! – pretty near hell, too, I guess. We're in a mighty bad line of life, us two, and ought to go easy with each other.'

He was maundering; yet it seemed as if he were maundering with some design, beating about the bush of some communication that he feared to make, or perhaps only talking against time in terror of what Herrick might say next. But Herrick had now spat his venom; his was a kindly nature, and, content with his triumph, he had now begun to pity. With a few soothing words, he sought to conclude the interview, and proposed that they should change their clothes.

'Not right yet,' said Davis. 'There's another thing I want to tell you first. You know what you said about my children? I want to tell you why it hit me so hard; I kind of think you'll feel bad about it too. It's about my little Adar. You hadn't ought to have quite said that – but of course I know you didn't know. She – she's dead, you see.'

'Why, Davis!' cried Herrick. 'You've told me a dozen times she was alive! Clear your head, man! This must be the drink.'

'No, *sir*,' said Davis. 'She's dead. Died of a bowel complaint. That was when I was away in the brig *Oregon*. She lies in Portland, Maine. "Adar, only daughter of Captain John Davis and Mariar his wife, aged five." I had a doll for her on board. I never took the paper off'n that doll, Herrick; it went down the way it was with the *Sea Ranger*, that day I was damned.'

The Captain's eyes were fixed on the horizon, he talked with an extraordinary softness but a complete composure; and Herrick looked upon him with something that was almost terror.

'Don't think I'm crazy neither,' resumed Davis. 'I've all the cold sense that I know what to do with. But I guess a man that's unhappy's like a child; and this is a kind of a child's game of mine. I never could act up to the plain-cut truth, you see; so I pretend. And I warn you square; as soon as we're through with this talk, I'll start in again with the pretending. Only, you see, she can't walk no streets,' added the captain, 'couldn't even make out to live and get that doll!'

Herrick laid a tremulous hand upon the captain's shoulder.

'Don't do that!' cried Davis, recoiling from the touch. 'Can't you see I'm all broken up the way it is? Come along, then; come along, old man; you can put your trust in me right through; come along and get dry clothes.'

They entered the cabin, and there was Huish on his knees prising open a case of champagne.

''Vast, there!' cried the captain. 'No more of that. No more drinking on this ship.'

'Turned teetotal, 'ave you?' inquired Huish. 'I'm agreeable. About time, eh? Bloomin' nearly lost another ship, I fancy.' He took out a bottle and began calmly to burst the wire with the spike of a corkscrew.

'Do you hear me speak?' cried Davis.

'I suppose I do. You speak loud enough,' said Huish. 'The trouble is that I don't care.'

Herrick plucked the captain's sleeve. 'Let him free now,' he said. 'We've had all we want this morning.'

'Let him have it then,' said the captain. 'It's his last.'

By this time the wire was open, the string was cut, the head of gilded paper was torn away; and Huish waited, mug in hand, expecting the usual explosion. It did not follow. He eased the cork with his thumb; still there was no result. At last he took the screw and drew it. It came out very easy and with scarce a sound.

''Illo!' said Huish. ''Ere's a bad bottle.'

He poured some of the wine into the mug; it was colourless and still. He smelt and tasted it.

'W'y, wot's this?' he said. 'It's water!'

If the voice of trumpets had suddenly sounded about the ship in the midst of the sea, the three men in the house could scarcely have been more stunned than by this incident. The mug passed round; each sipped, each smelt of it; each stared at the bottle in its glory of gold paper as Crusoe may have stared at the footprint, and their minds were swift to fix upon a common apprehension. The difference between a bottle of champagne and a bottle of water is not great; between a shipload of one or of the other lay the whole scale from riches to ruin.

A second bottle was broached. There were two cases standing ready in a stateroom; these two were brought out, broken open, and tested. Still with the same result: the contents were still colourless and tasteless, and dead as the rain in a beached fishing-boat.

'Crikey!' said Huish.

'Here, let's sample the hold!' said the captain, mopping his brow with a back-handed sweep; and the three stalked out of the house, grim and heavy-footed.

All hands were turned out; two Kanakas were sent below, another stationed at a purchase; and Davis, axe in hand, took his place beside the coamings.

'Are you going to let the men know?' whispered Herrick.

'Damn the men!' said Davis. 'It's beyond that. We've got to know ourselves.'

Three cases were sent on deck and sampled in turn; from each bottle, as the captain smashed it with the axe, the champagne ran bubbling and creaming.

'Go deeper, can't you?' cried Davis to the Kanakas in the hold.

The command gave the signal for a disastrous change. Case after case came up, bottle after bottle was burst, and bled mere water. Deeper yet, and they came upon a layer where there was scarcely so much as the intention to deceive; where the cases were no longer branded, the bottles no longer wired or papered, where the fraud was manifest and stared them in the face.

'Here's about enough of this foolery!' said Davis. 'Stow back the cases in the hold, Uncle, and get the broken crockery overboard. Come with me,' he added to his co-adventurers, and led the way back into the cabin.

Chapter Six

The Partners

Each took a side of the fixed table; it was the first time they had sat down at it together; but now all sense of incongruity, all memory of differences, was quite swept away by the presence of the common ruin.

'Gentlemen,' said the captain, after a pause, and with very much the air of a chairman opening a board-meeting, 'we're sold.'

Huish broke out in laughter. 'Well, if this ain't the 'ighest old rig!' he cried. 'And Dyvis 'ere, who thought he had got up so bloomin' early in the mornin'! We've stolen a cargo of spring water! Oh, my crikey!' and he squirmed with mirth.

The captain managed to screw out a phantom smile.

'Here's Old Man Destiny again,' said he to Herrick, 'but this time I guess he's kicked the door right in.'

Herrick only shook his head.

'O Lord, it's rich!' laughed Huish. 'It would really be a scrumptious lark if it 'ad 'appened to somebody else! And wot are we to do next? Oh, my eye! with this bloomin' schooner, too?'

'That's the trouble,' said Davis. 'There's only one thing certain: it's no use carting this old glass and ballast to Peru. No, *sir*, we're in a hole.'

'O my, and the merchant!' cried Huish; 'the man that made this shipment! He'll get the news by the mail brigantine; and he'll think of course we're making straight for Sydney.'

'Yes, he'll be a sick merchant,' said the captain. 'One thing: this explains the Kanaka crew. If you're going to lose a ship, I would ask no better myself than a Kanaka crew. But there's one thing it don't explain; it don't explain why she came down Tahiti ways.'

'W'y, to lose her, you byby!' said Huish.

'A lot you know,' said the captain. 'Nobody wants to lose a schooner; they want to lose her *on her course*, you skeericks! You seem to think underwriters haven't got enough sense to come in out of the rain.'

'Well,' said Herrick, 'I can tell you (I am afraid) why she came so far to the eastward. I had it of Uncle Ned. It seems these two unhappy devils, Wiseman and Wishart, were drunk on the champagne from the beginning – and died drunk at the end.'

The captain looked on the table.

'They lay in their two bunks, or sat here in this damned house,' he pursued, with rising agitation, 'filling their skins with the accursed stuff, till sickness took them. As they sickened and the fever rose, they drank the more. They lay here howling and groaning, drunk and dying, all in one. They didn't know where they were, they didn't care. They didn't even take the sun, it seems.'

'Not take the sun?' cried the captain, looking up. 'Sacred Billy! what a crowd!'

'Well, it don't matter to Joe!' said Huish. 'Wot are Wiseman and the t'other buffer to us?'

'A good deal, too,' says the captain. 'We're their heirs, I guess.'

'It is a great inheritance,' said Herrick.

'Well, I don't know about that,' returned Davis. 'Appears to me as if it might be worse. 'Tain't worth what the cargo would have been of course, at least not money down. But I'll tell you what it appears to figure up to. Appears to me as if it amounted to about the bottom dollar of the man in 'Frisco.'

''Old on,' said Huish. 'Give a fellow time; 'ow's this, umpire?'

'Well, my sons,' pursued the captain, who seemed to have recovered his assurance, 'Wiseman and Wishart were to be paid for casting away this old schooner and its cargo. We're going to cast away the schooner right enough; and I'll make it my private business to see that we get paid. What were W. and W. to get? That's more'n I can tell. But W. and W. went into this business themselves, they were on the crook. Now *we're* on the square, *we* only stumbled into it; and that merchant has just got to squeal, and I'm the man to see that he squeals good. No, *sir*! there's some stuffing to this *Farallone* racket after all.'

'Go it, cap!' cried Huish. 'Yoicks! Forrard! 'Old 'ard! There's your style for the money! Blow me if I don't prefer this to the hother.'

'I do not understand,' said Herrick. 'I have to ask you to excuse me; I do not understand.'

'Well now, see here, Herrick,' said Davis, 'I'm going to have a word with you anyway upon a different matter, and it's good that Huish should hear it too. We're done with this boozing business, and we ask your pardon for it right here and now. We have to thank you for all you did for us while we were making hogs of ourselves; you'll find me turn-to all right in future; and as for the wine, which I grant we stole from you, I'll take stock and see you paid for it. That's good enough, I believe. But what I want to point out to you is this. The old game was a risky game. The new game's as safe as running a Vienna Bakery. We just put this *Farallone* before the wind, and run till we're well to looard of our port of departure and reasonably well up with some other place, where they have an American Consul. Down goes the *Farallone*, and good bye to her! A day or so in the boat; the consul packs us home, at Uncle Sam's expense, to 'Frisco; and if that merchant don't put the dollars down, you come to me!'

'But I thought,' began Herrick; and then broke out: 'oh, let's get on to Peru!'

'Well, if you're going to Peru for your health, I won't say no!' replied the captain. 'But for what other blame' shadow of a reason you should want to go there, gets me clear. We don't want to go there with this cargo; I don't know as old bottles is a lively article anywheres; leastways, I'll go my bottom cent, it ain't Peru. It was always a doubt if we could sell the schooner; I never rightly hoped to, and now I'm sure she ain't worth a hill of beans; what's wrong with her, I don't know; I only know it's something, or she wouldn't be here with this truck in her inside. Then again, if we lose her, and land in Peru, where are we? We can't declare the loss, or how did we get to Peru? In that case the merchant can't touch the insurance; most likely he'll go bust; and don't you think you see the three of us on the beach of Callao?'

'There's no extradition there,' said Herrick.

'Well, my son, and we want to be extraded,' said the captain. 'What's our point? We want to have a consul extrade us as far as San Francisco and that merchant's office door. My idea is that Samoa would be found an eligible business centre. It's dead before the wind; the States have a consul there, and 'Frisco steamers call, so's we could skip right back and interview the merchant.'

'Samoa?' said Herrick. 'It will take us for ever to get there.'

'Oh, with a fair wind!' said the captain.

'No trouble about the log, eh?' asked Huish.

'No, *sir*,' said Davis. *'Light airs and baffling winds. Squalls and calms. D. R.: five miles. No obs. Pumps attended.* And fill in the barometer and thermometer off of last year's trip. "Never saw such a voyage," says you to the consul. "Thought I was going to run short . . ."' 'He stopped in mid career.' 'Say,' he began again, and once more stopped. 'Beg your pardon, Herrick,' he added with undisguised humility, 'but did you keep the run of the stores?'

'Had I been told to do so, it should have been done, as the rest was done, to the best of my little ability,' said Herrick. 'As it was, the cook helped himself to what he pleased.'

Davis looked at the table.

'I drew it rather fine, you see,' he said at last. 'The great thing was to clear right out of Papeete before the consul could think better of it. Tell you what: I guess I'll take stock.'

And he rose from table and disappeared with a lamp in the lazarette.

''Ere's another screw loose,' observed Huish.

'My man,' said Herrick, with a sudden gleam of animosity, 'it is still your watch on deck, and surely your wheel also?'

'You come the 'eavy swell, don't you, ducky?' said Huish. 'Stand away from that binnacle. Surely your w'eel, my man. Yah.'

He lit a cigar ostentatiously, and strolled into the waist with his hands in his pockets.

In a surprisingly short time, the captain reappeared; he did not look at Herrick, but called Huish back and sat down.

'Well,' he began, 'I've taken stock – roughly.' He paused as if for somebody to help him out; and none doing so, both gazing on him instead with manifest anxiety, he yet more heavily resumed. 'Well, it won't fight. We can't do it; that's the bed-rock. I'm as sorry as what you can be, and sorrier. But the game's up. We can't look near Samoa. I don't know as we could get to Peru.'

'Wot-ju mean?' asked Huish brutally.

'I can't 'most tell myself,' replied the captain. 'I drew it fine; I said I did; but what's been going on here gets me! Appears as if the devil had been around. That cook must be the holiest kind of fraud. Only twelve days, too! Seems like craziness. I'll own up square to one thing: I seem to have figured too fine upon the flour. But the rest – my land! I'll never understand it! There's been more waste on this twopenny ship than what there is to an Atlantic Liner.' He stole a glance at his companions; nothing good was to be gleaned from their dark faces; and he had recourse to rage. 'You wait till I interview that cook!' he roared and smote the table with his fist. 'I'll interview the son of a gun so's he's never been spoken to before. I'll put a bead upon the – !'

'You will not lay a finger on the man,' said Herrick. 'The fault is yours and you know it. If you turn a savage loose in your store-room, you know what to expect. I will not allow the man to be molested.'

It is hard to say how Davis might have taken this defiance; but he was diverted to a fresh assailant.

'Well!' drawled Huish, 'you're a plummy captain, ain't you? You're a blooming captain! Don't you set up any of your chat to me, John Dyvis: I know you now, you ain't any more use than a bloomin' dawl! Oh, you "don't know", don't you? Oh, it "gets you", do it? Oh, I dessay! W'y, weren't you 'owling for fresh tins every blessed day? 'Ow often 'ave I 'eard you send the 'ole bloomin' dinner off and tell the man to chuck it in the swill-tub? And breakfast? Oh, my crikey! breakfast for ten, and you 'ollerin' for more! And now you "can't 'most tell"! Blow me, if it ain't enough to make a man write an insultin' letter to Gawd! You dror it mild, John Dyvis; don't 'andle me; I'm dyngerous.'

Davis sat like one bemused; it might even have been doubted if he heard, but the voice of the clerk rang about the cabin like that of a cormorant among the ledges of the cliff.

'That will do, Huish,' said Herrick.

'Oh, so you tyke his part, do you? you stuck-up sneerin' snob! Tyke it then. Come on, the pair of you. But as for John Dyvis, let him look out! He struck me the first night aboard, and I never took a blow yet but wot I gave as good. Let him knuckle down on his marrow bones and beg my pardon. That's my last word.'

'I stand by the Captain,' said Herrick. 'That makes us two to one, both good men; and the crew will all follow me. I hope I shall die very soon; but I have not the least objection to killing you before I go. I should prefer it so; I should do it with no more remorse than winking. Take care – take care, you little cad!'

The animosity with which these words were uttered was so marked in itself, and so remarkable in the man who uttered them, that Huish stared, and even the humiliated Davis reared up his head and gazed at his defender. As for Herrick, the successive agitations and disappointments of the day had left him wholly reckless; he was conscious of a pleasant glow, an agreeable excitement; his head seemed empty, his eyeballs burned as he turned them, his throat was dry as a biscuit; the least dangerous man by nature, except in so far as the weak are always dangerous, at that moment he was ready to slay or to be slain with equal unconcern.

Here at least was the gage thrown down, and battle offered; he who should speak next would bring the matter to an issue there and then; all knew it to be so and hung back; and for many seconds by the cabin clock, the trio sat motionless and silent.

Then came an interruption, welcome as the flowers in May.

'Land ho!' sang out a voice on deck. 'Land a weatha bow!'

'Land!' cried Davis, springing to his feet. 'What's this? There ain't no land here.'

And as men may run from the chamber of a murdered corpse, the three ran forth out of the house and left their quarrel behind them, undecided.

The sky shaded down at the sea-level to the white of opals; the sea itself, insolently, inkily blue, drew all about them the uncompromising wheel of the horizon. Search it as they pleased, not even the practised eye of Captain Davis could descry the smallest interruption. A few filmy clouds were slowly melting overhead; and about the schooner, as around the only point of interest, a tropic bird, white as a snowflake, hung, and circled, and displayed, as it turned, the long vermilion feather of its tail. Save the sea and the heaven, that was all.

'Who sang out land?' asked Davis. 'If there's any boy playing funny-dog with me, I'll teach him skylarking!'

But Uncle Ned contentedly pointed to a part of the horizon, where a greenish, filmy iridescence could be discerned floating like smoke on the pale heavens.

Davis applied his glass to it, and then looked at the Kanaka. 'Call that land?' said he. 'Well, it's more than I do.'

'One time long ago,' said Uncle Ned, 'I see Anaa all-e-same that, four five hours befo' we come up. Capena he say sun go down, sun go up again; he say lagoon all-e-same milla.'

'All-e-same *what*?' asked Davis.

'Milla, sah,' said Uncle Ned.

'Oh, ah! mirror,' said Davis. 'I see; reflection from the lagoon. Well, you know, it is just possible, though it's strange I never heard of it. Here, let's look at the chart.'

They went back to the cabin, and found the position of the schooner well to windward of the archipelago in the midst of a white field of paper.

'There! you see for yourselves,' said Davis.

'And yet I don't know,' said Herrick, 'I somehow think there's something in it. I'll tell you one thing too, captain; that's all right about the reflection; I heard it in Papeete.'

'Fetch up that Findlay, then!' said Davis. 'I'll try it all ways. An island wouldn't come amiss, the way we're fixed.'

The bulky volume was handed up to him, broken-backed as is the way with Findlay; and he turned to the place and began to run over the text, muttering to himself and turning over the pages with a wetted finger.

'Hullo!' he exclaimed. 'How's this?' And he read aloud. '*New Island*. According to M. Delille this island, which from private interests would remain unknown, lies, it is said, in lat. 12°49′10″ S. long. 133°6′ W. In addition to the position above given, Commander Matthews H. M. S. *Scorpion*, states that an island exists in lat. 12°0′ S. long. 133°16′ W. This must be the same, if such an island exists, which is very doubtful, and totally disbelieved in by South Sea traders.'

'Golly!' said Huish.

'It's rather in the conditional mood,' said Herrick.

'It's anything you please,' cried Davis, 'only there it is! That's our place, and don't you make any mistake.'

' "Which from private interests would remain unknown," ' read Herrick, over his shoulder. 'What may that mean?'

'It should mean pearls,' said Davis. 'A pearling island the government don't know about? That sounds like real estate. Or suppose it don't mean anything. Suppose it's just an island; I guess we could fill up with fish, and cocoanuts, and native stuff, and carry out the Samoa scheme hand over fist. How long did he say it was before they raised Anaa? Five hours, I think?'

'Four or five,' said Herrick.

Davis stepped to the door. 'What breeze had you that time you made Anaa, Uncle Ned?' said he.

'Six or seven knots,' was the reply.

'Thirty or thirty-five miles,' said Davis. 'High time we were shortening sail, then. If it is an island, we don't want to be butting our head against it in the dark; and if it isn't an island, we can get through it just as well by daylight. Ready about!' he roared.

And the schooner's head was laid for that elusive glimmer in the sky, which began already to pale in lustre and diminish in size, as the stain of breath vanishes from a window pane. At the same time she was reefed close down.

PART TWO

The Quartette

Chapter Seven

The Pearl-Fisher

About four in the morning, as the captain and Herrick sat together on the rail, there arose from the midst of the night in front of them the voice of breakers. Each sprang to his feet and stared and listened. The sound was continuous, like the passing of a train; no rise or fall could be distinguished; minute by minute the ocean heaved with an equal potency against the invisible isle; and as time passed, and Herrick waited in vain for any vicissitude in the volume of that roaring, a sense of the eternal weighed upon his mind. To the expert eye the isle itself was to be inferred from a certain string of blots along the starry heaven. And the schooner was laid to and anxiously observed till daylight.

There was little or no morning bank. A brightening came in the east; then a wash of some ineffable, faint, nameless hue between crimson and silver; and then coals of fire. These glimmered a while on the sea-line, and seemed to brighten and darken and spread out, and still the night and the stars reigned undisturbed; it was as though a spark should catch and glow and creep along the foot of some heavy and almost incombustible wall-hanging, and the room itself be scarce menaced. Yet a little after, and the whole east glowed with gold and scarlet, and the hollow of heaven was filled with the daylight.

The isle – the undiscovered, the scarce-believed in – now lay before them and close aboard; and Herrick thought that never in his dreams had he beheld anything more strange and delicate. The beach was excellently white, the continuous barrier of trees inimitably green; the land perhaps ten feet high, the trees thirty more. Every here and there, as the schooner coasted northward, the wood was intermitted; and he could see clear over the inconsiderable strip of land (as a man looks over a wall) to the lagoon within – and clear over that again to where the far side of the atoll prolonged its pencilling of trees against the morning sky. He tortured himself to find analogies. The isle was like the rim of a great vessel sunken in the waters; it was like the embankment of an annular railway grown upon with wood: so slender it seemed amidst the outrageous breakers, so frail and pretty, he would scarce have wondered to see it sink and disappear without a sound, and the waves close smoothly over its descent.

Meanwhile the captain was in the four cross-trees, glass in hand, his eyes in every quarter, spying for an entrance, spying for signs of tenancy. But the isle continued to unfold itself in joints, and to run out in indeterminate capes, and still there was neither house nor man, nor the smoke of fire. Here a multitude of sea-birds soared and twinkled, and fished in the blue waters; and there, and for miles together, the fringe of cocoa-palm and pandanus extended desolate, and made desirable green bowers for nobody to visit, and the silence of death was only broken by the throbbing of the sea.

The airs were very light, their speed was small; the heat intense. The decks were scorching underfoot, the sun flamed overhead, brazen, out of a brazen sky; the pitch bubbled in the seams, and the brains in the brain-pan. And all the while the excitement of the three adventurers glowed about their bones like a fever. They whispered, and nodded, and pointed, and put mouth to ear, with a singular instinct of secrecy, approaching that island under-hand like eavesdroppers and thieves; and even Davis from the cross-trees gave his orders mostly by gestures. The hands shared in this mute strain, like dogs, without comprehending it; and through the roar of so many miles of breakers, it was a silent ship that approached an empty island.

At last they drew near to the break in that interminable gangway. A spur of coral sand stood forth on the one hand; on the other a high and thick tuft of trees cut off the view; between was the mouth of the huge laver. Twice a day the ocean crowded in that narrow entrance and was heaped between these frail walls; twice a day, with the return of the ebb, the mighty surplusage of water must struggle to escape. The hour in which the *Farallone* came there was the hour of flood. The sea turned (as with the instinct of the homing pigeon) for the vast receptacle, swept eddying through the gates, was transmuted, as it did so, into a wonder of watery and silken hues, and brimmed into the inland sea beyond. The schooner looked up close-hauled, and was caught and carried away by the influx like a toy. She skimmed; she flew; a momentary shadow touched her decks from the shoreside trees; the bottom of the channel showed up for a moment and was in a moment gone; the next, she floated on the bosom of the lagoon, and below, in the transparent chamber of waters, a myriad of many-coloured fishes were sporting, a myriad pale flowers of coral diversified the floor.

Herrick stood transported. In the gratified lust of his eye, he forgot the past and the present; forgot that he was menaced by a prison on the one hand and starvation on the other; forgot that he was come to that island, desperately foraging, clutching at expedients. A drove of fishes, painted like the rainbow and billed like parrots, hovered up in the shadow of the schooner, and passed clear of it, and glinted in the submarine sun. They were beautiful, like birds, and their silent passage impressed him like a strain of song.

Meanwhile, to the eye of Davis in the cross-trees, the lagoon continued to expand its empty waters, and the long succession of the shore-side trees to be paid out like fishing-line off a reel. And still there was no mark of habitation. The schooner, immediately on entering, had been kept away to the nor'ard where the water seemed to be the most deep; and she was now skimming past the tall grove of trees, which stood on that side of the channel and denied further view. Of the whole of the low shores of the island, only this bight remained to be revealed. And suddenly the curtain was raised; they began to open out a haven, snugly elbowed there, and beheld, with an astonishment beyond words, the roofs of men.

The appearance, thus 'instantaneously disclosed' to those on the deck of the *Farallone*, was not that of a city, rather of a substantial country farm with its attendant hamlet: a long line of sheds and store-houses; apart, upon the one side, a deep-veranda'ed dwelling-house; on the other, perhaps a dozen native huts; a building with a belfry and some rude offer at architectural features that might be thought to mark it out for a chapel; on the beach in front some heavy boats drawn up, and a pile of timber running forth into the burning shallows of the lagoon. From a flagstaff at the pierhead, the red ensign of England was displayed. Behind, about, and over, the same tall grove of palms, which had masked the settlement in the beginning, prolonged its roof of tumultuous green fans, and turned and ruffled overhead, and sang its silver song all day in the wind. The place had the indescribable but unmistakable appearance of being in commission; yet there breathed from it a sense of desertion that was almost poignant, no human figure was to be observed going to and fro about the houses, and there was no sound of human industry or enjoyment. Only, on the top of the beach and hard by the flagstaff, a woman of exorbitant stature and as white as snow was to be seen beckoning with uplifted arm. The second glance identified her as a piece of naval sculpture, the figure-head of a ship that had long hovered and plunged into so many running billows, and was now brought ashore to be the ensign and presiding genius of that empty town.

The *Farallone* made a soldier's breeze of it; the wind, besides, was stronger inside than without under the lee of the land; and the stolen schooner opened out successive objects with the swiftness of a panorama, so that the adventurers stood speechless. The flag spoke for itself; it was no frayed and weathered trophy that had beaten itself to pieces on the post, flying over desolation;

and to make assurance stronger, there was to be descried in the deep shade of the veranda, a glitter of crystal and the fluttering of white napery. If the figure-head at the pier-end, with its perpetual gesture and its leprous whiteness, reigned alone in that hamlet as it seemed to do, it would not have reigned long. Men's hands had been busy, men's feet stirring there, within the circuit of the clock. The *Farallones* were sure of it; their eyes dug in the deep shadow of the palms for some one hiding; if intensity of looking might have prevailed, they would have pierced the walls of houses; and there came to them, in these pregnant seconds, a sense of being watched and played with, and of a blow impending, that was hardly bearable.

The extreme point of palms they had just passed enclosed a creek, which was thus hidden up to the last moment from the eyes of those on board; and from this, a boat put suddenly and briskly out, and a voice hailed.

'Schooner ahoy!' it cried. 'Stand in for the pier! In two cables' lengths you'll have twenty fathoms water and good holding-ground.'

The boat was manned with a couple of brown oarsmen in scanty kilts of blue. The speaker, who was steering, wore white clothes, the full dress of the tropics; a wide hat shaded his face; but it could be seen that he was of stalwart size, and his voice sounded like a gentleman's. So much could be made out. It was plain, besides, that the *Farallone* had been descried some time before at sea, and the inhabitants were prepared for its reception.

Mechanically the orders were obeyed, and the ship berthed; and the three adventurers gathered aft beside the house and waited, with galloping pulses and a perfect vacancy of mind, the coming of the stranger who might mean so much to them. They had no plan, no story prepared; there was no time to make one; they were caught red-handed and must stand their chance. Yet this anxiety was chequered with hope. The island being undeclared, it was not possible the man could hold any office or be in a position to demand their papers. And beyond that, if there was any truth in Findlay, as it now seemed there should be, he was the representative of the 'private reasons', he must see their coming with a profound disappointment; and perhaps (hope whispered) he would be willing and able to purchase their silence.

The boat was by that time forging alongside, and they were able at last to see what manner of man they had to do with. He was a huge fellow, six feet four in height, and of a build proportionately strong, but his sinews seemed to be dissolved in a listlessness that was more than languor. It was only the eye that corrected this impression; an eye of an unusual mingled brilliancy and softness, sombre as coal and with lights that outshone the topaz; an eye of unimpaired health and virility; an eye that bid you beware of the man's devastating anger. A complexion, naturally dark, had been tanned in the island to a hue hardly distinguishable from that of a Tahitian; only his manners and movements, and the living force that dwelt in him, like fire in flint, betrayed the European. He was dressed in white drill, exquisitely made; his scarf and tie were of tender-coloured silks; on the thwart beside him there leaned a Winchester rifle.

'Is the doctor on board?' he cried as he came up. 'Dr Symonds, I mean? You never heard of him? Nor yet of the *Trinity Hall*? Ah!'

He did not look surprised, seemed rather to affect it in politeness; but his eye rested on each of the three white men in succession with a sudden weight of curiosity that was almost savage. 'Ah, *then!*' said he, 'there is some small mistake, no doubt, and I must ask you to what I am indebted for this pleasure?'

He was by this time on the deck, but he had the art to be quite unapproachable; the friendliest vulgarian, three parts drunk, would have known better than take liberties; and not one of the adventurers so much as offered to shake hands.

'Well,' said Davis, 'I suppose you may call it an accident. We had heard of your island, and read that thing in the Directory about the *Private Reasons*, you see; so when we saw the lagoon reflected in the sky, we put her head for it at once, and so here we are.'

"Ope we don't intrude!' said Huish.

The stranger looked at Huish with an air of faint surprise, and looked pointedly away again. It was hard to be more offensive in dumb show.

'It may suit me, your coming here,' he said. 'My own schooner is overdue, and I may put something in your way in the mean-time. Are you open to a charter?'

'Well, I guess so,' said Davis; 'it depends.'

'My name is Attwater,' continued the stranger. 'You, I presume, are the captain?'

'Yes, sir. I am the captain of this ship: Captain Brown,' was the reply.

'Well, see 'ere!' said Huish, 'better begin fair! 'E's skipper on deck right enough, but not below. Below, we're all equal, all got a lay in the adventure; when it comes to business, I'm as good as 'e; and what I say is, let's go into the 'ouse and have a lush, and talk it over among pals. We've some prime fizz,' he said, and winked.

The presence of the gentleman lighted up like a candle the vul-garity of the clerk; and Herrick instinctively, as one shields himself from pain, made haste to interrupt.

'My name is Hay,' said he, 'since introductions are going. We shall be very glad if you will step inside.'

Attwater leaned to him swiftly. 'University man?' said he.

'Yes, Merton,' said Herrick, and the next moment blushed scarlet at his indiscretion.

'I am of the other lot,' said Attwater: 'Trinity Hall, Cambridge, I called my schooner after the old shop. Well! this is a queer place and company for us to meet in, Mr Hay,' he pursued, with easy incivility to the others. 'But do you bear out . . . I beg this gentle-man's pardon, I really did not catch his name.'

'My name is 'Uish, sir,' returned the clerk, and blushed in turn.

'Ah!' said Attwater. And then turning again to Herrick, 'Do

you bear out Mr Whish's description of your vintage? or was it only the unaffected poetry of his own nature bubbling up?'

Herrick was embarrassed; the silken brutality of their visitor made him blush; that he should be accepted as an equal, and the others thus pointedly ignored, pleased him in spite of himself, and then ran through his veins in a recoil of anger.

'I don't know,' he said. 'It's only California; it's good enough, I believe.'

Attwater seemed to make up his mind. 'Well then, I'll tell you what: you three gentlemen come ashore this evening and bring a basket of wine with you; I'll try and find the food,' he said. 'And by the by, here is a question I should have asked you when I came on board: have you had smallpox?'

'Personally, no,' said Herrick. 'But the schooner had it.'

'Deaths?' from Attwater.

'Two,' said Herrick.

'Well, it is a dreadful sickness,' said Attwater.

''Ad you any deaths?' asked Huish, ''ere on the island?'

'Twenty-nine,' said Attwater. 'Twenty-nine deaths and thirty-one cases, out of thirty-three souls upon the island. – That's a strange way to calculate, Mr Hay, is it not? Souls! I never say it but it startles me.'

'Oh, so that's why everything's deserted?' said Huish.

'That is why, Mr Whish,' said Attwater; 'that is why the house is empty and the graveyard full.'

'Twenty-nine out of thirty-three!' exclaimed Herrick. 'Why, when it came to burying – or did you bother burying?'

'Scarcely,' said Attwater; 'or there was one day at least when we gave up. There were five of the dead that morning, and thirteen of the dying, and no one able to go about except the sexton and myself. We held a council of war, took the . . . empty bottles . . . into the lagoon, and . . . buried them.' He looked over his shoulder, back at the bright water. 'Well, so you'll come to dinner, then? Shall we say half-past six? *So* good of you!'

His voice, in uttering these conventional phrases, fell at once into the false measure of society; and Herrick unconsciously followed the example.

'I am sure we shall be very glad,' he said. 'At half-past six? Thank you so very much.'

> ' "For my voice has been tuned to the note of the gun
> That startles the deep when the combat's begun," '

quoted Attwater, with a smile, which instantly gave way to an air of funereal solemnity. 'I shall particularly expect Mr Whish,' he continued. 'Mr Whish, I trust you understand the invitation?'

'I believe you, my boy!' replied the genial Huish.

'That is right then; and quite understood, is it not?' said Attwater. 'Mr Whish and Captain Brown at six thirty without fault – and you, Hay, at four sharp.'

And he called his boat.

During all this talk, a load of thought or anxiety had weighed upon the captain. There was no part for which nature had so liberally endowed him as that of the genial ship-captain. But today he was silent and abstracted. Those who knew him could see that he hearkened close to every syllable, and seemed to ponder and try it in balances. It would have been hard to say what look there was, cold, attentive, and sinister, as of a man maturing plans, which still brooded over the unconscious guest; it was here, it was there, it was nowhere; it was now so little that Herrick chid himself for an idle fancy; and anon it was so gross and palpable that you could say every hair on the man's head talked mischief.

He woke up now, as with a start. 'You were talking of a charter,' said he.

'Was I?' said Attwater. 'Well, let's talk of it no more at present.'

'Your own schooner is overdue, I understand?' continued the captain.

'You understand perfectly, Captain Brown,' said Attwater; 'thirty-three days overdue at noon today.'

'She come and goes, eh? plies between here and . . . ?' hinted the captain.

'Exactly; every four months; three trips in the year,' said Attwater.

'You go in her, ever?' asked Davis.

'No, one stops here,' said Attwater, 'one has plenty to attend to.'

'Stop here, do you?' cried Davis. 'Say, how long?'

'How long, O Lord,' said Attwater with perfect, stern gravity. 'But it does not seem so,' he added, with a smile.

'No, I daresay not,' said Davis. 'No, I suppose not. Not with all your gods about you, and in as snug a berth as this. For it is a pretty snug berth,' said he, with a sweeping look.

'The spot, as you are good enough to indicate, is not entirely intolerable,' was the reply.

'Shell, I suppose?' said Davis.

'Yes, there was shell,' said Attwater.

'This is a considerable big beast of a lagoon, sir,' said the captain. 'Was there a – was the fishing – would you call the fishing anyways *good*?'

'I don't know that I would call it anyways anything,' said Attwater, 'if you put it to me direct.'

'There were pearls too?' said Davis.

'Pearls, too,' said Attwater.

'Well, I give out!' laughed Davis, and his laughter rang cracked like a false piece. 'If you're not going to tell, you're not going to tell, and there's an end to it.'

'There can be no reason why I should affect the least degree of secrecy about my island,' returned Attwater; 'that came wholly to an end with your arrival; and I am sure, at any rate, that gentlemen like you and Mr Whish, I should have always been charmed to make perfectly at home. The point on which we are now differing – if you can call it a difference – is one of times and seasons. I have some information which you think I might impart, and I think not. Well, we'll see tonight! By-by, Whish!' He stepped into his boat, and shoved off. 'All understood, then?' said he. 'The captain and Mr Whish at six thirty, and you, Hay, at four precise. You understand that, Hay? Mind, I take no denial. If you're not there by the time named, there will be no banquet; no song, no supper, Mr Whish!'

White birds whisked in the air above, a shoal of parti-coloured fishes in the scarce denser medium below; between, like Mahomet's coffin, the boat drew away briskly on the surface, and its shadow followed it over the glittering floor of the lagoon. Attwater looked steadily back over his shoulders as he sat; he did not once remove his eyes from the *Farallone* and the group on her quarter-deck beside the house, till his boat ground upon the pier. Thence, with an agile pace, he hurried ashore, and they saw his white clothes shining in the chequered dusk of the grove until the house received him.

The captain, with a gesture and a speaking countenance, called the adventurers into the cabin.

'Well,' he said to Herrick, when they were seated, 'there's one good job at least. He's taken to you in earnest.'

'Why should that be a good job?' said Herrick.

'Oh, you'll see how it pans out presently,' returned Davis. 'You go ashore and stand in with him, that's all! You'll get lots of pointers; you can find out what he has, and what the charter is, and who's the fourth man – for there's four of them, and we're only three.'

'And suppose I do, what next?' cried Herrick. 'Answer me that!'

'So I will, Robert Herrick,' said the captain. 'But first, let's see all clear. I guess you know,' he said with an imperious solemnity, 'I guess you know the bottom is out of this *Farallone* speculation? I guess you know it's *right* out? and if this old island hadn't been turned up right when it did, I guess you know where you and I and Huish would have been?'

'Yes, I know that,' said Herrick. 'No matter who's to blame, I know it. And what next?'

'No matter who's to blame, you know it, right enough,' said the captain, 'and I'm obliged to you for the reminder. Now here's this Attwater: what do you think of him?'

'I do not know,' said Herrick. 'I am attracted and repelled. He was insufferably rude to you.'

'And you, Huish?' said the captain.

Huish sat cleaning a favourite briar-root; he scarce looked up from that engrossing task. 'Don't ast me what I think of him!' he said. 'There's a day comin', I pray Gawd, when I can tell it him myself.'

'Huish means the same as what I do,' said Davis, 'When that man came stepping around, and saying "Look here, I'm Attwater" – and you knew it was so, by God! – I sized him right straight up. Here's the real article, I said, and I don't like it; here's the real, first-rate, copper-bottomed aristocrat. *"Aw! don't know ye, do I? God damn ye, did God make ye?"* No, that couldn't be nothing but genuine; a man got to be born to that, and notice! smart as champagne and hard as nails; no kind of a fool; no, *sir*! not a pound of him! Well, what's he here upon this beastly island for? I said. *He's* not here collecting eggs. He's a palace at home, and powdered flunkies; and if he don't stay there, you bet he knows the reason why! Follow?'

'O yes, I 'ear you,' said Huish.

'He's been doing good business here, then,' continued the captain. 'For ten years, he's been doing a great business. It's pearl and shell, of course; there couldn't be nothing else in such a place, and no doubt the shell goes off regularly by this *Trinity Hall*, and the money for it straight into the bank, so that's no use to us. But what else is there? Is there nothing else he would be likely to keep here? Is there nothing else he would be bound to keep here? Yes, sir; the pearls! First, because they're too valuable to trust out of his hands. Second, because pearls want a lot of handling and matching; and the man who sells his pearls as they come in, one here, one there, instead of hanging back and holding up – well, that man's a fool, and it's not Attwater.'

'Likely,' said Huish, 'that's w'at it is; not proved, but likely.'

'It's proved,' said Davis bluntly.

'Suppose it was?' said Herrick. 'Suppose that was all so, and he had these pearls – a ten years' collection of them? – Suppose he had? There's my question.'

The captain drummed with his thick hands on the board in front of him; he looked steadily in Herrick's face, and Herrick as steadily looked upon the table and the pattering fingers; there was a gentle oscillation of the anchored ship, and a big patch of sunlight travelled to and fro between the one and the other.

'Hear me!' Herrick burst out suddenly.

'No, you better hear me first,' said Davis. 'Hear me and understand me. *We*'ve got no use for that fellow, whatever you may have. He's your kind, he's not ours; he's took to you, and he's wiped his boots on me and Huish. Save him if you can!'

'Save him?' repeated Herrick.

'Save him, if you're able!' reiterated Davis, with a blow of his clenched fist. 'Go ashore, and talk him smooth; and if you get him and his pearls aboard, I'll spare him. If you don't, there's going to be a funeral. Is that so, Huish? does that suit you?'

'I ain't a forgiving man,' said Huish, 'but I'm not the sort to spoil business neither. Bring the bloke on board and bring his pearls along with him, and you can have it your own way; maroon him where you like, – I'm agreeable.'

'Well, and if I can't?' cried Herrick, while the sweat streamed upon his face. 'You talk to me as if I was God Almighty, to do this and that! But if I can't?'

'My son,' said the captain, 'you better do your level best, or you'll see sights!'

'O yes,' said Huish. 'O crikey, yes!' He looked across at Herrick with a toothless smile that was shocking in its savagery; and his ear caught apparently by the trivial expression he had used, broke into a piece of the chorus of a comic song which he must have heard twenty years before in London: meaningless gibberish that, in that hour and place, seemed hateful as a blasphemy: 'Hikey, pikey, crikey, fikey, chillingawallaba dory.'

The captain suffered him to finish; his face was unchanged.

'The way things are, there's many a man that wouldn't let you go ashore,' he resumed. 'But I'm not that kind. I know you'd never go back on me, Herrick! Or if you choose to, – go, and do it, and be damned!' he cried, and rose abruptly from the table.

He walked out of the house; and as he reached the door, turned and called Huish, suddenly and violently, like the barking of a dog. Huish followed, and Herrick remained alone in the cabin.

'Now, see here!' whispered Davis. 'I know that man. If you open your mouth to him again, you'll ruin all.'

Chapter Eight

Better Acquaintance

The boat was gone again, and already halfway to the *Farallone*, before Herrick turned and went unwillingly up the pier. From the crown of the beach, the figure-head confronted him with what seemed irony, her helmeted head tossed back, her formidable arm apparently hurling something, whether shell or missile, in the direction of the anchored schooner. She seemed a defiant deity from the island, coming forth to its threshold with a rush as of one about to fly, and perpetuated in that dashing attitude. Herrick looked up at her, where she towered above him head and shoulders, with singular feelings of curiosity and romance, and suffered his mind to travel to and fro in her life-history. So long she had been the blind conductress of a ship among the waves; so long she had stood here idle in the violent sun, that yet did not avail to blister her; and was even this the end of so many adventures? he wondered, or was more behind? And he could have found it in his heart to regret that she was not a goddess, nor yet he a pagan, that he might have bowed down before her in that hour of difficulty.

When he now went forward, it was cool with the shadow of many well-grown palms; draughts of the dying breeze swung them together overhead; and on all sides, with a swiftness beyond dragon-flies or swallows, the spots of sunshine flitted, and hovered, and returned. Underfoot, the sand was fairly solid and quite level, and Herrick's steps fell there noiseless as in new-fallen snow. It bore the marks of having been once weeded like a garden alley at home; but the pestilence had done its work, and the weeds were returning. The buildings of the settlement showed here and there through the stems of the colonnade, fresh painted, trim and dandy, and all silent as the grave. Only, here and there in the crypt, there was a rustle and scurry and some crowing of poultry; and from behind the house with the verandahs, he saw smoke arise and heard the crackling of a fire.

The store-houses were nearest him upon his right. The first was locked; in the second, he could dimly perceive, through a window, a certain accumulation of pearl-shell piled in the far end; the third, which stood gaping open on the afternoon, seized on the mind of Herrick with its multiplicity and disorder of romantic things. Therein were cables, windlasses and blocks of every size and capacity; cabin windows and ladders; rusty tanks, a companion hutch; a binnacle with its brass mountings and its compass idly pointing, in the confusion and dusk of that shed, to a forgotten pole; ropes, anchors, harpoons, a blubber-dipper of copper, green with years, a steering-wheel, a tool-chest with the vessel's name upon the top, the *Asia*: a whole curiosity-shop of sea-curios, gross and solid, heavy to lift, ill to break, bound with brass and shod with iron. Two wrecks at the least must have contributed to this random heap of lumber; and as Herrick looked upon it, it seemed to him as if the two ships' companies were there on guard, and he heard the tread of feet and whisperings, and saw with the tail of his eye the commonplace ghosts of sailor men.

This was not merely the work of an aroused imagination, but had something sensible to go upon; sounds of a stealthy approach were no doubt audible; and while he still stood staring at the lumber, the voice of his host sounded suddenly, and with even more than the customary softness of enunciation, from behind.

'Junk,' it said, 'only old junk! And does Mr Hay find a parable?'

'I find at least a strong impression,' replied Herrick, turning quickly, lest he might be able to catch, on the face of the speaker, some commentary on the words.

Attwater stood in the doorway, which he almost wholly filled;

his hands stretched above his head and grasping the architrave. He smiled when their eyes met, but the expression was inscrutable.

'Yes, a powerful impression. You are like me; nothing so affecting as ships!' said he. 'The ruins of an empire would leave me frigid, when a bit of an old rail that an old shellback leaned on in the middle watch, would bring me up all standing. But come, let's see some more of the island. It's all sand and coral and palm trees; but there's a kind of a quaintness in the place.'

'I find it heavenly,' said Herrick, breathing deep, with head bared in the shadow.

'Ah, that's because you're new from sea,' said Attwater. 'I daresay too, you can appreciate what one calls it. It's a lovely name. It has a flavour, it has a colour, it has a ring and fall to it; it's like its author – it's half Christian! Remember your first view of the island, and how it's only woods and woods and water; and suppose you had asked somebody for the name, and he had answered – *nemorosa Zacynthos*.'

'*Jam medio apparet fluctu!*' exclaimed Herrick. 'Ye gods, yes, how good!'

'If it gets upon the chart, the skippers will make nice work of it,' said Attwater. 'But here, come and see the diving-shed.'

He opened a door, and Herrick saw a large display of apparatus neatly ordered: pumps and pipes, and the leaded boots, and the huge snouted helmets shining in rows along the wall; ten complete outfits.

'The whole eastern half of my lagoon is shallow, you must understand,' said Attwater; 'so we were able to get in the dress to great advantage. It paid beyond belief, and was a queer sight when they were at it, and these marine monsters' – tapping the nearest of the helmets – 'kept appearing and reappearing in the midst of the lagoon. Fond of parables?' he asked abruptly.

'O yes!' said Herrick.

'Well, I saw these machines come up dripping and go down

again, and come up dripping and go down again, and all the while
the fellow inside as dry as toast!' said Attwater; 'and I thought we
all wanted a dress to go down into the world in, and come up
scatheless. What do you think the name was?' he inquired.

'Self-conceit,' said Herrick.

'Ah, but I mean seriously!' said Attwater.

'Call it self-respect, then!' corrected Herrick, with a laugh.

'And why not Grace? Why not God's Grace, Hay?' asked Attwater. 'Why not the grace of your Maker and Redeemer, He who
died for you, He who upholds you, He whom you daily crucify
afresh? There is nothing here,' – striking on his bosom – 'nothing
there' – smiting the wall – 'and nothing there' – stamping – 'nothing
but God's Grace! We walk upon it, we breathe it; we live and die
by it; it makes the nails and axles of the universe; and a puppy in
pyjamas prefers self-conceit!' The huge dark man stood over
against Herrick by the line of the diver's helmets, and seemed to
swell and glow; and the next moment the life had gone from him.
'I beg your pardon,' said he; 'I see you don't believe in God?'

'Not in your sense, I am afraid,' said Herrick.

'I never argue with young atheists or habitual drunkards,'
said Attwater flippantly. 'Let us go across the island to the outer
beach.'

It was but a little way, the greatest width of that island scarce
exceeding a furlong, and they walked gently. Herrick was like one
in a dream. He had come there with a mind divided; come prepared to study that ambiguous and sneering mask, drag out the
essential man from underneath, and act accordingly; decision
being till then postponed. Iron cruelty, an iron insensibility to the
suffering of others, the uncompromising pursuit of his own
interests, cold culture, manners without humanity; these he had
looked for, these he still thought he saw. But to find the whole
machine thus glow with the reverberation of religious zeal, surprised him beyond words; and he laboured in vain, as he walked,
to piece together into any kind of whole his odds and ends of

knowledge – to adjust again into any kind of focus with itself, his picture of the man beside him.

'What brought you here to the South Seas?' he asked presently.

'Many things,' said Attwater. 'Youth, curiosity, romance, the love of the sea, and (it will surprise you to hear) an interest in missions. That has a good deal declined, which will surprise you less. They go the wrong way to work; they are too parsonish, too much of the old wife, and even the old apple-wife. *Clothes, clothes,* are their idea; but clothes are not Christianity, any more than they are the sun in heaven, or could take the place of it! They think a parsonage with roses, and church bells, and nice old women bobbing in the lanes, are part and parcel of religion. But religion is a savage thing, like the universe it illuminates; savage, cold, and bare, but infinitely strong.'

'And you found this island by an accident?' said Herrick.

'As you did!' said Attwater. 'And since then I have had a business, and a colony, and a mission of my own. I was a man of the world before I was a Christian; I'm a man of the world still, and I made my mission pay. No good ever came of coddling. A man has to stand up in God's sight and work up to his weight avoirdupois; then I'll talk to him, but not before. I gave these beggars what they wanted: a judge in Israel, the bearer of the sword and scourge; I was making a new people here; and behold, the angel of the Lord smote them and they were not!'

With the very uttering of the words, which were accompanied by a gesture, they came forth out of the porch of the palm wood by the margin of the sea and full in front of the sun which was near setting. Before them the surf broke slowly. All around, with an air of imperfect wooden things inspired with wicked activity, the crabs trundled and scuttled into holes. On the right, whither Attwater pointed and abruptly turned, was the cemetery of the island, a field of broken stones from the bigness of a child's hand to that of his head, diversified by many mounds of the same material, and walled by a rude rectangular enclosure. Nothing grew there but a shrub or two with some white flowers; nothing but the number of the mounds, and their disquieting shape, indicated the presence of the dead.

'"The rude forefathers of the hamlet lie!"'

quoted Attwater as he entered by the open gateway into that unholy close. 'Coral to coral, pebbles to pebbles,' he said, 'this has been the main scene of my activity in the South Pacific. Some were good, and some bad, and the majority (of course and always) null. Here was a fellow, now, that used to frisk like a dog; if you had called him he came like an arrow from a bow; if you had not, and he came unbidden, you should have seen the deprecating eye and the little intricate dancing step. Well, his trouble is over now, he has lain down with kings and councillors; the rest of his acts, are they not written in the book of the chronicles? That fellow was from Penrhyn; like all the Penrhyn islanders he was ill to manage; heady, jealous, violent: the man with the nose! He lies here quiet enough. And so they all lie.

'"And darkness was the burier of the dead!"'

He stood, in the strong glow of the sunset, with bowed head; his voice sounded now sweet and now bitter with the varying sense.

'You loved these people?' cried Herrick, strangely touched.

'I?' said Attwater. 'Dear no! Don't think me a philanthropist. I dislike men, and hate women. If I like the islanders at all, it is because you see them here plucked of their lendings, their dead birds and cocked hats, their petticoats and coloured hose. Here was one I liked though,' and he set his foot upon a mound. 'He was a fine savage fellow; he had a dark soul; yes, I liked this one. I am fanciful,' he added, looking hard at Herrick, 'and I take fads. I like you.'

Herrick turned swiftly and looked far away to where the

clouds were beginning to troop together and amass themselves round the obsequies of day. 'No one can like me,' he said.

'You are wrong there,' said the other, 'as a man usually is about himself. You are attractive, very attractive.'

'It is not me,' said Herrick; 'no one can like me. If you knew how I despised myself – and why!' His voice rang out in the quiet graveyard.

'I knew that you despised yourself,' said Attwater. 'I saw the blood come into your face today when you remembered Oxford. And I could have blushed for you myself, to see a man, a gentleman, with these two vulgar wolves.'

Herrick faced him with a thrill. 'Wolves?' he repeated.

'I said wolves and vulgar wolves,' said Attwater. 'Do you know that today, when I came on board, I trembled?'

'You concealed it well,' stammered Herrick.

'A habit of mine,' said Attwater. 'But I was afraid, for all that: I was afraid of the two wolves.' He raised his hand slowly. 'And now, Hay, you poor lost puppy, what do you do with the two wolves?'

'What do I do? I don't do anything,' said Herrick. 'There is nothing wrong; all is above-board; Captain Brown is a good soul; he is a . . . he is . . .' The phantom voice of Davis called in his ear: 'There's going to be a funeral;' and the sweat burst forth and streamed on his brow. 'He is a family man,' he resumed again, swallowing; 'he has children at home – and a wife.'

'And a very nice man?' said Attwater. 'And so is Mr Whish, no doubt?'

'I won't go so far as that,' said Herrick. 'I do not like Huish. And yet . . . he has his merits too.'

'And, in short, take them for all in all, as good a ship's company as one would ask?' said Attwater.

'O yes,' said Herrick, 'quite.'

'So then we approach the other point of why you despise yourself?' said Attwater.

'Do we not all despise ourselves?' cried Herrick. 'Do not you?'

'Oh, I say I do. But do I?' said Attwater. 'One thing I know at least: I never gave a cry like yours. Hay! it came from a bad conscience! Ah, man, that poor diving-dress of self-conceit is sadly tattered! Today, if ye will hear my voice. Today, now, while the sun sets, and here in this burying-place of brown innocents, fall on your knees and cast your sins and sorrows on the Redeemer. Hay –'

'Not Hay!' interrupted the other, strangling. 'Don't call me that! I mean . . . For God's sake, can't you see I'm on the rack?'

'I see it, I know it, I put and keep you there, my fingers are on the screws!' said Attwater. 'Please God, I will bring a penitent this night before His throne. Come, come to the mercy-seat! He waits to be gracious, man – waits to be gracious!'

He spread out his arms like a crucifix; his face shone with the brightness of a seraph's; in his voice, as it rose to the last word, the tears seemed ready.

Herrick made a vigorous call upon himself. 'Attwater,' he said, 'you push me beyond bearing. What am I to do? I do not believe. It is living truth to you; to me, upon my conscience, only folklore. I do not believe there is any form of words under heaven, by which I can lift the burthen from my shoulders. I must stagger on to the end with the pack of my responsibility; I cannot shift it; do you suppose I would not, if I thought I could? I cannot – cannot – cannot – and let that suffice.'

The rapture was all gone from Attwater's countenance; the dark apostle had disappeared; and in his place there stood an easy, sneering gentleman, who took off his hat and bowed. It was pertly done, and the blood burned in Herrick's face.

'What do you mean by that?' he cried.

'Well, shall we go back to the house?' said Attwater. 'Our guests will soon be due.'

Herrick stood his ground a moment with clenched fists and teeth; and as he so stood, the fact of his errand there slowly swung clear in front of him, like the moon out of clouds. He had come to lure that man on board; he was failing, even if it could be said that he had tried; he was sure to fail now, and knew it, and knew it was better so. And what was to be next?

With a groan he turned to follow his host, who was standing with polite smile, and instantly and somewhat obsequiously led the way in the now darkened colonnade of palms. There they went in silence, the earth gave up richly of her perfume, the air tasted warm and aromatic in the nostrils; and from a great way forward in the wood, the brightness of lights and fire marked out the house of Attwater.

Herrick meanwhile resolved and resisted an immense temptation to go up, to touch him on the arm and breathe a word in his ear: 'Beware, they are going to murder you.' There would be one life saved; but what of the two others? The three lives went up and down before him like buckets in a well, or like the scales of balances. It had come to a choice, and one that must be speedy. For certain invaluable minutes, the wheels of life ran before him, and he could still divert them with a touch to the one side or the other, still choose who was to live and who was to die. He considered the men. Attwater intrigued, puzzled, dazzled, enchanted and revolted him; alive, he seemed but a doubtful good; and the thought of him lying dead was so unwelcome that it pursued him, like a vision, with every circumstance of colour and sound. Incessantly, he had before him the image of that great mass of man stricken down in varying attitudes and with varying wounds; fallen prone, fallen supine, fallen on his side; or clinging to a doorpost with the changing face and the relaxing fingers of the death-agony. He heard the click of the trigger, the thud of the ball, the cry of the victim; he saw the blood flow. And this building up of circumstance was like a consecration of the man, till he seemed to walk in sacrificial fillets. Next he considered Davis, with his thick-fingered, coarse-grained, oatbread commonness of nature, his indomitable valour and mirth in the old days of their starvation, the endearing blend of his faults and virtues, the sudden shining forth of a tenderness that lay too deep for tears; his children, Ada and her bowel complaint, and Ada's doll. No, death could not be suffered to approach that head even in fancy; with a general heat and a bracing of his muscles, it was borne in on Herrick that Ada's father would find in him a son to the death. And even Huish showed a little in that sacredness; by the tacit adoption of daily life they were become brothers; there was an implied bond of loyalty in their cohabitation of the ship and their passed miseries, to which Herrick must be a little true or wholly dishonoured. Horror of sudden death for horror of sudden death, there was here no hesitation possible: it must be Attwater. And no sooner was the thought formed (which was a sentence) than his whole mind of man ran in a panic to the other side: and when he looked within himself, he was aware only of turbulence and inarticulate outcry.

In all this there was no thought of Robert Herrick. He had complied with the ebb-tide in man's affairs, and the tide had carried him away; he heard already the roaring of the maelstrom that must hurry him under. And in his bedevilled and dishonoured soul there was no thought of self.

For how long he walked silent by his companion Herrick had no guess. The clouds rolled suddenly away; the orgasm was over; he found himself placid with the placidity of despair; there returned to him the power of commonplace speech; and he heard with surprise his own voice say: 'What a lovely evening!'

'Is it not?' said Attwater. 'Yes, the evenings here would be very pleasant if one had anything to do. By day, of course, one can shoot.'

'You shoot?' asked Herrick.

'Yes, I am what you would call a fine shot,' said Attwater. 'It is faith; I believe my balls will go true; if I were to miss once, it would spoil me for nine months.'

'You never miss, then?' said Herrick.

'Not unless I mean to,' said Attwater. 'But to miss nicely is the art. There was an old king one knew in the western islands, who used to empty a Winchester all round a man, and stir his hair or nick a rag out of his clothes with every ball except the last; and that went plump between the eyes. It was pretty practice.'

'You could do that?' asked Herrick, with a sudden chill.

'Oh, I can do anything,' returned the other. 'You do not understand: what must be, must.'

They were now come near to the back part of the house. One of the men was engaged about the cooking fire, which burned with the clear, fierce, essential radiance of cocoanut-shells. A fragrance of strange meats was in the air. All round in the verandahs lamps were lighted, so that the place shone abroad in the dusk of the trees with many complicated patterns of shadow.

'Come and wash your hands,' said Attwater, and led the way into a clean, matted room with a cot bed, a safe, a shelf or two of books in a glazed case, and an iron washing-stand. Presently he cried in the native, and there appeared for a moment in the doorway a plump and pretty young woman with a clean towel.

'Hullo!' cried Herrick, who now saw for the first time the fourth survivor of the pestilence, and was startled by the recollection of the captain's orders.

'Yes,' said Attwater, 'the whole colony lives about the house, what's left of it. We are all afraid of devils, if you please! and Taniera and she sleep in the front parlour, and the other boy on the verandah.'

'She is pretty,' said Herrick.

'Too pretty,' said Attwater. 'That was why I had her married. A man never knows when he may be inclined to be a fool about women; so when we were left alone, I had the pair of them to the chapel and performed the ceremony. She made a lot of fuss. I do not take at all the romantic view of marriage,' he explained.

'And that strikes you as a safeguard?' asked Herrick with amazement.

'Certainly. I am a plain man and very literal. *Whom God hath joined together*, are the words, I fancy. So one married them, and respects the marriage,' said Attwater.

'Ah!' said Herrick.

'You see, I may look to make an excellent marriage when I go home,' began Attwater, confidentially. 'I am rich. This safe alone' – laying his hand upon it – 'will be a moderate fortune, when I have the time to place the pearls upon the market. Here are ten years' accumulation from a lagoon, where I have had as many as ten divers going all day long; and I went further than people usually do in these waters, for I rotted a lot of shell, and did splendidly. Would you like to see them?'

This confirmation of the captain's guess hit Herrick hard, and he contained himself with difficulty. 'No, thank you, I think not,' said he. 'I do not care for pearls. I am very indifferent to all these . . .'

'Gewgaws?' suggested Attwater. 'And yet I believe you ought to cast an eye on my collection, which is really unique, and which – oh! it is the case with all of us and everything about us! – hangs by a hair. Today it groweth up and flourisheth; tomorrow it is cut down and cast into the oven. Today it is here and together in this safe; tomorrow – to-night! – it may be scattered. Thou fool, this night thy soul shall be required of thee.'

'I do not understand you,' said Herrick.

'Not?' said Attwater.

'You seem to speak in riddles,' said Herrick, unsteadily. 'I do not understand what manner of man you are, nor what you are driving at.'

Attwater stood with his hands upon his hips, and his head bent forward. 'I am a fatalist,' he replied, 'and just now (if you insist on it) an experimentalist. Talking of which, by the bye, who painted out the schooner's name?' he said, with mocking softness, 'because, do you know? one thinks it should be done again. It can still be partly read; and whatever is worth doing, is surely worth doing well. You think with me? That is so nice! Well, shall we step on the veranda? I have a dry sherry that I would like your opinion of.'

Herrick followed him forth to where, under the light of the hanging lamps, the table shone with napery and crystal; followed him as the criminal goes with the hangman, or the sheep with the butcher; took the sherry mechanically, drank it, and spoke mechanical words of praise. The object of his terror had become suddenly inverted; till then he had seen Attwater trussed and gagged, a helpless victim, and had longed to run in and save him; he saw him now tower up mysterious and menacing, the angel of the Lord's wrath, armed with knowledge and threatening judgment. He set down his glass again, and was surprised to see it empty.

'You go always armed?' he said, and the next moment could have plucked his tongue out.

'Always,' said Attwater. 'I have been through a mutiny here; that was one of my incidents of missionary life.'

And just then the sound of voices reached them, and looking forth from the veranda they saw Huish and the captain drawing near.

Chapter Nine

The Dinner Party

They sat down to an island dinner, remarkable for its variety and excellence: turtle-soup and steak, fish, fowls, a sucking pig, a cocoanut salad, and sprouting cocoanut roasted for dessert. Not a tin had been opened; and save for the oil and vinegar in the salad, and some green spears of onion which Attwater cultivated and plucked with his own hand, not even the condiments were European. Sherry, hock, and claret succeeded each other, and the *Farallone* champagne brought up the rear with the dessert.

It was plain that, like so many of the extremely religious in the days before teetotalism, Attwater had a dash of the epicure. For such characters it is softening to eat well; doubly so to have designed and had prepared an excellent meal for others; and the manners of their host were agreeably mollified in consequence. A cat of huge growth sat on his shoulder purring, and occasionally, with a deft paw, capturing a morsel in the air. To a cat he might be likened himself, as he lolled at the head of his table, dealing out attentions and innuendos, and using the velvet and the claw indifferently. And both Huish and the captain fell progressively under the charm of his hospitable freedom.

Over the third guest, the incidents of the dinner may be said to have passed for long unheeded. Herrick accepted all that was offered him, ate and drank without tasting, and heard without comprehension. His mind was singly occupied in contemplating the horror of the circumstances in which he sat. What Attwater knew, what the captain designed, from which side treachery was to be first expected, these were the ground of his thoughts. There were times when he longed to throw down the table and flee into the night. And even that was debarred him; to do anything, to say anything, to move at all, were only to precipitate the barbarous tragedy; and he sat spell-bound, eating with white lips. Two of his companions observed him narrowly, Attwater with raking, sidelong glances that did not interrupt his talk, the captain with a heavy and anxious consideration.

'Well, I must say this sherry is a really prime article,' said Huish, ''Ow much does it stand you in, if it's a fair question?'

'A hundred and twelve shillings in London, and the freight to Valparaiso, and on again,' said Attwater. 'It strikes one as really not a bad fluid.'

'A 'undred and twelve!' murmured the clerk, relishing the wine and the figures in a common ecstasy: 'O my!'

'So glad you like it,' said Attwater. 'Help yourself, Mr Whish, and keep the bottle by you.'

'My friend's name is Huish and not Whish, sir,' said the captain with a flush.

'I beg your pardon, I am sure. Huish and not Whish; certainly,' said Attwater. 'I was about to say that I have still eight dozen,' he added, fixing the captain with his eye.

'Eight dozen what?' said Davis.

'Sherry,' was the reply. 'Eight dozen excellent sherry. Why, it seems almost worth it in itself; to a man fond of wine.'

The ambiguous words struck home to guilty consciences, and Huish and the captain sat up in their places and regarded him with a scare.

'Worth what?' said Davis.

'A hundred and twelve shillings,' replied Attwater.

The captain breathed hard for a moment. He reached out far and wide to find any coherency in these remarks; then, with a great effort, changed the subject.

'I allow we are about the first white men upon this island, sir,' said he.

Attwater followed him at once, and with entire gravity, to the new ground. 'Myself and Dr Symonds excepted, I should say the only ones,' he returned. 'And yet who can tell? In the course of the ages some one may have lived here, and we sometimes think that some one must. The cocoa-palms grow all round the island, which is scarce like nature's planting. We found besides, when we landed, an unmistakable cairn upon the beach; use unknown; but probably erected in the hope of gratifying some mumbo-jumbo whose very name is forgotten, by some thick-witted gentry whose very bones are lost. Then the island (witness the *Directory*) has been twice reported; and since my tenancy, we have had two wrecks, both derelict. The rest is conjecture.'

'Dr Symonds is your partner, I guess?' said Davis.

'A dear fellow, Symonds! How he would regret it, if he knew you had been here!' said Attwater.

''E's on the *Trinity 'All*, ain't he?' asked Huish.

'And if you could tell me where the *Trinity 'All* was, you would confer a favour, Mr Whish!' was the reply.

'I suppose she has a native crew?' said Davis.

'Since the secret has been kept ten years, one would suppose she had,' replied Attwater.

'Well, now, see 'ere!' said Huish. 'You have everythink about you in no end style, and no mistake, but I tell you it wouldn't do for me. Too much of "the old rustic bridge by the mill"; too retired, by 'alf. Give me the sound of Bow Bells!'

'You must not think it was always so,' replied Attwater. 'This was once a busy shore, although now, hark! you can hear the solitude. I find it stimulating. And talking of the sound of bells, kindly follow a little experiment of mine in silence.' There was a silver bell at his right hand to call the servants; he made them a sign to stand still, struck the bell with force, and leaned eagerly forward. The note rose clear and strong; it rang out clear and far into the night and over the deserted island; it died into the distance until there only lingered in the porches of the ear a vibration that was sound no longer. 'Empty houses, empty sea, solitary beaches!' said Attwater. 'And yet God hears the bell! And yet we sit in this veranda on a lighted stage with all heaven for spectators! And you call that solitude?'

There followed a bar of silence, during which the captain sat mesmerized.

Then Attwater laughed softly. 'These are the diversions of a lonely man,' he resumed, 'and possibly not in good taste. One tells oneself these little fairy tales for company. If there *should* happen to be anything in folk-lore, Mr Hay? But here comes the claret. One does not offer you Lafitte, captain, because I believe it is all sold to the railroad dining-cars in your great country; but this Brâne-Mouton is of a good year, and Mr Whish will give me news of it.'

'That's a queer idea of yours!' cried the captain, bursting with a sigh from the spell that had bound him. 'So you mean to tell me now, that you sit here evenings and ring up . . . well, ring on the angels . . . by yourself?'

'As a matter of historic fact, and since you put it directly, one does not,' said Attwater. 'Why ring a bell, when there flows out from oneself and everything about one a far more momentous silence? the least beat of my heart and the least thought in my mind echoing into eternity for ever and for ever and for ever.'

'O look 'ere,' said Huish, 'turn down the lights at once, and the Band of 'Ope will oblige! This ain't a spiritual séance.'

'No folk-lore about Mr Whish – I beg your pardon, captain: Huish not Whish, of course,' said Attwater.

As the boy was filling Huish's glass, the bottle escaped from his hand and was shattered, and the wine spilt on the veranda floor. Instant grimness as of death appeared in the face of Attwater; he smote the bell imperiously, and the two brown natives fell into the attitude of attention and stood mute and trembling. There was just a moment of silence and hard looks; then followed a few savage words in the native; and, upon a gesture of dismissal, the service proceeded as before.

None of the party had as yet observed upon the excellent

bearing of the two men. They were dark, undersized, and well set-up; stepped softly, waited deftly, brought on the wines and dishes at a look, and their eyes attended studiously on their master.

'Where do you get your labour from anyway?' asked Davis.

'Ah, where not?' answered Attwater.

'Not much of a soft job, I suppose?' said the captain.

'If you will tell me where getting labour is!' said Attwater with a shrug. 'And of course, in our case, as we could name no destination, we had to go far and wide and do the best we could. We have gone as far west as the Kingsmills and as far south as Rapa-iti. Pity Symonds isn't here! He is full of yarns. That was his part, to collect them. Then began mine, which was the educational.'

'You mean to run them?' said Davis.

'Ay! to run them,' said Attwater.

'Wait a bit,' said Davis, 'I'm out of my depth. How was this? Do you mean to say you did it single-handed?'

'One did it single-handed,' said Attwater, 'because there was nobody to help one.'

'By God, but you must be a holy terror!' cried the captain, in a glow of admiration.

'One does one's best,' said Attwater.

'Well, now!' said Davis, 'I have seen a lot of driving in my time and been counted a good driver myself; I fought my way, third mate, round the Cape Horn with a push of packet-rats that would have turned the devil out of hell and shut the door on him; and I tell you, this racket of Mr Attwater's takes the cake. In a ship, why, there ain't nothing to it! You've got the law with you, that's what does it. But put me down on this blame' beach alone, with nothing but a whip and a mouthful of bad words, and ask me to . . . no, *sir*! it's not good enough! I haven't got the sand for that!' cried Davis. 'It's the law behind,' he added; 'it's the law does it, every time!'

'The beak ain't as black as he's sometimes pynted,' observed Huish, humorously.

'Well, one got the law after a fashion,' said Attwater. 'One had to be a number of things. It was sometimes rather a bore.'

'I should smile!' said Davis. 'Rather lively, I should think!'

'I daresay we mean the same thing,' said Attwater. 'However, one way or another, one got it knocked into their heads that they *must* work, and they *did* . . . until the Lord took them!'

''Ope you made 'em jump,' said Huish.

'When it was necessary, Mr Whish, I made them jump,' said Attwater.

'You bet you did,' cried the captain. He was a good deal flushed, but not so much with wine as admiration; and his eyes drank in the huge proportions of the other with delight. 'You bet you did, and you bet that I can see you doing it! By God, you're a man, and you can say I said so.'

'Too good of you, I'm sure,' said Attwater.

'Did you – did you ever have crime here?' asked Herrick, breaking his silence with a pungent voice.

'Yes,' said Attwater, 'we did.'

'And how did you handle that, sir?' cried the eager captain.

'Well, you see, it was a queer case,' replied Attwater. 'It was a case that would have puzzled Solomon. Shall I tell it you? yes?'

The captain repturously accepted.

'Well,' drawled Attwater, 'here is what it was. I daresay you know two types of natives, which may be called the obsequious and the sullen? Well, one had them, the types themselves, detected in the fact; and one had them together. Obsequiousness ran out of the first like wine out of a bottle, sullenness congested in the second. Obsequiousness was all smiles; he ran to catch your eye, he loved to gabble; and he had about a dozen words of beach English, and an eighth-of-an-inch veneer of Christianity. Sullens was industrious; a big down-looking bee. When he was spoken to, he answered with a black look and a shrug of one shoulder, but the thing would be done. I don't give him to you for a model of manners; there was nothing showy about Sullens; but he was strong and steady, and ungraciously obedient. Now Sullens got into trouble; no matter how; the regulations of the place were broken, and he was punished accordingly – without effect. So, the next day, and the next, and the day after, till I began to be weary of the business, and Sullens (I am afraid) particularly so. There came a day when he was in fault again, for the – oh, perhaps the thirtieth time; and he rolled a dull eye upon me, with a spark in it, and appeared to speak. Now the regulations of the place are formal upon one point: we allow no explanations; none are received, none allowed to be offered. So one stopped him instantly, but made a note of the circumstance. The next day, he was gone from the settlement. There could be nothing more annoying; if the labour took to running away, the fishery was wrecked. There are sixty miles of this island, you see, all in length like the Queen's Highway; the idea of pursuit in such a place was a piece of single-minded childishness, which one did not entertain. Two days later, I made a discovery; it came in upon me with a flash that Sullens had been unjustly punished from beginning to end, and the real culprit throughout had been Obsequiousness. The native who talks, like the woman who hesitates, is lost. You set him talking and lying; and he talks, and lies, and watches your face to see if he has pleased you; till at last, out comes the truth! It came out of Obsequiousness in the regular course. I said nothing to him; I dismissed him; and late as it was, for it was already night, set off to look for Sullens. I had not far to go: about two hundred yards up the island, the moon showed him to me. He was hanging in a cocoa-palm – I'm not botanist enough to tell you how – but it's the way, in nine cases out of ten, these natives commit suicide. His tongue was out, poor devil, and the birds had got at him; I spare you details, he was an ugly sight! I gave the business six good hours of thinking in this veranda. My justice had been made a fool of; I don't suppose that I was ever angrier. Next day, I had the conch sounded and all hands out before sunrise. One took one's gun, and led the way, with Obsequiousness.

He was very talkative; the beggar supposed that all was right now he had confessed; in the old schoolboy phrase, he was plainly 'sucking up' to me; full of protestations of good-will and good behaviour; to which one answered one really can't remember what. Presently the tree came in sight, and the hanged man. They all burst out lamenting for their comrade in the island way, and Obsequiousness was the loudest of the mourners. He was quite genuine; a noxious creature, without any consciousness of guilt. Well, presently – to make a long story short – one told him to go up the tree. He stared a bit, looked at one with a trouble in his eye, and had rather a sickly smile; but went. He was obedient to the last; he had all the pretty virtues, but the truth was not in him. So soon as he was up, he looked down, and there was the rifle covering him; and at that he gave a whimper like a dog. You could hear a pin drop; no more keening now. There they all crouched upon the ground, with bulging eyes; there was he in the tree-top, the colour of lead; and between was the dead man, dancing a bit in the air. He was obedient to the last, recited his crime, recommended his soul to God. And then . . .'

Attwater paused, and Herrick, who had been listening attentively, made a convulsive movement which upset his glass.

'And then?' said the breathless captain.

'Shot,' said Attwater. 'They came to ground together.'

Herrick sprang to his feet with a shriek and an insensate gesture.

'It was a murder,' he screamed. 'A cold-hearted, bloody-minded murder! You monstrous being! Murderer and hypocrite – murderer and hypocrite – murderer and hypocrite –' he repeated, and his tongue stumbled among the words.

The captain was by him in a moment. 'Herrick!' he cried, 'behave yourself! Here, don't be a blame' fool!'

Herrick struggled in his embrace like a frantic child, and suddenly bowing his face in his hands, choked into a sob, the first of many, which now convulsed his body silently, and now jerked from him indescribable and meaningless sounds.

'Your friend appears over-excited,' remarked Attwater, sitting unmoved but all alert at table.

'It must be the wine,' replied the captain. 'He ain't no drinking man, you see. I – I think I'll take him away. A walk'll sober him up, I guess.'

He led him without resistance out of the veranda and into the night, in which they soon melted; but still for some time, as they drew away, his comfortable voice was to be heard soothing and remonstrating, and Herrick answering, at intervals, with the mechanical noises of hysteria.

''E's like a bloomin' poultry yard!' observed Huish, helping himself to wine (of which he spilled a good deal) with gentlemanly ease. 'A man should learn to beyave at table,' he added.

'Rather bad form, is it not?' said Attwater. 'Well, well, we are left *tête-à-tête*. A glass of wine with you, Mr Whish!'

Chapter Ten

The Open Door

The captain and Herrick meanwhile turned their back upon the lights in Attwater's veranda, and took a direction towards the pier and the beach of the lagoon.

The isle, at this hour, with its smooth floor of sand, the pillared roof overhead, and the prevalent illumination of the lamps, wore an air of unreality like a deserted theatre or a public garden at midnight. A man looked about him for the statues and tables. Not the least air of wind was stirring among the palms, and the silence was emphasized by the continuous clamour of the surf from the sea-shore, as it might be of traffic in the next street.

Still talking, still soothing him, the captain hurried his patient on, brought him at last to the lagoon side, and leading him down the beach, laved his head and face with the tepid water. The paroxysm gradually subsided, the sobs became less convulsive and then ceased; by an odd but not quite unnatural conjunction, the captain's soothing current of talk died away at the same time and by proportional steps, and the pair remained sunk in silence. The lagoon broke at their feet in petty wavelets, and with a sound as delicate as a whisper; stars of all degrees looked down on their own images in that vast mirror; and the more angry colour of the *Farallone*'s riding lamp burned in the middle distance. For long they continued to gaze on the scene before them, and hearken anxiously to the rustle and tinkle of that miniature surf, or the more distant and loud reverberations from the outer coast. For long speech was denied them; and when the words came at last, they came to both simultaneously.

'Say, Herrick . . .' the captain was beginning.

But Herrick, turning swiftly towards his companion, bent him down with the eager cry: 'Let's up anchor, captain, and to sea!'

'Where to, my son?' said the captain. 'Up anchor's easy saying. But where to?'

'To sea,' responded Herrick. 'The sea's big enough! To sea – away from this dreadful island and that, oh! that sinister man!'

'Oh, we'll see about that,' said Davis. 'You brace up, and we'll see about that. You're all run down, that's what's wrong with you; you're all nerves, like Jemimar; you've got to brace up good and be yourself again, and then we'll talk.'

'To sea,' reiterated Herrick, 'to sea tonight – now – this moment!'

'It can't be, my son,' replied the captain firmly. 'No ship of mine puts to sea without provisions, you can take that for settled.'

'You don't seem to understand,' said Herrick. 'The whole thing is over, I tell you. There is nothing to do here, when he knows all. That man there with the cat knows all; can't you take it in?'

'All what?' asked the captain, visibly discomposed. 'Why, he received us like a perfect gentleman and treated us real handsome, until you began with your foolery – and I must say I seen men shot for less, and nobody sorry! What more do you expect anyway?'

Herrick rocked to and fro upon the sand, shaking his head.

'Guying us,' he said, 'he was guying us – only guying us; it's all we're good for.'

'There was one queer thing, to be sure,' admitted the captain, with a misgiving of the voice; 'that about the sherry. Damned if I caught on to that. Say, Herrick, you didn't give me away?'

'Oh! give you away!' repeated Herrick with weary, querulous scorn. 'What was there to give away? We're transparent; we've got rascal branded on us: detected rascal – detected rascal! Why, before he came on board, there was the name painted out, and he saw the whole thing. He made sure we would kill him there and then, and stood guying you and Huish on the chance. He calls that being frightened! Next he had me ashore; a fine time I had! *The two wolves*, he calls you and Huish. – *What is the puppy doing with the two wolves?* he asked. He showed me his pearls; he said they might be dispersed before morning, and *all hung by a hair* – and smiled as he said it, such a smile! O, it's no use, I tell you! He knows all, he sees through all; we only make him laugh with our pretences – he looks at us and laughs like God!'

There was a silence. Davis stood with contorted brows, gazing into the night.

'The pearls?' he said suddenly. 'He showed them to you? he has them?'

'No, he didn't show them; I forgot: only the safe they were in,' said Herrick. 'But you'll never get them!'

'I've two words to say to that,' said the captain.

'Do you think he would have been so easy at table, unless he was prepared?' cried Herrick. 'The servants were both armed. He was armed himself; he always is; he told me. You will never deceive his vigilance. Davis, I know it! It's all up, I tell you, and keep telling you and proving it. All up; all up. There's nothing for it, there's nothing to be done: all gone: life, honour, love. Oh, my God, my God, why was I born?'

Another pause followed upon this outburst.

The captain put his hands to his brow.

'Another thing!' he broke out. 'Why did he tell you all this? Seems like madness to me!'

Herrick shook his head with gloomy iteration. 'You wouldn't understand if I were to tell you,' said he.

'I guess I can understand any blame' thing that you can tell me,' said the captain.

'Well, then, he's a fatalist,' said Herrick.

'What's that, a fatalist?' said Davis.

'Oh, it's a fellow that believes a lot of things,' said Herrick, 'believes that his bullets go true; believes that all falls out as God chooses, do as you like to prevent it; and all that.'

'Why, I guess I believe right so myself,' said Davis.

'You do?' said Herrick.

'You bet I do!' says Davis.

Herrick shrugged his shoulders. 'Well, you must be a fool,' said he, and he leaned his head upon his knees.

The captain stood biting his hands.

'There's one thing sure,' he said at last. 'I must get Huish out of that. *He's* not fit to hold his end up with a man like you describe.'

And he turned to go away. The words had been quite simple; not so the tone; and the other was quick to catch it.

'Davis!' he cried, 'no! Don't do it. Spare *me*, and don't do it – spare yourself, and leave it alone – for God's sake, for your children's sake!'

His voice rose to a passionate shrillness; another moment, and he might be overheard by their not distant victim. But Davis turned on him with a savage oath and gesture; and the miserable young man rolled over on his face on the sand, and lay speechless and helpless.

The captain meanwhile set out rapidly for Attwater's house. As he went, he considered with himself eagerly, his thoughts racing. The man had understood, he had mocked them from the beginning; he would teach him to make a mockery of John Davis! Herrick thought him a god; give him a second to aim in, and the god was overthrown. He chuckled as he felt the butt of his revolver. It should be done now, as he went in. From behind? It was difficult to get there. From across the table? No, the captain preferred to shoot standing, so as you could be sure to get your hand upon your gun. The best would be to summon Huish, and when Attwater stood up and turned – Ah, then would be the moment. Wrapped in this ardent prefiguration of events, the captain posted towards the house with his head down.

'Hands up! Halt!' cried the voice of Attwater.

And the captain, before he knew what he was doing, had obeyed. The surprise was complete and irremediable. Coming on the top crest of his murderous intentions, he had walked straight into an ambuscade, and now stood, with his hands impotently lifted, staring at the veranda.

The party was now broken up. Attwater leaned on a post, and kept Davis covered with a Winchester. One of the servants was hard by with a second at the port arms, leaning a little forward, round-eyed with eager expectancy. In the open space at the head of the stair, Huish was partly supported by the other native; his face wreathed in meaningless smiles, his mind seemingly sunk in the contemplation of an unlighted cigar.

'Well,' said Attwater, 'you seem to me to be a very twopenny pirate!'

The captain uttered a sound in his throat for which we have no name; rage choked him.

'I am going to give you Mr Whish – or the wine-sop that remains of him,' continued Attwater. 'He talks a great deal when he drinks, Captain Davis of the *Sea Ranger*. But I have quite done with him – and return the article with thanks. Now,' he cried sharply. 'Another false movement like that, and your family will have to deplore the loss of an invaluable parent; keep strictly still, Davis.'

Attwater said a word in the native, his eye still undeviatingly fixed on the captain; and the servant thrust Huish smartly forward from the brink of the stair. With an extraordinary simultaneous dispersion of his members, that gentleman bounded forth into space, struck the earth, ricochetted, and brought up with his arms about a palm. His mind was quite a stranger to these events; the expression of anguish that deformed his countenance at the moment of the leap was probably mechanical; and he suffered these convulsions in silence; clung to the tree like an infant; and seemed, by his dips, to suppose himself engaged in the pastime of bobbing for apples. A more finely sympathetic mind or a more observant eye might have remarked, a little in front of him on the sand, and still quite beyond reach, the unlighted cigar.

'There is your Whitechapel carrion!' said Attwater. 'And now you might very well ask me why I do not put a period to you at once, as you deserve. I will tell you why, Davis. It is because I have nothing to do with the *Sea Ranger* and the people you drowned, or the *Farallone* and the champagne that you stole. That is your account with God; He keeps it, and He will settle it when the clock strikes. In my own case, I have nothing to go on but suspicion, and I do not kill on suspicion, not even vermin like you. But understand! if ever I see any of you again, it is another matter, and you shall eat a bullet. And now take yourself off. March! and as you value what you call your life, keep your hands up as you go!'

The captain remained as he was, his hands up, his mouth open: mesmerized with fury.

'March!' said Attwater. 'One – two – three!'

And Davis turned and passed slowly away. But even as he went, he was meditating a prompt, offensive return. In the twinkling of an eye, he had leaped behind a tree; and was crouching there, pistol in hand, peering from either side of his place of ambush with bared teeth; a serpent already poised to strike. And already he was too late. Attwater and his servants had disappeared; and only the lamps shone on the deserted table and the bright sand about the house, and threw into the night in all directions the strong and tall shadows of the palms.

Davis ground his teeth. Where were they gone, the cowards? to what hole had they retreated beyond reach? It was in vain he should try anything, he, single and with a second-hand revolver, against three persons, armed with Winchesters, and who did not show an ear out of any of the apertures of that lighted and silent house. Some of them might have already ducked below it from the rear, and be drawing a bead upon him at that moment from the low-browed crypt, the receptacle of empty bottles and broken crockery. No, there was nothing to be done but to bring away (if it were still possible) his shattered and demoralized forces.

'Huish,' he said, 'come along.'

''S lose my ciga',' said Huish, reaching vaguely forward.

The captain let out a rasping oath. 'Come right along here,' said he.

''S all righ'. Sleep here 'th Atty-Attwa. Go boar' t'morr',' replied the festive one.

'If you don't come, and come now, by the living God, I'll shoot you!' cried the captain.

It is not to be supposed that the sense of these words in any way penetrated to the mind of Huish; rather that, in a fresh attempt upon the cigar, he over-balanced himself and came flying erratically forward: a course which brought him within reach of Davis.

'Now you walk straight,' said the captain, clutching him, 'or I'll know why not!'

''S lose my ciga',' replied Huish.

The captain's contained fury blazed up for a moment. He twisted Huish round, grasped him by the neck of the coat, ran him in front of him to the pier-end, and flung him savagely forward on his face.

'Look for your cigar then, you swine!' said he, and blew his boat-call till the pea in it ceased to rattle.

An immediate activity responded on board the *Farallone*; faraway voices, and soon the sound of oars, floated along the surface of the lagoon; and at the same time, from nearer hand, Herrick aroused himself and strolled languidly up. He bent over the insignificant figure of Huish, where it grovelled, apparently insensible, at the base of the figure-head.

'Dead?' he asked.

'No, he's not dead,' said Davis.

'And Attwater?' asked Herrick.

'Now you just shut your head!' replied Davis. 'You can do that, I fancy, and by God, I'll show you how! I'll stand no more of your drivel.'

They waited accordingly in silence till the boat bumped on the furthest piers; then raised Huish, head and heels, carried him down the gangway, and flung him summarily in the bottom. On the way out he was heard murmuring of the loss of his cigar; and after he had been handed up the side like baggage, and cast down in the alleyway to slumber, his last audible expression was: 'Splen'l fl' Attwa'!' This the expert construed into 'Splendid fellow, Attwater'; with so much innocence had this great spirit issued from the adventures of the evening.

The captain went and walked in the waist with brief, irate turns; Herrick leaned his arms on the taffrail; the crew had all turned in. The ship had a gentle, cradling motion; at times a block piped like a bird. On shore, through the colonnade of palm stems, Attwater's house was to be seen shining steadily with many lamps. And there was nothing else visible, whether in the heaven above or in the lagoon below, but the stars and their reflexions. It might have been minutes or it might have been hours, that Herrick leaned there, looking in the glorified water and drinking peace. 'A bath of stars,' he was thinking; when a hand was laid at last on his shoulder.

'Herrick,' said the captain, 'I've been walking off my trouble.'

A sharp jar passed through the young man, but he neither answered nor so much as turned his head.

'I guess I spoke a little rough to you on shore,' pursued the captain; 'the fact is, I was real mad; but now it's over, and you and me have to turn to and think.'

'I will *not* think,' said Herrick.

'Here, old man!' said Davis, kindly; 'this won't fight, you know! You've got to brace up and help me get things straight. You're not going back on a friend? That's not like you, Herrick!'

'O yes, it is,' said Herrick.

'Come, come!' said the captain, and paused as if quite at a loss. 'Look here,' he cried, 'you have a glass of champagne. *I* won't touch it, so that'll show you if I'm in earnest. But it's just the pick-me-up for you; it'll put an edge on you at once.'

'O, you leave me alone!' said Herrick, and turned away.

The captain caught him by the sleeve; and he shook him off and turned on him, for the moment, like a demoniac.

'Go to hell in your own way!' he cried.

And he turned away again, this time unchecked, and stepped forward to where the boat rocked alongside and ground occasionally against the schooner. He looked about him. A corner of the house was interposed between the captain and himself; all was well; no eye must see him in that last act. He slid silently into the boat; thence, silently, into the starry water. Instinctively he swam a little; it would be time enough to stop by and by.

The shock of the immersion brightened his mind immediately. The events of the ignoble day passed before him in a frieze of pictures, and he thanked 'whatever Gods there be' for that open door of suicide. In such a little while he would be done with it, the random business at an end, the prodigal son come home. A very bright planet shone before him and drew a trenchant wake along the water. He took that for his line and followed it. That was the last earthly thing that he should look upon; that radiant speck, which he had soon magnified into a City of Laputa, along whose terraces there walked men and women of awful and benignant features, who viewed him with distant commiseration. These imaginary spectators consoled him; he told himself their talk, one to another; it was of himself and his sad destiny.

From such flights of fancy, he was aroused by the growing coldness of the water. Why should he delay? Here, where he was now, let him drop the curtain, let him seek the ineffable refuge, let him lie down with all races and generations of men in the house of sleep. It was easy to say, easy to do. To stop swimming: there was no mystery in that, if he could do it. Could he? And he could not. He knew it instantly. He was aware instantly of an opposition in his members, unanimous and invincible, clinging to life with a single and fixed resolve, finger by finger, sinew by sinew; something that was at once he and not he – at once within and without him; the shutting of some miniature valve in his brain, which a single manly thought should suffice to open – and the grasp of an external fate ineluctable as gravity. To any man there may come at times a consciousness that there blows, through all the articulations of his body, the wind of a spirit not wholly his; that his mind rebels; that another girds him and carries him whither he would not. It came now to Herrick, with the authority of a revelation. There was no escape possible. The open door was closed in his recreant face. He must go back into the world and amongst men without illusion. He must stagger on to the end with the pack of his responsibility and his disgrace, until a cold, a blow, a merciful chance ball, or the more merciful hangman, should dismiss him from his infamy. There were men who could commit suicide; there were men who could not; and he was one who could not.

For perhaps a minute, there raged in his mind the coil of this discovery; then cheerless certitude followed; and, with an incredible simplicity of submission to ascertained fact, he turned round and struck out for shore. There was a courage in this which he could not appreciate; the ignobility of his cowardice wholly occupying him. A strong current set against him like a wind in his face; he contended with it heavily, wearily, without enthusiasm, but with substantial advantage; marking his progress the while, without pleasure, by the outline of the trees. Once he had a moment of hope. He heard to the southward of him, towards the centre of the lagoon, the wallowing of some great fish, doubtless a shark, and paused for a little, treading water. Might not this be the hangman? he thought. But the wallowing died away; mere silence succeeded; and Herrick pushed on again for the shore, raging as he went at his own nature. Ay, he would wait for the shark; but if he had heard him coming! . . . His smile was tragic. He could have spat upon himself.

About three in the morning, chance, and the set of the current, and the bias of his own right-handed body, so decided it between them that he came to shore upon the beach in front of Attwater's. There he sat down, and looked forth into a world without any of the lights of hope. The poor diving-dress of self-conceit was sadly tattered! With the fairy tale of suicide, of a refuge always open to him, he had hitherto beguiled and supported himself in the trials of life; and behold! that also was only a fairy tale, that also was folk-lore. With the consequences of his acts he saw himself implacably confronted for the duration of life: stretched upon a cross, and nailed there with the iron bolts of his own cowardice. He had no tears; he told himself no stories. His disgust with himself was so complete, that even the process of apologetic mythology had ceased. He was like a man cast down from a pillar, and every bone broken. He lay there, and admitted the facts, and did not attempt to rise.

Dawn began to break over the far side of the atoll, the sky brightened, the clouds became dyed with gorgeous colours, the shadows of the night lifted. And, suddenly, Herrick was aware that the lagoon and the trees wore again their daylight livery; and he saw, on board the *Farallone*, Davis extinguishing the lantern, and smoke rising from the galley.

Davis, without doubt, remarked and recognized the figure on the beach; or perhaps hesitated to recognize it; for after he had gazed a long while from under his hand, he went into the house and fetched a glass. It was very powerful; Herrick had often used it. With an instinct of shame, he hid his face in his hands.

'And what brings you here, Mr Herrick-Hay, or Mr Hay-Herrick?' asked the voice of Attwater. 'Your back view from my present position is remarkably fine, and I would continue to present it. We can get on very nicely as we are, and if you were to turn round, do you know? I think it would be awkward.'

Herrick slowly rose to his feet; his heart throbbed hard, a hideous excitement shook him, but he was master of himself. Slowly he turned, and faced Attwater and the muzzle of a pointed rifle. 'Why could I not do that last night?' he thought.

'Well, why don't you fire?' he said aloud, with a voice that trembled.

Attwater slowly put his gun under his arm, then his hands in his pockets.

'What brings you here?' he repeated.

'I don't know,' said Herrick; and then, with a cry: 'Can you do anything with me?'

'Are you armed?' said Attwater. 'I ask for the form's sake.'

'Armed? No!' said Herrick. 'O yes, I am, too!'

And he flung upon the beach a dripping pistol.

'You are wet,' said Attwater.

'Yes, I am wet,' said Herrick. 'Can you do anything with me?'

Attwater read his face attentively.

'It would depend a good deal upon what you are,' said he.

'What I am? A coward!' said Herrick.

'There is very little to be done with that,' said Attwater. 'And yet the description hardly strikes one as exhaustive.'

'Oh, what does it matter?' cried Herrick. 'Here I am. I am broken crockery; I am a burst drum; the whole of my life is gone to water; I have nothing left that I believe in, except my living horror of myself. Why do I come to you? I don't know; you are cold, cruel, hateful; and I hate you, or I think I hate you. But you are an honest man, an honest gentleman. I put myself, helpless, in your hands. What must I do? If I can't do anything, be merciful and put a bullet through me; it's only a puppy with a broken leg!'

'If I were you, I would pick up that pistol, come up to the house, and put on some dry clothes,' said Attwater.

'If you really mean it?' said Herrick. 'You know they – we – they . . . But you know all.'

'I know quite enough,' said Attwater. 'Come up to the house.'

And the captain, from the deck of the *Farallone*, saw the two men pass together under the shadow of the grove.

Chapter Eleven

David and Goliath

Huish had bundled himself up from the glare of the day – his face to the house, his knees retracted. The frail bones in the thin tropical raiment seemed scarce more considerable than a fowl's; and Davis, sitting on the rail with his arm about a stay, contemplated him with gloom, wondering what manner of counsel that insignificant figure should contain. For since Herrick had thrown him off and deserted to the enemy, Huish, alone of mankind, remained to him to be a helper and oracle.

He considered their position with a sinking heart. The ship was a stolen ship; the stores, whether from initial carelessness or ill administration during the voyage, were insufficient to carry them to any port except back to Papeete; and there retribution waited in the shape of a gendarme, a judge with a queer-shaped hat, and the horror of distant Noumea. Upon that side, there was no glimmer of hope. Here, at the island, the dragon was roused; Attwater with his men and his Winchesters watched and patrolled the house; let him who dare approach it. What else was then left but to sit there, inactive, pacing the decks – until the *Trinity Hall* arrived and they were cast into irons, or until the food came to an end, and the pangs of famine succeeded? For the *Trinity Hall* Davis was prepared; he would barricade the house, and die there defending it, like a rat in a crevice. But for the other? The cruise of the *Farallone*, into which he had plunged, only a fortnight before, with such golden expectations, could this be the nightmare end of it? The ship rotting at anchor, the crew stumbling and dying in the scuppers? It seemed as if any extreme of hazard were to be preferred to so grisly a certainty; as if it would be better to up-anchor after all, put to sea at a venture, and, perhaps, perish at the hands of cannibals on one of the more obscure Paumotus. His eye roved swiftly over sea and sky in quest of any promise of wind, but the fountains of the Trade were empty. Where it had run yesterday and for weeks before, a roaring blue river charioting clouds, silence now reigned; and the whole height of the atmosphere stood balanced. On the endless ribbon of island that stretched out to either hand of him its array of golden and green and silvery palms, not the most volatile frond was to be seen stirring; they drooped to their stable images in the lagoon like things carved of metal, and already their long line began to reverberate heat. There was no escape possible that day, none probable on the morrow. And still the stores were running out!

Then came over Davis, from deep down in the roots of his being, or at least from far back among his memories of childhood and innocence, a wave of superstition. This run of ill luck was something beyond natural; the chances of the game were in themselves more various; it seemed as if the devil must serve the pieces. The devil? He heard again the clear note of Attwater's bell ringing abroad into the night, and dying away. How if God . . . ?

Briskly, he averted his mind. Attwater: that was the point. Attwater had food and a treasure of pearls; escape made possible in the present, riches in the future. They must come to grips with Attwater; the man must die. A smoky heat went over his face, as he recalled the impotent figure he had made last night, and the contemptuous speeches he must bear in silence. Rage, shame, and the love of life, all pointed the one way; and only invention halted: how to reach him? had he strength enough? was there any help in that misbegotten packet of bones against the house?

His eyes dwelled upon him with a strange avidity, as though he would read into his soul; and presently the sleeper moved, stirred uneasily, turned suddenly round, and threw him a blinking look. Davis maintained the same dark stare, and Huish looked away again and sat up.

'Lord, I've an 'eadache on me!' said he. 'I believe I was a bit swipey last night. W'ere's that cry-byby, 'Errick?'

'Gone,' said the captain.

'Ashore?' cried Huish. 'Oh, I say! I'd 'a gone, too.'

'Would you?' said the captain.

'Yes, I would,' replied Huish. 'I like Attwater. 'E's all right; we got on like one o'clock when you were gone. And ain't his sherry in it, rather? It's like Spiers and Ponds' Amontillado! I wish I 'ad a drain of it now.' He sighed.

'Well, you'll never get no more of it – that's one thing,' said Davis, gravely.

''Ere! wot's wrong with you, Dyvis? Coppers 'ot? Well, look at *me*! *I* ain't grumpy,' said Huish; 'I'm as plyful as a canary-bird, I am.'

'Yes,' said Davis, 'you're playful; I own that; and you were playful last night, I believe, and a damned fine performance you made of it.'

''Allo!' said Huish. ''Ow's this? Wot performance?'

'Well, I'll tell you,' said the captain, getting slowly off the rail.

And he did: at full length, with every wounding epithet and absurd detail repeated and emphasized; he had his own vanity and Huish's upon the grill, and roasted them; and as he spoke, he inflicted and endured agonies of humiliation. It was a plain man's masterpiece of the sardonic.

'What do you think of it?' said he, when he had done, and looked down at Huish, flushed and serious, and yet jeering.

'I'll tell you wot it is,' was the reply, 'you and me cut a pretty dicky figure.'

'That's so,' said Davis, 'a pretty measly figure, by God! And, by God, I want to see that man at my knees.'

'Ah!' said Huish. ''Ow to get him there?'

'That's it!' cried Davis. 'How to get hold of him! They're four to two; though there's only one man among them to count, and that's Attwater. Get a bead on Attwater, and the others would cut and run and sing out like frightened poultry – and old man Herrick would come round with his hat for a share of the pearls. No, *sir*! it's how to get hold of Attwater! And we daren't even go ashore; he would shoot us in the boat like dogs.'

'Are you particular about having him dead or alive?' asked Huish.

'I want to see him dead,' said the captain.

'Ah, well!' said Huish, 'then I believe I'll do a bit of breakfast.' And he turned into the house.

The captain doggedly followed him.

'What's this?' he asked. 'What's your idea, anyway?'

'Oh, you let me alone, will you?' said Huish, opening a bottle of champagne. 'You'll 'ear my idea soon enough. Wyte till I pour some cham on my 'ot coppers.' He drank a glass off, and affected to listen. ''Ark!' said he, ''ear it fizz. Like 'am fryin', I declyre. 'Ave a glass, do, and look sociable.'

'No!' said the captain, with emphasis; 'no, I will not! there's business.'

'You p'ys your money and you tykes your choice, my little man,' returned Huish. 'Seems rather a shyme to me to spoil your breakfast for wot's really ancient 'istory.'

He finished three parts of a bottle of champagne, and nibbled a corner of biscuit, with extreme deliberation; the captain sitting opposite and champing the bit like an impatient horse. Then Huish leaned his arms on the table and looked Davis in the face.

'W'en you're ready!' said he.

'Well, now, what's your idea?' said Davis, with a sigh.

'Fair play!' said Huish. 'What's yours?'

'The trouble is that I've got none,' replied Davis; and wandered for some time in aimless discussion of the difficulties in their path, and useless explanations of his own fiasco.

'About done?' said Huish.

'I'll dry up right here,' replied Davis.

'Well, then,' said Huish, 'you give me your 'and across the table, and say, "Gawd strike me dead if I don't back you up."'

His voice was hardly raised, yet it thrilled the hearer. His face seemed the epitome of cunning, and the captain recoiled from it as from a blow.

'What for?' said he.

'Luck,' said Huish. 'Substantial guarantee demanded.'

And he continued to hold out his hand.

'I don't see the good of any such tomfoolery,' said the other.

'I do, though,' returned Huish. 'Gimme your 'and and say the words; then you'll 'ear my view of it. Don't, and you don't.'

The captain went through the required form, breathing short, and gazing on the clerk with anguish. What to fear, he knew not; yet he feared slavishly what was to fall from the pale lips.

'Now, if you'll excuse me 'alf a second,' said Huish, 'I'll go and fetch the byby.'

'The baby?' said Davis. 'What's that?'

'Fragile. With care. This side up,' replied the clerk with a wink, as he disappeared.

He returned, smiling to himself, and carrying in his hand a silk handkerchief. The long stupid wrinkles ran up Davis's brow, as he saw it. What should it contain? He could think of nothing more recondite than a revolver.

Huish resumed his seat.

'Now,' said he, 'are you man enough to take charge of 'Errick and the niggers? Because I'll take care of Hattwater.'

'How?' cried Davis. 'You can't!'

'Tut, tut!' said the clerk. 'You gimme time. Wot's the first point? The first point is that we can't get ashore, and I'll make you a present of that for a 'ard one. But 'ow about a flag of truce? Would that do the trick, d'ye think? or would Attwater simply blyze aw'y at us in the bloomin' boat like dawgs?'

'No,' said Davis, 'I don't believe he would.'

'No more do I,' said Huish; 'I don't believe he would either;

and I'm sure I 'ope he won't! So then you can call us ashore. Next point is to get near the managin' direction. And for that I'm going to 'ave you write a letter, in w'ich you s'y you're ashymed to meet his eye, and that the bearer, Mr J. L. 'Uish, is empowered to represent you. Armed with w'ich seemin'ly simple expedient, Mr J. L. 'Uish will proceed to business.'

He paused, like one who had finished, but still held Davis with his eye.

'How?' said Davis. 'Why?'

'Well, you see, you're big,' returned Huish; ' 'e knows you 'ave a gun in your pocket, and anybody can see with 'alf an eye that you ain't the man to 'esitate about usin' it. So it's no go with you, and never was; you're out of the runnin', Dyvis. But he won't be afryde of me, I'm such a little un! I'm unarmed – no kid about that – and I'll hold my 'ands up right enough.' He paused. 'If I can manage to sneak up nearer to him as we talk,' he resumed, 'you look out and back me up smart. If I don't, we go aw'y again, and nothink to 'urt. See?'

The captain's face was contorted by the frenzied effort to comprehend.

'No, I don't see,' he cried, 'I can't see. What do you mean?'

'I mean to do for the Beast!' cried Huish, in a burst of venomous triumph, 'I'll bring the 'ulkin' bully to grass. He's 'ad his larks out of me; I'm goin' to 'ave my lark out of 'im, and a good lark too!'

'What is it?' said the captain, almost in a whisper.

'Sure you want to know?' asked Huish.

Davis rose and took a turn in the house.

'Yes, I want to know,' he said at last with an effort.

'W'en your back's at the wall, you do the best you can, don't you?' began the clerk. 'I s'y that, because I 'appen to know there's a prejudice against it; it's considered vulgar, awf'ly vulgar.' He unrolled the handkerchief and showed a four-ounce jar. 'This 'ere's vitriol, this is,' said he.

The captain stared upon him with a whitening face.

'This is the stuff!' he pursued, holding it up. 'This'll burn to the bone; you'll see it smoke upon 'im like 'ell fire! One drop upon 'is bloomin' heyesight, and I'll trouble you for Attwater!'

'No, no, by God!' exclaimed the captain.

'Now, see 'ere, ducky,' said Huish, 'this is my bean feast, I believe? I'm goin' up to that man single-'anded, I am. 'E's about seven foot high, and I'm five foot one. 'E's a rifle in his 'and, 'e's on the look out, 'e wasn't born yesterday. This is Dyvid and Goliar, I tell you! If I'd ast you to walk up and face the music I could understand. But I don't. I on'y ast you to stand by and spifflicate the niggers. It'll all come in quite natural; you'll see, else! Fust thing you know, you'll see him running round and 'owling like a good un . . .'

'Don't!' said Davis. 'Don't talk of it!'

'Well, you *are* a juggins!' exclaimed Huish. 'What did you want? You wanted to kill him, and tried to last night. You wanted to kill the 'ole lot of them and tried to, and 'ere I show you 'ow; and because there's some medicine in a bottle you kick up this fuss!'

'I suppose that's so,' said Davis. 'It don't seem someways reasonable, only there it is.'

'It's the happlication of science, I suppose?' sneered Huish.

'I don't know what it is,' cried Davis, pacing the floor; 'it's there! I draw the line at it. I can't put a finger to no such piggishness. It's too damned hateful!'

'And I suppose it's all your fancy pynted it,' said Huish, 'w'en you take a pistol and a bit o' lead, and copse a man's brains all over him? No accountin' for tystes.'

'I'm not denying it,' said Davis, 'it's something here, inside of me. It's foolishness; I daresay it's dam foolishness. I don't argue, I just draw the line. Isn't there no other way?'

'Look for yourself,' said Huish. 'I ain't wedded to this, if you think I am; I ain't ambitious; I don't make a point of playin' the lead; I offer to, that's all, and if you can't show me better, by Gawd, I'm goin' to!'

'Then the risk!' cried Davis.

'If you ast me straight, I should say it was a case of seven to one and no takers,' said Huish. 'But that's my look-out, ducky, and I'm gyme. Look at me, Dyvis, there ain't any shilly-shally about me. I'm gyme, that's wot I am: gyme all through.'

The captain looked at him. Huish sat there, preening his sinister vanity, glorying in his precedency in evil; and the villainous courage and readiness of the creature shone out of him like a candle from a lantern. Dismay and a kind of respect seized hold on Davis in his own despite. Until that moment, he had seen the clerk always hanging back, always listless, uninterested, and openly grumbling at a word of anything to do; and now, by the touch of an enchanter's wand, he beheld him sitting girt and resolved, and his face radiant. He had raised the devil, he thought; and asked who was to control him? and his spirits quailed.

'Look as long as you like,' Huish was going on. 'You don't see any green in my eye! I ain't afryde of Attwater, I ain't afryde of you, and I ain't afryde of words. You want to kill people, that's wot *you* want; but you want to do it in kid gloves, and it can't be done that w'y. Murder ain't genteel, it ain't easy, it ain't safe, and it tykes a man to do it. 'Ere's the man.'

'Huish!' began the captain with energy; and then stopped, and remained staring at him with corrugated brows.

'Well, hout with it!' said Huish. ''Ave you anythink else to put up? Is there any other chanst to try?'

The captain held his peace.

'There you are then!' said Huish with a shrug.

Davis fell again to his pacing.

'Oh, you may do sentry-go till you're blue in the mug, you won't find anythink else,' said Huish.

There was a little silence; the captain, like a man launched on a swing, flying dizzily among extremes of conjecture and refusal.

'But see,' he said, suddenly pausing. 'Can you? Can the thing be done? It – it can't be easy.'

'If I get within twenty foot of 'im it'll be done; so you look out,' said Huish, and his tone of certainty was absolute.

'How can you know that?' broke from the captain in a choked cry. 'You beast, I believe you've done it before!'

'Oh, that's private affyres,' returned Huish, 'I ain't a talking man.'

A shock of repulsion struck and shook the captain; a scream rose almost to his lips; had he uttered it, he might have cast himself at the same moment on the body of Huish, might have picked him up, and flung him down, and wiped the cabin with him, in a frenzy of cruelty that seemed half moral. But the moment passed; and the abortive crisis left the man weaker. The stakes were so high – the pearls on the one hand – starvation and shame on the other. Ten years of pearls! the imagination of Davis translated them into a new, glorified existence for himself and his family. The seat of this new life must be in London; there were deadly reasons against Portland, Maine; and the pictures that came to him were of English manners. He saw his boys marching in the procession of a school, with gowns on, an usher marshalling them and reading as he walked in a great book. He was installed in a villa, semi-detached; the name, *Rosemore*, on the gateposts. In a chair on the gravel walk, he seemed to sit smoking a cigar, a blue ribbon in his buttonhole, victor over himself and circumstances, and the malignity of bankers. He saw the parlour with red curtains and shells on the mantelpiece – and with the fine inconsistency of visions, mixed a grog at the mahogany table ere he turned in. With that the *Farallone* gave one of the aimless and nameless movements which (even in an anchored ship and even in the most profound calm) remind one of the mobility of fluids; and he was back again under the cover of the house, the fierce daylight besieging it all round and glaring in the chinks, and the clerk in a rather airy attitude, awaiting his decision.

He began to walk again. He aspired after the realization of these dreams, like a horse nickering for water; the lust of them burned in his inside. And the only obstacle was Attwater, who had insulted him from the first. He gave Herrick a full share of the pearls, he insisted on it; Huish opposed him, and he trod the opposition down; and praised himself exceedingly. He was not going to use vitriol himself; was he Huish's keeper? It was a pity he had asked, but after all! . . . he saw the boys again in the school procession, with the gowns he had thought to be so 'tony' long since . . . And at the same time the incomparable shame of the last evening blazed up in his mind.

'Have it your own way!' he said hoarsely.

'Oh, I knew you would walk up,' said Huish. 'Now for the letter. There's paper, pens and ink. Sit down and I'll dictyte.'

The captain took a seat and the pen, looked a while helplessly at the paper, then at Huish. The swing had gone the other way; there was a blur upon his eyes. 'It's a dreadful business,' he said, with a strong twitch of his shoulders.

'It's rather a start, no doubt,' said Huish. 'Tyke a dip of ink. That's it. *William John Hattwater, Esq. Sir:*' he dictated.

'How do you know his name is William John?' asked Davis.

'Saw it on a packing case,' said Huish. 'Got that?'

'No,' said Davis. 'But there's another thing. What are we to write?'

'O my golly!' cried the exasperated Huish. 'Wot kind of man do *you* call yourself? *I'm* goin' to tell you wot to write; that's *my* pitch; if you'll just be so bloomin' condescendin' as to write it down! *William John Attwater, Esq., Sir:*' he reiterated. And the captain at last beginning half mechanically to move his pen, the dictation proceeded: '*It is with feelings of shyme and 'artfelt contrition that I approach you after the yumiliatin' events of last night. Our Mr 'Errick has left the ship, and will have doubtless communicated to you the nature of our 'opes. Needless to s'y, these are no longer possible: Fate 'as declyred against us, and we bow the 'ead. Well awyre as I am of*

354

the just suspicions with w'ich I am regarded, I do not venture to solicit the fyvour of an interview for myself, but in order to put an end to a situuation w'ich must be equally pyneful to all, I 'ave deputed my friend and partner, Mr J. L. Huish, to l'y before you my proposals, and w'ich by their moderytion, will, I trust, be found to merit your attention. Mr J. L. Huish is entirely unarmed, I swear to Gawd! and will 'old 'is 'ands over 'is 'ead from the moment he begins to approach you. I am your fytheful servant, John Dyvis.'

Huish read the letter with the innocent joy of amateurs, chuckled gustfully to himself, and reopened it more than once after it was folded, to repeat the pleasure; Davis meanwhile sitting inert and heavily frowning.

Of a sudden he rose; he seemed all abroad. 'No!' he cried. 'No! it can't be! It's too much; it's damnation. God would never forgive it.'

'Well, and 'oo wants him to?' returned Huish, shrill with fury. 'You were damned years ago for the *Sea Rynger*, and said so yourself. Well then, be damned for something else, and 'old your tongue.'

The captain looked at him mistily. 'No,' he pleaded, 'no, old man! don't do it.'

''Ere now,' said Huish, 'I'll give you my ultimytum. Go or st'y w'ere you are; I don't mind; I'm goin' to see that man and chuck this vitriol in his eyes. If you st'y I'll go alone; the niggers will likely knock me on the 'ead, and a fat lot you'll be the better! But there's one thing sure: I'll 'ear no more of your moonin', mullygrubbin' rot, and tyke it stryte.'

The captain took it with a blink and a gulp. Memory, with phantom voices, repeated in his ears something similar, something he had once said to Herrick – years ago it seemed.

'Now, gimme over your pistol,' said Huish. 'I 'ave to see all clear. Six shots, and mind you don't wyste them.'

The captain, like a man in a nightmare, laid down his revolver on the table, and Huish wiped the cartridges and oiled the works.

It was close on noon, there was no breath of wind, and the heat was scarce bearable, when the two men came on deck, had the boat manned, and passed down, one after another, into the stern-sheets. A white shirt at the end of an oar served as flag of truce; and the men, by direction, and to give it the better chance to be observed, pulled with extreme slowness. The isle shook before them like a place incandescent; on the face of the lagoon blinding copper suns, no bigger than sixpences, danced and stabbed them in the eyeballs; there went up from sand and sea, and even from the boat, a glare of scathing brightness; and as they could only peer abroad from between closed lashes, the excess of light seemed to be changed into a sinister darkness, comparable to that of a thundercloud before it bursts.

The captain had come upon this errand for any one of a dozen reasons, the last of which was desire for its success. Superstition rules all men; semi-ignorant and gross natures, like that of Davis, it rules utterly. For murder he had been prepared; but this horror of the medicine in the bottle went beyond him, and he seemed to himself to be parting the last strands that united him to God. The boat carried him on to reprobation, to damnation; and he suffered himself to be carried passively consenting, silently bidding farewell to his better self and his hopes.

Huish sat by his side in towering spirits that were not wholly genuine. Perhaps as brave a man as ever lived, brave as a weasel, he must still reassure himself with the tones of his own voice; he must play his part to exaggeration, he must out-Herod Herod, insult all that was respectable, and brave all that was formidable, in a kind of desperate wager with himself.

'Golly, but it's 'ot!' said he. 'Cruel 'ot, I call it. Nice d'y to get your gruel in! I s'y, you know, it must feel awf'ly peculiar to get bowled over on a d'y like this. I'd rather 'ave it on a cowld and frosty morning, wouldn't you? (Singing) " '*Ere we go round the mulberry bush on a cowld and frosty mornin'.*" (Spoken) Give you my word, I 'aven't thought o' that in ten year; used to sing it at a hinfant school in 'Ackney, 'Ackney Wick it was. (Singing) *"This is the way the tyler does, the tyler does."* (Spoken) Bloomin' 'umbug. 'Ow are you off now, for the notion of a future styte? Do you cotton to the tea-fight views, or the old red 'ot boguey business?'

'Oh, dry up!' said the captain.

'No, but I want to know,' said Huish. 'It's within the sp'ere of practical politics for you and me, my boy; we may both be bowled over, one up, t'other down, within the next ten minutes. It would be rather a lark, now, if you only skipped across, came up smilin' t'other side, and a hangel met you with a B.-and-S. under his wing. 'Ullo, you'd s'y: come, I tyke this kind.'

The captain groaned. While Huish was thus airing and exercising his bravado, the man at his side was actually engaged in prayer. Prayer, what for? God knows. But out of his inconsistent, illogical, and agitated spirit, a stream of supplication was poured forth, inarticulate as himself, earnest as death and judgment.

'Thou Gawd seest me!' continued Huish. 'I remember I had that written in my Bible. I remember the Bible too, all about Abinadab and parties. Well, Gawd!' apostrophizing the meridian, 'you're goin' to see a rum start presently, I promise you that!'

The captain bounded.

'I'll have no blasphemy!' he cried, 'no blasphemy in my boat.'

'All right, cap,' said Huish. 'Anythink to oblige. Any other topic you would like to sudgest, the ryne-gyge, the lightnin' rod, Shykespeare, or the musical glasses? 'Ere's conversation on tap. Put a penny in the slot, and . . . 'ullo! 'ere they are!' he cried. 'Now or never! is 'e goin' to shoot?'

And the little man straightened himself into an alert and dashing attitude, and looked steadily at the enemy.

But the captain rose half up in the boat with eyes protruding.

'What's that?' he cried.

'Wot's wot?' said Huish.

'Those – blamed things,' said the captain.

And indeed it was something strange. Herrick and Attwater,

both armed with Winchesters, had appeared out of the grove behind the figure-head; and to either hand of them, the sun glistened upon two metallic objects, locomotory like men, and occupying in the economy of these creatures the places of heads – only the heads were faceless. To Davis between wind and water, his mythology appeared to have come alive, and Tophet to be vomiting demons. But Huish was not mystified a moment.

'Diver's 'elmets, you ninny. Can't you see?' he said.

'So they are,' said Davis, with a gasp. 'And why? Oh, I see, it's for armour.'

'Wot did I tell you?' said Huish. 'Dyvid and Goliar all the w'y and back.'

The two natives (for they it was that were equipped in this unusual panoply of war) spread out to right and left, and at last lay down in the shade, on the extreme flank of the position. Even now that the mystery was explained, Davis was hatefully pre-occupied, stared at the flame on their crests, and forgot, and then remembered with a smile, the explanation.

Attwater withdrew again into the grove, and Herrick, with his gun under his arm, came down the pier alone.

About half-way down he halted and hailed the boat.

'What do you want?' he cried.

'I'll tell that to Mr Attwater,' replied Huish, stepping briskly on the ladder. 'I don't tell it to you, because you played the trucklin' sneak. Here's a letter for him: tyke it, and give it, and be 'anged to you!'

'Davis, is this all right?' said Herrick.

Davis raised his chin, glanced swiftly at Herrick and away again, and held his peace. The glance was charged with some deep emotion, but whether of hatred or of fear, it was beyond Herrick to divine.

'Well,' he said, 'I'll give the letter.' He drew a score with his foot on the boards of the gangway. 'Till I bring the answer, don't move a step past this.'

And he returned to where Attwater leaned against a tree, and gave him the letter. Attwater glanced it through.

'What does that mean,' he asked, passing it to Herrick. 'Treachery?'

'Oh, I suppose so!' said Herrick.

'Well, tell him to come on,' said Attwater. 'One isn't a fatalist for nothing. Tell him to come on and to look out.'

Herrick returned to the figure-head. Half-way down the pier the clerk was waiting, with Davis by his side.

'You are to come along, Huish,' said Herrick. 'He bids you look out, no tricks.'

Huish walked briskly up the pier, and paused face to face with the young man.

'W'ere is 'e?' said he, and to Herrick's surprise, the low-bred, insignificant face before him flushed suddenly crimson and went white again.

'Right forward,' said Herrick, pointing. 'Now your hands above your head.'

The clerk turned away from him and towards the figure-head, as though he were about to address to it his devotions; he was seen to heave a deep breath; and raised his arms. In common with many men of his unhappy physical endowments, Huish's hands were disproportionately long and broad, and the palms in particular enormous; a four-ounce jar was nothing in that capacious fist. The next moment he was plodding steadily forward on his mission.

Herrick at first followed. Then a noise in his rear startled him, and he turned about to find Davis already advanced as far as the figure-head. He came, crouching and open-mouthed, as the mesmerized may follow the mesmerizer; all human considerations, and even the care of his own life, swallowed up in one abominable and burning curiosity.

'Halt!' cried Herrick, covering him with his rifle. 'Davis, what are you doing, man? *You* are not to come.'

Davis instinctively paused, and regarded him with a dreadful vacancy of eye.

'Put your back to that figure-head, do you hear me? and stand fast!' said Herrick.

The captain fetched a breath, stepped back against the figure-head, and instantly redirected his glances after Huish.

There was a hollow place of the sand in that part, and, as it were, a glade among the cocoa-palms in which the direct noon-day sun blazed intolerably. At the far end, in the shadow, the tall figure of Attwater was to be seen leaning on a tree; towards him, with his hands over his head, and his steps smothered in the sand, the clerk painfully waded. The surrounding glare threw out and exaggerated the man's smallness; it seemed no less perilous an enterprise, this that he was gone upon, than for a whelp to besiege a citadel.

'There, Mr Whish. That will do,' cried Attwater. 'From that distance, and keeping your hands up, like a good boy, you can very well put me in possession of the skipper's views.'

The interval betwixt them was perhaps forty feet; and Huish measured it with his eye, and breathed a curse. He was already distressed with labouring in the loose sand, and his arms ached bitterly from their unnatural position. In the palm of his right hand, the jar was ready; and his heart thrilled, and his voice choked, as he began to speak.

'Mr Hattwater,' said he, 'I don't know if ever you 'ad a mother . . .'

'I can set your mind at rest: I had,' returned Attwater; 'and henceforth, if I might venture to suggest it, her name need not recur in our communications. I should perhaps tell you that I am not amenable to the pathetic.'

'I am sorry, sir, if I 'ave seemed to trespass on your private feelin's,' said the clerk, cringing and stealing a step. 'At least, sir, you will never pe'suade me that you are not a perfec' gentleman; I know a gentleman when I see him; and as such, I 'ave no 'esita-tion in throwin' myself on your merciful consideration. It *is* 'ard lines, no doubt; it's 'ard lines to have to hown yourself beat; it's 'ard lines to 'ave to come and beg to you for charity.'

'When, if things had only gone right, the whole place was as good as your own?' suggested Attwater. 'I can understand the feeling.'

'You are judging me, Mr Attwater,' said the clerk, 'and God knows how unjustly! *Thou Gawd seest me*, was the tex' I 'ad in my Bible, w'ich my father wrote it in with 'is own 'and upon the fly leaf.'

'I am sorry I have to beg your pardon once more,' said Attwater; 'but, do you know, you seem to me to be a trifle nearer, which is entirely outside of our bargain. And I would venture to suggest that you take one – two – three – steps back; and stay there.'

The devil, at this staggering disappointment, looked out of Huish's face, and Attwater was swift to suspect. He frowned, he stared on the little man, and considered. Why should he be creeping nearer? The next moment, his gun was at his shoulder.

'Kindly oblige me by opening your hands. Open your hands wide – let me see the fingers spread, you dog – throw down that thing you're holding!' he roared, his rage and certitude increasing together.

And then, at almost the same moment, the indomitable Huish decided to throw, and Attwater pulled the trigger. There was scarce the difference of a second between the two resolves, but it was in favour of the man with the rifle; and the jar had not yet left the clerk's hand, before the ball shattered both. For the twinkling of an eye the wretch was in hell's agonies, bathed in liquid flames, a screaming bedlamite; and then a second and more merciful bullet stretched him dead.

The whole thing was come and gone in a breath. Before Herrick could turn about, before Davis could complete his cry of horror, the clerk lay in the sand, sprawling and convulsed.

Attwater ran to the body; he stooped and viewed it; he put his finger in the vitriol, and his face whitened and hardened with anger.

Davis had not yet moved; he stood astonished, with his back to the figure-head, his hands clutching it behind him, his body inclined forward from the waist.

Attwater turned deliberately and covered him with his rifle.

'Davis,' he cried, in a voice like a trumpet, 'I give you sixty seconds to make your peace with God!'

Davis looked, and his mind awoke. He did not dream of self-defence, he did not reach for his pistol. He drew himself up instead to face death, with a quivering nostril.

'I guess I'll not trouble the Old Man,' he said; 'considering the job I was on, I guess it's better business to just shut my face.'

Attwater fired; there came a spasmodic movement of the victim, and immediately above the middle of his forehead, a black hole marred the whiteness of the figure-head. A dreadful pause; then again the report, and the solid sound and jar of the bullet in the wood; and this time the captain had felt the wind of it along his cheek. A third shot, and he was bleeding from one ear; and along the levelled rifle Attwater smiled like a red Indian.

The cruel game of which he was the puppet was now clear to Davis; three times he had drunk of death, and he must look to drink of it seven times more before he was despatched. He held up his hand.

'Steady!' he cried; 'I'll take your sixty seconds.'

'Good!' said Attwater.

The captain shut his eyes tight like a child: he held his hands up at last with a tragic and ridiculous gesture.

'My God, for Christ's sake, look after my two kids,' he said; and then, after a pause and a falter, 'for Christ's sake, Amen.'

And he opened his eyes and looked down the rifle with a quivering mouth.

'But don't keep fooling me long!' he pleaded.

'That's all your prayer?' asked Attwater, with a singular ring in his voice.

'Guess so,' said Davis.

'So?' said Attwater, resting the butt of his rifle on the ground, 'is that done? Is your peace made with Heaven? Because it is with me. Go, and sin no more, sinful father. And remember that whatever you do to others, God shall visit it again a thousandfold upon your innocents.'

The wretched Davis came staggering forward from his place against the figure-head, fell upon his knees, and waved his hands, and fainted.

When he came to himself again, his head was on Attwater's arm, and close by stood one of the men in diver's helmets, holding a bucket of water, from which his late executioner now laved his face. The memory of that dreadful passage returned upon him in a clap; again he saw Huish lying dead, again he seemed to himself to totter on the brink of an unplumbed eternity. With trembling hands he seized hold of the man whom he had come to slay; and his voice broke from him like that of a child among the nightmares of fever: 'O! isn't there no mercy? O! what must I do to be saved?'

'Ah!' thought Attwater, 'here is the true penitent.'

Chapter Twelve

A Tail-Piece

On a very bright, hot, lusty, strongly blowing noon, a fortnight after the events recorded, and a month since the curtain rose upon this episode, a man might have been spied, praying on the sand by the lagoon beach. A point of palm-trees isolated him from the settlement; and from the place where he knelt, the only work of man's hand that interrupted the expanse, was the schooner *Farallone*, her berth quite changed, and rocking at anchor some two miles to windward in the midst of the lagoon. The noise of the Trade ran very boisterous in all parts of the island; the nearer palm-trees crashed and whistled in the gusts, those farther off contributed a humming bass like the roar of cities; and yet, to any man less absorbed, there must have risen at times over this turmoil of the winds, the sharper note of the human voice from the settlement. There all was activity. Attwater, stripped to his trousers and lending a strong hand of help, was directing and encouraging five Kanakas; from his lively voice, and their more lively efforts, it was to be gathered that some sudden and joyful emergency had set them in this bustle; and the Union Jack floated once more on its staff. But the suppliant on the beach, unconscious of their voices, prayed on with instancy and fervour, and the sound of his voice rose and fell again, and his countenance brightened and was deformed with changing moods of piety and terror.

Before his closed eyes, the skiff had been for some time tacking towards the distant and deserted *Farallone*; and presently the figure of Herrick might have been observed to board her, to pass for a while into the house, thence forward to the forecastle, and at last to plunge into the main hatch. In all these quarters, his visit was followed by a coil of smoke; and he had scarce entered his

364

boat again and shoved off, before flames broke forth upon the schooner. They burned gaily; kerosene had not been spared, and the bellows of the Trade incited the conflagration. About half way on the return voyage, when Herrick looked back, he beheld the *Farallone* wrapped to the topmasts in leaping arms of fire, and the voluminous smoke pursuing him along the face of the lagoon. In one hour's time, he computed, the waters would have closed over the stolen ship.

It so chanced that, as his boat flew before the wind with much vivacity, and his eyes were continually busy in the wake, measuring the progress of the flames, he found himself embayed to the northward of the point of palms, and here became aware at the same time, of the figure of Davis immersed in his devotion. An exclamation, part of annoyance, part of amusement, broke from him: and he touched the helm and ran the prow upon the beach not twenty feet from the unconscious devotee. Taking the painter in his hand, he landed, and drew near, and stood over him. And still the voluble and incoherent stream of prayer continued unabated. It was not possible for him to overhear the suppliant's petitions, which he listened to some while in a very mingled mood of humour and pity: and it was only when his own name began to occur and to be conjoined with epithets, that he at last laid his hand on the captain's shoulder.

'Sorry to interrupt the exercise,' said he; 'but I want you to look at the *Farallone*.'

The captain scrambled to his feet, and stood gasping and staring. 'Mr Herrick, don't startle a man like that!' he said. 'I don't seem someways rightly myself since . . .' he broke off. 'What did you say anyway? O, the *Farallone*,' and he looked languidly out.

'Yes,' said Herrick. 'There she burns! and you may guess from that what the news is.'

'The *Trinity Hall*, I guess,' said the captain.

'The same,' said Herrick; 'sighted half-an-hour ago, and coming up hand over fist.'

'Well, it don't amount to a hill of beans,' said the captain with a sigh.

'O, come, that's rank ingratitude!' cried Herrick.

'Well,' replied the captain, meditatively, 'you mayn't just see the way that I view it in, but I'd 'most rather stay here upon this island. I found peace here, peace in believing. Yes, I guess this island is about good enough for John Davis.'

'I never heard such nonsense!' cried Herrick. 'What! with all turning out in your favour the way it does, the *Farallone* wiped out, the crew disposed of, a sure thing for your wife and family, and you, yourself, Attwater's spoiled darling and pet penitent!'

'Now, Mr Herrick, don't say that,' said the captain gently; 'when you know he don't make no difference between us. But, O! why not be one of us? why not come to Jesus right away, and let's meet in yon beautiful land? That's just the one thing wanted; just say, Lord, I believe, help thou mine unbelief! And He'll fold you in His arms. You see, I know! I been a sinner myself!'

Three Contemporary Reviews

1) An Unsigned Notice, 'Academy'

1 December 1883, xxiv, 362

The reviewer is unidentified, but in a letter to Stevenson dated 25 November (B, 4772) Henley remarks that a 'friend' hopes to write the 'Academy' review.

Mr Stevenson has treated a well-worn theme with freshness. His story is skilfully constructed, and related with untiring vivacity and genuine dramatic power. It is calculated to fascinate the old boy as well as the young, the reader of Smollett and Dr Moore and Marryat as well as the admirer of the dexterous ingenuity of Poe. It deals with a mysterious island, a buried treasure, the bold buccaneer, and all the stirring incidents of a merry life on the Main. Mr Stevenson's buccaneers are not of the heroic age that Kingsley sang; they know nothing of pleasant isles in the glowing tropic seas; their traditions are not of good Queen Bess and the hated Spaniard; they do not swagger in picturesque attire and drink canary; they belong, in short, to the more prosaic era of the Georges. But they are not less individual and rather more entertaining. They are, for the most part, superlative and consistent villains. They cannot inspire the most enthusiastic youth with a desire for the return of the glorious age of buccaneering. Their profession is not set forth in a dangerous halo of romance, nor are their deeds made alluring through a familiar moral process by which crimes are mitigated with the milk of sophistry. Mr Stevenson deserves praise not alone for this. He has dared to depict an island the sole attraction of which lies in its hidden treasure. With a healthy realism he has avoided that false and specious luxuriance which denaturalises the action of a story by placing its actors out of harmony with their surroundings. His island is no garden of Eden, where all the products of all the zones thrive in happy ignorance, and where the modern representatives of the Swiss Family Robinson may find all to their liking and life certainly worth living. It has its drawbacks as well as its piratical hoard, but it is portrayed in several vivid pictures with the truth and precision of nature. In the opening chapters only may be detected a discordant touch. Here the events are a little too melodramatic and the narrative somewhat strained. The affray with the revenue officers and the discovery of the chart of the island are cleverly managed and form an ingenious prelude. The blind sailor, Pew, is an exception to the author's otherwise excellent delineations. After we have recovered from the thrilling shudder he causes, we feel that he is an anomaly, monstrous, irrelevant – a transitory spasm of nightmare in a coherent story. This, however, is a slight matter. The dramatic verse of the narrative is not less striking than its unflagging spirit. The invention is rich and ready, the dialogue abounds in pith and humour, while the characters – particularly the sailors – are drawn with great force and distinction. Among these is one who stands out with the prominence of one of Cooper's or Marryat's heroes. Long John Silver is a creation. There is not so much of the salt about him as might be desired, but there is no gainsaying his merit. We may long to hang him, or wish him a bad end, in the final chapter, but it is impossible not to be interested in him. With all our knowledge of this abandoned ruffian, of his treachery, his craft, and his abominable wickedness, it is surprising how his humour and cynicism move us to admiration. There is not a false touch in the portrait; the character has all the complexity of a humorist, and is painted with unerring consistency. The scheme by which this cold-blooded villain seduces the crew to mutiny is detailed with admirable irony and humour. The owner of the ship treats his men with a leniency that almost parallels that of Capt. Reece, commander of the *Mantelpiece*. How their ingratitude and criminal designs are divulged – how the island is reached, and becomes the theatre of the most exciting events – and how Long John eventually comes off – the book must tell. We can only add that we shall be surprised if 'Treasure Island' does not satisfy the most exacting lover of perilous adventures and thrilling situation; he can scarcely fail to share in the anticipations of Jim Hawkins, the relater of this sea yarn, when he finds himself on board the *Hispaniola*, 'with a piping boatswain and pig-tailed singing seamen, bound for an unknown island and to seek for buried treasure.'

2) W. E. Henley, Unsigned Review, 'Saturday Review'

8 December 1883, lvi, 737–8

Buried treasure is one of the very foundations of romance. To our thinking, there are no such enchanting passages in the 'Arabian Nights' themselves as those in which the hero, alone in the mysterious desert, comes suddenly, even promiscuously, on an iron ring in the earth, and, lifting the trapdoor to which it is attached, descends by a neat stone staircase into a subterranean chamber chastely furnished with brazen jars, which on examination prove to be filled to the brim with sequins, or gold-dust, or diamonds and emeralds of the largest size and the purest water. Aladdins's lamp and ring are, after all, no more than talismanic introductions to the hoard of the djinns, which is an example of buried treasure on the largest and costliest scale; the secret of the cave where Ali Baba spoiled the forty robbers of their ill-gotten gains is but a variation on the same delightful theme – at the back of it there is buried treasure in its most romantic shape. What is El Dorado itself but an ideal of discovery and hidden wealth? To many of us The Gold Beetle is Poe's best story. To many of us the interest of 'Monte Cristo' culminates in the discovery of the hoards of Caesar Borgia. To many of us Facino Cane lighting on the secret bank of the Venetian Republic is one of the most striking of Balzac's many wonderful and moving inventions. The scheme looks noble and adventurous which has for its object the rescue of doubloons and ingots from between the ribs of tall galleons, sunk long ages back in mysterious nooks of ocean. The pirate who so far respected himself as to deal in treasure-hiding becomes at once heroic. To have buried moidores and pieces-of-eight in islets off the Spanish Main is to have deserved well of romance and the arts. Kidd is a hero by virtue of his buried gold; and the memory of Execution Dock itself is powerless to break the spell and ruin the tradition.

This is the theory on which Mr Stevenson has written 'Treasure Island.' Primarily it is a book for boys, with a boy-hero and a string of wonderful adventures. But it is a book for boys which will be delightful to all grown men who have the sentiment of treasure-hunting and are touched with the true spirit of the Spanish Main. It is the story of the monstrous pile which Flint, the great pirate, buried, with extraordinary circumstances of secresy and ferocity, on an unknown islet; and it sets forth, with uncommon directness and dexterity, the adventures of certain persons who went in search of the cache, and returned to Bristol city with seven hundred thousand pounds in all the coinages of the world. It contains a delightful map (a legacy from Flint himself), a hoard that will bear comparison with Monte Cristo's own, a fort, a stockade, a maroon, and one of the most remarkable pirates in fiction. Like all Mr Stevenson's good work, crisp, choice, nervous English of which he has the secret – with such a union of measure and force as to be in its way a masterpiece of narrative. It is rich in excellent characterization, in an abundant invention, in a certain grim romance, in a vein of what must, for want of a better word, be described as melodrama, which is both thrilling and peculiar. It is the work of one who knows all there is to be known about 'Robinson Crusoe,' and to whom Dumas is something more than a great *amateur*; and it is in some ways the best thing he has produced.

Mr Stevenson deals but sparingly in landscape and the emotional analysis of emotion. He makes his personages explain themselves. (What he is most interested in is his story.) In his very first paragraph he gives us a foretaste of all the many delights of the book. 'I take up my pen,' says Jim Hawkins, the boy-hero, 'in the year of grace 17—, and go back to the time when my father kept the "Admiral Benbow" inn, and the brown old seaman with the sabre cut first took up his lodgings under our roof.' The brown old seaman is a tremendous and ferocious rascal; 'a tall, strong, heavy, nut-brown man,' Jim Hawkins writes, with a 'tarry pigtail,' hands 'ragged and scarred, with black, dirty nails,' and 'the sabre cut across his face a dirty, livid white.' He consumes immense quantities of rum; he settles his score in blasphemies and threats; he is always singing, to himself or the 'Admiral Benbow's' guests, in 'a high old tottering voice that seemed to have been tuned and broken at the capstan bars,' a certain reckless and desperate shanty –

> Fifteen men on the dead man's chest,
> Yee-ho-ho and a bottle of rum,
> Drink and the Devil had done for the rest –

and so forth; he is full of oaths and wicked stories – 'about hanging, and walking the plank, and storms at sea, and the Dry Tortugas, and wild deeds and places on the Spanish Main.' What is more, he is in daily and nightly terror of men of his own profession; he is always looking out to sea through a brass telescope; and he engages Jim Hawkins at fourpence a month (the only debt he ever pays) to keep his 'weather' eye open for a seafaring man with one leg.' For some time the captain (so he dubs himself) pursues his wicked way unchecked; he roars, he swaggers, he bullies the company, he takes down unlimited rum, he even ventures on a brash with Dr Livesey, the village physician, and is severely worsted. But at last, though not in the shape he had feared, his fate swoops down upon him. One day there comes to the 'Admiral Benbow' a leering, evil-looking mariner, with two fingers slashed from his left hand. This gentleman, who answers to the name of Black Dog, beards the captain, though with visible reluctance. He is presently put to flight by that awful shipman, who gashes him badly on the shoulder, and, after pursuing him for some little distance, comes back to the inn and has a fit on the parlour floor. When Dr Livesey, of whom he is much afraid, strips his arm to bleed him, he find it neatly tattooed with piratical devices – a gallows, 'Billy Bones his Fancy,' and such like; and when, restored to something like his right mind and threatened with death if he persists in his habit of rum, he finds he is too weak to get away, as he is wild to do, he breaks into strange and tremendous confidences.

As it falls out, these confidences are more or less useless. Jim's father, who is ailing, dies that same night; and the next day the pirate comes downstairs, and goes to work on the rum. He gets weaker and angrier and more drunken than ever; but his time is up, and he has death and terror on every hand of him. The day after the funeral Jim is standing at the inn door, when he sees 'some one drawing slowly near along the road. He was plainly blind, for he tapped before him with a stick, and wore a great green shade over his eyes and nose; and he was hunched, as if with age or weakness, and wore a huge old tattered sea cloak with a hood, that made him appear positively deformed.' Addressing him in the true blind man's whine, this dreadful apparition implores to be led into the 'Admiral Benbow.' No sooner, however, does Jim take hands with him than 'the horrible, soft-spoken, eyeless creature' grips him as in a vice, playfully wrenches his joints for him, and, in a voice 'so cruel and cold and ugly' that he never heard the like of it, commands him to take him in to the captain. That mariner is absolutely overwhelmed by the visit. He allows the black spot – 'that's a summons, mate' – to be put upon him without resistance; and, as soon as his guest has withdrawn (which he does 'with incredible accuracy and nimbleness'), he falls 'from his whole height face foremost to the floor.' That is the end of old Flint's first mate, the redoubtable Billy Bones. Of course Jim Hawkins knows that there is worse than death behind, that the black spot has been passed, and that in a very little while all Flint's crew will be down at the inn after Billy Bones's chest. He tells his mother all he knows; and she, after vainly asking help of her neighbours, determines to search the chest, and pay the pirate's score with whatever she may find. By the pirate's corpse they pick up the dreaded spot – 'a little round of paper blackened on one side,' and on the other, 'written in a very good, clear hand,' the words, 'You have till ten to-night.' Tied to the dead man's neck they find the key of the chest. It is only six o'clock, and they have a good four hours before them; so they at once proceeded to make an inventory of Billy Bones's assets. Among these are a very good suit of clothes, 'carefully brushed and folded – they had never been worn, my mother said; 'a quadrant, a tin canikin, several sticks of tobacco, two brace of very handsome pistols, a piece of bar silver, an old Spanish watch and some other trinkets of little value and mostly of foreign make, a pair of compasses mounted with brass, and five or six curious East Indian shells'; 'an old boat cloak, whitened with salt on many a harbour bar', with 'a bundle tied up in oil-cloth and looking like papers,' and 'a canvas bag that gave forth, at a touch, the jungle of gold.' Mrs Hawkins is obstinate to take no more than her due; and while she is hunting out the English coins in Billy Bones's very miscellaneous savings something happens. 'I suddenly put my hand upon her arm,' says Jim, 'for I had heard in the silent frosty air a sound that brought my heart into my mouth – the tap-tapping of the blind man's stick upon the frozen road.' What follows shall be told by none but Mr Stevenson himself. It is too good and alarming to be paraphrased; and, besides, to take it out piecemeal would spoil the excitement and interest of the book.

As yet, it will be noted, the terrible seafaring man with one leg has not yet put in an appearance. When he does, he is so fascinating, and looks so innocent, that Jim Hawkins fails to recognize him. He turns up in Bristol, in the person of a certain John Silver, landlord of the 'Spyglass,' a tavern frequented by seamen. He is a big fellow, 'very tall and strong, with a face as big as a ham; plain and pale, but intelligent and smiling'; his left leg is cut off at the hip, and he carries a crutch, which he manages with 'wonderful dexterity, hopping about on it like a bird.' He has travelled all the world over; he has a black wife; he is master of a parrot named Captain Flint; he is so helpful and clever, so smooth-spoken and powerful and charming, that everybody is deceived in him, and that to have him as cook aboard the *Hispaniola*, searching for Treasure Island and Flint's hoard, is to the leaders of the expedition the greatest piece of luck imaginable. Of course he makes himself the most useful of men while the ship is fitting out, and of course a considerable proportion of the crew are of his discovery and recommendation. The consequences are plain to the meanest capacity. There is a mutiny and they hoist the black flag, the noble Jolly Roger; there are fights and murders and adventures; only a few of the expedition escape with their lives; and it is all John Silver's doing. John Silver, in fact, is Flint's old quartermaster, and the bloodiest and most dangerous villain of all Flint's crew of villains. His wickedness is the wickedness of a man of genius; he has no heart, but he has any amount of character and brains; he is a desperado of the worst type, but entirely passionless – a kind of buccaneering Borgia; in victory and defeat alike he maintains a magnificent intellectual superiority – to himself, his comrades, and his circumstances; and when at last he disappears from the story, you are glad that he has not gone the way of his companions (shot, drowned, stabbed, marooned), but has got off to his old negress with a whole skin and a bagful of pieces-of-eight. There are many good characters and sketches of character in the book – Dr Livesey, Squire Trelawney, Captain Smollett, Billy Bones, Ben Gunn the maroon (a study of singular freshness and originality), the horrible blind pirate, Jim Hawkins himself; but Long John, called Barbecue, is incomparably the best of all. He, and not Jim Hawkins, nor Flint's treasure, is Mr Stevenson's real hero; and you feel, when the story is done, that the right name of it is not 'Treasure Island,' but 'John Silver, Pirate.'

3) I. Zangwill In Defence Of 'Ebb-Tide', Review, 'Critic' (New York)

24 November 1894, xxii n.s., 342–3

To judge by the reviews and the advertisement columns, a great new novel is published every week. It is depressing to be told by the same reviewers who discover these great new novels that Mr Stevenson's new romance, 'The Ebb-Tide,' is badly constructed, a mere random series of adventures, sliced out of a chain of heterogeneous episodes that might have gone on forever. In reality, the story is so symmetrical that it is perhaps the best constructed of all Mr Stevenson's books, and it might therefore seem surprising that critics could be found blind to so striking a unity as the book manifests. But the reason why they have failed to recognize it is easily discoverable. It is not constructed on what I have called the parlor-game formula, to which the stock British novel invariably reduces itself; the said formula being, as in the parlor-game of 'Consequences,' entirely connected with the recontre of the hero and the heroine under peculiar circumstances, and with their ultimate union in the bonds of matrimony. As, to start with, Mr Stevenson dispenses with a heroine altogether, it is plain that the acutest vision can detect no trace of the stereotyped form in 'The Ebb-Tide.' The poor critics! Mr Stevenson has really set them too hard a task. To abolish the petticoat, and yet expect them to discover the coherency of his composition! Why, *cherchez la femme* is their first thought in hunting for a scheme! They have yet to learn that a story, short or long, is merely the evolution of an idea, that (*pace* Lord Chesterfield) it has no necessary connection with marriage or even with women, and that, when the author has developed his theme, his task is completed. What that theme is need not be clearly stated on the first page. Often it is part of the plot interest of the story to keep its point secret till the last page. Then, however, the conclusion is a flash-light upon all that has gone before. This is exactly the case with 'The Ebb-Tide.' The theme is not formally stated, and the book ends so abruptly that if the reader closes it and writes a review of it instead of reviewing it, he is likely to fall into the error of supposing his author to be a fool rather than himself. Let us examine the texture of 'The Ebb-Tide' by the light of these remarks, and by the flashlight thrown on the whole book by the abrupt close. It begins with the picture of three men in the South Seas. They are 'on the beach,' which is equivalent to sleeping on the Embankment, as, according to Mr David Christie Murray, (1) himself and so many other lights of the day have done in their time. These three men have come by very different routes to this common lodging-house of poverty *à la belle étoile*. One of them is a University man, who has fallen lower and lower through want of backbone. Another is a captain who has lost his ship through drunkenness, and the last of the trio is a cockney cad of the most brutal type. It was a conception of genius to unite in a desperate adventure these strange bed-fellows whom misery has made acquainted.

The theme of the book, then, is the inter-relations of these three curiously-assorted characters during their joint criminal enterprise; and it is supplemented by their individual relations to a fourth man – for whom General Gordon might well have been the model – with whom the course of their adventure connects their lives. When the adventure is over, when the mutual relations of the quartette have been exhausted, when the interaction and revelation of character are complete, the book is finished, and the author wisely lays aside the pen. He has taken the affairs of his men at the ebb-tide, he has shown to what fortune it led on, he has exhibited his characters in every light, and turned them inside out – and so *voilà tout*. There are two species of novels, the novel of character and the novel of adventure. Mr Stevenson loves adventure, but he is also a student of character (using character almost in its technical theatrical signification of 'highly colored'). And so it has naturally occurred to him to combine the two species in one, and to have flesh and-blood figures acted on by incidents, and reacting on them, instead of lay figures buffeted about by the winds of romance. In the preface to 'The Wrecker' (likewise written in collaboration with Mr Lloyd Osbourne) he explained that his idea was to interest the reader in his personages preliminarily to their embarking on the adventure with which the book was really concerned. But in that book he was only groping for the true method, for 'The Wrecker' is merely a novel of character and a novel of adventure pieced together, so that one may put one's finger on the seam.

It is only in 'The Ebb-Tide' that he has struck the true method and achieved a true unity, and fused character and adventure intimately from the first page to the last. The varying turns of his characters' fortunes are cunningly contrived to lay bare their hearts and souls, and the result is, not only an enthralling romance, but a subtle study of the psychology of blackguardism in divers shades and degrees; a study which is convincing except in the case of Huish, the cockney, whose desperate courage in the latter stages has at least not been sufficiently 'prepared' in the original introduction of him, though, for the rest, he is the most vivid figure of all. This little masterpiece – for, by virtue of its construction, its beautiful English, its virile force, and its creation of four new characters, 'The Ebb-Tide' is nothing less – strikes several of the dominant notes which have haunted Mr Stevenson's later work, apart from the deserted islands and the hidden treasures which have always fascinated him and his readers. One of these *Leit-motifs*, as one might almost call them, is the intense interest in villains, whose more genial side our broadly human artist delights to exhibit, dwelling, though not in the spirit of Mr Gilbert, upon the coster's innocent *penchant* for basking in the sun after he has finished jumping on his mother. Another of these later *Leit-motifs* is the illustration of the social possibilities of the most despised human individual, when he is the only companionable being in peculiar and perilous circumstances. The disreputable 'shyster' in 'The Wrecker,' when he was the sole companion in misfortune of his contemptuous enemy, was discovered to have a pleasing fondness for sentimental poetry; and in 'The Ebb-Tide' the University man and the Captain find the intolerable Cockney endurable, if only from the primitive human instinct of gregariousness. There is here quite a field to be worked by story-writers in search of stories. One might develop the relations of the most incongruous couples isolated together on desert islands – say one of 'the souls' and a 'suburban' corn-factor, an impressionist artist and a Royal Academician, a minor poet and a prizefighter, a czar and a nihilist, a dramatist and a critic. How each would cling to the other in their joint loneliness! – for the dread of solitude is the touch of nature that makes the whole world kin. Yet another of Mr Stevenson's *Leit-motifs* is the romance of the modern, which exists this very day contemporaneously with type-writers and county-councils, though it would have been a greater achievement to have found it here at home and not gone questing to the South Seas for it as for a buried treasure.

The treasure lies here, under our eyes, at our very feet. Every alley and byway is swarming with romance. The great dramas of life are working themselves out under every roof in the most prosaic of streets. Never was there more romance than to-day, with its ferment of problems and propaganda, its cosmopolitan movement, its contrasts of wealth and poverty, its shock and interactions of populations and creeds, its clash of mediaeval and modern. The ends of the ages meet in every Atlantic liner. It will be an eternal pity if a writer like Stevenson passes away without having once applied his marvellous gifts of vision and sympathy to the reproduction and transfiguration of every-day human life, if he is content to play perpetually with wrecks and treasures and islands, and to be remembered as an exquisite artist in the abnormal.

PENGUIN ENGLISH
LIBRARY

OTHER TITLES IN THIS SERIES

The Adventures of Huckleberry Finn
MARK TWAIN

> **"I'm unfavorable to killin' a man as long as you can git around it; it ain't good sense, it ain't good morals. Ain't I right?"**

The original Great American Novel, an incomparable adventure story and a classic of anarchic humour, Twain's masterpiece sees Huckleberry Finn and Jim the slave escape their difficult lives by fleeing down the Mississippi on a raft. There, they find steamships, feuding families, an unlikely Duke and King and vital lessons about the world in which they live.

With its unforgettable cast of characters, Hemingway called this 'the best book we've ever had'.

PENGUIN ENGLISH
LIBRARY

OTHER TITLES IN THIS SERIES

Ivanhoe
SIR WALTER SCOTT

"Fight on, brave knights! Man dies, but glory lives!"

Banished from England for seeking to marry against his father's wishes, Ivanhoe joins Richard the Lionheart on a crusade in the Holy Land. On his return, his passionate desire is to be reunited with the beautiful but forbidden Lady Rowena, but he soon finds himself playing a more dangerous game as he is drawn into a bitter power struggle between the noble King Richard and his evil and scheming brother John. The first of Scott's novels to address a purely English subject, *Ivanhoe* is set in a highly romanticized medieval world of tournaments and sieges, chivalry and adventure where dispossessed Saxons are pitted against their Norman overlords, and where the historical and fictional seamlessly merge.

PENGUIN ENGLISH
LIBRARY

OTHER TITLES IN THIS SERIES

The Hound of the Baskervilles
ARTHUR CONAN DOYLE

"Mr Holmes, they were the footprints of a gigantic hound!"

The terrible spectacle of the beast, the fog of the moor, the discovery of a body: this classic horror story pits detective against dog, rationalism against the supernatural, good against evil. When Sir Charles Baskerville is found dead on the wild Devon moorland with the footprints of a giant hound nearby, the blame is placed on a family curse. It is left to Sherlock Holmes and Doctor Watson to solve the mystery of the legend of the phantom hound before Sir Charles's heir comes to an equally gruesome end. *The Hound of the Baskervilles* gripped readers when it was first serialized and has continued to hold its place in the popular imagination.

OTHER TITLES IN THIS SERIES

The Private Memoirs and Confessions of a Justified Sinner
JAMES HOGG

> 'He was constantly harrassed with the idea, that the next time he lifted his eyes, he would to a certainty see that face, the most repulsive to all his feelings of aught the earth contained'

A nightmarish tale of religious fanaticism and darkness, this chilling classic of the macabre tells the tale of Robert Wringhim, drawn in his moral confusion into committing the most monstrous acts by an evil doppelgänger.

James Hogg's masterpiece is as troublingly duplicitous as Wringhim himself, and was ignored and bowdlerized before becoming a hugely influential work of Scottish literature.

PENGUIN ENGLISH
LIBRARY

OTHER TITLES IN THIS SERIES

Lady Audley's Secret
MARY ELIZABETH BRADDON

**'Lady Audley uttered a long, low, wailing cry, and threw her
arms above her head with a wild gesture of despair'**

In this outlandish, outrageous triumph of scandal fiction, a new Lady Audley
arrives at the manor: young, beautiful – and very mysterious. Why does she
behave so strangely? What, exactly, is the dark secret this seductive outsider
carries with her?

A huge success in the nineteenth century, the book's anti-heroine – with
her good looks and hidden past – embodied perfectly the concerns of the
Victorian age with morality and madness.

PENGUIN ENGLISH
LIBRARY

OTHER TITLES IN THIS SERIES

Wuthering Heights
EMILY BRONTË

> **"May you not rest, as long as I am living. You said I killed you — haunt me, then"**

Lockwood, the new tenant of Thrushcross Grange on the bleak Yorkshire moors, is forced to seek shelter one night at Wuthering Heights, the home of his landlord. There he discovers the history of the tempestuous events that took place years before: of the intense passion between the foundling Heathcliff and Catherine Earnshaw, and her betrayal of him. As Heathcliff's bitterness and vengeance are visited upon the next generation, their innocent heirs must struggle to escape the legacy of the past.

PENGUIN ENGLISH
LIBRARY

OTHER TITLES IN THIS SERIES

David Copperfield
CHARLES DICKENS

'Whether I shall turn out to be the hero of my own life, or whether that station will be held by anybody else, these pages must show'

Dickens's epic, exuberant novel is one of the greatest coming-of-age stories in literature. It chronicles David Copperfield's extraordinary journey through life, as he encounters villains, saviours, eccentrics and grotesques, including the wicked Mr Murdstone, stout-hearted Peggotty, formidable Betsey Trotwood, impecunious Micawber and odious Uriah Heep.

Dickens's great *Bildungsroman* (based, in part, on his own boyhood, and which he described as a 'favourite child') is a work filled with life, both comic and tragic.

PENGUIN ENGLISH
LIBRARY

OTHER TITLES IN THIS SERIES

> "You talk very easily of hours, sir! How long do you suppose, sir, that an hour is to a man who is choking for want of air?"

A masterly evocation of the state and psychology of imprisonment, *Little Dorrit* is one of the supreme works of Dickens's maturity.

When Arthur Clennam returns to England after many years abroad, he takes a kindly interest in Amy Dorrit, his mother's seamstress, and in the affairs of Amy's father, a man of shabby grandeur, long imprisoned for debt in the Marshalsea. As Arthur discovers, the dark shadow of the prison stretches far beyond its walls to affect many lives, from Mr Panks, the reluctant rent-collector of Bleeding Heart Yard, to Merdle, an unscrupulous financier.

PENGUIN ENGLISH
LIBRARY

OTHER TITLES IN THIS SERIES

Melmoth the Wanderer
CHARLES MATURIN

"My hour is come ... the clock of eternity is about to strike, but its knell must be unheard by mortal ears!"

This violent, profound, baroque and blackly humorous novel is the story of Melmoth, who has sold his soul in exchange for immortality in a satanic bargain, and now preys on the helpless in their darkest moments, offering to ease their suffering if they will take his place and release him from his centuries of tortured wanderings.

Melmoth the Wanderer (1820) blended Gothic fiction and psychological realism to create a work of hallucinatory power.

PENGUIN ENGLISH
LIBRARY

OTHER TITLES IN THIS SERIES

Shirley
CHARLOTTE BRONTË

> 'Alas, Experience! No other mentor has so wasted and frozen
> a face as yours: none wears a robe so black, none bears a rod
> so heavy ... '

A powerful, heatfelt depiction of conflict between classes, sexes and generations, *Shirley* is the story of struggling, debt-ridden Robert Moore, whose decision to try to save his Yorkshire mill by sacking workers sparks a riot. When
Robert considers marriage to the wealthy Shirley Keeldar to solve his financial
problems, he discovers instead that both their hearts ultimately lie elsewhere.

Charlotte Brontë's strange and beautiful novel brilliantly recreates the world
of early industrial Britain, and the shocking impact it had on both landscape
and society. It also contains, in the penniless dependent Caroline Helstone,
one of the most touching and engaging of all nineteenth-century portraits of
women.

PENGUIN ENGLISH
LIBRARY

OTHER TITLES IN THIS SERIES

Pamela
SAMUEL RICHARDSON

> **'O the deceitfulness of the heart of man! This John, whom I
> took to be the honestest of men ... this _very_ fellow was all the
> while a vile hypocrite, and a perfidious wretch, and helping
> to carry on my ruin'**

A tale of seduction and 'Virtue Rewarded', this early epistolary novel tells
of the maidservant Pamela, abducted and abused by her master before she
eventually falls in love with him.

Although _Pamela_ was a bestseller and became hugely influential, it caused
a scandal on its publication in 1740; not for the plotline of kidnap and at-
tempted rape, but for Richardson's idea that social and class roles could be
overcome by morality and love.